MIC

Michael Arnold lives in Petersfield, Hampshire, with his wife and son. After childhood holidays spent visiting castles and battlefields, he developed a lifelong fascination with the Civil Wars. *Devil's Charge* is the second in a planned series of over ten books that will follow the fortunes of Captain Stryker through one of the most treacherous periods of English history. *Traitor's Blood* and *Hunter's Rage* are also available from John Murray.

PRAISE FOR THE CIVIL WAR CHRONICLES

'Michael Arnold's *Devil's Charge* featuring the battle-hardened English Civil War veteran Captain Stryker, skilfully blends the author's own inventions with the real events of 1643' *Sunday Times*, Historical Fiction Books of the Year

'In this dark-hued romp of a historical novel, livid with the scents, sounds and colours of a country on the brink of implosion, Arnold combines real and imaginary events as in many novels of this sort, identifiable characters of the period with fictional players. His grasp of the minutiae of mid-seventeenth-century combat is impressive' *Daily Express*

'Pushed as "the Sharpe of the Civil War", Captain Stryker is a character well able to attract readers on his own merits . . . Many of the most famous engagements of the Civil

War are still to come, and the enigmatic Stryker's involvement in them promises much entertainment' *Sunday Times*

'A thumping good read. With considerable skill, Arnold has reached back in time to create a living, breathing depiction of seventeenth-century England. From his vividly described battle scenes to the richly drawn descriptions of everyday life, from the earthy vernacular of its characters to the precise details of military equipment, every last part of this book oozes authenticity. Fans of Cornwell's Sharpe novels will love Captain Innocent Stryker – he's uglier, meaner and cleverer than Sharpe. Tremendous!' Ben Kane, author of *The Forgotten Legion* Chronicles

'If you love Sharpe, you'll be knocked out by the . . . adventures of Captain Innocent Stryker, who is just as tough, merciless and fearless in battle. In fact, at times this one-eyed veteran makes Sharpe look rather civilized' *Peterborough Evening Telegraph*

'You can smell the gunpowder and hear the cannon fire . . . Arnold's passion for the period suffuses every page' Robyn Young, author of the *Brethren* trilogy

'Michael Arnold's superb Civil War Chronicles . . . have reached the thrilling second instalment and the trumpet blasts, battle cries and howls of execration are filling the air again. At the forefront of all the heart-thumping action is Stryker with his narrow, feral face and its ragged patch of swirling scar tissue . . . he's wily, dangerous, too often thinks with his fists and can kill a man in the twinkling of his one demonic eye . . . Arnold brings to colourful life the English

Civil War with all its conflicting passions, raw brutality and blood-curdling passions' *Lancashire Evening Post*

'Captures the grittiness, as well as the doomed glamour, of the Royalist cause' Charles Spencer, author of *Prince Rupert*

'Arnold is at his best describing real events . . . As it says on the blurb, if you like Cornwell you will like Arnold' *Historical Novels Review*

'Mike Arnold hooks the reader with the clash of steel and the roar of gunpowder. Rollicking action and proper history combine in this cracking series' Anthony Riches, author of the *Empire* series

'Read this book for historical entertainment backed by extensive research of the time we love and you will not be disappointed' *English Civil War Society*

'Powerfully visualized battle scenes which can certainly stand in comparison with the best of Cornwell' *Yorkshire Post*

'I loved Sharpe. I am going to be equally at home with Captain Stryker' *Historical Novels Review*

'Michael Arnold has caught all of the passion, urgency, fear and exhilaration of men in battle. Not only that, he's writing in a period that he obviously knows intimately and in to which he has breathed new life' *Patrick Mercer*, author of *To Do and Die* and *Dust and Steel*

Also by Michael Arnold

Traitor's Blood
Hunter's Rage

DEVIL'S CHARGE

MICHAEL ARNOLD

JOHN MURRAY

First published in Great Britain in 2011 by John Murray (Publishers)
An Hachette UK Company

First published in paperback in 2012

2

Maps drawn by Rosie Collins

A CIP catalogue record for this title is available from the British Library

ISBN 978-1-84854-408-6
Ebook ISBN 978-1-84854-409-3

Typeset in Sabon by Hewer Text UK Ltd, Edinburgh
Printed and bound by Clays Ltd, St Ives plc

John Murray policy is to use papers that are natural, renewable and
recyclable products and made from wood grown in sustainable forests. The
logging and manufacturing processes are expected to conform to the
environmental regulations of the country of origin.

John Murray (Publishers)
338 Euston Road
London NW1 3BH

www.johnmurray.co.uk

To John and Gerry Arnold –
the best parents ever

Early 1643

- Royalist territory
- Parliamentarian territory
- Neutral territory

Inverness

Aberdeen

Perth

Edinburgh

Newcastle

Carlisle

Bridlington

York

Lincoln

Newark

Chester

Nottingham

Lichfield

Worcester

Colchester

Pembroke

Gloucester

Oxford

Cirencester

London

Bristol

Taunton

Portsmouth

Plymouth

N
W · E
S

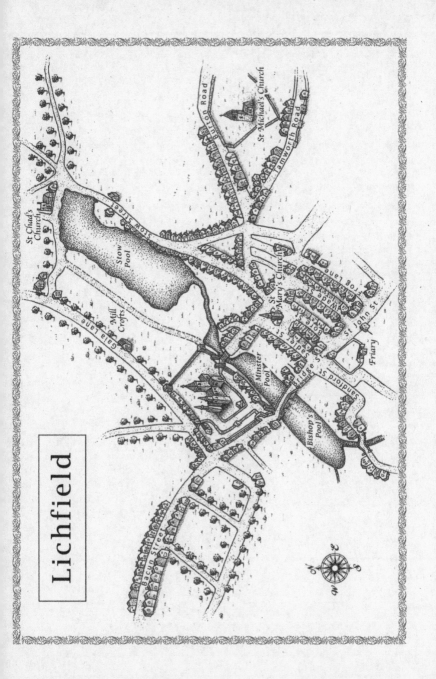

Lichfield

St Chad's Church

Stow Pool

Stow Street

Burton Road

St Michael's Church

Tamworth Road

Fog Lane

St Mary's Church

Wade St

Mill Crofts

Gaia Lane

Minster Pool

Bird St

Dam St

St John St

Friary

Bishop's Pool

Sandford St

Bridge St

Bacon Street

N

PROLOGUE

It was a good place for an ambush.

The road was turned to swamp by a night-long deluge, making the going desperately slow, while at its flanks grew thick forests shrouded in a mist that made the great trunks appear as sentries guarding an otherworldly realm.

Indeed, it was a very good place for an ambush.

Three men, waiting expectantly in the murky half-light beneath the bough of an ancient oak, glanced at one another. They had all heard the distant rumble of wheels and hoofbeats cut into the dawn. Finally the coach was here. Finally they could set about their work.

The tallest of the three, a middle-aged man of impressive stature and pallid, warty complexion, swallowed hard. He was not a man given to anxiety, but this assignment had burrowed its way beneath his skin like a tick.

He forced himself to study the bend in the road, anxious for the coach to appear, but was startled as one of the advancing horses whinnied from the depths of the gloom. He thumped his thigh viciously, angry at his own timidity, and glanced again at his companions. Like him, they were prepared for the morning's work: black-clad, heavily armed and resolute.

'Ready?' he hissed, running gloved fingers quickly over the firing mechanism of his musket. 'Remember,' he added, neck sinews convulsing in a violent spasm as he spoke, 'the Lord guides us. He sends our fire true and deadly. We do *His* work. We cannot fail.'

The others nodded, fingering their weapons.

His confidence growing, the leader strode out from the shelter of the oak and approached the edge of the road. The ground sucked at his boots, though he was thankful the sleety rain had finally abated.

As he took up a kneeling position, chilling damp immediately stabbing at his knee, he silently praised God for giving him the foresight to use firelocks instead of matchlocks. He cocked the weapon; there would be no telltale match light for his prey to spy in the darkness.

More sharp clicks nearby told him that his men had made their own weapons ready.

The leader stared back at the road, his body tense as he waited for the coach to appear. It was close now, and he knew the sound of bouncing wheels and pounding hooves would be thunderously loud, but he could hear only the rushing of blood in his own ears.

And then, like a ghoulish apparition, the coach-horses finally materialized from the darkness, their eyes floating like something conjured by witchcraft, nostrils flaring as they pumped gouts of swirling steam into the air around their heads. And there, careening along in the wake of the furious animals, was the prey.

'Now!' the tall man snarled, squeezing the firelock's well-oiled trigger. It eased back smoothly, as he knew it would, and the dawn was shattered by the scream of a dying horse.

The second and third muskets cracked into life, their leaden balls whipping across the short range before the coach driver had time to react, and slamming into the terrified animals, sending blood spraying into the grey air and across the sodden road. The horses stumbled, fell and rolled, and the coach clattered across their broken bodies, throwing the driver and the roof-stacked baggage skyward.

The vehicle itself seemed to take flight for an instant, gliding almost serenely above the bullet-riddled beasts, but then it crashed down in a symphony of splintered wood, sliced chains and shattered axles. The wheels came away as though the coach was no more than a child's toy, speeding madly into the undergrowth at the road's verge, and the carriage, now simply a large box, hit the ground, skidding across the mud, spinning once, twice, until it left the road and slammed into the trunk of a gnarled tree.

The tall man stood up, discarding his spent musket and reaching for the spare that was slung on his back. 'Tom!'

'Sir!' the response came from somewhere to the rear.

The leader did not look back, but called over his shoulder as he began to run towards the battered carriage, 'See to the driver! Micky!'

'Aye, Major!' the second man replied.

'With me!'

As he reached what was left of the vehicle, the tall major cocked and levelled his second firelock, pointing it at the deeply scratched door. 'Out!' he called.

Nothing stirred. No voices called, nor figures emerged.

'Shall I?' Micky asked, eagerly.

The major nodded. 'Bring him out.'

Micky, a stocky man whose eye level did not even reach his superior's shoulders, raised his musket and stepped forward carefully. He shoved the black barrel through the window of the coach, and called again. Still no response. Micky leaned in, poking his head through the frame to inspect the dead passenger within.

The shot that followed almost immediately was more like an explosion within the confines of the coach. From several paces away, the major saw only the bright orange flash, followed by a black pall of smoke that billowed manically out of the windows, rising quickly to mingle with the bare branches of the surrounding oaks. And with the smoke came Micky's heavy torso, flung back with so much force it was as though God himself had slapped him.

The major looked on in disbelief and horror as Micky came to rest in the sopping grass and rotten bracken, his face a mess of torn flesh and gushing blood.

The major raced forwards. He yanked open the battered door, wisps of dirty smoke still playing around him, and shoved his musket into the gloomy interior, pulling the trigger as he did so.

The ball thudded home, tearing a hole in one of the empty seats. Of the passenger, there was no sign.

The major had made great efforts to cleanse his language since the true faith had cleansed his soul, but now he screamed his fury to the dawn in a stream of oaths. He cast down the empty firelock, twisting away to snatch up Micky's still-loaded weapon, and bolted into the dense forest after his quarry.

He kept his step artificially high to avoid tripping on the winter debris, praying aloud with each breathless moment, beseeching Christ to forgive his failure and show him the path his enemy had taken.

And there, some twenty paces ahead, lumbering like a terrified bullock between bent trunks and beneath the grabbing claws of branches, was the man he had come to kill. The fat, sweating, despicable, Popish excuse for a man he had dreamt of dispatching for so long.

But, to his surprise, he saw a second person in the misty distance. A slighter, hooded figure, gripping a pistol in one hand. The other hand tore at the fat man's bulky arm, urging him on, forcing him deeper into the mist's protection.

The major wondered then at Tom's whereabouts, for he had but a single shot, and could not hope to take down both fugitives. But the report of a musket somewhere to his left told him that the young man was still busy making an end of the coach driver.

He would have to choose which of the two fleeing figures was to die. The thought rankled, for, though the fat man was his intended target, he dearly wished to put a bullet in Micky's killer.

He resolved to place duty before vengeance. He halted, levelled Micky's firelock, and finding his target along its slim barrel, pulled the trigger.

For a moment the fugitives vanished in the cloud of smoke that belched from the musket. But the major knew his business and was confident of the shot. As the scene cleared, he thanked God for His providence. Only the thinner figure was weaving its way further into the safety of the wood.

'Driver's a dead'un, Major,' a voice broke into the tall man's thoughts.

The major turned, seeing Tom emerge from the trees to his left. 'Well done, lad.'

Tom frowned. 'You get him, sir?'

'I did. Praise the good Lord, I did.'

Tom squinted as he scanned the scene before them. He saw the distant figure disappear into the depths of the forest, his form gradually swallowed by the mist. 'There were two?'

'Aye, there were. Romish coward had a bodyguard.'

'Shall I go after 'im?' Tom asked eagerly.

The major scratched a wart on his pointed chin. He shook his head. 'We shan't catch him now. Let him go. Our work today is done.' He turned away.

Tom stared after him. 'Today, sir?'

'Sir Samuel gave us two targets,' the major replied, not looking back. 'Lazarus is no more. Now we must locate the other. Fetch the horses, Corporal.'

CHAPTER 1

It was perhaps three hours after midnight, and the town was still and silent.

The sky was crammed with thick, grey clouds and the earth was ankle-deep in snow. The scant moonlight danced brightly on the sparkling white blanket, illuminating streets and rooftops with an ethereal glow.

And gliding like a wraith in that strange half-light, shoulders hunched, eyes keenly attentive, was a tall, cloaked man. He moved swiftly along the outside of the town's ramshackle defences, tracing the path of the ancient walls, the legacy of a long since fallen empire, rows of densely packed streets always on his left, fields and hills rising away to the right. He was wary of patrols, acutely aware of the fatal consequences capture would bring.

At length he came to a halt where the crumbling walls had been built up with new stone and topped with wooden stakes to form a makeshift palisade. This, he remembered, was where the road from the south-west pierced the town limits. He stared into the darkness for several moments, until he was able to discern the road from the fields at its flanks. There was a pile of rubble nearby, left over from

7

the day's frantic rebuilding, and the man dropped down and scrambled towards it on hands and knees. Here, in this place of relative concealment, he scrutinized the road, eyes straining to distinguish its path, until his gaze settled on a group of shapes some three hundred paces away. It resolved into walls, buildings, rooftops. A farm.

'There she is,' he whispered.

The man waited for a few moments, ensuring there were no movements on the exposed ground between his hiding place and the distant buildings, before breaking forwards again.

He ran beside the road, following it away from the town walls, praying silently, desperately, that he would not be seen.

He reached the farm's outer wall, dropping with his back against it, chest heaving rhythmically, yearning for his nerves to calm. Footsteps crunched through the brittle snow close by. They were shockingly close, the other side of the wall, and he held his breath sharply, gritting his teeth as icy air needled labouring lungs.

The steps seemed to be heading away from his position, but, then, in a moment of utter terror, he heard voices to his right. They had circled round, and were now on his side of the wall. Like ghostly apparitions, their bodies gradually resolved from the darkness just a few paces away. There were half a dozen; soldiers all. Lord Stamford's men. They stood chatting, a couple leaning on the very wall he was crouched beside. He smelled the smoke from their pipes, heard their inane banter.

He did not move, praying the soldiers would fail to notice him in his shadowy place. He allowed air into his lungs again, for fear they would burst, but kept his breathing shallow, lest he send plumes of vapour into the air like a hideous beacon.

The soldiers did not spot him. He heard them speak of the large force encamped a mile away from the hastily bolstered walls of this newly garrisoned farmyard, but they were not expecting the enemy to be sneaking about on this side of their pickets.

The soldiers left, heading towards the farm's central cluster of buildings, and the ghostly figure was finally able to edge out of his protective shadows.

He reached the farm's first structure, flattening himself against its wattle and daub wall, then edging carefully to peer out beyond the gable end. Satisfied there were no more patrols, nor common folk abroad that might accidentally catch sight of him, the figure took his first steps into the dangerously exposed area between the farmhouse and its outbuildings.

A screech startled him before he had taken a dozen strides, and his stomach twisted violently, but no soldiers burst from secret hiding places, no priming pans flared, no halberds sliced at his head. As his pulse settled, and the prickling of skin began to fade, he realized with a gush of relief that the sound was not human. Perhaps a fox, perhaps not, but certainly not the alarm his anxious mind had conjured.

Pulling the long cloak tighter about his shoulders, the man set forth once again, this time at a run. His goal was up ahead, less than twenty paces away, and the sooner he reached it the sooner this damnable mission would be complete.

A stout barricade was the target. The farm sat adjacent to the south-west road and, on hearing of the enemy's return, Stamford's men had decided that it would make the most logical place of defence. They had erected a barrier of stakes and wagons and bushels, of old fences and of commandeered furniture, and, as an attacking force spent their energy against its dense strength, the defenders would pour fire upon them from the walls and buildings of the farm complex.

He reached the makeshift barricade without obstruction and studied the tightly packed array of objects which comprised it. Presently his eyes fixed upon a large cart, stacked full of mouldering hay. It was wedged at the very centre of the temporary defensive work.

The vehicle had been destined for the town the previous evening as dusk had closed in. But the soldiers manning the ever-growing barricade had stepped into the road, unbridled the two scrawny oxen, and ignored the driver's pleas.

'Please, sirs!' the old man, bent and withered by age, had spluttered through a wracking cough that sent large globules of spittle to rest on the settling snow. 'Please, sirs, have mercy! She's me livelihood! I'll perish without her to carry me wares.'

The sentries had been deaf to his appeal, stating in surly tones that the rickety vehicle would be used for the good of the town. He had grasped at their sleeves, begged them to relent, but they just thrust him aside.

The old man had wept. 'Jus' let me warm these old bones while the snow falls,' he had pleaded. 'Let me find shelter in the town, sirs!'

The sentries had growled and cursed their displeasure at the old fool's ramblings, for no pilgrims were to be granted freedom of the town while the great army threatened its very existence, but it was snowing hard and they had no wish to stand and argue when they could be warming their hands at the farm's hearths.

'I swear I'll not see mornin' else!' the old man had whined, though the sergeant in command was already stalking back to the shelter of his billet, thinking of the plump whore waiting within.

'I want you gone by this time on the morrow!' he had barked over his shoulder at the cart's driver. 'Dusk on the morrow, you old palliard, hear me?'

The snowfall had faded since then, and the carter had found an inn. But after the tired oxen were led away by a spotty stableboy, the carter had not slept and had taken only small beer. Instead of resting, he sharpened the dirk hitherto concealed within a filthy boot, and rather than sheltering from the foul weather, he had waited for the dead of night and crept out into the snow once more.

The man was not old. Nor was he infirm, though it had pleased him to give that impression to the sentries. He was a man of war; a *petardier*.

Now, as he crunched his way across the last few paces and climbed up into the cart, burrowing his way beneath the damp, snow-encrusted hay, nostrils overwhelmed by the ripe stench of putrefaction, the petardier knew that the wheels of victory had been set in motion.

He almost pitied the rebellious townsfolk.

Almost.

—m—

Captain Innocent Stryker, of Sir Edmund Mowbray's Regiment of Foot, was not a pious man. Indeed, he was not sure he believed in any higher power than a loaded gun and a keen blade. But today he prayed. He prayed for a white flag. He yearned to see it flutter tentatively from the town's beleaguered walls, a grimy symbol of the citizens' submission. But, as he watched the black funnels of smoke thicken as they rose from the defenders' belching artillery to smudge the pale horizon, he knew that God would not answer his prayer.

One of Stryker's officers came to stand at his shoulder. A man whose fluff-covered upper lip was at odds with his confident bearing and weather-beaten skin. Andrew Burton might have still been in his teens, but he had seen more fighting than most witnessed in a lifetime. His right arm was withered, propped close against his ribcage within a tight leather sling, the shoulder shattered months earlier by a pistol ball. 'Men are ready, sir,' Burton said, glancing back at the ranks. 'It's past noon. Will we advance, do you think?'

Stryker removed his hat, fiddling with the once bright feathers at its band, careful to have them in good order for the inevitable assault. Somehow it was important. 'Imminently, Lieutenant.'

Burton stared at the earthworks hedging the town. 'I had hoped we might pound them a while,' he said wistfully.

'Aye,' Stryker agreed. Royalist ordnance had softened the town's resolve during late morning, the damage becoming increasingly visible amid the low rooftops, but here, at the south-western entrance, the defences were left unscathed. 'It seems the prince will require an escalade.' He regarded the younger man with interest. 'Frightened?'

Burton's neck convulsed as he swallowed thickly. 'Aye, sir.'

'All is well then,' Stryker said. 'You'll not get yourself killed for misplaced bravery.'

'Sir?'

'The colonel did not promote you so that you could dash away your life against this damned town's barricades. Caution, Andrew. There'll be time enough for valour, lad, but you must choose your moment.'

Lieutenant Burton nodded solemnly, and paced back to the men at his command. Stryker frowned slightly. His protégé had proven himself more than once since joining Stryker on their suicidal mission to arrest Sir Randolph Moxcroft in the weeks after Kineton Fight, and had been rewarded for his bravery and rapidly increasing skill, but a streak of recklessness had also shown itself. Burton was now second-in-command of the company. Stryker needed a man with a level head as much as he needed one of stout heart.

The drums rolled.

They rumbled low and ominous across the snow-blanketed fields, lingering in echo as they climbed the white summits of hills beyond.

Stryker studied the nearest buildings. They were not within the town's dilapidated walls, but outside, straddling the road. It was, he had been told, a small farm known as the Barton. It was there that the defenders would stage their first attempt to repel the closing horde. By the look of the old Roman walls that surrounded the town, he imagined the Barton would be the most difficult obstacle. Once they were beyond it, the town would quickly fall. He wondered whether the inhabitants had had the good sense to bury their valuables and flee into those high, sheep-crowded crests. Somehow he doubted it.

'Capital of the Cotswolds,' Captain Lancelot Forrester said as he came to stand at Stryker's side. All but Colonel Mowbray had dismounted for the day's action, the horses corralled at the rear by the dour wagon-master, Yalden.

Stryker's thin lips twitched in amusement as he acknowledged Forrester. 'Not much to crow about, is it?'

'Perhaps not,' Forrester agreed, absently fingering the gold trim of his blood-red sash.

Stryker frowned. 'Should you not be with your lads?'

'They're neat, tidy and ready for the off, old boy, worry not!' Forrester exclaimed brightly. He had been with Stryker and Burton on that terrible mission the previous autumn, had shared those same dangers and carved his own swathe though the hellish barricades of New and Old Brentford. His reward had been the posting of his choice, and the death of Mowbray's fourth captain in a skirmish outside Banbury had provided a vacant position serving with his old comrade.

Stryker stared down the line of pike and musket to cast an appraising eye over his friend's new command. 'A good group, Forry. You've done well with them.'

'Kind in you to say,' Forrester said simply, though his big cherubic face became a little pink. He hastily rummaged in the snapsack slung at his shoulder, eventually plucking out a short, tooth-worn clay pipe.

Stryker's lone brow shot up. 'You lost the game, Forry.'

Forrester glanced at the pipe. 'I did, I did. And I had not forgotten the forfeit.'

'No sotweed for a month.'

Forrester propped the pipe stem in the corner of his mouth. 'The chirurgeon prescribed it for reasons of health.' He pulled a hurt expression. 'You would have me give up tobacco, to the detriment of my lungs, for a little game of dice?'

Stryker laughed and turned back to point towards the Barton. Forrester followed his companion's gaze as he touched a smouldering length of match to the pipe bowl, eyes resting on the walls of stacked clods and stout barrels that formed the deep works. Those works were crowned by a palisade of sharpened stakes, behind which would doubtless be as many immovable objects as the townsfolk could gather. He remembered this method of defence from that terrible day west of London where the men of Holles and Brooke had proved so damnably difficult to shift.

'Bloody waste to dash them against those works,' Stryker said bluntly.

Forrester sighed, cheeriness eroding. 'I'd prayed we'd avoid a climb.'

'Prayed?' Stryker said, failing to keep the surprise from his tone. 'Hardly a religious man, are you?'

Forrester smiled weakly, pipe smoke wreathing his round face. 'No, I'm not. But when faced with imminent death, one's thoughts do turn to one's saviour.'

Stryker kept his tongue still, though he could not help but agree.

'The good news,' Forrester added, forcing brightness back into his voice, 'is that they're seriously under strength.'

Stryker knew that was true, and knew that he should have been elated by the news, but the prospect of witnessing the town's inevitable demise was not one he relished. Once the Royalist force had breached the Barton and the ancient walls beyond, they would give no quarter to those inside. He let out a heavy breath that obscured his face in roiling vapour. 'Why do they not surrender, damn them, and save us all a bloodbath?'

'Parliament heartland, Stryker. The good citizens are misguided souls, harbouring rebel sympathies. Every man-jack of 'em. The whole shire's rife with it.' Forrester chuckled blackly. 'Like French-welcome in a bawdy-house.'

Stryker turned to him. 'The townsfolk will fight?'

Forrester nodded slowly, ruddy cheeks bright. 'No bloody doubt about it. When they turned the prince away last month they declared they would die for *the True Religion*.' He blew out his cheeks at the thought of the day's almost inevitable blood-letting. 'They're ready for the slaughter, Stryker. Now Stamford's buggered off with most of his men to Sudeley Castle, and he's mired in snow and mud. They'll never make it back in time. So the town has what's left of his force bolstering the walls, while the streets 'll be lined with pitchfork-wielding peasants.'

Stryker shook his head. 'God's teeth.'

Forrester shrugged. 'Worry not, Stryker, we'll be warming our arses by their hearths in short order.'

'It's not the assault that worries me most, Forry, but what follows.' He looked back to the settlement and the buildings huddled within, remembering well the horrors inflicted on so many similar towns and villages in Germany and the Low Countries. 'Bloody town.'

Cirencester had grown rich from its wool, and sat between Charles's new court at Oxford and his hotbed of support in Wales and Cornwall. It was a fat, juicy apple crying out to be plucked. But if its wealth and geography made it a logical prize for the Royalist army, a forthright defiance of the king had made Cirencester a personal target for their commander, Prince Rupert. So he had brought a horde to its walls. Stryker knew the price to be paid for defying men like Rupert of the Rhine. By dusk, so would the folk of Cirencester.

'*Bloody, bloody* town.'

Cirencester was surrounded. Prince Rupert held a large division of horse, dragoons and foot, of which Mowbray's men formed only a fraction, before the town's south-west entrance. There were several units further out on the Stroud road, and, Stryker knew, more bristling companies to the east. On the road leading south-west towards Bristol, Lord Wentworth had three companies of infantry, one of dragoons and one of light cavalry, while to the north-east, in the direction of Sudeley and Winchcombe, the Earl of Carnarvon led a similar number. It was a force to be reckoned with.

The Royalist artillery had pounded away with little reply as the assault troops moved into position, gnawing at the defences, reducing them to nothing more than a display of pitiful insolence. If the attackers were able to force their way inside the town, it would be short work, Stryker knew, for the remains of Stamford's troops would be spread pathetically thin manning the perimeter of the town while patching up the myriad breaches in the fortifications.

'And all the while Robert the Devil intends to gallop straight through the main gate,' Forrester's well-educated tones startled Stryker from his thoughts.

'You read my mind,' Stryker said grimly, taking the pipe from Forrester and inhaling deeply. Carnarvon would lead an assault against Spitalgate to the north, while, according to the orders hammered out by Rupert's drummers, the prince would take his cavalry directly through the Barton and on into the town. The strategy baffled Stryker, for, though entering Cirencester by the south-west road was the shortest route to the town's heart, a cavalry charge against the only heavily fortified point in the relatively weak perimeter seemed futile.

'You try and teach prudence to the youth of today,' Forrester went on, snatching back the tobacco-filled clay stem and twitching his head at Lieutenant Burton, 'and our good commander proves himself entirely devoid of the stuff.'

Stryker's laugh was more like a bark. 'Aye, the prince has a way about him. They won't expect him to make for the front door.'

'The surprise alone'll win him the day, I'd wager. He's mad, Stryker. Quite mad.'

'But you're glad he's on our side,' Stryker replied.

Forrester slapped his friend on the back. 'I thank God for it daily!'

'And I thank Him for the two of you, though I can't comprehend why, what with all your whining!'

Forrester's face turned cherry red with embarrassment as Prince Rupert of the Rhine reined in behind the officers. The young General of Horse seemed like a giant atop his great stallion, an impression only enhanced by his russetted armour and thick buff-coat. The portly captain stared up at King Charles's nephew, snatching off his hat in rapid salute to reveal sandy hair that only made his cheeks appear more livid. He stuttered the beginnings of an apology, but the prince stopped him with a great bellow of laughter. 'At your ease, Captain Forrester! We will indeed make for the front door, as your one-eyed compatriot so eloquently put it.'

Stryker met the prince's gaze. Rupert seemed to be fidgeting in his saddle, such was his unbridled excitement. 'May I ask as to your plans, General?'

Rupert offered another beaming grin, his neat white teeth bright beneath the sliding nasal bar of his Dutch-style pot helmet. 'Plans, Stryker? I plan to toast a great victory this evening. Find me after! We'll share a bottle, if the God-bothering stiffs ain't poured every drop o' drink in the Churn!'

'After, sir? We attack soon?'

'We do, we do. Carnarvon strikes to the north even now. We'll take the southern entrance while their heads are turned.'

Stryker frowned. 'Beg' pardon, General, but the southern defences are stout. Do you not require infantry to first clear that barricade? We—'

To Stryker's surprise, the young prince's eye twitched a conspiratorial wink. 'They say I use sorcery, Stryker.' He indicated the giant white poodle that stood, as ever, beside his horse. The dog had been a gift from Lord Arundell during the prince's time in an Austrian prison after the battle of Vlotho in 1638, and was now Rupert's constant shadow, even joining its master's often death-defying cavalry charges. 'They say Boye, here, is my familiar. Would you countenance such puritanical drivel?' Rupert laughed at the notion, though his sharp features hardened a fraction of a second later, his eyes darkening with a steely seriousness. 'Well today, Captain, I mean to show 'em some *real* magic! Look to the barricade!'

19

In moments the prince was gone, galloping away down the line, Boye in tow, to find his famed cavalry.

The drums sounded again.

Stryker turned to Forrester, noting the sheen of sweat that had already crept across his fellow captain's plump jowls despite the oppressive cold. 'That's our order to advance.'

Forrester upturned his pipe, letting the still smoking contents litter the snow, and shook the proffered hand. 'Godspeed. I must see to my own lads. Once more unto the breach an' all that, what?' He stared back at the Barton, perhaps imagining the rows of muskets that must wait behind the piled wall. It seemed almost inevitable that those muskets would repel the cavalry charge with devastating ease, leaving the task of assault to his infantrymen. 'Rather wish there were a breach to assault.'

Stryker shrugged. 'Watch the barricade.'

Forrester shot him a wan smile. 'I'll watch it. By God, I'll be watching nothing but.'

Stryker set his jaw, determination puckering the ragged tissue that covered his long-shattered eye socket. 'Fare you well, Forry.' He turned away. 'Sergeant!'

A tall man appeared from where he had been waiting patiently some distance behind the officers. His sinewy frame and weather-hewn face marked him as a seasoned winter campaigner. 'Sir!'

Stryker craned his neck up to look into the sergeant's face. 'Make them ready, Will. He'll send in his beloved horse first, but we'll sweep behind right enough.'

''Bout bleedin' time,' Sergeant William Skellen murmured.

'What was that?'

'Men'll have a grand old time, sir,' said Skellen, his voice suddenly finding clarity in the crisp air. 'Armed and eager, Mister Stryker.'

Stryker jerked his head back towards the ranks of brown-coated infantry, pike files bristling, musketeers blowing on match-cords to prick bright holes in the gloomy day. 'Get on with it then, Sergeant.'

Skellen gave a curt nod and turned away.

'And Sergeant?'

Skellen looked back. 'Sir?'

'Try not to come back dead.'

The sergeant grinned ferociously, showing stumps of mottled amber. 'Never did yet, sir.'

The first cavalry units began to move. Of the four thousand men at Prince Rupert's disposal, the majority were harquebusiers, and they surged forward, raggedly at first, but soon forming into a great wave of armour and hooves as the charge gathered momentum.

Stryker watched the horsemen go, and he felt the land shake beneath his tall boots. He wished he could be in that great assault. But, as the elation of battle prickled along the nape of his neck and quickened his pulse, he bit it down savagely, forcing himself to focus on his own command. He knew them for hard, confident men, men who had followed him into the terrors below the ridge at Edgehill and had survived. Fifty-three musketeers, thirty-six pikemen, two commissioned officers, two sergeants, three corporals and two drummers: Stryker's company. Ninety-eight men that would take on the entire rebel army if he asked it of them.

'Ensign Chase!' Stryker bellowed at a stocky, full-bearded fellow stood at the front of the company. 'Hold that bloody colour high, man! Let 'em see who they face!'

Chase had not been Stryker's ensign long, but he knew his business well enough. With a powerful heave, he lofted the banner as high as he might, so that the square of red taffeta caught the breeze, its pair of white diamonds flickering taut and proud.

The dense swathe of horse was a hundred paces away now, charging inexorably towards the ominously robust barricade. The Royalist infantry units to Stryker's flanks began to move. Colonel Mowbray was out in front, standing tall in bright stirrups, proudly urging his regiment to the fray. In turn, Stryker sucked air deep into his lungs and bellowed, 'Forward!'

The men of Sir Edmund Mowbray's Regiment of Foot took their first steps towards Cirencester.

'They have artillery, sir,' Burton, away to Stryker's left, chirped uncertainly.

Stryker snorted. 'They dragged their culverins over to pound Sudeley Castle. And their best crews, to boot. What they have left are half a dozen small pieces. Don't sound a deal more than drakes. It is not their guns you should fear, Lieutenant, but their bloody muskets poking at us from beyond that barricade.'

Burton's brow creased in consternation as he assessed the grim task ahead. 'Our horse will never break that.'

Stryker understood what he meant. It seemed as if the cavalry and infantry would take it in turn to hammer uselessly upon the thick barricade, only to be shot at by jeering defenders. And yet something in Rupert's nervous energy had infected him, made him dare to share in the young general's confidence.

'Have faith, Lieutenant.'

Burton briefly sketched a crucifix across his chest with his left arm, the right hanging uselessly in its strap. 'I do, sir. I do.'

Stryker grinned. 'Not in God, Burton. In Rupert.'

'Sir?' Burton seemed baffled.

'I believe the general has something hidden up one of those long sleeves of his.'

Burton said something in reply, but Stryker did not catch a single word for, in a single great, ear-splitting, earth-shuddering second Cirencester vanished from view.

It was a matter of moments before the cavalry hit home. But they did not blunt their blades against the earthworks or hurl pathetic insults up at the men safe behind the palisade. Instead, the horsemen whooped and cheered and screamed their thanks to God. They stood high in their stirrups and vanished into the red flame and black smoke that billowed about the Barton.

'Fuck me,' Sergeant Skellen said quietly from somewhere behind Stryker.

'A petard,' Stryker breathed. He was as astonished as every other man in the company.

'How the blazes did 'e get a petard in there?' Skellen replied.

'Magic,' Stryker replied softly, staring ahead. A mighty explosion had reduced the barricade to a jagged mass of gigantic splinters. And between those great, raw stakes streamed the exultant Royalist horsemen.

The company had slowed in the aftermath of the explosion, amazement breaking the usually measured stride, and Stryker blinked himself back to the duty at hand. He turned quickly, facing the stunned ranks as his tall boots kicked up the churned snow. 'Prince Rupert's in the town, lads! Do we join him inside?'

The men cheered and the sergeants growled. Stryker drew his sword, a fine weapon of Spanish steel, with a swirling half-basket hilt to protect the hand and a pommel decorated with a large, crimson garnet.

In less than a minute they were at the farm, following in the wake of the horsemen, searching for men to kill. But there were none. The defenders had fled with Rupert's exultant cavalrymen slashing at their backs. Those that remained were dead, blown to pieces by the initial explosion, and Stryker stepped over scorched limbs and splintered weapons as he led his company on.

Cirencester was a vision of hell.

Bodies lay strewn in the streets, twisted and broken, blood freezing in pools beneath them, faces describing final, horrific moments. Some were clearly soldiers, the unfortunates Lord Stamford had left behind, but it was clear that many – rough-hewn clubs or kitchen utensils still clutched in stiffening fingers – were ordinary folk. Butchers and coopers, tanners and merchants. These were common men sucked into a war against their own kind. And not just men; to Stryker's right, emerging into view as he turned his head repeatedly to make full use of his one remaining eye, was the body of a woman. Stryker felt little sympathy, since the blood-gleaming scythe, held tight in a grotesquely curled hand, spoke plainly of her willingness to defy the Royalist attackers. But her waxen features and golden hair reminded him of Lisette. His stomach turned.

This lapse angered him, and he swore bitterly. 'On!' he snarled, and the company surged forwards, picking their way across the obstacles of rubble and flesh. It soon became clear there were no enemies to confront. Rupert's lightning charge had had the desired effect. The soldiers and townsfolk manning the initial defences had fallen back into the muddy streets that scored the town, narrow tributaries of the impressive marketplace at Cirencester's heart, a gigantic cobbled spider in a web of roads and alleys.

Hooves sounded, the ground vibrating beneath Stryker's feet, and from the direction of the town centre, a place still hidden from Stryker's view by Cirencester's close-cropped buildings, came the cavalrymen who had inflicted such damage in that opening assault. This time, though, those men were not yelling in victory, nor standing triumphantly in their stirrups.

A harquebusier came near. One gloved fist gripped a long cavalry sword, blood tracing its way in gleaming beads from tip to hilt, while the other snapped expertly at his mount's reins, jerking the beast's muscular neck round to regroup with his troop. Stryker hailed him, but the man paid no heed, absorbed as he was in the moment.

He knew the horseman would probably hear nothing above the rush of his own pulse, a rhythmic, persistent waterfall flowing hard within his skull, but Stryker wanted information. He reached up to take the horse's bridle in a cold hand. The animal responded by turning fractionally towards him, and the trooper's face instantly clouded.

'Damn your pox'n ballocks, you bliddy plodder!' the trooper snarled, his right arm instinctively lifting the long sword in furious reaction.

'Captain Stryker! Mowbray's!' Stryker barked quickly, hoping his action would not result in a cleaved scalp.

The trooper faltered, blade easing to his side. 'Pardon, Cap'n, sir.'

Stryker did not know whether it was his rank that had cooled the horseman's ire, or his name. Nor did he care. 'No matter. What news, man?'

The trooper stared down at him, chest heaving as he regained composure after what had evidently been a hot fight. 'Buggers are 'oled up good 'n proper, sir.'

'Holed up? They have barricades?'

The trooper snorted ruefully. 'Harrows, sir. Big buggers, stretched 'cross all the roads into the square. And plenty else. Bastards are on the thatches an' up the church tower. Shootin' at our fuckin' heads, sir!'

'Jesus,' Stryker whispered, releasing the bridle. Forrester's assessment of pitchfork-wielding peasants might have been accurate, but they were peasants ready and willing to fight. And fight hard. A harrow may have been more typically seen on a farm, but the heavy, spiked chains were lethal barriers for horses to negotiate.

'Mowbray's!' Another voice snapped sharp and crisp above the din of the milling Royalist infantry. 'Mowbray's, to me! Form up!'

Stryker saw it was his commanding officer, Sir Edmund. The armour-clad colonel had finally managed to negotiate the dense mass of men still pouring from the direction of Barton Farm and was now cantering his grey gelding to the head of his regiment. The silver-streaked auburn of his hair and beard shone bright above the dark-coated infantrymen, a beacon his men might follow. The colonel would never consider the fact that his appearance, and pale horse, would also draw the eye of a potential sniper.

'Cavalry are stalling, sir!' Stryker bellowed at Mowbray.

Sir Edmund caught the familiar voice and scanned the mass of men for sight of his second captain. 'Stalling? Why? We're goddamned through!'

'Chained harrows, sir!'

Mowbray paused as thoughts raced through his mind. He fixed Stryker with a hard stare. 'Take your boys, Captain!' He pointed to where the cavalryman had come. 'Take 'em down that road and find those harrows. The general has cutters, but he'll need covering fire!'

The sharp reports of musket fire carried to Stryker's ears as he led the way. The road curved to the right, and, as it finally began to straighten, the company saw the full horror of their task. Up ahead was the marketplace, the vast parish church of St John looming beside it. It was here that the rebels would make their final stand. And it was here that they had draped their vicious harrows from one side of the street to the other.

Stryker saw Prince Rupert standing tall in silver stirrups, bellowing orders, desperate to break through the unexpected obstacles. If Mowbray was right and the prince's men had brought cutting tools, then they would probably make light work of the harrows, but how could they hope to get close enough to conduct the task?

Muskets coughed from the thatched roofs all around, spitting deadly venom down on the attackers. The range was far enough that their bullets did not find a mark, but it kept the Royalists at bay.

'Musketeers!' Stryker ordered, and the men wielding primed long-arms hastened to the front of the company.

'Get up to that bloody harrow and give fire! The horse'll deal with the chains if you cover their heads!'

The montero-capped musketeers surged forward, splitting to the left and right of the street, until they were up against the harrow. From there they aimed their weapons into the great open space that was the marketplace, finding targets amongst the wooden barricades and up in the windows that looked out upon the town centre.

Prince Rupert surged forward, waving his own men on, for they knew their work would be unhindered as soon as Mowbray's infantrymen opened fire.

'Cut that bloody chain, goddamn you! Cut that bloody chain!' Rupert thundered, eyes wild, sword tip tracing manic circles above his head.

The musketeers gave fire. It was no ordered volley, but then this was not open battle. It was hard, vicious street fighting that required nothing more than guts and brutality.

Sure enough, the rebel fire seemed to ebb in the face of this new assault. Perhaps Mowbray's men had found their marks, or perhaps the enemy snipers possessed little skill and ancient weapons.

The harrow was cut. The chains fell. Rupert and his horsemen surged through like avenging angels. They fanned out, picking off the easiest prey first, leaving the bulk of the rebels at the centre of the open ground.

'A gift for us, is it?' Sergeant Skellen droned to Stryker's right.

Stryker ignored him. He ran forward, jumping the pile of cut chains that had been hitherto so formidable. He shouted at his men, and knew they were at his back as he burst through to sweep the final defenders aside. But those defenders did not know when they were beaten, and they strode out from behind their makeshift shields – wagons and barrels and table-tops and wooden chests – to meet the Royalists, and Stryker's men, bolstered now by Mowbray's other companies.

It might have been the fair-meadow below Edgehill, or the barricades of Old Brentford, or the killing fields of Lützen. It was always the same. Always melee; always chaos. Pick a man, bring him down, move on. Cut, thrust, parry, slash. The natural rhythm of men groomed in warfare.

Skellen was there. Stryker could not see him in the mass of snarling faces and slashing weaponry, but he heard his guttural roar and knew the halberd would be scything a path through the enemy for others to follow.

A woman was on her knees, cradling a man's head in her blood-drenched hands, and Stryker stepped over her, deaf to her wails. A youngster came at him, no more than a boy, toting a thick table leg that had already seen action, judging by its scarred surface and bloody sheen. Stryker ducked the wild swipe, ducked the reverse swing, and jammed the ornate hilt of his sword into the lad's mouth. He heard teeth smash, felt the wet spray of fresh blood course across his fingers, saw the boy fall to his knees. Stryker cursed, for a bloody hilt was no aid to effective swordsmanship. He kicked the boy in the face, and moved quickly on.

Mowbray's men enjoyed massively superior numbers and already the defenders were beginning to thin. Many lay where they had fought, while others took flight into the surrounding alleys, only to be tracked down like foxes by Rupert's huntsmen.

'You men!' A shout came from somewhere to the rear, and Stryker turned to see Lancelot Forrester, red-faced and sweating like a roast hog, hailing a group of his men. 'Get up in that fucking church, Tobin! Clear out those blasted snipers!'

The day was won. Rupert's vast force had ultimately swamped Cirencester's courageous but outnumbered defenders, and, from the moment the Barton's barricade had been blown, their victory was assured.

Some of the conquering soldiers were already looting. Stryker saw one of his own pikemen lay down his weapon and crouch beside one of Lord Stamford's fallen men. Ordinarily he would not frown upon the practice of emptying a vanquished enemy's pockets, but the fight had not finished, and he suddenly felt a surge of anger. He strode over and kicked the pikeman hard in the ribs, snarling a furious rebuke.

All around them Cirencester began to burn. Some of the houses had been subjected to grenadoes, the small incendiaries tossed through windows and doors where snipers were suspected. Other buildings were fired as a simple means of instilling terror into the townsfolk. Stryker stared at the fires, watching the burgeoning flames lap indiscriminately at thatch and beam.

The rebel came unseen from the direction of the church, darting out from its shadows, across the marketplace and barrelling into Stryker, sending them both to the hard cobbles. Stryker was first to recover, but found he was without his sword, for his grip on the slippery hilt had failed him. The blade went skittering away and he had no time to retrieve it, for his assailant was quickly on his feet, holding out a broad-bladed knife, teeth bared in a grimace of pure hatred.

The man was young, his body thin, his clothes those of a peasant, and fury had transformed him into a formidable opponent.

He came at him in a series of arcing swipes, and Stryker swayed out of the weapon's reach, stepping ever backwards. But luck was not on his side, and his heels met, perhaps inevitably, with a prone body. His balance gone, Stryker was sent tumbling backwards, clattering on to the ice-cold cobbles for a second time. The townsman was instantly upon him, stabbing down with all the force he could muster.

Stryker was not heavily muscled like some of his pikemen, but he was stronger than most. He fended off the wild young man, gripping at wrists and at the throat, scrabbling at eyes, anything to put the man off his killing stride, but one stab made it through his desperate defence. One blow, clean and hard, found the flesh of his left shoulder. He felt the blood pulse warm and steaming down his arm, and for a moment he thought he saw death approaching, but the youth, even in his second of triumph, had frozen. His eyes were locked on the wound he had inflicted, and his hands were rooted at the blade's hilt, unable to draw it from his victim.

'Never seen blood before?' Stryker hissed, and launched upwards, pulverizing the man's face with his forehead. The blow sent fresh pain streaking through Stryker's own skull, blurring his vision, but the weight suddenly lifted from him and he was able to scramble to his feet. When the mist cleared, he saw the youth was lying flat on his back, nose gushing crimson, eyelids fluttering feebly.

'Christ's robes, Stryker!' Forrester appeared at Stryker's side.

31

Stryker followed his friend's gaze, only to find a pair of iron shears protruding from the flesh of his shoulder. 'Not pitchforks, Forry,' he said quietly, jerking the unlikely weapon free with a wince and a fresh spout of blood, 'but you weren't far off.'

CHAPTER 2

The final defenders of Cirencester fled south and east in the direction of Cricklade and Lechlade, Byron's troop of horse close at their heels. The unfortunate folk left behind in the broken settlement scuttled like rats from the terrier of Royalist retribution, seeking shelter behind barred doors and deep within cellars.

Stryker stood in the marketplace, surveying the scene. Already discipline was dissolving. The Royalists, revelling in the heady mix of victory and promised riches, were breaking ranks to form gangs that would seek ale and plunder. The cavalry were long gone, galloping into the streets and lanes to find easy kills and easier treasure, but many of the infantry, slower and more tired as they were, had not yet disappeared.

He stooped to retrieve his sword, blood gleaming in wet streaks from tip to hilt, and raised it high, bellowing into the rapidly dispersing throng. 'Stryker's! Stryker's!'

The sergeants and corporals within earshot followed suit, bawling oath-laden threats to the soldiers standing close, and gradually the light of bloodlust and greed began to fade from those red-ringed eyes as pikemen and musketeers acknowledged their officer.

Feeling he had but a few moments before thoughts would turn back to pillage, Stryker stalked into the mass of weary men that marched to his command. They were battered and bloodied, chests heaving with exhaustion. They had been part of a great victory, and he was never more proud of them. 'You deserve ale and food, lads!'

'And loot!' an unidentified voice chirped from within the mass of brown-coated infantry. The words were greeted with a low cheer.

Stryker nodded. 'Aye, loot too!'

Another cheer, heartier this time.

'But,' he continued, his one eye meeting the gaze of each of his men in turn, 'do not allow just reward to become unjust revenge. Any man murders when blood's cold, or takes a woman against her will, you shall have me to answer to.'

Will Skellen, standing a full head above any other in the company, strolled up to Stryker's side and glowered at the milling soldiers. He was leaning, lazy and relaxed, against his halberd, but the threat was clear in his glinting dark eyes and the pole-arm's scarlet stained shaft. Flanking Skellen was his fellow sergeant, Moses Heel, the bullock-shaped Devonshire farmhand who prayed as hard as he fought.

'Now,' Stryker shouted into the crowd, content the implication had been understood, 'enough of care! Be gone!'

'How quickly nature falls into revolt when gold becomes her object,' said a voice on Stryker's blind side.

The latter did not turn to look at his friend. 'Henry the Fourth.'

Captain Lancelot Forrester brayed. 'Got to offer up an easy one now and again, Stryker!'

'Shakespeare was in the right of it,' Stryker said absently, still watching his men melt into the alleyways leading away from the marketplace. 'I had hoped, after Brentford, that the prince might have seen sense. It does not help our cause to destroy everything to cross our path. With every town sacked, we turn countless folk against our cause.'

'The cropheads will sack their conquered towns too,' Forrester replied. 'Mind you, though, we've all heard the tales.'

There were rumours of the more pious elements in Parliament's ranks recruiting none but the godliest men. Those men, it was said, proved more courageous, more chivalrous and more disciplined than their Royalist counterparts.

'Stories,' Stryker replied. 'Nicely embellished to put the fear of a vengeful Christ into our rakish Cavaliers.'

'Aye, well. Good thing that gutter-mouthed sergeant of yours had the good sense to follow you into the king's service.' Forrester had raised his voice so that Skellen would hear.

Stryker agreed.

The sacking continued into the night. Gangs of soldiers roamed the cobbled thoroughfares, cramming pockets and snapsacks with what loot they might, bellies full with the bounty of ransacked kitchens, heads foggy with plundered ale.

Having spent the early evening propped on a low stool receiving the ministrations of Mowbray's chirurgeon, George Whorlebatt, Stryker paced into the crisp night – shoulder bound tight beneath grimy bandages – and made his way back towards the billet chosen by Sir Edmund for his officers.

Stryker stalked quickly across the marketplace. Marauding gangs of soldiers quarrelled over plunder, their language ripe and threats deadly. The intermittent smash of a splintered door or shattered window rang out as new loot was discovered, while raucous tones drifted from the taphouses as men toasted their victory again and again.

It was ever thus. Townsfolk, instilled with a courageous heart and a preacher's zeal, would believe themselves indestructible. They would gather behind their walls and shout oaths to their enemies and prayers to their God, and genuinely begin to feel that they could, through some divine power, repel an army. But then that army would come, and it would not be a host of demons, dissolving amid the citizens' projected piety, but men. Real men with real cannon and real muskets and real blades, and they would prick the self-righteous bubble, breach the walls and burn the town. Stryker had seen it many times, and now it was happening in his homeland.

He glanced in on stores and homes, many with their doors caved inwards, splintered by savage boot heels and the butts of muskets. Several were illuminated, their insides glowing orange where small fires were taking hold, and he could see the destruction within. Nothing of value was left: tables were upended and cupboards flung open, their innards disgorged haphazardly across bloody floorboards. Chairs – used to batter open strongboxes and locked doors – were smashed into a myriad jagged shards and shelves were swept violently clean.

Passing one such smallholding, Stryker drew close to a group of men – perhaps five or six – gathered at the street's edge to rifle through a large chest. It was lighter out in the open, for the debris-strewn road was bathed in the glow of the smouldering town, and one of the group had evidently had the forethought to drag the prize from within the dishevelled building.

Stryker took a wide berth as he reached the men. He understood their behaviour, had partaken of it in younger days, and knew that they would be dangerous to engage, strong drink and plunder transforming them from soldiers to a pack of wolves. He drew his cloak tight, dipping his head so that the brim of his hat cast shadows across his face.

One of the men looked up. 'Hold, cully.'

Stryker ignored him, though he felt his pulse gather pace.

'I said,' the man repeated, the threat in his tone unmistakable as he stood, moving sideways to block Stryker's path, 'hold.'

The man was big, as tall as Stryker, and broad of shoulder and neck. Stryker did not recognize the uniform, but then many in the king's ranks were merely clothed in what they had stood up in when they first enlisted. Even so, a lack of regimental recognition did not prevent Stryker detecting the danger the man presented. The aggressor was clearly muscular, and the gleam in his dark eyes had at least a modicum of intelligence. Most ominously, the broad, bucktoothed grin was that of a man supreme in confidence.

Stryker met the bucktooth's gaze levelly. 'None of your concern. Out of my way.'

'Oh, I thinks it is, cully,' the bucktooth said in low tones. He was close enough for Stryker to smell the stench of wine on his breath. 'I thinks it sore is, an' no mistake.' He ran small eyes from the feathers at Stryker's hat band down to his tall cavalry boots. 'Got a pretty penny, I'd say. Turn out yer pockets. You'll pay a toll to me an' my fedaries.'

'I'm in a rare black mood,' Stryker said slowly, making to move past, 'and wish only to press on.'

A thick-fingered hand jerked up to press against Stryker's sternum. 'Makes not a fig o' fuckin' difference to me, General,' the bucktooth growled. 'Every man for 'imself tonight.'

The rest of the group were standing now, revelling in a confrontation.

'Last chance, you beef-brained router,' Stryker said, lifting his chin slightly so that his features were bathed in the smouldering building's glow.

The bucktooth's beady eyes widened in sudden alarm as he gazed into a face he had never before seen, yet instantly recognized. An unmistakable face, narrow and feral, its ragged patch of swirling scar tissue appearing demonic in the livid orange light.

'I—I'm sorry, sir,' was all he could say as he stepped quickly out of Stryker's path.

Stryker turned to the rest of the looters, who stared at him with slack expressions. 'Anyone else?' he snarled. 'You have the advantage of numbers, gentlemen. Do you wish to be as courageous as your friend, here?'

To a man, the looters shot wide-eyed glances at the bucktooth. The big soldier simply stared at his boots, all trace of bravery long gone, shoulders sagging as though he were a giant set of empty bellows.

Stryker removed his hat, rearranging the feathers carefully, before returning it and flattening down his crusty coat. 'I thought as much.'

'Find his company commander,' Lancelot Forrester said as he inspected the spur of an upturned boot.

Stryker glanced up from his tankard of small beer. 'To what end?'

Forrester was seated opposite Stryker at the low table, and his small teeth gleamed white in the guttering candle glow as he grinned wolfishly. 'Gauntlet the insubordinate bastard.'

The friends, along with four of Colonel Mowbray's other company captains, were in a small room above the Golden Goose taphouse. It was a good building to occupy, overlooking the marketplace and at a relatively safe distance from any of the town's fires. Mowbray had commandeered the entire building for his officers' billets, and the captains, as befitted the dignity of their rank, would share the group of smaller rooms on the first of three floors. They had congregated in one such room to share a drink, toasting their collective survival.

'I probably would,' Stryker said, considering the idea. Making the bucktooth's own company whip him with gloves filled with musket-balls was a tempting punishment. 'But he did not know who I was at first.'

'You're too lenient,' Forrester said, turning his attention back to the long, black boot.

'If he'd decided to take me on, things would have been different, I assure you.'

'I do not think anyone doubts that,' said a tall, willowy man as he strode into the chamber, the candle flames casting shadows over a head of tight, golden curls and severely crooked nose.

'Captain Kuyt.' Stryker stood hurriedly to greet the most senior of Mowbray's captains. His four comrades stood too, snatching off hats in salute.

First Captain Aad Kuyt went to the nearest table, lifted a pewter goblet and drained its contents, letting a small belch escape between thin lips. 'Sit, gentlemen,' he said, his voice smooth in confidence but distinct in origin. His tone was similar to that of Prince Rupert, but more pronounced, its source more definitely rooted in the Netherlands. 'Sir Edmund informs me we are to follow the general to Gloucester.'

Stryker stared up at him. 'Follow, sir?'

Kuyt sighed deeply before continuing. 'Prince Rupert wishes his army to be—' He chewed the inside of his mouth as the most apt word proved elusive. 'Fast.' The word ended up being uttered more as a question than a statement.

'Flying,' another voice interceded. It was Bottomley, the regiment's third-ranked captain. Bottomley was vastly corpulent, with yellow-bagged eyes and milky skin that seemed to glow against the coke blackness of his thick hair and neat whiskers. 'I overheard the colonel speaking with Lieutenant-Colonel Baxter. Prince Rupert means to have a flying column moving across the Midlands with stealth, attacking before the enemy's made its defences properly stout.'

Kuyt offered a slight bow. 'Thank you, Job. A flying column. And to have speed, Rupert must ride. He cannot wait upon infantry. So we follow his wake.'

'And Gloucester is his next target?' Stryker asked.

'Aye,' confirmed Kuyt. 'He will take his horse and dragooners nor'-west at dawn and call upon the town to surrender. Some foot are to form rearguard. Some must stay.'

'We go,' said a man sat on a three-legged stool in the room's far corner. Lettis Fullwood was newly commissioned, and as the regiment's sixth captain, was the lowest ranked of the company commanders. The man, in his mid twenties, had a sickly countenance of sallow skin and dense pockmarks. 'Sir,' he added, immediately looking abashed.

Captain Kuyt nodded. 'We go. Gloucester first, and then perhaps Bristol. Blunt Bob has been made aware, so your mounts will be prepared by sun-up.'

Stryker thought of Vos, his giant sorrel-coated stallion, and felt a mighty sense of relief that Blunt Bob was overseeing his care during their stay in this precarious town. Vos was an excellent horse, one that had been with him for many years. True, he had been captured by Captain Tainton in the killing ground of Shinfield Forest the previous autumn, but had been discovered, to Stryker's great joy, tethered with other captured mounts in a barn at the eastern edge of Old Brentford, after that fierce battle had finally ended.

'So tonight we round up our lads,' Kuyt went on. 'They must be ready for our march.'

Stryker rubbed rough fingers across his prickly chin. 'No easy task.'

Kuyt shot him a hard look. 'Problem?'

'No, sir, but you have been a soldier as long as I.'

'Longer,' Kuyt corrected.

Stryker dipped his head. 'So you will know that to deny a man his right to plunder is to invite trouble.'

'Then you will inform Prince Rupert that his infantry cannot do as they are ordered?'

Stryker stood up, wincing as his shoulder twinged at the sudden movement. 'No, sir. Of course not.'

Kuyt nodded curtly, eyes flicking to each man in turn. 'Then you have your orders, gentlemen.'

Forrester was bent forward, red-faced, hauling at the long sleeve of leather swathing his lower leg. 'Damn these new boots! I'll see to the men as soon as I can get this ill-fitting bloody thing on to my foot.'

'It's those enormous calves,' Stryker said, seeing the others stifle smirks.

Forrester glared up at him. 'Enormous due to muscle, Stryker! Too much cursed marching!'

'Oberon does all your marching, Forry,' Stryker said, keeping his face blank. 'Poor beast.'

'I am cut to the quick,' Forrester protested, though without conviction. Finally the boot jerked upwards and he grinned triumphantly. 'There!'

The company commanders filed out of the room under the gaze of Mowbray's First Captain. Stryker was last out, and Kuyt hailed him, compelling him to turn back. 'I have one other task for you, Stryker.'

They were alone now, and Stryker raised his scarred brow. 'Sir?'

'There is a man here, in this building, we are safeguarding.' His voice was low, conspiratorial. 'He has been ordered to Prince Rupert's billet. I want you to escort him.'

'I don't understand, sir. The general's quarters are only a matter of three of four hundred yards away. Just across the marketplace.'

'The man is important,' Kuyt said simply.

'And the town is dangerous,' another voice suddenly interrupted from out in the corridor.

Stryker turned to the doorway, to see two men enter the room, neither of whom he recognized. The first was in his early forties, tall, square-jawed and bright-eyed. Golden hair fell from beneath the brim of his hat to his shoulders, thick, coarse and straight, like a straw thatch. 'The name is Jonathan Blaze,' he said in a loud, confident tone.

Stryker shook the proffered hand, noticing the swirling, mottled skin of the man's fingers. 'You deal in ordnance?'

Blaze grinned, bearing long, white teeth. 'Keenly observed, Captain. I am a fireworker, yes. More than that. I deal in all types of explosive. Artillery, grenadoes, petards.' With a small nod, Blaze indicated his companion. 'My assistant Jesper Rontry.'

Rontry was a man of similar age to Blaze but of far smaller stature, with thinning, mousy hair above his ears, a completely bald pate and a disposition as dissimilar to his master's as Stryker could imagine possible. He seemed sickly, frail, and flinched at every scream or crash coming from outside the tavern, while his eyelids were perpetually screwed down, as if he could not help but wince in the presence of such warlike men.

Rontry's nose was pinched and red at the tip, made to run thick with sticky mucus by the cold. 'Captain,' he acknowledged, wiping a dirty sleeve across his upper lip. 'I am pleased to make your—'

'Enough of your twittering, Jes,' Blaze interrupted suddenly, waving a big hand towards his assistant as if swatting a fly. Rontry dropped his gaze to the straw beneath his boots. Blaze stared at Stryker. 'The prince

43

would undermine any city that defies him. Blow their walls to kingdom come. For that he requires my expertise.'

'Which is why you must keep him alive,' Kuyt said.

Stryker glanced at his superior. 'Escort Master Blaze to the general's billet?'

Kuyt nodded. 'Only that, Stryker. Then you may see to your men.' He pulled a mildly apologetic expression. 'It is a simple task, I admit, but I am a mercenary, Stryker. I do not easily trust.'

'I'll see him safe, sir.'

'My apologies for dragging you from your duties, Captain,' Blaze said, addressing Stryker as the trio crossed the debris-strewn marketplace, 'but I am quite sure Jesper and I would not fair well on our own tonight.'

That was true, Stryker thought, as he looked at the booming-voiced fireworker. 'The streets are not safe,' he agreed. 'After a storming, our men are akin to wild animals.'

'It is not only the king's men we fear, sir,' Blaze replied.

'Oh?'

'Parliament's supporters in the town would have me flayed alive if they could,' Blaze explained, his wide face almost glowing with pride. 'I am a wanted man, you know.'

'A criminal?' Stryker asked, Blaze's haughty tone already beginning to grate.

He noticed Rontry wince.

'Not a bit of it, Captain,' Blaze said, evidently taking no offence at Stryker's curtness.

'A genius!' Rontry blurted.

44

'Hush, Jes,' Blaze commanded, again making the swatting gesture at his assistant.

Stryker sensed that the way had been left open for him to ask Blaze about his supposed genius. He kept his mouth shut.

'Master Blaze,' Jesper Rontry began, his legs scuttling rapidly to keep pace with the taller men, 'is an expert in his field. There are very few in the land as capable as he. Consequently the enemy would pay dear to be rid of him.'

Stryker thought back to the approach towards Cirencester, remembering all too well the daunting prospect of breaching the web of defences protecting the town's south-western entrance. But those barriers had vanished in great tongues of flame and clouds of filthy smoke, the explosion ringing hours later in his ears. 'It was you,' he said suddenly, stride faltering. 'You blew the barricades at the Barton, didn't you?'

Blaze revealed those dazzling teeth again. 'An odious task, I don't mind telling you,' he said. 'Or do I mean odorous? Hid myself all that night in a cart full of rotting mulch with nought but the petard as company.'

'I'd have stayed with you,' Rontry interrupted.

Blaze wrinkled his long nose. 'Bloody freezing it was.'

'You placed a petard in a cart,' Stryker said, for it was all beginning to make sense, 'and left the cart against the barricade.'

'Aye,' Blaze nodded. 'I'd already packed the thing full of black powder, so it simply remained for me to listen for Rupert's trumpets, light the bugger and run like hell.'

'Run like hell?' Stryker repeated as they picked up the pace again. 'That's a brave act in itself, Master Blaze,

45

for you might have found a musket-ball between your shoulders.'

Blaze casually picked grime from beneath his broad fingernails. 'They'd be lucky to hit a man from forty yards, Captain,' he said, a wry smile turning up the corner of his mouth. 'By the time they realized what I was about, I was out of any effective range.'

Stryker touched a finger to his hat in acknowledgement of the feat. 'Odious or odorous, Master Blaze, it worked us a miracle.'

'You are most welcome, Captain,' Blaze said, and Rontry, while saying nothing, looked like he might burst with pride.

'We are here, sir,' Stryker said after a short while. He pointed at a big stone building, once home, he presumed, to a wealthy member of the local mercantile class. Armed men in blue clothing guarded the door. 'The prince's headquarters.'

Blaze shook Stryker's hand. 'Thank you, Captain. Perhaps our paths will cross in the future.'

'One never knows, sir.'

Stryker returned to the Golden Goose and stepped into its capacious taproom.

'Sir,' a voice snapped from the gloom.

It took a few moments for Stryker's vision to become accustomed to the gloomier surroundings, but, sure enough, the man he had expected to see was standing, straight-backed and square-shouldered against the bar. Skellen had been drinking, for there was a wooden cup beside him, but he stood upright and looked sober. Around him were a handful of Stryker's men, and he indicated that they should all follow.

Stryker shoved open the tavern's heavy oaken door. 'With me.'

'Off for a stroll, sir?' Skellen asked, his expression blank but his tone wry.

'Don't be so bloody impudent.'

'Sorry, sir, but that's what Cap'n Forrester said.'

'Of course he did. We're to gather the men. The Prince intends to march on Gloucester at first light.'

They were out in the street now, the glow of fires affording the night a strange luminosity. Skellen and Heel walked shoulder to shoulder with Stryker, followed by his standard-bearer, Ensign Chase, and two of his corporals, Tresick and Shephard.

'Where's the lieutenant?' Stryker asked.

'Ain't seen 'im, sir,' Skellen replied, almost too quickly.

Stryker shot him a hard glance. 'Are you covering for him?'

Skellen fixed his gaze on a point just above Stryker's shoulder. ''Course not, sir.'

'Think carefully, Moses,' Stryker said, turning to Sergeant Heel. He knew attempting to break through Skellen's well-practised impassivity would be futile, but Heel was easier to coerce. 'Where is Lieutenant Burton? If you lie to me, Sergeant, it will not go well for you.'

Heel swallowed thickly. 'He's over at some boozin' ken near the abbey, sir.' Skellen cast Heel a sour look, but the burly man from Tiverton shrugged helplessly.

Stryker glowered. 'You saw him? How was he?'

'Gage in his fist, an' eyes like a couple o' piss-holes in the snow, sir.'

'I'll deal with him later,' Stryker said sharply, already striding away, the party corralled at the Golden Goose in tow.

47

The group strode out into the marketplace and immediately identified a group of soldiers from Stryker's company gathered across the street. 'You men!'

Heads turned at the sound of Stryker's voice. 'Sir?' one replied.

'Back to billets! We march at dawn!'

Stryker stalked away before the men could argue, and led his group to the nearest alley. They passed more men, ordering them back to their quarters and ensuring the message would be passed on.

When the alley opened out into a wider thoroughfare, they saw a large group of men, carts and horses. At first Stryker wondered if the looting had increased to a far more sophisticated scale, but then a voice he knew well emanated from the party. It was a gravelly tone, made coarse by London's streets and laced with the possibility of violence.

'Bob!' Stryker shouted at the men around the cart. 'Bob!'

At length, a heavy-jowled man with fat on his stomach and muscle on his arms stepped from the crowd. 'Gabriel's beard, Stryker, but this gaggle o' lazy, piss-brained nanny hens are good for nothin' but whorin' and sleepin', I swear it!'

Stryker grinned at Robert Yalden, or Blunt Bob as he was known to the men. Sir Edmund Mowbray's regimental wagon-master was famously short-fused and impressive in a fight, and, to Stryker's mind, one of the colonel's most wisely picked staff officers. 'Where are the horses, sir?'

'Satan's stones, man, am I your bloody mother?' Yalden snarled. 'Am I?'

48

'No, sir,' Stryker said quickly, 'but you are the most knowledgeable and efficient wagon-master in the entire army.'

'Well fuck me backwards if your nose ain't covered in my dung!' He pointed a gnarled hand in the direction of a large building of timber frame and low roof. 'Old storehouse. When we got here it was full o' tallow candles and dragoons. Now the candles are in the lads' snapsacks, and the store's full o' horses!'

'And the dragoons?'

'Out on their ear.' Yalden patted his sword-hilt. 'Took some persuading, but they saw sense.'

'Thank you, Bob,' Stryker said, as Skellen smirked in the background.

'*Sir* to you!' Yalden snarled.

'Sir,' Stryker replied with a wry smile and turned away, leaving the wagon-master to berate his unfortunate subordinates. 'I mean to check on the horses,' he said to his men. 'Rest of you go out into the town. Warn the men they'll deal directly with me if they're not ready to march by sun-up.'

Stryker covered the fifty paces to the storehouse in short order, passing at least half a dozen homes whose doors had been flung open so violently that pale wood had been exposed where the hinges were ripped away. Skellen was at his heel, as Stryker knew he would be. A scream rang out from somewhere nearby. It split the air with its startling pitch, sharp and blood-curdling. There were many screams that night. Screams of the wounded, of the frightened and of the angry, and neither man paid any heed.

The storehouse's rectangular frontage stretched out before them. At its centre was a wide doorway, large

49

enough for a cart to pass through. Yalden, as always, had chosen well.

Flanking the doorway were four of Mowbray's musketeers, grim-faced and watchful.

'Captain Stryker and Sergeant Skellen,' Stryker announced as he drew close.

The musketeers stepped aside, one of them unlocking the great door as the pair passed.

The temporary stable was wide and long, but its low ceiling and ripe stench made it feel suffocating. Skellen followed Stryker into its depths, staring about the gloomy building. There were somewhere in the region of thirty horses tethered to the upright beams of the walls. Greys and blacks and bays and chestnuts. All standing nervously, all staring at the newcomers.

'Strange,' Skellen murmured at Stryker's side. 'They're not eating.'

Stryker looked at the untouched hay strewn around the beasts. 'You're right.'

'Somethin's spooked 'em.'

Stryker moved further into the long room, caution ringing like church bells in his mind. At the far corner was a small table, piled high with various items of tack. 'Where's the stable hand?'

Skellen looked at him. 'Not somethin' Blunt Bob would have forgotten, is it?'

Stryker shook his head. And, as he moved deeper into the musty room, he noticed a leg jutting out from behind the table. He ran forward, crouching down beside the prone form of a young lad, a deep gash glistening at his temple. He removed his glove and felt for a pulse at the boy's neck. It was there, faint but steady.

'Sir!' Skellen said, urgency inflecting his voice.

Stryker stood, looking across the room to where the sergeant pointed. There was a door set into the wall, presumably leading to some kind of antechamber. The door was ajar, and, from beyond it, low voices could be heard.

'Alert the guards, Will,' Stryker ordered and, as the sergeant quickly obeyed, ran to the door and pushed it open. What he saw took him utterly by surprise. There in front of him was his own horse, Vos. The huge, red-coloured stallion was being coaxed through the antechamber to another door that, Stryker now saw, opened out on to the street beyond.

'He won't go, Saul,' the coaxer was saying. 'Won't move a blinkin' muscle.'

'What the bloody hell do you think you're doing?' Stryker said, striding by Vos's muscular bulk to accost the yellow-coated man who gripped his bridle.

The man simply gaped, and another spoke for him. 'None o' yer goddamned business!'

Stryker spun to his left to see a second man dressed in yellow step into his field of vision. This, he presumed, was the one named Saul. 'It is my goddamned business,' Stryker said, keeping his tone level, 'because it's my goddamned horse.'

The yellowcoats glanced at one another, each searching the other's face for a response, but Stryker had seen enough. The guards at the front of the building were obviously unaware of the yellow-coated intruders, while the unconscious stableboy and use of such a furtive exit route told him only one thing.

Stryker hammered his fist into the first man's chin. The man released Vos's looped reins, and, though it felt to

51

Stryker as though he had punched an anvil, went crashing on to the messy hay.

Stryker turned immediately on the one named Saul, lashing up at the man's meaty midriff with the sharp toe-end of his boot. It connected in a dull thud, hard and fast, and Saul doubled forward with a howl of agony and surprise. When he straightened, his face was a mask of rage. One hand remained pressed to his injured guts, a knife appearing in the other. 'Come, sir,' he challenged, crouching slightly like a cat about to pounce.

Stryker advanced quickly, hoping Saul had lost some of his wits with the blow, and moved a hand to the tacky shark-skin grip of his sword-hilt. The blade, his most prized possession, hung from its long scabbard, inviting him to reveal its lethal edge, but the room was small, especially so with the huge stallion stood patiently at its centre, and Stryker could not be sure that its length would prove help not hindrance.

'Stick 'im, Saul!' the first man, sitting up now, screamed, voice high and desperate as he hurried to regain his feet. 'Hew 'n punch the fucker!'

'Get off yer blasted arse, Caleb, and help me!' Saul snarled, lunging forward as he finished the sentence.

Stryker was ready for the attack. Saul had struck high, as Stryker knew he would, aiming the dagger for the exposed windpipe, and Stryker twisted away, performing an about-turn on the balls of his feet. He finished behind his attacker, and kicked savagely at the yellowcoat's broad back. Saul careered into Vos's solid flank, bouncing off the horse as though he had run into a tree.

As Saul went sprawling on to the hay, Stryker turned his attention to Caleb, noticing how alike this pair were. Both had broad, flat noses and thick auburn beards. Both were of stocky frame, but significantly shorter than Stryker.

'Not going to help your brother, Caleb?' Stryker said. He glanced back at Saul's inert body. 'He'd be glad of the assistance, I think.'

Caleb looked from Stryker to Saul and back to Stryker. A small whimper escaped his mouth, a whimper that became a bellow of rage. He leapt forward with the fury of a wounded bull, and Stryker had to react rapidly lest he be trampled by the crazed yellowcoat. This time he drew his long sword. It might not have been effective in a duel, but now it would most certainly suffice. He would not even have to deliver a stroke.

Caleb ran straight on to the blade, the expensive Spanish steel piercing his clothing and flesh with little difficulty. Stryker was forced to use all his strength to keep a grip on the hilt, and he leaned in, putting his full weight behind the weapon. For a moment it seemed as though Caleb would keep coming, run through the sword and place meaty hands around Stryker's throat. But then, as if time itself slowed, his momentum dwindled. It was as though he waded through slurry. And then he stopped. Stopped and sagged. The light faded from his pale-blue eyes and the breath wheezed its way through the fresh hole in his chest.

For a moment man and corpse stared at one another. Caleb was gone, but Stryker could not take his eyes from the man he had killed. The yellowcoat was hanging on the blade, blood blooming in all directions where the weapon had entered. He was held up only by the strength in Stryker's hands.

'Captain!'

The warning was almost too late, for Saul had regained his wits and was bearing down upon him from the other side of the room. There was no time to pull the sword from Caleb's broad frame, so Stryker released it, twisting away to face the new assault, and thanking God his assailant had lost his dagger during their first altercation. He ducked below Saul's heavy punch, and rammed his own fist low and solid into the stocky man's guts. Saul was unhurt, but it made him step back a pace, and Stryker followed him, unyielding, aggressive.

Saul doubled over in a great bellow of anguish as Stryker kicked him in the balls, then grasped his shoulders in a grip of iron, lifting a knee savagely into his face.

He howled as blood sprayed in a fine mist from his shattered nose, then he was stumbling backwards, reeling from the attack, retreating from an enemy that seemed unable to relent. Hands were at his shoulders again. He was being propelled rearwards, step by inexorable step, halting only when something hard met the small of his back. Then his eyes, fixed though they were on Stryker's narrow face, seemed to glaze.

Stryker looked down, staring at the trio of long iron prongs that filled the space between their bodies. Tattered pieces of Saul's intestines hung from their sharp points like some implement used at a city shambles.

'Thank you, Will,' Stryker said, acknowledging Skellen's timely intervention. 'I owe you one.'

The sergeant jerked the pitchfork free. 'I'll add it to the list, sir.'

Stryker let Saul's body drop to the floor and cast his eye across the carnage of the room. Vos still stood, impassive and immovable, but all around the horse it looked as though a petard had been ignited within the small chamber's confines. Caleb's body was slumped near the stallion's front hooves, the sword still protruding from his sternum, blood escaping in a thick lake to stain the hay. Stryker walked across to the dead man and bent to grasp the basket-hilt of his sword, placing a boot against the already stiffening shoulder. 'Hew and punch.'

'Beg pardon?' Skellen replied.

'That's what this bastard,' Stryker said, with a gentle kick of the corpse, 'urged the other to do.' He glanced at Saul's inert body. 'I assumed *that* bastard would heed his advice. Luckily for me I was right.'

'The old neck slash and belly slit,' Skellen said grimly. 'I know it well.'

Stryker thought better than to ask for the sergeant to elaborate. He wiped the blade on Caleb's breeches, leaving a long red smear across the bright yellow fabric, and slid it back into its scabbard. 'Get those guards round here, Sergeant,' he ordered, taking hold of Vos's reins. 'Tell the buggers to man the back door as well!'

The hours went quickly by, for the night brought a ceaseless stream of duties. The sacking continued unabated, and with it came tales of drink-fuelled brawls, rape and murder. But the sack of a town was – by tradition if not law – accepted as the right of a victorious soldier, and Stryker could only curtail the acts of his own men, hoping that they would muster in time for the morning departure.

It was still dark when he and Skellen made their way back to the marketplace to take a look at the number of prisoners the bitter storming had ensnared. They paced across the cobbles, seeing disparate groups of men huddled together at sword-point, waiting, Stryker assumed, to be herded to a central location where they might be held in the short term.

A large, dirty-white dog ran across their path. It had beady black eyes and a coat of tight curls. It trotted to where Stryker stood, pausing to sniff at his boots and breeches, and if Stryker had not recognized the animal instantly, it might have earned a sharp kick for its curiosity. Instead Stryker straightened his back instinctively.

'Ah, if it ain't the rather-less-than-innocent Innocent!' Prince Rupert of the Rhine's mildly accented English barked from some distance behind Stryker. The latter turned to see the extraordinarily tall general striding, head and shoulders above all others in the marketplace, from the direction of the parish church.

Stryker gave a low bow, but Rupert ignored it. Instead he pointed at the blackened remains of a workshop facing on to the street. 'In there,' he said abruptly, before casting a look of distaste in the direction of the rapidly growing number of prisoners.

'To your duty, Sergeant,' Stryker called back to Skellen as he followed Prince Rupert – and the dog, Boye – into the fired chandlery. 'By dawn!'

Once beneath the precarious beams, Stryker snatched off his wide-brimmed hat, partly out of respect and partly because he was suddenly aware that the garment, a gift from Rupert, was looking some distance beyond its best. 'Your Highness,' he began, 'I trust you are well?'

'S'precious blood, Captain! Do not bow and scrape.'

Stryker looked up, meeting that dark, intimidating gaze.

'And put your bloody hat on,' the prince snapped before Stryker could formulate a sensible response. For the first time, Rupert seemed to notice the guards that had followed them into the room. 'Leave.'

When the pair were alone, Rupert's long face became impish as his keen eyes twinkled. 'How was it? The blade, I mean?'

Stryker could not withhold a smile when he thought of his new double-edged broadsword. 'Incredible, General. Well balanced, strong and as sharp a thing as I've used.'

Rupert grinned excitedly. 'Did I not tell you? Spanish steel, Captain. Toledo, to be precise. The best of the best.'

'And I thank Her Majesty for it daily, sir,' Stryker said genuinely.

'We were all grateful for your yeoman service last year,' Rupert said. 'In fact, Stryker, my aunt is quite taken with you. I will tell her you are pleased with the token.'

'Token?' Stryker brushed fingertips across the pommel's twinkling garnet. 'It is an incredible gift, sir.'

Rupert nodded. 'Quite so.' He fished in his doublet briefly, eventually producing a silver drinking flask. 'It is good to see you survived the fight, Stryker, damn me it is.'

'Likewise, sir,' Stryker said, accepting the flask and unscrewing the lid, 'but this is a strange place to be toasting our victory, if I may be so bold.'

As Stryker took a draught of the fiery liquid, Rupert glanced left and right as if the Earl of Essex himself might be crouched behind one of the black beams. He paused to rifle once more inside the doublet, which,

57

Stryker could tell in the moonlight, was a mix of green and silver, its silks and satins shimmering with each movement. When his hand reappeared it gripped a small apple. Rupert sunk his teeth into its pale flesh, a bead of juice tracing a path down his pointed chin. When he had finished chewing, the prince met Stryker's expectant gaze, his own eyes suddenly hard. 'I have lost something, Stryker. Some*one*, to be precise. One of my agents. The very best.'

'And you wish me to find him?'

Rupert nodded slowly.

'Where, sir?' Stryker asked with a sense of foreboding. His last mission for the prince, which had cost three of his men their lives, and barely left him with his own, had been one of the most perilous undertakings of his military career, and he was not eager to experience anything similar.

Rupert stooped to ruffle Boye's coarse fur. 'Staffordshire.'

Stryker thought for a moment. 'I was told Mowbray's were marching on Gloucester with you, Highness.'

Rupert nodded. 'And they are. But without you.'

'This mission is secret?'

'Well, it ain't public knowledge, Stryker, naturally!' He took another bite of the apple. 'When the main force marches west, to Gloucester, you will instead travel north.' Gnawing away the last pieces of flesh from the fruit, he tossed it into the charred ruins at his feet, ignoring the panting Boye, who darted across the room to snaffle the core. 'This agent was escorting an important man,' Rupert's voice echoed about the chandler's smoke-stinking shell, 'to Stafford. It is crucial to our cause. We have the south-west and Wales. And we have much of the north. The enemy hold the south and east. But who owns the middle?'

'No one,' was Stryker's reply.

The prince nodded sombrely. 'Neither side and yet both sides. It is a *kookketel*, Stryker. A cauldron. Stirred and bubbling. We must take it, inch by bloody inch if need be. Stafford is garrisoned by king's men. It must stay that way. The man my agent escorted was—'

'*Was?*'

'Was—is—I do not know. He's a man of rare knowledge, sent to aid our supporters in that garrison. Something must have happened, for they never reached Stafford.' Rupert had shrugged helplessly. 'Vanished.'

'Then how will I begin to find them?'

'It appears my agent has resurfaced in nearby Lichfield. Wounded, but alive. If you find the agent, you may discover what happened to the expert. And if he lives, it is crucial that he is found.'

The idea took shape in Stryker's mind, bringing with it a deep sense of foreboding. Damn the prince! Since his successful mission to capture a dangerous turncoat in the weeks after Kineton Fight, he had become Rupert's man, the prince's agent, assigned to conduct the general's more dangerous tasks whenever the mood took him. And Stryker resented it.

'It would make me most grateful, Captain,' Rupert said, perhaps noting the reluctance in Stryker's hard face. 'And besides, I'd wager you, above all men, have a certain interest in seeing this job successfully executed.'

Stryker stared up into the prince's eyes, intelligence glinting bright from their brown depths. 'Your Highness?'

'Did I not mention before? My agent,' Rupert said softly, 'is Mademoiselle Gaillard.'

Stryker swallowed hard, a knot forming tight and sickeningly in the very pit of his guts. 'Lichfield, you say?'

CHAPTER 3

Stryker was arrested at dawn. It had been a busy night. He had not slept and was in a mood of high irritation when he returned to the Golden Goose to breakfast. His shoulder still smarted from the graze received amid the remnants of the chained harrow, and his eye felt sore from powder grit and exhaustion. Most of all, he wanted to be away from this town and on the road north. To Lichfield. To Lisette.

He stepped across the threshold, dipping his head to clear the oaken lintel. He expected to find some of his fellow officers similarly at rest within the dark room, sheltering from the swirling anarchy outside. The room was pitch black to his eye, for the night had been lurid with flame and the sudden contrast was blinding. As he waited for clarity to return, he considered what he might do after taking well-earned victuals. Catch up on some sleep, or take time to sharpen his sword.

But as his raw eye adjusted to the gloom, it fixed upon six shapes, ghostly at first, but rapidly gathering form so that swords and muskets began to resolve before him. Soldiers, armed and purposeful.

He watched them with interest because, while it was no surprise to see armed men, their yellow uniforms reminded him instantly of that devastated stable block, its straw drenched red.

One of them stepped forward. 'Captain Stryker. You're to accompany us, sir.'

'Accompany?'

The yellowcoat stepped forward a pace, his bearded face grave. 'I am to place you under arrest, sir.'

'By whose order?' was Stryker's sharp retort as he rested a hand at the pommel of his sword.

The lead yellowcoat was a sergeant, and he lowered his halberd so that its three-bladed head was level with Stryker's chest. 'Order o' Prince Rupert, sir,' he said, tone sliding from steady calm to growled threat. 'You're to come now.'

'I'faith, man,' another voice snapped from the doorway through which Stryker had stepped, 'I suggest you back down, before I knock you down.'

Stryker turned and was pleased to see a friendly face.

The sergeant, flanked by equally confrontational subordinates, was unrelenting in the face of two senior officers. 'I have m'orders . . . sir?'

'Captain Lancelot Forrester,' Forrester introduced himself. His affable face was creased in anger. 'Now put those rusty tucks away, or I shall be obliged to ram 'em up your arses!'

The sergeant flinched but remained truculent. 'Can't do that, sir. Captain Stryker, here, must attend the inquiry.'

Forrester's face was reddening as only it could. 'Inquiry? Goddamn it, asinine bloody ape, what inquiry?'

The sergeant turned his attention back to Stryker. He nodded at the open doorway. 'If you'll come wi' us, sir.'

'Go,' another man spoke from deeper within the dark taproom, cutting across the exchange before Forrester could muster another salvo. Stryker squinted to see the tired face of Captain Kuyt. 'These men have provided their papers. They are within their rights, Stryker. I will inform the colonel, do not worry.' The Dutchman's calm gaze flicked to Forrester. 'But make no trouble, gentlemen. It cannot help matters.'

Stryker saw that another man stood next to Kuyt, and he recognized the gun-metal grey whiskers and angular jaw of the regiment's provost-marshal, Humfrey Patience, the man charged with keeping discipline in Sir Edmund's ranks. Stryker held his eye meaningfully, hoping the prov-ost-marshal might intervene on his behalf, but Patience simply returned the look with a glower. 'Just bloody go, Captain,' he snapped irritably. 'Or would you defy the Prince?'

With the stench of Cirencester's burnt-out buildings hanging in his nostrils, Stryker paced nervously into the hallway of the grandiose town house chosen by Prince Rupert as his headquarters.

The place fairly bristled with armed guards. In addition to the yellow-coated arrest party that still flanked their charge closely, Stryker passed sentries at the large entrance, surly faces scanning the street in grim warning, and members of various units patrolling the long corridors and protecting the winding staircase. The prince was evidently taking no chances in the unashamedly rebel town.

Stryker rubbed his jaw. It was sore, the muscles afflicted by the familiar dull ache that would always appear the day following battle. The result, he supposed, of gritting his teeth with such savagery during those furious moments when a lapse in concentration could prove fatal. His smarting shoulder reminded him that it almost had.

The nearest door opened suddenly, its creaking hinges unnaturally loud in the corridor, and a montero-capped head poked round to fix eyes upon Stryker. 'The general bids you enter, Captain Stryker,' the white-whiskered man said.

'There's the churl! The stink of murder verily wafts from him!'

The voice was high, and Stryker almost had to take a step back, such was the malevolence inflecting the tone. Instead, he paced with deliberate composure into the room.

It was small for the headquarters of a general, but that lack of size only served to magnify Stryker's discomfort, for the sombre faces that regarded him were so awkwardly close. Two musketeers behind, guarding the door, three men seated before him, bare-headed and solemn, and a clerk, taking the role of scribe, he presumed, sat to his right. Too many bodies for such a small space. It seemed to thicken the atmosphere tenfold.

At the end of the room was a table, a low piece, plain and unprepossessing, containing nothing on its surface but a pot helmet in the Dutch style, with distinctive fixed peak and sliding nose guard. A helmet Stryker remembered from the nervous moments before assaulting Cirencester and its doomed barricade.

Sat behind that helmet its owner was resplendent in gold-laced buff-coat over a rich green-and-silver uniform. His sleeves billowed open like unbuttoned cassocks, displaying a fine shirt of pristine white linen, while the golden lace of the aiguillettes at his shoulders seemed to shimmer amid the otherwise drab surroundings. His long face, however, was a darker affair, for the king's nephew positively glowered at Stryker, brown eyes smaller, harder than Stryker had ever seen them.

But it was not the prince that had spoken with such shrill fury. Seated to the left of the table was a man who Stryker could see would be fairly short when standing, for the top of his bare head did not reach Rupert's collar. He was stocky at the shoulder, with bushy white brows, a thick white beard and fat, wet lips.

Stryker met the man's gaze. He recognized detestation, had encountered it too many times to mention on battle-fields and in towns across Europe and now England. And here it was again, staring back at him, twinkling behind eyes of the palest blue, wrinkling the flat, bulbous nose, bringing trembling tension to those amphibian lips. Such intensity. Unbridled, seething, bubbling, as if the man's very skin might melt.

Stryker chose to ignore him. 'Your Highness, I—'

Rupert held up a hand. 'Please. No rhetoric, Captain.'

The man to Rupert's side visibly bristled, leaning suddenly forward as if shot in the back. '*Captain*?' he spat. 'No longer, sir. No longer . . .'

Rupert held up a curtailing hand. 'And no diatribes either, Artemas.' The young general turned to his left. 'Sir Edmund, would you please, for the record, confirm that this man is, indeed, Captain Innocent Stryker, Second Captain to your own Regiment of Foot?'

'Of course, Highness,' Sir Edmund Mowbray said, absently twisting the waxed tip of his neat beard. 'This is he.' Mowbray was a far smaller man than either Rupert or Artemas. He made Stryker think of a rodent, slender-faced and delicate-featured, but imbued with a frenetic energy that made him a fine fighter and competent leader.

'Stryker,' Rupert was saying. 'What the devil have you done?'

'Sir, I—' Stryker began, but was cut off as Artemas suddenly shot to his feet.

'Cowardly, soul-rotten, pelting churl! You're a disgrace to your rank, sir! A disgrace to this army!'

Stryker remained silent.

Artemas gritted his teeth, the skin of his cheeks a deep crimson beneath the mop of white hair that sprouted unevenly from his narrow skull. One stubby hand rifled within the folds of his yellow doublet, until finally, triumphantly, it appeared with a great flourish, brandishing a small, well-thumbed book. 'You're destined for hell's inferno, Stryker,' the man hissed. 'Your wicked-hearted sergeant too. You'll burn, sir. Burn! Or are you so mired in sin that murder is nothing to you?' The small eyes gleamed like nuggets of jet as they swivelled to stare at Rupert. 'Perhaps he kills so many men, he thinks it of no more account than scratching his arse.'

Rupert's face remained impassive. 'Perhaps. But put the Bible away, there's a good chap.' He looked at Stryker. 'You have met Colonel Crow? Raised a regiment of dragoons for my uncle.'

Stryker shook his head. 'No, sir.'

'The colonel brings a charge of murder against you and Sergeant Skellen. The sergeant,' he added, seeing Stryker's eye widen, 'is already under lock and key.'

Prince Rupert leaned back in his chair, exposing the broad red and silver sash at his waist and interlinking his hands behind his head. 'It is alleged that you disposed of two of Colonel Crow's men last night.'

Stryker could barely hear his own thoughts above the pounding of his heart. He considered lying, but that course seemed futile. Instead, he kept his gaze fixed on a crack in the wall somewhere above and behind Prince Rupert. 'Yes, sir. To be precise, I ran one through, and the other fell on to a pitchfork. Sergeant Skellen played no part in it.'

Rupert removed his hands from behind his head, leaning slowly forward.

'There!' Crow's shrill cry was triumphal, and he thumped a fist on to the tabletop. 'You have it, General. From the devil's own lips!'

'They were stealing our horses, sir,' Stryker added hastily. 'Blunt B— that is to say Wagon-Master Yalden had evicted the dragoons from the building and turned it to stabling. I can only assume they were vexed by such treatment and returned to seek revenge.' There were no witnesses, he thought, so the dragoons must have stayed in the vicinity and seen Stryker and Skellen enter the stable.

'He lies!' Crow almost screamed. 'Slanders as well as murders!'

'Jesu, Colonel Crow,' Rupert snapped with sudden ferocity. 'Must I ask you to leave? Must I?'

Crow, with visible effort, took his seat once more. 'No, Highness.'

'Then keep that firebrand tongue still, sir, or I swear—'

Colonel Mowbray cleared his throat with little subtlety.

Rupert dipped his head in acknowledgement. 'Quite right, Sir Edmund.' He glared at Stryker. 'You are charged with the murder of Dragoon Caleb Potts.'

'They were stealing our goddamned horses, General!' Stryker protested. 'I startled them, and they attacked me. Of course I murdered the thieving bastards!'

'And of his brother,' Rupert went on morosely, his voice flat and low, '*Lieutenant* Saul Potts.'

It was as if Rupert had stabbed Stryker with a red-hot dirk. 'They were stealing,' he said again, though the revelation that he had killed an officer made it feel as though his throat was suddenly stuffed full of flax. 'They came at me first. I—'

'Stealing horses?' Colonel Crow barked. 'Insidious, barefaced lies, told by a man with less breeding than my dogs!' His glassy eyes swivelled to the prince. 'He'll be murdering half your army if he has his way, sir!'

'It's not true, sir,' Stryker argued weakly.

'And what of my witness, eh?' Crow went on, like a hound sensing the kill. 'Will you deny his word, too?'

'Witness?' Stryker said, truly baffled.

Crow waved a thick-fingered hand at the guards, and they ushered a man into the room. He was a big man, taller than Stryker and clearly well muscled, with a thick blond moustache and long straw-coloured hair. He, too, wore the yellow garb of Crow's regiment. 'I saw the fight,' the man said in an accent Stryker guessed was Scandinavian in origin.

'And you are?' Stryker asked, utterly thrown by this new twist.

'Major Henning Edberg.' The Scandinavian's ocean-blue eyes fixed on him. 'Saul and Caleb Potts, loyal soldiers both, were plundering the building, naturally, but not stealing your horses. I saw you and your sergeant murder them in cold blood.'

'I'm telling you, Your Highness,' Stryker protested, 'they were trying to take the animals!'

'Scandalous lies!' Crow interjected harshly, his face aglow, a bead of spittle escaping down his clean-shaven chin. 'If they plundered, then it was only from the enemy.'

The prince held up his hand again, his hard stare drilling into Stryker. 'It is not within even my power to deny the men their just reward.'

'But they attacked me first, Your Highness, it was self defence.'

Rupert sighed heavily. 'And yet Major Edberg, a man who outranks you, do not forget, says different.'

Without warning, Prince Rupert took to his feet, snatching up the helmet and thrusting the chair out behind him to clatter noisily against the wall. 'I haven't time for this. I ride for Gloucester as soon as I am able.'

A thought struck Stryker then, twisting his guts to knots. 'What of Lichfield, sir?'

Rupert shot Stryker a grim look. 'Due to your actions, Captain, that business will have to be postponed for the time being. You'll be sentenced upon my return.'

'But General,' Crow spluttered, 'the man is a murderer of the lowest kind. The *Orders and Articles for the Better Ordering of His Majesty's Army* are clear in such matters. The sentence is for the bounder to be shot through!'

Rupert rounded on the indignant Crow. 'Do not presume to quote the *Articles* at me, Colonel! By God, it will not stand!' He waited until Crow had had the wisdom to lower his bellicose stare, before continuing in a more controlled manner. 'I am well aware of the gravity of this man's alleged crime, Artemas, but Captain Stryker is a respected, loyal officer.'

'The *Orders and Articles*,' Sir Edmund Mowbray added when he had gained Crow's attention, 'also state that no man shall presume to lift up his hand to strike a superior officer, upon pain of death. Captain Stryker maintains he was not the aggressor.'

'And *Major* Edberg refutes the claim,' Crow growled.

'Clearly I must ponder this case a while longer,' Rupert said, pushing his way out from behind the table and making his way towards the door, only turning to say, 'Upon my return, when the town's fires have gone cold and more potential witnesses have been sought, we will see this sorry incident dealt with, I swear it. In the interim, Stryker and his sergeant will be placed under lock and key.'

Stryker was a prisoner, and, to all intents and purposes, soon to be a dead man. He dropped his gaze in the silence that followed the prince's departure, making no effort to resist the rough hands that took away his sword, wondering how victory had turned to personal defeat in so short a time. When he looked up, he was staring into the baleful face of Colonel Artemas Crow.

'Sleep lightly, Captain,' Crow said, his voice no greater than a whisper.

As Stryker was led away by Rupert's guards, he felt Crow's stare like a blade in his spine.

'Snout-fair gaol, if ever there was one,' William Skellen said as he craned his long neck to stare out of the little window.

Stryker came to stand beside the sergeant. He had been taken from Rupert's quarters and marched, under heavy guard, to the only building large enough to incarcerate the huge number of captives taken during the Royalist storming: St John's church.

Stryker and Skellen were being held in a small room facing out on to the marketplace, while the rebel soldiers and townsmen had been locked in the long nave, but now those frightened men were being led out on to the slushy road. Stryker followed Skellen's gaze, peering through the small window crammed with vertical iron bars. 'I don't imagine they had prison duty in mind when it was built,' he said, as he watched the mass of bedraggled captives file past, each squinting at the sudden light after a night in the church's sepulchral gloom.

To his surprise, some of the men set the task of corralling the unfortunate prisoners were members of his own company. Lieutenant Burton, as Stryker's second-in-command, was overseeing their work, ably assisted by the likes of Heel and Tresick. Skellen had watched them through the little window as pikemen and musketeers formed up during dawn's first pallid hour, the time when Stryker was facing the wrath of a prince. Now, as the morning reached its feeble zenith of drab grey, Stryker's company were busy tethering the prisoners, neck to neck, like knots in a vast rope.

Checking that no other officers were around, Stryker hailed Burton, and the young man, after a furtive glance left and right, ran across the cobbles to stand beside the window.

'What news?' Stryker asked, chin resting on the sill.

'This lot,' Burton replied, 'are to be made to march all the way to Oxford.'

'Through mud and snow?' Stryker said, shocked. 'Barefoot and fettered?'

'Aye, sir. To beg forgiveness for their treason.'

Stryker watched the prisoners, realizing that their futures were as precarious as his own. As he stared out on to the sorry scene, a pungent aroma hit his nostrils and he looked at Burton. 'What happened to you last night?'

Lieutenant Burton pulled a slack-jawed expression, evidently intended to give the appearance of puzzled innocence. 'Sir? I was patrolling, sir. Ensuring the men refrained from anything immoral.'

'Patrolling?' Stryker's tone dripped with incredulity. 'Then why might your brow sweat so? And how are you taken so pale?'

Burton lifted a gloved hand to scratch at the downy beard that fringed his narrow chin. 'I have a fever, sir.'

'By Christ, Andrew, you are a brazen bloody liar! The air reeks of cheap wine!'

Burton paused for a moment, considering his response, before adopting the merest flicker of a smile. 'Not cheap, sir.'

Skellen snorted.

Stryker rounded on him. 'You have something to say, Sergeant?'

The tall man straightened up. 'Not a word, sir.'

For several moments Stryker intently searched the sergeant's impassive face.

And Skellen grinned.

'Goddamn it, Sergeant!' Stryker exclaimed, though he could already feel his anger dissipating.

Burton leaned close to the window suddenly, his gaze serious. 'I'm sorry, sir. I should have been there.'

'At my arrest? Christ, Andrew, what would you have done?'

'Knocked some 'eads together?' Skellen suggested.

'Precisely,' Burton agreed.

Stryker almost laughed. 'Not certain that would have helped my cause.'

'All the same, though, sir,' said Burton. He looked back to the crowded marketplace. 'It's all around the town. The men aren't happy. They don't believe you're guilty.'

Stryker met the younger man's eyes. 'Believe it, Andrew. And tell them not to cause trouble.'

Burton grimaced. 'Bit late for that, sir. They're angry.'

And suddenly Stryker understood. 'That's why you're going with the prisoners, isn't it?'

Burton nodded. 'They're separating the regiment, for they fear a riot, sir. Some go to Gloucester with the prince. Others to Oxford with the prisoners and that loud-mouthed fire-worker.'

'Blaze?'

'That's him, sir.' Burton's voice became husky. 'I would stay, sir, but they are adamant I leave Cirencester immediately.'

'And what would you do if you stayed?'

'Free you both,' Burton replied in a tone suggesting the answer was obvious.

'Then can you blame them for wanting rid of you?'

'I suppose not.'

The leather-faced Sergeant Skellen, with hands rough as bark and eyes hard as iron, stared at the ground, his voice soft. 'Funny old world, sir.'

Stryker looked across at him.

Skellen glanced up. 'After all this bloody fightin', we're to be shot by our own side.'

Stryker offered a weary smile. 'Makes you wonder why we bother.'

'How many we got, then, Mister Burton, sir?' Skellen asked, forcing the issue back to the prisoners lining up outside.

Lieutenant Burton cast an appraising eye across the long line of disconsolate souls that now stretched from one side of the cobbled marketplace to the other. Ragged and barely clothed, the beaten rebels stared dejectedly at their naked feet as they were shoved and prodded by sneering guards.

'Eleven hundred,' he replied after a time. 'Some are Stamford's, but a fair few are townsfolk. We even have five clergymen!'

Skellen grinned wickedly. 'I'll say a prayer for 'em, sir, if they'll say one for me.'

The officers chuckled.

'Still,' Skellen continued, his face returned to its typically expressionless state. 'They're all ballock-out Roun'eads after a fashion, sir, soldiers or no.'

Burton abruptly tensed, stepping away from the bars behind which his comrades stood. 'Sorry, sir,' he hissed over his shoulder. 'Can't be seen fraternizing. But do not worry. All is not lost!' As he paced back towards the prisoners, a group of yellow-coated dragoons trotted past, malevolent glances flickering between the lieutenant and the church.

Stryker and Skellen watched as Burton paced along the line of despairing humanity, his face a cold mask, any natural revulsion buried deep. Here and there he would lean in to pull at the ropes binding the captives' wrists, ensuring no unnecessary slack had been allowed, while his corporals – Tresick, Shephard and Mookes – tugged roughly at the ropes fastened at their charges' necks. The rebels might have been unarmed and threadbare, but this many men were still a force to be reckoned with, and Burton had had the good sense to order them bound tight and guarded close.

As the lieutenant moved slowly across the slush-blanketed cobbles, his attention was apparently caught by a moaning sound further up the line. Stryker watched as he made his way towards the spot where a young man stood, his bulrush-thin frame shaking against the cold. He was probably no more than twenty, though it was hard to tell given his battered state.

'Stone me,' Stryker said, for a vision came to him of a skinny lad brandishing a pair of rusty shears.

'What is it, sir?' asked Skellen.

Stryker said nothing, but touched a finger to the spot where the shears had snagged his shoulder.

Skellen whistled softly. 'Why that fuckin' doddypoll! Should have torn 'im a new—'

'Just a whelp, Sergeant,' Stryker replied calmly. 'Not a great deal more than a child.'

And then the discussion was drowned out by the beat of drums. The captives watched through their tiny window, winter breeze stinging their eyes, as Stryker's company and their miserable human chain marched briskly out of the marketplace. To Oxford.

As the grey light of midday spread across the beech forests and steep coombs of the wold plateau, the column from Cirencester snaked ever eastward. Mowbray's men, two of his companies, formed vanguard, rearguard and flanks. They had six wagons packed tight with arms and provisions taken from the town, another smaller cart to convey the fourteen captured Parliamentarian colours, and several horse crews to drag the five captured cannon. Ahead of those vehicles trudged the prisoners, with a slow step born of despair and exacerbated by mired roads. The winter's snowfall had been a sporadic affair, frequent and heavy but quick to thaw, leaving roads choked with filth and difficult enough for any man to negotiate, let alone one forced to march barefoot.

'We'll lose a few before we reach Oxford, sir,' Ensign Chase said, seemingly reading his lieutenant's thoughts.

The man temporarily commanding Stryker's company instinctively glanced down at the large square of red taffeta held proudly by the bull-necked ensign. 'They're fortunate to've survived the sacking, Matthew,' Lieutenant Andrew Burton said. He adjusted the reins briefly, ensuring they were looped tightly around his withered right arm. 'They may live yet.'

Burton studied the distant terrain as wintry land met pale sky. Not an inch of soil could be considered friendly in this war, and, though they headed for the king's temporary capital, he did not take his eye from a horizon that might yet betray the glint of an enemy pike.

They marched along the Lechlade road, the tethered prisoners silent, traipsing with bovine acquiescence to an uncertain fate.

Burton rode at the head, his chestnut gelding, Bruce, loping uneasily across the terrain. At his side was the regiment's most senior captain, Aad Kuyt, while behind him the squelching of bare feet in muddy slush filled the crisp air, punctuated only by the occasional bark of a corporal as a rebel slid off the pace.

A pang of concern gripped him as he thought of Stryker and Skellen. By God, he hoped the plan would work.

It was dusk by the time the human chain reached the outskirts of Lechlade. Ordinarily they might have expected to cover that small distance in perhaps four or five hours, but the prisoners, encumbered by ropes and knee-deep in mud, were reduced to a painfully slow pace. To make matters worse, the five cannon, small though they were, proved near impossible to draw along the clogged roads.

'We rest a short while,' Captain Kuyt said, ordering the brown-coated soldiers to stand down. As the instruction rippled along the column, setting forth a wave of appreciative mutterings from men finally able to take refreshment or light up a pipe, the Dutch mercenary summoned Lieutenant Burton.

The pair, followed by two other mounted and hooded men, walked their horses some distance down the cloying road, plunging into the gathering darkness, careful to be away from eavesdroppers.

When they had reached a point where Kuyt felt comfortable, he turned his horse to face the group. 'Now is the time. We are far enough away from Cirencester's prying eyes.'

The two men who had followed Kuyt out of the column drew back their cowls.

'Thank you, Captain,' fire-worker Jonathan Blaze said. 'I hear Parliament's new spymaster has placed a considerable price on my head.'

'Sir Samuel Luke,' Jesper Rontry added, his tone laced with loathing. 'A vile creature.'

Blaze ignored his assistant. 'Which way now?'

Kuyt twisted round to point further eastwards along the road. 'Lechlade is up ahead. The road forks in the village. Take the left-hand route, it leads north.' He glanced at Burton. 'The lieutenant, here, knows the way.'

'Sir?' Burton said suspiciously.

'Stryker believed you'd make a good leader,' Kuyt replied. 'Now is your chance to prove him right. You will escort Master Blaze to Kenilworth Castle.'

Burton's eyes widened. 'He is not bound for Oxford, sir?'

'No, Lieutenant.'

Blaze looked Burton up and down, though he addressed Kuyt. 'You send a cripple for my protection?'

Burton's mouth opened to deliver a stinging retort, but Kuyt intervened. 'This man is one of our best, Master Blaze. He will see you safe.'

Blaze wrinkled his big nose. 'Can he ride?'

Kuyt nodded. 'Better than most, sir.'

'I possess enough strength in this arm to hold Bruce's reins,' Burton said, tapping right hand with left.

'And when you draw your sword?' Blaze replied incredulously.

'When I fight my knees command the horse.'

Kuyt offered an appreciative smile. 'It is quite something to behold, I can assure you. But let us hope you will

78

not have need of the lieutenant's blade. Besides,' he said, waving towards the main column, the gesture causing a group of horsemen to emerge from the gloom, 'Prince Rupert has given seven of his best cavalrymen for this task, so you will be a formidable party.'

Blaze nodded slowly, replacing his hood. 'Then let us be away, gentlemen.'

CIRENCESTER, GLOUCESTERSHIRE, 9 FEBRUARY 1643

The wine sloshed over the goblet's pewter rim like the crest of a miniature wave. It hit the flagstones, splashing widely, speckling the corporal's shoes in glistening crimson.

'Bugger it!' the corporal said, though with little conviction. 'They's m' new latchets.' He stared down at the damp leather, nearly pitching forwards with the movement, then quickly straightened up, deciding to ignore the spill. 'Deal with it in mornin'.'

'Quite right, sir!' the corporal's fat companion exclaimed, raising his own cup in a hearty toast. 'Drink up, good man, and leave your cares for the morrow!'

The corporal grinned and quaffed the last of his wine, red beads tracing their way down his chin to add to the mess on the floor. When the goblet was empty, he slumped back in his chair, letting out a vast, rumbling belch, and gazed about the room. At his feet lay the inebriated form of his fellow corporal, while the two musketeers sat either side of the small, heavy-barred door were slumped forwards, heads lolling between knees, snoring like a pair of sows.

'More wine, Corporal Dove?' the fat man said, lifting a wooden jug.

The room spun as the corporal looked at his new acquaintance. He held out his goblet. 'One more to ward off the chill, Barnaby, eh?'

'That's the spirit, sir! A man after my own heart, and that's God's honest truth!' Barnaby tilted the jug, filling Corporal Dove's cup to the brim.

'Mus' say,' Dove slurred, 'you're the kin'est fedary a man could meet.'

The round face, pulpy, boil-infested and loose, creased in a grin. 'Kind in you to say, sir.'

Dove took another huge gulp. 'You're sure y'ain't required at yon alehouse? Mus' be busy as a Southwick bawdy.'

Barnaby set down the jug and scratched at his hooded head. 'Damned pox. Left m' skin falling off in clumps.'

Corporal Dove shuddered.

'Anyhow,' Barnaby went on, 'the advantage o' tapsterin' is being master of your own domain.' He paused to release a juddering hiccup. 'The girls'll take great care o' my beloved Jolly Drover, do not worry. My duty is to refresh the brave lads what took this town back from Stamford's Bible-thumpin' bloody Puritanicals.'

Dove raised the goblet to his purple-stained lips. 'Amen to that.' He swallowed the luxurious liquid down. 'Well, I'm glad you brought your wares here, Barnaby, for we couldn't have left our posts, les' we wanted to be on a charge.' He glanced at the table where a small wine barrel had been propped at midnight. An hour had since elapsed, and that vessel, he suspected, was now almost empty. 'Guard duty's fuckin' tiresome, an' no mistake. We been watchin' these buggers all o' five nights now.'

'Sounds like you lads done the crime, sir!'

'Aye, you're in the right of it,' Dove replied bitterly. 'We're to hold this pair till their trial. An' that can't 'appen till young Longshanks returns.'

'A bad business.' The disease-ridden tapster patted Dove's swaying shoulder. 'But as I say, sir, m' first duty is to you. I'm simply pleased you saw sense to let me in here.' He upturned the jug, watching a solitary bead drop from its grooved spout.

Dove watched the last vestige of wine fall to the floor at his feet, and frowned. 'We've drunk the place dry, Barnaby.'

'Alas, Corporal, it would seem so,' the tapster replied, standing hastily.

Dove stared up at him through blurry vision. 'Where'ya goin', B—Barnaby?'

The tapster jerked his head towards the small door at the rear of the guardroom. 'In there.'

For a moment Dove failed to comprehend. He looked from Barnaby to the door and back again, trying to fathom the puss-faced tapster's meaning through the fog of strong drink. 'You what?'

Barnaby lifted the jug above his head, swiping it downwards in a rapid arc that connected with Dove's temple.

And all went black.

CHAPTER 4

'Life, as the poet Cowley tells us, is an incurable disease,' Captain Lancelot Forrester said brightly as he and his two companions made their way north. It was late evening, the sky was cloudy and dark, and the ground was covered in snow. 'But fortunately spiced pottage is not!'

The fugitives had galloped out of Cirencester in the predawn darkness, immediately finding progress difficult in the inclement weather, and now, after almost an entire day tramping through terrain that seemed more like treacle, they began to feel safe enough to let their voices break the countryside's silence.

'Pottage?' Stryker echoed incredulously. 'That's what you used?'

'A little trick I picked up when playing the part of a plague sufferer for the Candlewick Street theatre troupe.' He lifted a hand to scratch at the crusty residue left on his cheeks and brow. 'Smear the stuff on, let it dry a tad, and you have a ready-made affliction of the skin.'

Stryker laughed. 'You never cease to amaze me, Forry.'

Forrester beamed with pride. 'Those thirsty musketeers didn't look beyond the face and the wine, as I predicted.

82

Barnaby Last, my newest creation, was as real to them as the wicked men they were supposed to be guarding. As soon as they were nicely in their cups, I took the keys and here we are.'

Stryker thought back to Burton's parting words as the prisoners were marched away. 'He knew you were planning to help us escape, didn't he?'

'You think he'd have willingly left the town otherwise? That boy's more reckless than I.'

'How did you get away from Gloucester, sir?' Skellen asked.

'I wasn't in Gloucester,' Forrester replied matter-of-factly.

Stryker stared at him. 'Rupert failed?'

Forrester nodded, his mouth a tight line. 'We called on the town to surrender. It duly declined.'

'And it is a far more difficult prospect than Cirencester,' Stryker said.

'We didn't have the numbers or resources to storm the place, so to Oxford we went.'

'Thank Christ he didn't decide to stop in Cirencester,' Skellen muttered.

Forrester looked at the sergeant. 'He was summoned back to the King's capital, whether he liked it or not. Besides, I think he is reticent to have to deal with you. Word from his staff is that your imprisonment gave him no pleasure. Your executions would give him even less.'

Stryker instinctively kicked his bay horse's sides, asking more speed of the labouring beast, though the effect was minimal. 'But he'll send men to recapture us as soon as he hears.'

Forrester and Skellen caught up with him easily. 'Men will come, of course, Stryker,' Forrester said, 'but not immediately. Rupert will be up to his neck in politics now that he's been ensnared at Oxford.'

'Whoever he sends,' Skellen added, 'will be slow as a lame mule anyway. The roads are buggered.'

Stryker sucked his teeth. 'What of Crow?'

Forrester pulled a face that showed little concern. 'Safely out of the way. He's in Oxford too.'

Stryker looked at his friend, his gaze serious. 'Thank you, Forry.'

Suddenly embarrassed, Forrester scratched again at the dried pottage that had formed such a convincing disguise. 'Thought you'd rather be free and hunted, than wing-clipped and caged.'

'You know me well.'

'Just a shame I couldn't bring Vos and Bess back for you,' Forrester went on.

'Might have given the game away a bit,' Skellen said.

'Indeed,' agreed Forrester, leaning forward to pat the neck of his own horse, Oberon. 'So you'll have to make do with those nags. They were all I could afford at such short notice.'

Stryker moved a hand to the hilt of his Spanish sword. 'At least you found our weapons.'

Forrester nodded. 'Simple enough. They were piled in the guardroom.'

The three men were bound for the Midlands, a part of the country emphatically for Parliament, so Stryker was reassured by the muskets at their backs, blades at their waists and a brace of carbines holstered at each saddle.

'So how do we find Mam'oiselle Lisette?' Skellen said after several minutes of silence. Stryker had told them of

Rupert's request, issued before the altercation with Saul and Caleb Potts, and they had immediately agreed to travel with him to Lichfield. After all, there was nowhere else for them to go.

Stryker thought back to Cirencester, and the conversation with Prince Rupert in the chandler's blackened shell. 'We ask Philip Stanhope.'

'Who?'

'The Earl of Chesterfield.'

Forrester looked across at his leader. 'He holds Lichfield?'

Stryker nodded. 'Rupert told me that Stanhope wrote to him claiming to have a young woman in his care. She held a letter of authority, bearing the general's personal seal. His description of her matched Lisette.' Stryker was aware concern must have strained every line of his face, but he did not care. 'She is dire wounded. Unable to speak.'

Forrester frowned. 'Why does the earl not convey her to Oxford?'

'The locals are poor disposed to our cause. He claims he cannot spare the men for such an errand.'

'So Rupert wished you to go to Lichfield,' Forrester replied, 'and, if this wounded girl proved to be our Norman firebrand, you were to bring her home?'

Stryker shook his head. 'If the girl proved to be Lisette, I was ordered to discover what happened to the man she was protecting. That was my task.'

'Though Longshanks would prefer it if she survived, I'd reckon,' Skellen said flatly. 'The only thing Rupert fears is his aunt, and she'd flog 'im all the way back to 'olland if Lisette died in his service.'

Stryker did not answer. He stared out at the rolling hills, stomach coiling in dread. At least, he thought, he was no longer encumbered with Rupert's original mission. The man Lisette was escorting was an irrelevance. His only concern was the Frenchwoman's fate.

When he looked back to the tree-flanked bridleway ahead, he noticed Forrester staring at him, and realized his anxiety must have been etched into his expression. He gritted his teeth angrily, chiding himself for the weakness. It annoyed him that he was so enamoured of a woman who entered his life for moments of fleeting joy, but would always walk out again, placing him second behind her duty to the Crown.

'We'll find her,' Forrester said.

Stryker nodded mutely.

'Match, sir!' It was Skellen's voice, sharp with alarm.

Stryker and Forrester turned back to see that Skellen was pointing to a place beyond them, some fifty paces diagonally ahead. They followed his outstretched finger, searching the grey dusk, their eyes straining to decipher one form from the next.

And there it was; a minute flicker of orange hovering in the twilight. The glowing tip of a match poised in an unseen firing mechanism.

'Well spotted, Sergeant,' Forrester murmured absently, attention transfixed on the pinprick of light.

And then, in a blast that, though compact and sharp, seemed to split open the night, the unknown gun was fired.

The shock of the noise startled Skellen's mount, and she reared wildly, flinging the tall sergeant to the mud. Stryker briefly caught sight of him flailing against the sucking mire, but quickly turned his focus on the origin of the shot.

'Down!' he hissed at Forrester, and the portly officer slid from his saddle with surprising agility, moving behind the horse's bulk for protection.

Stryker stared into the descending darkness, searching for a telltale plume of smoke or the ghostly outline of men hidden in the shadows. 'Where the bloody hell are they?'

'Flash was small, smothered,' Forrester said from somewhere to his right. 'They're beyond the bend.'

Stryker saw that Forrester's explanation was correct. The bridleway did not run north in a straight line, but curved to the left, and dense woodland prevented sight of the road on the bend's far side. The shot was certainly close, for its report had been impressively loud in the gloom, but the flash of gunpowder had been muted, as though their line of sight was blocked, and they could see no smoke roiling into the flanking trees.

'He's not shooting at us,' Stryker said.

'Beggin' your pardon, sirs,' a voice snarled from behind Stryker, 'but would one o' yer gentlemen mind gettin' me out of this fuckin' slop?'

A second shot split the night air.

Stryker and Forrester struggled to where Skellen was writhing, legs and arms thrashing skywards like a giant upturned beetle, the sticky ground sucking at his clothes.

'They're not after us,' Stryker said as he hauled Skellen up by one of his long arms.

'I can't see the buggers, though,' Forrester said, taking the other arm. 'Too many trees 'tween here and the road beyond the bend.'

'Then can we get ourselves over there, sir?' Skellen growled. 'Someone needs to pay for this clobber.'

ST NEOTS, CAMBRIDGESHIRE, 9 FEBRUARY 1643

The young soldier hammered on the solid door with a gloved fist.

A metal slat, set in the centre of the door, slid violently open. 'Yes?' the speaker snapped, eyes darting left and right as he peered through the hole.

'Lieutenant Trim to see the major,' the soldier replied. He fixed calm eyes upon the hostile sentry, knowing the hidden man was assessing him from head to toe, deciding whether he posed any great danger. The thick brown cloak he wore over his buff-coat and breastplate went some way to providing an image of strength, while the carbine and cavalry sword hanging at his waist showed him to be a warrior. But Trim knew he did not cut an imposing figure, for he was slender in the shoulders and his face, framed by thick black curls, was pasty. His beard, even at the age of twenty-four, was still little more than fluff.

The door creaked open.

'Use' be 'ome to an old Papist,' the sentry said conversationally, as he showed the newcomer into the building. Trim was glad to be out of the chilling night air. The sentry led the way along a narrow, oak-panelled corridor, dimly lit by stinking tallow candles every few yards. 'But the mob drove 'em out this Yule past. Well rid, I says.'

The corridor ended at a low door, and the sentry knocked, listened for a response from within, and then pushed it gently open.

The room's interior was sparse, save three stools arranged before a roaring hearth. Two of the stools were occupied, and, as Trim stepped into the room, the sentry shutting the door firmly in his wake, the nearest man nodded to the vacant seat.

'Welcome, Lieutenant. Please sit.'

Trim had imagined Major Zacharie Girns differently. Vastly tall and bearded, like Goliath, with a face full of scars and eyes that burned red. A Parliamentarian killing machine. The man himself was tall, certainly, and clad in expensive garments of black that made the pallid skin of his face appear somewhat alarming, but he was not the descendant of the biblical nephilim the Royalists would have folk believe. The skin was patchy and irregular, probably marked by a dose of the pox, and sat on his bony features as though someone had spread an uneven layer of soft cheese across his face. Lank tendrils of black hair gleamed greasily at his cheeks in the dim firelight, while clusters of warts protruded from his nose and chin.

Lieutenant Trim sat on the vacant stool, prising the stiff buff-gloves from his fingers. He was mightily pleased to be feeling the warmth of the fire, but Girns unsettled him. His eyes were not ruby-red as the stories would have it, but emerald green, and held a glint of ruthlessness in their depths.

'God has brought you to me,' Major Girns said unexpectedly.

Trim bowed his head awkwardly. 'My captain says you have need of me, sir.'

Girns's eyes remained fixed on Trim. 'I have an itch I need to scratch. His name is Blaze.'

89

Girns's companion stirred then, and spoke for the first time. 'Blaze? Same as the fatty?'

Girns glanced at the speaker. He was dressed in the same black garments but was far younger than the major, probably not yet eighteen years old. His frame was slight and his face unblemished, but he had a bulbous, syphilitic nose and rotten teeth.

'Astute as ever, Tom. They were brothers.' Girns turned back to Trim. 'We have already dispatched Lazarus, the younger sibling, to his maker. May he receive his just celestial reward.'

The black-toothed youngster grinned maliciously. 'Or look at it this way. One less cock to strut up Charlie's shit-heap.'

Girns raised a hand. 'Profanity, Tom.'

'Forgive me, Major,' the lad said easily.

'This urchin is Corporal Thomas Slater,' Girns told Trim. 'Reports direct to me for this task.' He looked at the corporal. 'This, Mister Slater, is Lieutenant Josiah Trim.' Girns paused while Trim and Slater exchanged a nod, before addressing the older of the pair. 'In the action against Lazarus Blaze, I lost one of my men. I require a replacement. Captain Cromwell tells me you are devout, honest, and professional. He also says you are his best tracker.'

Trim found his voice with difficulty. 'The captain pays me a great compliment.'

Girns's green gaze darkened. 'Pride is a terrible sin, Lieutenant.'

Trim swallowed hard. 'Beg pardon, sir. I am yours to command.'

Girns paused motionless for a second, then twisted his thin mouth as though tasting acid. 'Devout Papists. The

90

Blazes are highly skilled in the use of black powder. Explosives, artillery, anything you might name. Served across the breadth of the Continent, learning their trade from men like La Riviere and La Roche. Before long they eclipsed their tutors. They had no equal, not even in France or Spain. When war was declared here, they spied a chance to fight for Popery upon the shores of their birth. To spread its poison. It is our duty, *my* duty, to rid this land of their foul presence.'

Slater hawked up a globule of mucus and spat it into the hearth. 'And Luke's offered a big reward for them!'

'Quite,' Girns confirmed. 'The Scoutmaster General wants them dead. We will see him happy, and God's will done.'

'We heard Lazarus was in Charlie's pay down in Wiltshire,' Slater said.

Girns nodded slowly. 'Micky was my previous tracker. A good one,' he added pointedly. 'News reached us that Lazarus Blaze was bound for Stafford, and we ran him down, intercepted him, and dispatched him. We have since heard that his older brother Jonathan, who is perhaps even more talented, enlisted with the king's whore at Paris.'

Trim chewed the inside of his mouth. 'Henrietta? She has not returned?' The queen's mission on the Continent was public knowledge. If she were allowed to return to England, she would bring armaments, money and men with her.

'Not yet, Praise God. The good Lord sends gales to turn her away.' Girns's lids fell until his eyes were almost closed. His lips moved silently. 'But Jonathan is here. In England,' he said, abruptly ending his whispered entreaty and taking a lingering look into the flames. When he looked up suddenly, his eyes carried a frightening intensity from which Trim found he could not turn away. 'Blaze can train gunners and their assistants – so-called mattrosses – to be a hundredfold the superior of our own. His aim is steadfast. We are told that with the right cannon, Blaze could destroy an army before the first charge, or reduce a city to rubble.'

'Forgive me, sir,' Trim ventured, 'but is he so great a threat? We have the Weald, sir. The great furnaces. And we hold the ports. They cannot import guns any more readily than they can make them.'

Girns scratched at one of the large warts that jutted from the end of his chin. 'Believe me, Lieutenant, the Cavaliers have enough work even now for Blaze. Not the sakers and falcons you have already faced. But culverins, demi-cannon and cannon. They're behind the walls of castles for the winter, guarded by large garrisons. But come spring they'll be dragged out to wreak havoc. I shudder to imagine the damage a man of Blaze's skill could inflict with such beasts. The enemy will muster with the coming of spring. If Jonathan Blaze marches with them – with their great cannon – his very name will probably persuade our supporters to surrender before there is even a fight. I see your incredulity,' Girns said sharply. 'But trust me when I say that when Blaze comes before a town, its walls are liable not to stand for long.'

'A modern-day Joshua,' Trim said.

Girns's face was a set mask of gravity. 'No town will wish to be known as the next Jericho. Instead, they will open their gates to the king, looking to safeguard their property before their souls.' He stood, his spine cracking as he stretched.

'We fear Blaze.'

The speaker had been Thomas Slater, and Girns rounded savagely on him. 'No, Tom, we do not fear him, for we know Christ's will is at our backs! To fear the Papists is to sin against God!' Girns grabbed a glass from the nearby mantelpiece, and crushed it in his gloved hand. Shards showered to the floor like glimmering grains of sand.

Slater looked away, unable to hold the major's gaze. Girns breathed deeply for a few moments before continuing, more calmly this time. 'But Blaze *must* be removed.' He fixed Trim with that sparkling stare. 'My expertise lies in rooting out Popery in all its forms, and ridding it from God's earth. Slater, here, is a crack shot, and you are a renowned tracker. The three of us will join to exterminate the Lord's enemy.'

'And to share the reward,' Slater said with relish.

Girns sat down again, appearing not to have heard the corporal.

'Where is he now, sir?' Trim asked.

'We await news.'

Josiah Trim was waiting too. He had been enlisted by Girns, Captain Cromwell's friend and, it seemed, God's own assassin, to perform a great service to the rebellion. And yet they did not appear to possess any knowledge as to their quarry's whereabouts.

Girns closed his eyes. 'The Lord will provide, Lieutenant. You must have faith. Now, join us in prayer.'

Trim looked stoical. 'Thank you, sir. I'd enjoy that.'

When Stryker, Forrester and Skellen rounded the dark bend, mud sucking at their ankles, they were greeted by a scene of utter chaos.

Four men, each armed with a brown-barrelled caliver, stood about a small wagon. The wagon was tipped on its side, upper wheels still spinning, contents disgorged haphazardly across the road. A scrawny palfrey lay at the road's edge, legs splayed at bizarre angles, great red stains blooming like rose petals at its head and chest where a brace of bullets had been to work. Sacks of grain had been stabbed open, spilling a myriad of kernels on to the mud, while bags containing clothing, food and other effects had been similarly ransacked.

Several paces from the vehicle was, Stryker presumed, the wagon's driver. His features were hard to make out in the murky evening, but certainly he was no comrade of the four armed men. He was curled tight on the ground, like a foetus, his small voice unintelligible from thirty paces away.

The picture was clear. An ambush.

Stryker darted forwards, confident the thieves were focussed upon their prey. He held his sword in his right hand, one of the carbines in his left, pleased his own weapon's flintlock mechanism would not act as a beacon announcing his arrival.

At ten paces, the detail of the ambush became clearer. The driver, still prostrate, held a hand to a wound on his temple, blood leaking through shaking fingers. Two of the four armed men were busy rifling through the baggage, while the second pair were standing over the man, one at his head and the other at his feet. The latter was speaking, growling some ultimatum at the prone form cowering before him, a caliver trained on the driver's body.

And then Stryker was behind him. The robber began to turn, but Stryker dug his blade in between the man's shoulder blades. As one, the other three startled thieves raised their own weapons, but two clicks nearby alerted them to the presence of Forrester and Skellen as their carbines were shifted from half- to full-cock.

No one moved.

'Shoot and he dies,' Stryker ordered, prodding a little harder with his sword.

'Don't like your odds.' The man pinned at the end of Stryker's blade was doing his best to sound unafraid.

'Your mates at the cart have fired already,' Stryker replied. 'We have the advantage by my reckoning.'

Wincing at the searing pain in the flesh of his back, the captive tossed his firearm into the mud, its match immediately fizzling out. The pair at the baggage followed suit, letting their spent weapons fall away and slap wetly into the ground.

But the man standing above the driver's head was not so easily cowed. He had raised his caliver so that the narrow muzzle was trained on the space just above his comrade's shoulder, the space now occupied by Stryker's face.

'Drop it,' Stryker said calmly, 'or my friends will see you dead before you can pull that trigger.'

The robber, a stocky brute with jug ears and thick copper-coloured hair, merely winked. 'A brave gamble.' His voice was calm, and, as Stryker stared at the levelled long-arm, noting how it did not waver, he began to have his doubts. The shot would be difficult. For the robber to be sure of hitting Stryker's head, even at such close range, would take great skill, and yet the hand clutching the weapon was steady, the man behind it determined.

The wagon's driver kicked out, his foot jabbing savagely upwards, the sharp point of his boot, powerful and unexpected, meeting with the robber's groin. The movement caught everyone off guard, not least the big-eared gunman who had held his ground so belligerently.

The man screamed, but still did not relinquish his weapon. He let his arm drop to blast a hole in his surprise attacker, but the driver was rolling rapidly away, scrambling into the scrub at the road's edge, where the moon failed to penetrate. The caliver, fired wildly amid the man's pain-wracked cries, spent its fury straight into the deep mud.

Stryker's captive saw his opportunity and spun round, reaching for a dagger at the small of his back, but Stryker was too fast and ran him through. As the new-made corpse slumped to its knees, Stryker heard two more shots, the distinct coughs of carbines, and the men at the baggage dropped limply on to the sticky earth.

'Traitor!' the copper-haired robber, caliver in one hand, balls in the other, was screeching frantically as he swept the empty long-arm like a club in great arcs just inches from the ground. It was so difficult to see in the darkness, but Stryker knew the man must be hunting for the driver of the wagon, hoping the heavy wooden stock would meet flesh in the confused gloom. 'Fucking traitor! I'll split your 'ead like—'

Stryker's sword curtailed the last arc with an arm-shaking clang as he stepped into the man's path. 'Drop it!'

The man ignored him, instead taking his spare hand from his injured groin to grasp the caliver with both hands. He screamed, and lofted the makeshift club vertically above his head, intending to slam it down in a blow that would crush Stryker's skull as though it were eggshell.

Stryker was prepared, and stepped backwards as quickly as the treacherous ground would allow, confident the attack would fall short.

It never came. As the frantic assailant summoned all his reserves of strength, the lethal point of another sword had darted from the gloom to take him at his exposed armpit. The blow was heavy, crunching through skin and bone, finding its way between ribs, not stopping until several inches of sleek steel had disappeared inside its target.

Air sighed from the wound with the sound of a blacksmith's bellows. The robber's grip failed, the caliver falling from his paralysed fingers, and only then did William Skellen jerk his blade free.

The robber's eyes became suddenly dull. And then he fell, face first, into the mud.

The wagon-driver introduced himself as Abel Menjam when he had eventually been coaxed from his hiding place within the dense trees. The wound at his head was superficial, a gash sustained as the wagon overturned, and Skellen quickly stemmed the bleeding with a tightly bound strip of cloth.

'I'm in the corn trade,' Menjam had said as Stryker and his men dragged the four bodies into the thick undergrowth at the side of the bridleway. He described how his vehicle had collided with a great branch, unseen as it lay across the night-shrouded earth, and, as he had been thrown from the upturned wagon, his assailants had burst from the shadows.

'A farmer, sir?' Skellen asked.

Menjam's high-pitched laughter was like the yap of a small dog. 'No fear, sir! I sell it. Far simpler than growing the stuff!'

Stryker kicked at the spilled kernels. 'I'm sorry you have lost your wares, Master Menjam.'

Menjam, a head shorter than Stryker, extended a hand. 'I have my life, sir. For that you have my deepest thanks, Colonel—?'

Stryker shook the dainty hand, noting the soft skin of a man unused to hardship. For a moment he had considered pretence that they were not soldiers, but the way in which their paths had crossed had precluded such a lie. 'Captain Grant,' he replied, thinking quickly. 'For King Charles. We could not ignore your plight.'

Menjam grinned through thin, purple lips. 'Well I am glad of it, sir.'

Stryker looked at the small man, from his wisp of grey hair, past his twitching black eyes and his clean-shaven chin, to the tips of diminutive feet that pointed from beneath the hem of a long cloak. And irritation stirred within him. Menjam's perverse joviality was jarring in the wake of so much death. 'Why were they trying to kill you?' he asked bluntly.

'Common padders, sir,' the smaller man said lightly. 'Godless brigands. Jumped out from the trees. They were after money, but no doubt they'd have dispatched me for sheer sport.'

Stryker frowned. 'You will ride with us.' He nodded to the upturned wagon. 'Your cart has a broken axle and your horse is dead.'

Menjam bobbed his head brightly. 'I should be grateful, Captain Grant. For as far as your own journey allows.'

'Lichfield,' Stryker said. 'We make for the town of Lichfield.'

Menjam threw his arms skyward, exclaiming his thanks to God. 'Then we are bound for the selfsame place, sir! The Maker truly looks kindly upon me!'

The wind bit hard as they took to the road, hunched into cloaks drawn high and tight. Vaporous tentacles rose from the horses' flanks like the fingers of phantoms, grabbing at the black night above them.

Two hours before dawn Stryker took the decision to rest. The moon stole only fleeting peaks through clouds threatening snow as they lit a small fire in a clearing at the road's fringe. Skellen had blasted a hole in a decent-sized rabbit as it fed the previous dusk, and he now hung it from a branch by long hind paws and skinned it from tail to shoulder.

Abel Menjam helped Forrester forage for kindling, and the pair made a small pile of it. From the corner of his eye, he noticed Stryker rummaging at the foot of a broad ash. 'What have you there, Captain Grant?'

Stryker straightened and held out a hand, in which sat what looked to be a piece of coal. 'King Alfred's Cake, they call it.'

Stryker threw it suddenly, sending the semi-spherical black lump tumbling across the clearing towards Skellen. The sergeant extended a wiry arm, plucking the projectile out of the air and holding it up to Menjam. 'God's own tinderbox.'

Forrester came to stand beside Menjam. '*Daldinia concentrica*,' he said. 'It's a fungus, the flesh of which will take a spark if dry enough.'

'Get it lit before the snow, Mister Dove,' Stryker said, 'and it should take fine.'

Forrester nodded, betraying no sign of his amusement at the name. 'Burns slowly,' he said to Menjam, 'but it'll get our twigs going with any luck. And it'll save our powder and match.'

When the embers began to spring from the black fungus and on to the kindling, the rabbit's bare flesh was spitted along Skellen's sword and the blade propped over the flames by gnarled branches. The men gathered cross-legged before the fire, drawing as close as the heat would allow and sniffing the air eagerly as the rabbit sizzled and spat, its aroma tantalizing.

Stryker stared into the dancing flames. 'I never thanked you,' he said to Skellen when Menjam had paced into the undergrowth to urinate.

'For Potts? I thought he'd kill you, sir,' Skellen's sardonic voice drifted back across the flames. 'So I got 'im first. I'll be sure an' wait for orders next time.'

Stryker opened his mouth to rebuke the sergeant, but Forrester, fat snowflakes beginning to speckle his wide-brimmed hat, snorted with laughter. 'Quite right, William!'

'Well I hope we have seen the last of Colonel Crow,' Stryker said.

'Do have a care,' Forrester replied, his usually open features screwed tight, serious. 'He thumps his Bible with the very best preachers, but I hear the bugger's frantic as a bloody bedlamite. And he leads a fine troop of dragoon-ers, all of which would gladly do his bidding and employ your back as target practice.'

Stryker tossed a twig into the flames, the damp bark hissing madly. 'I'm not concerned with Crow. When the

Prince finds out we've escaped we'll have the whole army after our hides.'

'May I ask of your business in Lichfield?' enquired Menjam casually as he stepped out of the tree line.

Stryker watched as the corn seller came to sit, holding childlike palms to the tremulous flames. 'Army business, sir.'

Menjam was unperturbed. 'Forgive my simple curiosity, Captain. My, I am famished. Can't wait for a bite of that tasty-looking coney.'

Stryker kept his eyes on Menjam. 'Curiosity can see a caliver pointed at your head.'

'I have told you,' Menjam persisted earnestly, 'I am a seller of corn, nothing more. I cause no trouble, nor seek it out. At least until last night, when my produce was sown in the mud by that pack of ruffians and my trusty old pony cruelly shot.'

Stryker nodded, though his grey eye did not flinch from Menjam's face.

CHAPTER 5

Away to the south and east, in the commandeered home of an ousted Parliamentarian, a barrel-shaped officer with ruddy features and hair spiked like hackles rubbed the dregs of sleep from his glassy eyes.

'What is it?' Colonel Artemas Crow said as he shoved himself out of the rocking chair that had served as bed for the night, blinking at the big silhouette leaning casually against the frame of the open doorway.

'You summon me?'

Crow looked at the newcomer with disfavour. 'I summoned you last night, Major Edberg.'

The man addressed removed his red-ribboned hat and ruffled his hair with a handful of thick fingers. 'A hard night, Co-lo-nel,' he said.

Crow squinted as Edberg spoke. The major's English was good, but heavily accented, and it grated that he struggled to wrap his tongue around Crow's own title. He watched Edberg step into the room. The man was broad and tall, like an ancient oak, looming, intimidating. He wore the same clothes as Crow, the yellow coat and breeches, the dark riding boots, the sword and pistol, though the red scarf about his waist was shabbier, and there were no feathers in his hat.

Unlike Crow's bristle-topped pate, the major's hair was long and golden. It was not curled in the fashion of so many of the king's rakehells – those men who brought about the derisive Cavalier monicker – but fell in tousled clumps, matted by the sweat of long rides and tough fights.

A blade had nicked Edberg's cheek, leaving a scarlet wound, puffy and livid, running horizontally above his golden moustache. The major's boots, bucket-tops pulled up to protect his thighs, were covered in filth where he had ridden through the sticky terrain, while a myriad droplets of blood speckled his buff-coat's skirts and sleeves.

'Losses?' Crow asked dubiously.

'*Ja*. Two. Ran into the *oäkting* to the south. Killed five.'

The colonel tugged angrily at his spiky hair. 'You lost two men?'

Edberg's expression betrayed nothing. 'You want to build a reputation for this troop? I win you fights.'

Crow sighed heavily, but relented. A victory, however costly, was all that mattered. 'And are the men improving?'

Edberg gave an almost imperceptible nod. 'We continue daily evolutions, sir. And I hammer them.'

Crow's pale stare lingered on the barrel-chested mercenary. 'I bet you do.'

Edberg picked his nose, wiping the contents on the greasy sleeves of his buff-coat. 'What news?'

Crow stood, moving to a table on the room's far side. He gathered up his cross-belt, sword and scabbard. 'I pay you well, do I not?'

Edberg watched with blank disinterestedness as his colonel buckled the belt just below his right shoulder and attached the scabbard at his left hip. 'You do.'

'But you are a mercenary. You would like more.'

'*Naturligt*,' Edberg agreed. 'The killing in England is not going to end. Not any time soon. And where there is killing, there is money to be made.'

'War is business,' Crow said, knowing the Stockholm-born major had fought for the Protestant Union at virtually every major engagement of the last fifteen years. 'It is why I hired you.' He waited for a moment. 'But how about I give you something better?'

Edberg bunched his upper lip so that his coarse moustache touched his nostrils. 'What can be better than coin, Co-lo-nel?'

'Rank.'

Edberg's left eye twitched a fraction.

A ghost of a smile crossed Crow's face. 'I am a very powerful man, Major. This troop is bankrolled from my own purse. What say you to a regiment of your own? Perhaps you should learn to pronounce—Colonel?'

Edberg sucked thoughtfully at his moustache. 'The price?'

'A death.'

Edberg did not flinch. 'Who's? A Scotch'un, I hope. I was at Newburn. Scotch fucked us right in our arses.' The battle of Newburn had been a terrible defeat for King Charles's armies at the hands of the Scottish Covenanters. 'I hate those bastards. Hate their hides. If he's Scots, I'll kill him gladly.'

Crow rolled his eyes. This swash-and-buckler was as taciturn as a statue, but mention the Scots and he would happily recount the lurid details of that rout on the banks of the River Tyne. 'Our man is English, Major. Stryker.'

The big man sucked at the matted hair of his top lip again. 'Stryker. That *skitstövel* from Cirencester.'

Crow clenched his teeth so that his jaw pulsed in pain. 'I want rid of him, Major. I want him rotting in the ground.' He paced past Edberg, striding out into the bustling courtyard on to which the house fronted. The small area of churned mud had been home to Crow's dragoons since they had followed Prince Rupert back from Gloucester, and the whole area stank of horse flesh and leather tack, unwashed bodies and stale drink.

'But he'll be shot,' the mercenary was saying as he followed Crow across the ankle-deep slop. 'We saw to that at the hearing. Why did you want him dead, anyhow?'

Crow rounded on the Swede. 'The man murdered Saul and Caleb Potts, Major!'

'But they *were* stealing those mounts.'

'Irrelevant.'

The pair had passed between two of the courtyard's properties and out on to some common land, where a small barn rose from the wet grass. Crow entered the barn without ceremony, causing a dozen hats to be snatched off dipped heads, but he ignored the deference, instead singling out one man. 'Is my horse ready?'

'Aye, she is, sir,' the trooper replied, darting off to take the bridle of a big grey.

Crow turned back to Edberg. 'News has reached the Prince. Disturbing news.'

'Oh?'

Crow's face seemed to redden further. 'It transpires the murderous churl has escaped.'

Now Henning Edberg's face cracked in a slight frown.

Crow's mount had been led to stand beside him, and he hauled himself expertly into the well-buffed saddle. 'Rupert is embroiled in his usual court intriguing, and has authorized me to oversee Stryker's capture,' he said, gathering up the reins.

'He won't be in Cirencester now, sir.'

'Of course he won't,' Crow snapped. 'But I know where he went.'

The cobalt eyes widened a fraction. 'He talked of Lichfield. At the hearing.'

'You recall it too. Whatever business he had there seemed dire urgent, did it not?'

'It did.'

'Go there, Major Edberg. Find the swaggering devil.' He leaned down so that his mouth would be closer to Edberg's ear when he spoke. 'But do not bring him back.'

'You want me to kill him,' Edberg replied, 'against the general's orders?'

Crow nodded slowly. 'And in return I will make you *Colonel* Henning Edberg.' He grinned wolfishly. 'How does that sound?'

'Good,' Edberg said bluntly. 'But I want one other thing.'

'Oh?'

'Tell me why. Why did I lie at the hearing? Why must I kill him now? Why do you hate him so?'

Crow straightened, nodding towards the stable entrance. 'Close the door.'

A minute later, when the door swung open again, Colonel Artemas Crow nudged his horse out of the stable and into a tentative canter. Mud began to spray up at him, but, for the first time this vile winter, he did not mind. He almost laughed aloud, for he was about to have the revenge he so craved. And Captain Stryker was going to die.

The fitful snow cleared by mid morning, and the arduous progress of Stryker's small group was much improved under cloudless skies. They cantered where they could, pleased finally to give the horses a run after so many days of snail-paced drudgery. Abel Menjam maintained his almost constant ebullience, despite looking laughably incongruous atop Oberon. He gripped Forrester's coat tightly as the captain urged the enormous beast over the frozen ground, only releasing a hand to adjust the crusty bandage encircling his head.

'You never did tell,' Menjam said over Forrester's shoulder.

Stryker, in the lead, twisted to look at him. 'Tell?'

'Your reason for visiting Lichfield, Captain Grant. That is to say,' he added quickly as he saw Stryker glower, 'that Staffordshire is a place of hot rebellion. The Midlands are for Parliament, town by town.'

'It is not so risk-fraught,' Forrester answered before Stryker could think of a suitably noncommittal response. 'Lichfield remains for the King.'

'Aye, that's as maybe,' Menjam replied, 'but many of the common folk are ardent rebels, mark, 'tis a matter of religion.'

Stryker shrugged. 'We'll take our chances.'

They negotiated a narrow, moss-fringed bridge that took them across a brook of clear water, stickleback dancing beneath the amber current like minuscule shadows.

'Have you ever seen the Prince Palatine? They say he is a warlock,' Menjam said when they were safely on the north bank, his voice hissing with conspiratorial excitement.

'We have seen him,' Stryker said guardedly.

'You have seen the dog? It is said to be his familiar. Does it truly ride to battle with him?'

'You would insult my general?' Stryker said, leaning forward slightly to ensure the ground was not too rutted for the skittering hooves.

'Of course not!' Menjam spluttered from behind Forrester. 'I merely relay what I hear!'

Stryker stared back at him, his expression granite-hewn. 'You relay what you hear now, and I'll hunt you down and flay you alive. Understand?'

Menjam grinned broadly. 'Captain Grant! I may have no allegiance to your army, but I would never betray the men who saved my life! Never sir!'

'It doesn't ride, Master Menjam,' Forrester said. 'Boye, Prince Rupert's dog. It doesn't ride into battle.'

'It glides,' Skellen offered flatly.

Menjam turned to stare at the tall man, evidently trying to read the truth in Skellen's blank face. 'You mock me, Sergeant Wilks,' he said incredulously.

Skellen's face was unreadable.

'Perhaps a little,' Stryker replied.

'I'm afraid the flea-bitten animal does nothing more exciting than pant and scratch,' Forrester put in.

'And shit,' added Skellen.

'Thank you, Sergeant,' said Stryker.

'But it joins the great charge with its master, yes?' Menjam asked.

'Aye, but you're mistook, Master Menjam, I can see,' Forrester replied. 'It does not jump at rebels, tearing throats like some four-pawed monster.'

'No,' Skellen sneered, 'it yaps like a scolded pup!'

Menjam tilted back his small head and burst forth in shrill laughter. 'The Roundheads make such drama of it. One cannot pass town or village without resting eyes upon a pamphlet decrying the Prince's sorcery.'

'Lies, Master Menjam,' said Stryker. 'Boye is no demon puckrel, and Prince Rupert no warlock or witch. He is a soldier, a good one. Skilled in musketry and swordplay, on foot or in the saddle.'

'Aye. A fearsome brawler,' Skellen agreed.

Forrester nodded. 'His enemies fear the very ground on which he treads, so they weave tall tales to drum up enmity towards him.'

'And those enemies' voices are many,' Stryker said. 'He has as many detractors at Oxford as at Parliament. The rebels fear him, while the King's courtiers envy him.'

In the adjacent field a pair of dogs delighted in harrying sheep. Their master whistled shrill commands, though Stryker never saw him. The shepherd, he supposed, had grown accustomed to staying out of sight when riders came near. 'We discuss the lot of great men,' Menjam said, following Stryker's gaze, 'when it is the meanest folk who suffer in this.'

They saw the three slender spires of the great cathedral while they were still two hours away. Those spires climbed ostentatiously into the sky, pointing the way to heaven and calling pilgrims to the small marshland city.

Stryker spurred his horse into a gallop for the final miles, following a slow-running stream as it meandered into the gentle valley that enfolded Lichfield.

'Christ,' Skellen said, as they reached the outskirts of the settlement. 'Is it a church or a fortress?'

Stryker followed the sergeant's impressed gaze to see that the Gothic church was enclosed within a circuit of vast walls rising, grey and daunting, above the clustered houses of the city.

Forrester whistled softly as he took in the towers and turrets that punctuated the walls. 'The legacy of some jittery bishop, I'd imagine. Perhaps he swindled a king, and holed himself up here.'

'Whatever its origin,' Menjam said, staring at the cathedral's great bulk, 'the Close – that's the part within those thick walls – is the single defendable place in the city.'

Stryker twisted to address the diminutive man with whom he shared his saddle. 'How does a seller of corn understand town defences?'

Menjam sighed heavily. 'You are a born sceptic, sir, my word you are. I have visited Lichfield countless times, for I have kin here. The city lies within a ditch and rampart, but they are ancient works. Sturdy barriers in their time, Captain Grant, I am certain, but easily swatted aside by today's armies. Even I may recognize the Close as the only place of reasonable fortification. It does not take a general to fathom. In any case,' he continued archly, 'I had a perfectly reasonable point to make.'

Stryker blew out his cheeks. 'Do enlighten us, Master Menjam.'

'The Earl of Chesterfield holds Lichfield for the King,' Menjam explained, 'but only because he may hide within the Close.'

Forrester chewed his upper lip as he considered the statement. 'You warn us to have a care in the town?'

Menjam nodded sternly. 'Right enough, sir, right enough. There are those well disposed to Charles and his court, naturally, but the larger part shift for the Parliament. Chesterfield might have control with his guns and walls, but do not rely on sympathy from the common folk. As you know, I have no particular truck with your cause, but I would not see the three of you harmed.'

Lichfield was a well-appointed little city of pretty thatches and paved streets. The entire settlement was, as Menjam had said, surrounded by a deep ditch, though roads had been cut through it in recent years, rendering it ineffective as a means of defence.

There were sentries at the places where those roads crossed into the city and, after a brief discussion with one of the Earl of Chesterfield's bored-looking guards, they were waved through with little ceremony.

They passed on to St John Street and headed north. 'My cousin Richard is a butcher,' Abel Menjam, still propped behind Forrester on Oberon's massive back, declared happily as they turned right on to Bore Street. He pointed past Forrester's shoulder, indicating a small church up ahead. 'St Mary's. A pleasant house of God, if a tad dwarfed by its looming sibling. Cousin Richard's shop lies beyond it, beside the market cross.'

'We'll see you safe to him,' Stryker said, doing his best to ignore the frightened glances garnered by his scar. He supposed he would never be entirely used to the feeling of being reviled at first sight by naturally superstitious folk. 'But we cannot stay further. I have urgent business that must be attended to.'

'As you wish,' Menjam replied.

The market cross was a stone structure of thick pillars and vaulted roof, topped by finely carved figures of the Apostles and a crucifix at each end. 'The market bell sits within,' Menjam said, pointing to a small turret rising from the market cross's roof.

'And there's always room for a nice set o' harmans,' Skellen said ruefully, his gaze fixed on the wooden stocks that sat, squat and forbidding, between two of the stout pillars.

'Indeed, William!' Menjam chirped happily. Stryker had not wished to be accosted by Parliamentarian sympathisers before he could get safely inside the Close, so Christian names had been adopted. 'And up here, just on the left, is Richard's house and livelihood!'

'Cousin Abel! By all that is holy, it's good to lay eyes upon you!'

The speaker came bustling from the side of the street. He was a short, fat man with thick beard and bald head. A long, scarlet-encrusted apron swathed his huge belly, finishing at his ankles, and he rubbed red hands across the filthy material.

Abel Menjam practically leapt from the saddle and ran to embrace his cousin. 'Richard! How fair you? And Lizzy? She keeps well?'

Richard beamed, exposing small, sharp teeth. 'She is well, Abel, praise God, as am I. Little Ben thrives, bless his boots!'

'Well thank the gracious Lord, cousin, thank Him indeed!' Abel exclaimed, pulling away from his excited kin and gesturing at the three mounted men. 'These are my travelling companions. William, Lancelot and Innocent. They saved my very life upon the road. I praise Jesus for them hourly!'

Stryker and his men dismounted and offered hands for the stout butcher to shake.

'My cousin's saviours! I thank you then, sirs, by God I do!' He turned to Stryker, failing to conceal the look of concern that ghosted across his features when he laid eyes upon Stryker's mutilated face. 'Innocent?' The butcher raised an eyebrow with interest, evidently deciding it was safer to discuss the fearsome-looking man's name than his face. 'A Banbury-man then?'

Stryker cringed at the name. 'No Puritan, sir. A mother's choice.'

'Mothers!' the butcher yapped happily. 'Well met, sirs. I am Richard Gunn. Come.' He nodded towards a building on the corner of the marketplace. 'Lizzy is not home, so I cannot provide you with victuals of any quality. But the house opposite is a fair establishment. Will you all join me for a jar of ale?'

Menjam announced that they would gladly, and he followed his cousin across the street. Stryker was reluctant, but the expressions on Skellen and Forrester's faces spoke volumes. He nodded permission and his old friends coaxed their mounts across the road, the happiest he had seen them in days.

'Come, Innocent!' Forrester called back to him.

Stryker's gritted teeth elicited a snort of amusement from Skellen.

'They have lads here who'll tend to your horses. Might be prudent to leave your weapons too,' Gunn said as they reached the alehouse door, shooting a wry glance at the muskets and swords. Stryker opened his mouth to explain, but the butcher interrupted swiftly, 'Say no more, Friend Innocent. A man who gives back Cousin Abel's life need never explain himself to the likes of me.'

'Call me Grant, sir, please,' Stryker hissed, acutely aware that he was beginning to sound desperate. Aware, too, of the low chortles coming from Forrester's direction.

Suddenly, the door of the inn was thrust open and a trio of armed men burst out on to the street. One led the way, while the others carried a large wine barrel between them. They ignored Stryker and his companions, instead marching quickly up the street towards the cathedral.

The George and Dragon tavern was warm and comfortable, its ceilings low and its fire blazing. Well-worn tables were dotted around the place, while a pair of ancient swords crossed above the wide hearth, flanked by half a dozen pottkilps from which various cooking pots hung. A couple of locals sat in one corner sucking at their clay pipe stems, but neither paid the group much attention.

Stryker, having tethered his horse in the small yard at the rear of the building, crossed to the taps with his four companions in tow. 'Five pots, sir,' he said, fishing some coins from his doublet.

A sullen man at the casks folded thick forearms. 'Lay 'em down, sir, or there'll be none for you.'

Stryker did as he was told, though his instinct was to reach out and smash the tavern keeper's face into one of his precious barrels.

The tapster's expression mellowed. 'Thank you, sir. The old bastard in the Close spouts the same drivel daily, mark me. There'll be not a smidge o' credit here, an' that's the final truth.'

'The old bastard?' said Stryker.

'Baron Stanhope!' the tapster exclaimed.

'The Earl of Chesterfield?' Forrester asked.

'The very same cozener!' the tapster nodded eagerly, scratching at the thick stubble of his jaw with filthy fingers. 'His men must have passed you on their way out.'

'They were Chesterfield's soldiers?'

'Aye,' the tapster responded morosely. 'They'd bleed me till I were bone dry and stick thin. Bloody Cavaliers.'

'They do not pay you?' Stryker said.

'Pay?' The tavern keeper tilted his head back in an open-mouthed parody of laughter. 'You jest, surely, sir. They pay in threat and promise, but never coin. The townsmen are all amort, and it ain't right. Sooner the King's thieving brabblers take 'emselves away from here the better for us all.'

'But the King still holds this town, Master Tapster,' Forrester said. 'Do you not fear your words will be taken for treason?'

The stubble-faced man shrugged and began filling five pewter jugs with ale from one of his casks. 'By which fool, sir? A man might repeat my words to Charlie's men in the Close, but the God-fearin' folk o' Lichfield'll have him swingin' from a rope before he can recant his Popish ways. You ain't one o' their swaggerin' sort, is ya?'

Forrester proffered his most charming smile. 'No, Master Tapster. We most certainly are not.'

'Glad to hear it,' the tapster said as he slid the brimming pots across his work surface. 'No halfcon here, sirs. Full measures only, and be sure an' tell your friends.'

The group took their drinks and gathered around one of the tables.

'How can Chesterfield send men into the town,' Stryker asked in a low voice, 'when the folk here hate him so?'

Richard Gunn leaned in close. 'We are not all for the Parliament, sir. But people here have long memories.'

Menjam interjected, 'You have heard of Edward Wightman?'

Stryker nodded. 'Yes.' He looked at Gunn.

'Aye,' Gunn confirmed. 'Burned at the stake, in this very town, for speaking out against the King and his Popery.'

'Charlie weren't even in charge then,' Skellen said.

'No, William,' Gunn agreed, 'but old wounds run deep. The people blamed King James and his clergy for what they saw as a terrible wrong. Charles inherited many of those same clergymen. They mistrust him.'

'And old James weren't Popish either,' Skellen persisted. 'Nor's Charlie.'

'Catholic or High Church, it is all the same to those who yearn for more purity in worship and doctrine. A large number in Lichfield are of that persuasion, William. And they watched a good man burn for that same kind of faith all those years back.' The butcher leaned back in his chair, placing chubby hands on his vast belly. 'Many townsfolk remember it well, and that memory disposes them to Parliament above the King. Lichfield is a troubled place, sir, have no doubt.'

Stryker led the way along Sadler Street and on to Bridge Street. Having drained their cups, the group parted company in affable fashion with much hand-shaking and pleasantries exchanged.

Lichfield's cathedral filled the skyline to the north of the city. Separating that Gothic colossus from the busy streets over which it loomed were two large bodies of water: the Bishop's Pool and Minster Pool.

'In days long past,' Abel Menjam had said as he bade his friends farewell, 'it took a ferry to cross them. But some worthy bishop built up the road so it may be traversed safely by foot.'

Sure enough, at the end of Bridge Street the three men trotted across a raised stone causeway, staring down at their tremulous reflections amid the water's ripples. At the north side of the pools they found themselves at the Close's south-west gate. That gate was a squat affair of grey stone, with portcullis and drawbridge, and guarded by a pair of surly sentries wielding stout pole-arms.

'Hold!' the older of the guards – a sergeant, to judge by his halberd – said lazily as the group approached. He cast searching eyes across the newcomers, noting their weapons and bearing. 'What business 'ave you?'

Stryker dismounted quickly, offering a curt bow. 'My name is Stryker. Captain. Sir Edmund Mowbray's Regiment of Foot. For God and King Charles,' he added, in case the guards had not heard of Mowbray's regiment.

At once, he sensed the twin gazes of Skellen and Forrester bore into his back as they wondered why he had given his real name. He fished inside a small pocket woven into the lining of his doublet. 'Here is my letter of authority.'

The sergeant stepped forward, taking Stryker's folded square of parchment. He squinted at it for a while, turning it over to stare at the embossed seal set into a blob of cracking red wax.

'It orders every loyal subject to assist my work in any possible way,' Stryker said impatiently.

The sergeant glowered. 'I have me letters, sir.'

'My compliments,' Forrester put in.

The sergeant's eyes narrowed as though he were mustering a retort, but he evidently thought better of it. 'Better let you in, sir,' he said, handing back the parchment.

'Better had,' Stryker said.

The sentries parted, the younger man waving them through the gate, while the older accompanied them for a few paces. 'You'll find my lord Chesterfield in the palace, thither,' he pointed a black-nailed finger towards the north-east corner of the cathedral's wall-ringed complex.

'Thank you, Sergeant,' Stryker said, handing the man a small coin for his trouble.

The sergeant nodded his thanks, calling to some men at his command. A handful came, taking the head collars of Oberon and the two mounts purchased for the escape, and leading the animals off to nearby stabling.

'Couldn't read a word,' Forrester said, highly amused.

'He recognizes a royal seal when he sees one,' replied Stryker.

'I take it our esteemed General of Horse gave you that letter when he told you of Lisette's plight?'

'But forgot to ask for it back.'

'And I suppose,' Forrester went on, 'it explicitly states your name.'

Stryker nodded. 'So we will take our chances here; hope word has not spread this far; and get Lisette out of Lichfield before it does.'

The cathedral sat in the centre of the Close, at once both imposing and beautiful, and Stryker, Forrester and Skellen skirted the magnificent building with more than a little awe. Intricate stone carvings of saints and gargoyles covered the edifice, the legacy of masons of almost boundless skill, while the scores of lifelike statues, set high on the West Front, were a rare sight to behold.

'Nice pile,' Skellen said as they reached the palace.

'Your eloquence leaves me astounded once again, William,' Forrester said with a smirk.

'Do me best,' replied Skellen. 'Strange sort o' church what don't 'ave Bible boys though.'

Stryker and Forrester exchanged a surprised glance, for neither had been as observant as the tall sergeant. But he was right, nevertheless. There did not seem to be a single clergyman in sight.

'Told you it were more of a fortress, didn't I?' Skellen went on.

'Aye, you did,' Stryker said. He realized that Skellen's assertion had been more accurate than any of them had imagined. In the absence of stout fortifications encircling the city, Baron Stanhope, the Earl of Chesterfield, had evidently decided to garrison the cathedral, relying on the impressive walls enclosing the Close for protection. 'Not a bad decision,' he said, accepting that, in similar circumstances, he would have done the same.

'I suppose he's kicked the churchmen out on their collective ear,' Forrester added.

Skellen gave a guttural grunt of amusement. 'Not a bad decision either.'

CHAPTER 6

The Bishop's Palace was a splendid group of buildings dominated by a handsome rectangular structure that a gangly musketeer confirmed to be the Great Hall.

'More gargoyles,' Forrester muttered as they followed the musketeer to where a pair of sentries flanked a formidable wooden doorway.

The sound of a heavy iron bar shifting out of place carried to them from the far side, and then the door gradually creaked open to reveal the large chamber beyond. The musketeer showed Stryker, Forrester and Skellen into the high-ceilinged room and led them down its length, footfalls echoing like distant chatter in the high beams, to the far end, where a fire blazed, flames leaping erratically in response to the gusty draft.

Men milled in the area immediately before the fire. A large group, more than a dozen, splintered into factions of two or three apiece, laughter bursting sporadically from some, while others seemed deep in whispered debate. A couple smoked long clay pipes, their writhing tobacco smoke playing up the walls, obscuring the many hanging tapestries that warmed the cold stone. Most cradled pewter goblets, stealing sips between gossip.

'The earl has his own court, I see,' Forrester said disparagingly. 'I'd wager more intrigue abounds before that grate than anywhere else in the county.'

'That him?' Skellen said quietly as his eyes settled upon the only man seated before the red-bricked hearth. His corpulent frame was swathed in a heavy cloak fringed about the neck by a thick russet animal pelt. Shards of silver and blue poked through where the cloak's string ties were loose at his chest, giving away the presence of a remarkably fine doublet.

'I'd say so,' Forrester replied, almost enviously, watching servants rush about the big man like bees at a hive. 'You don't get a belly like that without being lord of the manor.'

Philip Stanhope, Earl of Chesterfield, turned to face the newcomers as they drew close. He remained seated, but shifted his stout chair beneath him, wincing as he did so. One leg remained jutting out at his side, even as his huge bulk turned, and a pair of retainers darted forward to lift it – one cupping hands at the ankle, the other at the thigh – and manhandled the limb into position. Chesterfield scolded them as they rested it back on the compacted straw. When they backed away hastily, he turned his attention to Stryker.

'What—have we—' the earl laboured as pain racked him, 'here?'

Stryker stepped forward a pace, removed his hat, and cleared his throat. 'Captain Stryker, my lord. Mowbray's Foot.'

Chesterfield eyed him for a second, and with a sudden lurch Stryker thought news of their escape from Cirencester must have reached Lichfield. But, to his heart-pounding relief, when the earl spoke it was not to order an arrest.

'Welcome to my humble abode, Captain,' he said, spreading chubby palms. The gesture gave rise to a chorus of polite chortles from a now silent and watchful retinue.

Uncomfortable under so many interested stares, Stryker steeled himself and offered a low bow. 'I am grateful, my lord.'

'My garrison here is small,' Chesterfield went on, the words coming quickly now that the pain in his leg had abated, each one almost punching from his mouth. 'I have, perhaps, three hundred. Gentlemen and their retainers in the main, yes? Not real soldiers, I'm sad to say. I'd welcome reinforcements.'

'That is not—'

'Oxford army, yes?' Chesterfield interrupted, though his attention had turned to a small table, dragged to his side by a pair of servants. On its surface sat a wooden trencher, a lump of meat the size of a man's head at its centre. Chesterfield began carving at it with a small knife.

Stryker shook his head. 'Not as such, sir.'

'How many?' Chesterfield said with difficulty as he eagerly crammed chunks of meat through greasy lips.

Stryker was bemused. 'My lord?'

Chesterfield finally looked up from his repast, swallowing hard so that his mouth was almost empty. 'Do you bring?' He leaned forward suddenly, trails of glistening fat tracing their way from the corners of his thick-lipped mouth to drip slowly from a chin lacking any definition. 'How many accompany you, sir, *hmm*? S'blood, man, tell, do! Toad! Copper!'

At the sound of his call, a pair of fearsomely built mastiffs bounded to the earl's side from somewhere near the hearth. One had a coat of reddish colour, the other brindle, and they began snaffling up scraps of meat as he tossed them to the floor.

'I confess, my lord,' Stryker replied, his voice flat, though he could not help but notice Forrester's shoulders trembling faintly at the corner of his vision, 'it is the three of us only.'

The room fell to dead silence. Even the mastiffs seemed to look up. The earl's hazel eyes, minuscule in such a large head, widened dramatically. 'Three? Three you say?'

Stryker thought it politic to drop his gaze. 'Alas.'

Chesterfield let out a small squeak of distress. 'Then tell me how his majesty means me to prevail here. I strive to protect his honour in this county, yes? In this rebellious town, yes? How would he have me do it with so paltry a force? How, sir, how?' There were rings on three of the fingers of his right hand, and he studied them now, twisting each one in turn, as though something profound could be divined from within their precious metals. 'That vile creature Drafgate stirs trouble with his every breath. Whispers treason to the townsfolk any chance he gets. Still, we're fortunate to defend these great walls, yes?'

Stryker did not know how to respond. 'My lord.'

'The walls are not impregnable, my lord.'

The new voice had cut across Chesterfield's diatribe just as Stryker sensed it was gathering pace, and the earl's face darkened in anger. The speaker was one of his entourage, but he did not turn to face the verbal intruder. He physically could not. But he seemed to know the man to berate regardless.

'Damn it all, Sir Richard, but I'm tired of your insidious chatter, by God I am!' Chesterfield barked, eyes still fixed upon Stryker. 'The local populace are Puritanical traitors and I pray to Christ that you'll learn that lesson before one of 'em sticks a dirk in your trusting back, yes? We must stay within the Close. Leave the streets to the enemy. They will never dig us out.'

The men of Chesterfield's retinue seemed to move suddenly, those at the forefront parting to allow one of their number through. A man emerged; tall, slim and soberly dressed, swathed as he was in black tunic and white shirt, the collar of which framing a thin face of stern countenance and wide, intelligent eyes. He paced confidently from the group to draw up at the earl's left side.

'As Steward of Lichfield, my lord, I am concerned only for the town and your person,' he said, respectfully enough, though Stryker detected the merest hint of frustration in that level tone. 'Heed me, my lord, I urge you.' A thin-fingered hand rose to scratch at the neat beard that came to a sharp point at his narrow chin. It was dark brown, like the hair that fell in wavy strands to just below his ear lobes.

The earl glared up at him. 'You must learn caution, yes? Your recklessness has already cost you a spell in Parliament's dungeons once this winter.'

The tall man, Sir Richard, furrowed thick eyebrows. 'That was through no recklessness, my lord. After Kineton—'

The name rang a mighty bell in Stryker's mind. 'You were at Kineton Fight, sir?'

Sir Richard turned to him, looking somewhat bashful. 'Aye. Well, I witnessed it, 'tis fair to say. I was sent to the King with a message from the city.'

'*Ha*!' Chesterfield scoffed. 'A message denying him the city's support, no less!'

'But not denying him *my* support, my lord,' Sir Richard added, eager to qualify the earl's rant. He threw Stryker a look withered by disappointment. 'The King ordered the city, at the war's outset, to raise for him money, plate and fighting men. There was a meeting,' he continued with a resigned shrug, 'at which Parliament's adherents carried the day. The order was denied.'

'Denied!' Chesterfield bellowed, as though the very notion could be met only with disbelief. 'They disobeyed their sovereign, yes? Unfathomable! Truly, truly.'

'I was sent to give King Charles the city's response,' Sir Richard said, unable to keep the sadness from his voice. 'With that message I took all the gold I – and my fellow loyal subjects – could muster, so that the King might see that not all Lichfield was of a treasonous mind.'

'And you raised your own troop o' horse, do not forget,' Chesterfield added.

Sir Richard nodded. 'While giving our miserable message to the King, his forces engaged the enemy at Kineton. I was too old to fight myself. But my troop were with Prince Rupert's regiment.'

'You stayed to watch?' Stryker asked.

'My son Anthony commands them,' Sir Richard replied.

Stryker nodded. It was explanation enough. 'My lord Chesterfield mentioned imprisonment.'

'Captured on my way home from the battle, Captain. I was taken by rebel horsemen at Southam and held at the Marshalsey in Coventry. They released me this new year.'

'And now he is back,' Chesterfield interjected. 'This flea in my ear,' he said, addressing Stryker, 'is Sir Richard

Dyott. He has harangued me these last weeks. Urges me to unnecessary action. To throw caution to the wind, and risk losing what few men I have at my command. A man of Lichfield, mark, yet he does not trust these walls to protect us.'

'Walls can only stave off cannon balls for so long, my lord,' Dyott said. 'I have seen what modern ordnance can do. You must fight, my lord. Send for reinforcements from local garrisons, send to Oxford, even, but grow your forces. Make this town formidable, my lord. We have but three hundred men here. It will not be enough when the enemy comes.'

Chesterfield shook his head, sweaty jowls wobbling vigorously. 'No, no, no. It is folly. It is all folly. And what makes you certain they will come at all, Sir Richard, *hmmm*?'

'Lord Brooke moves from Warwick Castle.'

Chesterfield smiled witheringly as though he addressed a child. 'And he will choose to sink those Satan-sharpened teeth into a juicier apple than little Lichfield. No, sir, Brooke will pass us by. We must stay within the protection of the Close. Hold the city for the King's cause. Protect these loyal men for service when it is truly needed. It is our only choice. Our sacred duty.'

Dyott's voice became more urgent now, as, Stryker guessed, he covered ground well trodden since his return from prison. 'But we do not hold the town from in here, my lord. Many of the common folk are set against us. If a rebel force marches into Lichfield, it will be welcomed. And we will be caught here, trapped and impotent in Cathedral Close. We will live, but the town will fall. Where is the sense in that?'

That was enough for Chesterfield. He leaned forward slowly, gaze hard. 'You question my judgement, Dyott?'

Dyott raised his long-fingered hands in supplication. 'No, my lord, of course not. But I—'

Stryker cleared his throat noisily.

The Earl of Chesterfield's sheen-glimmering brow rose at the intrusion. 'You have something to say, sir? Speak it.'

Stryker did have something to say. He wanted to throttle the Earl of Chesterfield. To storm forward and scream into his round face, shake him by those vast shoulders and make him see that Dyott was right. They could not simply sit idle, for such inertia would spell the end of a Royalist presence in Lichfield. It was sheer madness to wait in the hope that inconspicuousness would keep them safe. If anything, it would present the earl's meagre force as an easy target for ambitious enemies. But he was not here for the king's cause, and had no wish to cross swords with the man who held the key to his flight north from Cirencester. He would have to swallow his annoyance.

'My lord, we are not here on king's business.'

Chesterfield's eyes narrowed to slits. 'Oh?'

Stryker thrust a hand into his cloak, drawing out the letter. 'Rather, Prince Rupert's.' The earl gestured he should approach, and Stryker did so, handing the parchment out for Chesterfield to grasp.

An age seemed to pass as all eyes watched Chesterfield examine the royal seal, before his stubby fingers went to work unravelling the scroll. He examined the few lines of black ink briefly, and glanced up. 'To give every assistance, eh?'

Stryker did not wish to waste time. 'Beg pardon for my directness, my lord, but might you have a woman here?'

The retinue chuckled at Chesterfield's back. 'We have many, sir. This is a garrison. Our families are with us.'

'My lord,' Stryker said, attempting to remain respectful, but struggling to keep the urgency from his voice. 'It is a particular woman I seek.' He held a hand out at shoulder-height. 'She is perhaps this tall, with golden hair. And she is French. The Prince told me you had written to him, alerting him of her presence.'

Chesterfield drummed his ringed fingers on the small table's surface as he thought. 'A Frenchy you say. Don't think we've seen such a creature in Lichfield since the Conqueror's days. Hardly something I'd forget, yes?'

And that was it. The words he had both feared and expected since leaving Cirencester. Prince Rupert had been wrong. The victim of some cruel game.

He turned to Forrester and Skellen in turn, realising for the first time the terrible price they would both pay for following him on this damned fool's errand. 'I'm sorry.'

Skellen shrugged nonchalantly. 'Bugger all else to do, sir.'

'Besides,' Forrester whispered, 'I'll simply tell the provosts you kidnapped me.'

Just as Stryker prepared to take his leave, a hollow chasm opening in the pit of his stomach, a figure emerged from the crowd. He was small, his head scarcely rising above the dogs that now skittered sheepishly out of his way, and Stryker watched, bemused, as the fellow approached Chesterfield, whispering hurriedly in the earl's ear.

'He takes council from children?' Skellen spoke quietly at Stryker's flank.

'Look closer, Will,' Stryker replied in equally hushed tones. 'It is no child.'

Skellen did look closer, eyes widening as he studied the earl's diminutive courtier. He took in the grey woollen uniform of a soldier, the shaven pate, and the abnormally large hands, gnarled with age and use. He saw the mottled, pulpy skin of an old scar that swathed the fellow's entire neck from ear to ear, stark in its pink hue and lack of stubble, and the blades – a tuck and two daggers – at his waist. This was no child. Skellen blew out his cheeks. 'Jesu. It's a bloody dwarf.'

The collective intake of breath from the men of Chesterfield's retinue told Skellen he had spoken a little too loudly. Stryker elbowed him sharply.

The small man, who, to Stryker's eye, might have been anywhere between the ages of twenty-five and fifty – looked up from Chesterfield's ear and stepped forward, a hand playing at the hilt of one of his daggers.

'Dwarf is it?' he hissed in an accent not native to Staffordshire, fixing Skellen with the flintiest of stares. His voice was faint, rasping, though it carried not a hint of trepidation. 'You think me some mythical creature, Sir Crannion?'

Skellen remained silent, clearly unsure how to react to being likened to a huge spider by a man whose head barely reached beyond the sergeant's own waistline.

'Well, this mythical creature'll spill your fuckin' guts over those big boots,' the little man challenged, not at all daunted by Skellen's vast size advantage, 'if you'd care to call me dwarf again.' His eyes held a rich amber hue, bright against the grey of his woollen coat and breeches, surrounding pupils of deepest black, giving him a feral, almost feline appearance. They burned with unbridled intensity, but not a trace of fear. The scarring below his chin seemed to glow scarlet with his rising ire, appearing all the more livid against the white of his falling band collar.

Stryker stepped forward. 'Calm yourself, sir,' he said, trying his best to ignore Forrester, whose shoulders were trembling again. 'My sergeant meant no offence, I can assure you. He lets his tongue run away on occasion. A mistake.'

The small man did not relent. 'Many have made a similar mistake, sir, and I've taught 'em not to make it twice.'

Judging by the nervous silence of the men gathered behind Chesterfield, Stryker did not doubt it. He made to speak, but the earl's voice cut across him.

'Enough of this! Relent, Simeon! I said relent, you cloth-eared dolt!'

The dwarf, Simeon, seemed to regain control of himself at the sound of Chesterfield's voice.

'Ignore him, Captain,' the earl said, 'his temper's short as his body. But a good man, mark. A loyal man, yes?'

'If you say so, my lord,' Stryker said, as Simeon resumed position at the earl's ear.

'You're right, Simeon,' Chesterfield was saying as the little man whispered hurriedly again. 'Bless my soul if I'd forgotten entirely with all our recent tribulations. Yes, yes, yes, we do. A beauty if I'm not sore mistook.' He looked up suddenly, surprising Stryker with a broad smile. 'We have one. A girl. Bad way, though, Captain, yes?'

Stryker's heart was racing, and he strained to keep emotion from his voice. 'Bad way?'

The earl nodded, jowls wobbling furiously. 'Fell to sickness when she arrived. I was inclined to 've slung her out 'pon the cobbles, truth be told, but she was clearly not a common sort, yes? Only after several days did we find her papers.'

Simeon leaned close, whispering to the earl again.

Chesterfield nodded. 'Indeed, Simeon, indeed.' He looked at Stryker. 'I am reminded she chatters in her fever. Chatters in French, no less.'

'She is here, my lord?' Stryker said eagerly, spirits soaring.

'Aye. Doctor Chambers tends her.'

Philip Stanhope, Earl of Chesterfield, glanced down at the prince's letter, taking one final opportunity to be sure that he should help his visitors. 'Every assistance,' he read aloud, before turning to the little man at his side. 'Take 'em thither, Simeon.'

'You do not look as naive as most, sir,' Simeon said as he led Stryker through the complex corridors that formed the arteries of the Bishop's Palace. Even with temper now cooled, his words were more rasped than spoken, like a pair of steel blades scraping together, and Stryker realized that this was the man's natural voice, strange though it was.

Stryker looked down at him. 'Naive?'

'Most of the king's men I encounter are green as new shoots. You have a different manner. You all do.' He looked up into Stryker's grey eye. 'You have seen war.'

Stryker nodded. 'We have, Mister—'

'Barkworth,' the dwarf answered. 'Simeon Barkworth. I thought as much. Your experience, I mean. I am a veteran also.'

Stryker could not help but raise his lone eyebrow in surprise, and was greeted with a caustic scowl.

'Do not let my stature play you false, Captain. Let me see: Boizenburg, Ekernforde, Wolgast, Coberg, Mainz. Need I go on?'

Skellen and Forrester were interested now. 'Scots Brigade?' the latter asked, fascinated by the small man's revelation.

Barkworth nodded. 'MacKay's Foot. I was Sir Donald's personal guard.'

Skellen could only whistle. It was an impressive past. The Scots Brigade, of which Sir Donald MacKay's famed highlanders were an integral part, had fought all over the Continent in the recent wars, proving themselves resourceful and granite-hard fighters for first the Danes and then the Swedes in the brutal struggle against the Catholic League.

'Then how did you come to be here?' Stryker asked, finally able to place the accent. It had been difficult to fathom, but now he understood: Barkworth was a Scot. His service with the brigade would also explain the grey clothing.

Barkworth offered a grin of brown, splintered teeth. Stryker noticed he seemed to be missing a few, for the survivors were spread out like so many mouldering tombstones across his gums. 'A woman. How else? She was working in London when I arrived back from Germany.'

'Working?'

Barkworth's cheeks burned as his perpetually simmering anger began to boil again. 'We cannot all marry gentlewomen, sir!' As quickly as it had come, Barkworth's temper disappeared as he evidently revelled in an old memory. 'Quite a beauty. We married.'

'And she is from Lichfield?' Stryker asked.

'*Was*—aye. Well, from nearby, sir. Burton-on-Trent. I had some money after my service with the brigade. She left her life in London and we came back to her childhood home to settle. She took up a post as maidservant to Baron Stanhope, his seat is at Bretby Park, and I went into service as the baron's protector.'

'But she died?'

Barkworth nodded. 'God rest her soul. When Stanhope left Bretby to garrison Lichfield, I followed, naturally. He is my lord now. My livelihood. I had hoped to avoid further battles, if I'm truthful, for I'd seen more than my gutful of horrors on the Continent. But if war comes to this city I shall defend it to my last breath.'

'You'll be on your own then,' Skellen said.

Barkworth stopped in his tracks, turning back to face the tall sergeant. 'You have something to say?'

Skellen frowned as though the answer was obvious. 'Seems your baron does a mighty lot of talkin' for one what sits tight behind his walls while his city lies so exposed.'

Barkworth visibly bristled. 'You call us cowards, sir?'

'Not them what're outside the Close, no,' Skellen replied.

'Then you're mistaken,' Barkworth rasped, and immediately a knife was in his hand, its tip stone still in the air, pointing directly at Skellen's long neck. 'And I'll be glad to tutor you in your manners.'

Skellen sighed in exasperation, but his hand dropped to his sword-hilt. 'Never did get any schoolin'. Be my guest, little friend.'

Stryker stepped between them. 'Stand down, Barkworth.'

133

Barkworth's eyes did not so much as flicker away from his opponent's face. 'I am not yours to order, Captain,' his hissing tones retorted. 'No piker on the king's shillin'. I answer only to my earl, and he'd tell me to teach this lanky streak o' nag's piss some respect.'

Stryker held up placating hands. It was a bizarre scene, for Skellen loomed so imposingly above the aggressive Scot that it seemed as though he were about to fight a child in warrior's clothing, but if the Earl of Chesterfield's personal guard had the martial pedigree he claimed, to pick a fight with the man would be foolhardy, even for a man such as Skellen. 'No such tutelage is necessary, brave Master Barkworth. I assure you Sergeant Skellen meant no offence of any kind.'

Barkworth did not move. Did not waver. He was poised, crouching slightly, prepared to counter any attack.

And William Skellen grinned. 'Praps not every man in this Close is cowardly after all.'

The infirmary was located in one of the smaller buildings at the rear of the palace. Having formed an uneasy truce with Skellen, his anger cooling as quickly as it had flared, Barkworth seemed happy to talk as he led them through a range of drafty corridors. He told them of the city's history and of the arguments amongst the earl's courtiers as to whether or not they should be hoarding food in preparation for a siege.

'Never mind all that,' Forrester exclaimed. 'Where are the women?'

'They're in the old homes of the prebendaries and canons, sir.'

Forrester's face lit up. 'You mean to tell me that instead of priests, we have wenches? Well, it's the most attractive cathedral I've ever visited!'

'And what of Lisette?' Stryker asked sombrely, cutting short Barkworth's chortle.

'She came to us not long after the year turned,' the Scot said. 'Barely conscious at first. Whispered some things that served only to confuse, and promptly passed out. She has a fever, sirs. A nasty one. It may yet prove her undoing.'

'May?'

'She is strong, Captain. I would not leap to wager against her.'

Stryker considered Barkworth's tone, for it was suddenly inflected with softness not present until now. 'You were the one who saved her, weren't you?'

Barkworth did not look back. 'My earl is a righteous and loyal man, and I shan't abide a word against him.'

'But?'

'But he has been wronged. Left here to rot, defending a town that doesn't want him. His time is taken with more pressing matters.'

Stryker understood. 'He would not have kept her within his walls.'

Now Barkworth turned to look up at him. 'No, he would not,' he said, and for the first time a hint of apology crept into his coarse voice, 'even after we discovered the letter of authority tucked into her boot. But I heard her words, and convinced him to write to the Prince.'

'Her words?'

'French words. I would have saved her for her faith alone.'

'You are Catholic?' Stryker asked, surprised. The Scots Brigade had been one of the most fearsome defenders of Protestantism Europe had ever seen.

Barkworth's shaven head shook. 'But I dislike Puritan zeal. It drives men to evil.'

A flash of memory came to Stryker. An image of a German hamlet, backlit by the glow of burning buildings and resounding with the death howls of women and children. 'As does Papist zeal.'

'Aye, maybe.' Barkworth stopped abruptly, a hand rising to rub the ruined skin of his throat. 'Though it was not a Papist noose did this.'

Stryker's jaw dropped. 'You were hanged?'

Barkworth's yellow eyes were glassy for a moment, but, just as Stryker thought he would reply, he blinked rapidly, forcing himself back to the here and now. He turned away suddenly, pointing to a low door at the end of the corridor. 'But we are here, gentlemen.'

'You are a loyal man, Barkworth,' Stryker said calmly, though his heart pounded uncontrollably. 'And astute. I thank you.'

The yellow eyes narrowed. 'Who is she, Captain?'

'A person of great import,' Stryker said non-committally.

'To our cause?' replied Barkworth. 'Or to *you*?'

Stryker could not stifle a rueful smile. 'Yes, Master Barkworth. You are astute, I give you that.'

The rectangular-shaped room was suffocated in oppressive gloom, its three glassless windows too small to allow enough daylight into such a large space. It might well have served as a bishop's bedchamber in early life, but now its furnishings were chosen for function rather than comfort. Rows of simple palliasses – tightly packed mattresses of straw – ran down the sides of the infirmary, while the roaring hearth at the far end was flanked by bushels, out of which jutted the handles of various metal implements that presumably frequented the red flames.

'It's a pissin' torture chamber,' Skellen murmured uneasily as the group waited for Barkworth to close the door in their wake.

'For the cauterisation of wounds,' a voice suddenly erupted from somewhere nearby, making Skellen jump in alarm. The speaker had been stooped over the prone form of a man on one of the adjacent palliasses, and they had not noticed his presence. He straightened up and nodded towards the far end of the room, evidently indicating the bushels. 'And every fighting man should thank the Lord for their presence.' The speaker wiped big hands down the front of an ominously stained apron and skirted the palliasse to welcome his visitors. He was tall, able to meet Skellen eye to eye, but vastly fat, so that, when stood at full height, his enormous frame seemed to make the room shrink. He indicated a table that sat, squat and forbidding, in the centre of his domain. It had short, stout legs and a scarred top on which a collection of darkly stained, serrated implements lay. 'Without the irons, I'd require my saws all too often.' He winked at the sergeant. 'Now the work I do with *those* tools is akin to torture, I grant you.'

Skellen visibly shuddered.

'We're here for the Frenchy, Doctor,' Barkworth said, impatient with the big man's ghoulish chatter.

The doctor clapped his hands. '*Ah ha*! 'Bout bloody time someone came to collect.' He wiped his giant paws again and offered one for the newcomers to shake. 'Gregory Chambers, at your service. Stanhope's resident sawbones.'

As soon as Stryker had introduced himself and his companions, Chambers turned on his heel. 'Follow me, gentlemen, if you'd be so kind.'

Barkworth loitered by the door, the room's only entrance or exit, while the other four men paced quickly down the length of the infirmary, Chambers in the lead. There were not many patients occupying the thirty or so palliasses, half a dozen at most, and Stryker scrutinized each as they passed, wondering with trepidation which one would prove to be Lisette.

'Poor bastard's dog-lock blew up in his face,' the doctor said as they paced by the first bed. The occupant's face was obscured by thickly bound bandages, but they could still hear his feeble moans. 'Took half his jaw away. He'll be gone before dawn, mark me. And that one,' Chambers continued as they reached another, 'has a canker in his belly. It spreads like the plague. Eats him alive. His body will let him down before long.' He scratched the thinning wisps of mousy hair that had been plastered horizontally across his scalp to give a more hirsute appearance. 'Alas, I am entirely powerless.'

He led them on, skirting the portentous form of the operating table and down to the far end of the room. Soon, when they were almost at the fireplace, Chambers came to an abrupt halt beside the last of the palliasses. He looked down at the patient, then moved so that his bulk did not obscure Stryker's view.

'And last, but absolutely not least,' the doctor said, 'our resident mystery.'

*

The patient in the knee-high bed was covered to the shoulders by a sheet of white. Stryker stepped closer, feeling tentative in the extreme, his eye fixed on the face before him.

Skin waxen, highlighted only by the sheen of sweat covering her brow and cheeks, Lisette Gaillard seemed ethereal, somehow otherworldly. Her hair was still lustrous where its thick golden tresses fell haphazardly around her shoulders, spreading outwards on the palliasse to frame her head like a halo, but at the edges where those strands met skin, they were dark and matted. For a moment Stryker thought she must be dead, so pale was the form before him, but, as his grey eye traced the contours of her narrow face, past the small white scar at her chin and down beyond the thin neck, he saw that Lisette's body trembled. The movement was barely detectable beneath the sheets, but definite all the same.

'Captain?' Chambers prompted after a time.

Stryker did not take his gaze away from the woman before him. 'It is her. Thank you, Doctor.'

'What happened to her?' Skellen asked.

'A puzzle, sir,' Chambers replied. 'A real puzzle. She arrived with nothing but the clothes she stood up in. Save this.' The doctor stooped to collect something from beneath the bed. It was a thin piece of silver the length of his hand, from wrist to the tip of his forefinger, no wider than a musket's scouring stick and tapering to a wickedly sharp point at one end. He handed it to Stryker.

'Her hairpin,' Stryker said, recognising the object, and choosing not to mention the fact that it had been embedded in more than hair over the years. He bent down, pushing the large pin into the side of his boot.

'She was in a terrible state,' Chambers went on. 'Gibbering madly, bleeding profusely, but couldn't tell us who she was or why she came to be here.'

'She was wounded, then?' Forrester prompted.

'Aye,' confirmed Chambers. 'Quite badly. And the scrap of parchment we eventually found told us nothing other than she had dealings with the prince palatine. And that scrap, I must confess, was in such a state that we imagined she had somehow found it. Or pinched it.'

Stryker felt as though he was deep within the surreal world of a dream. The voices of those stood behind him were clear and at once faint, as though spoken from inside a barrel. He could hear Chambers's jovial prattle, could discern the questions of Skellen and Forrester, yet could not engage in the conversation. His gaze – his very consciousness – was transfixed upon the woman before him.

'It was a splinter,' Chambers continued, meeting Skellen's darkly hooded gaze, 'for want of a better word. A big one. Almost a stake, I suppose. It was lodged deep in the flesh at her collar. Took me an age to remove the confounded thing. A blessing she was not compos mentis, if I'm honest. Still have the vicious little bastard. Look here.'

At that, Stryker finally managed to drag himself away from Lisette's silent form. He stood, knees shaky, and watched as Chambers strode purposefully over to the much scarred operating table and grasped something in his meaty fingers.

'Keepsake,' the doctor said brightly when he returned to the bed. He was holding a dark wedge of wood, and held it up proudly.

'May I?' Forrester asked.

Chambers handed the wedge to him, and Forrester turned it slowly in his hand. It was big – stretching completely across his palm – and every bit as vicious as the doctor had described. One end was thick, the other wickedly sharp and jagged.

'In her collar?' Stryker managed to say, aghast at the horrific notion that such a thing had somehow been thrust into Lisette's body.

Chambers nodded. 'Where the bone meets the shoulder. How the devil she came by it, I haven't the faintest idea. The procedure to remove the thing, and all the little rot-inducing splinters it left in her flesh, seemed to take an age. Painstaking stuff, and it took a mighty toll. I thought she'd expire there and then. But, as you can see, she was tougher than I had predicted.' Forrester handed the stake back, and Chambers held it up as he spoke. 'Left the skin and muscle somewhat ruinous, mind. I patched her up, and she seemed to be recovering from the wound. Even got some colour back in her cheeks. But then the wound turned, began to go bad, and the fever came hard on its heels. And here we are.'

Stryker turned back to Lisette. She seemed ghostly pale in the oppressively gloomy room. He stared at her, horrified at her stark fragility and disquieted by his own reaction to her plight. Injury and death were commonplace in his life, and he thought himself numb to it, yet the very sight of this pathetic form sent his pulse frantic and his skin crawling. Stryker did not react, did not weep or fall to his knees – but, by God, he wanted to.

As he stared at her, he noticed a certain lopsidedness to Lisette's frame, as though the left portion of her torso carried more bulk than the right. He pointed to it mutely.

Chambers waved a hand at the bed. 'Not a great deal to see, but you're welcome.'

Stryker bent down, taking careful hold of the sheet's edge just below Lisette's chin, and tentatively drew it back, revealing the thick layers of tightly wound bandages that gave her ordinarily slim shoulder so much extra mass.

'The wound is now clean, you'll be pleased to hear,' Chambers said.

'Stank some?' Skellen asked flatly.

Chambers let out a rueful chuckle. 'It did, it did. Dark and putrid. But my beauties cleaned her up.'

Forrester's brow rose, and he glanced around the infirmary with sudden interest. 'Your beauties?'

Chambers bestowed upon him a grin that revealed a cavernous gap between his two front teeth, giving him the air of a gigantic rabbit. He rifled in a pocket, eventually producing a pair of spectacles, which he propped on his large face. The lenses were wide and thick, and he secured them by clamping his crimson nose between the two riveted lens rims. Even then, he struggled to keep them on, and was forced to keep his head tilted slightly back so as to maintain their precarious perch. He turned away, moving between two of the nearest beds, and reached up to pluck a large jar from a shelf nailed high on the stone wall. 'My beauties,' he said proudly, hefting the transparent vessel to the wan light so that his guests could see its contents.

Skellen snorted. 'Maggots. Better 'an any chirurgeon if you ask me.'

'You're a man after my own heart, Sergeant Skellen. Many a bad wound's been healed up by a handful of these plump little lovelies.'

Stryker peered at the jar. At first there seemed nothing of note within, it was simply half-filled with some off-white potion, but as his eye adjusted, it became clear that the potion was in fact a mass of fat, writhing maggots. The sight was hardly pleasant, for he had seen too many bloated corpses infested with the ravenous larvae over the years, but he recognized their usefulness. Maggots applied to a festering wound would devour only the rotting flesh, stripping away the bad and leaving the good intact and with an opportunity to heal.

'My very best crop,' Chambers went on proudly. 'They've delivered me many a happy – or should I say living – customer. We can only pray that your fine-looking Frank, here, will be one.'

CHAPTER 7

NEAR CHIPPING NORTON, OXFORDSHIRE,
23 FEBRUARY 1643

The quill scratched quickly across the old vellum frag-
ment, specks of ink spurting haphazardly in its wake.
The writer paused, squinting at the candlelit page, review-
ing what he had written so far. He glanced up, staring out
into the stable's dark interior, ready to snuff out the glowing stub of beeswax at the first hint of his companions'
waking. Nothing.

He stared back down at the vellum. What was the next
character in the sequence? With reluctance, he set down
the quill and rifled in a pocket sown into the lining of his
woollen breeches, feeling for the hard square of parchment within. He withdrew it as silently as possible and
hurriedly unfolded the square.

His eyes, small and pale, scanned the faded scrawl.
He hated having to remove the parchment from its
hiding place, for to have it on view was to invite the
worst kind of trouble, but his memory for the intrica-
cies of such complex cipher had never been good. He
processed the ranks of letters, numbers and Roman
numerals as fast as he could, holding the page of codes
as close to the small flame as possible without singeing

its edge, all the while keeping half an eye on the snoring bodies around him.

Eventually, and with palpable relief, he found what he was searching for. The symbols representing the letters he needed. He took up the quill again, scratching out the word in the agreed code, so that only the man carrying the identical legend sheet would be able to decipher the message.

Task complete, the man opened the snapsack that lay at his side and returned the quill and ink pot. His heart thudded heavily in his chest as he quickly folded the pieces of parchment into small, tightly packed squares and crammed them both into the secret pocket. With one last check of the room, he snuffed out the candle with tongue-moistened thumb and forefinger, careful not to allow any smoke to trail up into the rafters and stir the slumbering soldiers' nostrils, and whispered a soundless prayer of thanks. There was still the small matter of finding a willing carrier to transport the message to its intended recipient, but men were beginning to starve in a country where grain stores were regularly stripped clean by marauding and hungry soldiers. It would not be difficult to find a willing fellow for a coin or two.

And then he lay down silently, a single breath of unadulterated relief taking the tension from his body.

Because it was done. And Jonathan Blaze would die.

LICHFIELD, STAFFORDSHIRE, 24–27 FEBRUARY 1643

Dawn sent grey light into the infirmary to creep up the stone walls and stir Stryker from a fitful sleep. He had stayed at Lisette's side during the night, Skellen and

Forrester taking up spare palliasses nearby. Part of him had wanted to abandon her here as she had abandoned him so brutally before. But then he would remember the scar on his face, and the way she had cared for him in the wake of the explosion that had deprived him of his eye and nearly his life. Despite whatever conflicting emotions he might feel for this woman, he would tend to her as she had once done for him.

He perched on the mattress beside Lisette. She shivered constantly. It was not violent, but a gentle tremor, a vibrating undercurrent that betrayed the fever's grip, and though its presence announced a very real danger, it served also to calm him, for he knew then that she was – for now at least – alive.

'Will she—?' he asked as Gregory Chambers appeared to perform his daily duties.

'Die?' Chambers pursed his lips as he studied the patient. 'Quite possibly, I'd say. She does not fair well with this fever, and our attempts at feeding her have not met with any degree of success. But, then again, I have been mistaken before. Do not lose hope, sir.'

Simeon Barkworth was with the doctor, and Stryker presumed the little man had been stationed at the door throughout the night, as he had every night since their arrival. It was no surprise, for the earl would have been foolish to leave three armed strangers at liberty within his domain.

Barkworth nodded down at Lisette. 'She's tough as a cart-horse, Captain.'

The ragged patch of scar tissue occupying Stryker's left eye socket crinkled slightly. 'And twice as stubborn.'

'I was right, then?' Barkworth said, hoarse tones reverberating against the stone walls in jarring echo. 'To bring her here?'

'More than you know, Master Barkworth. More than you know.'

Stryker stood, stretched his aching spine, and walked to a nearby chair, dragging it up against the palliasse. He was aware of Chambers speaking, chirping cheerfully about the best way to break a fever, but the words were dull, somehow distant. He sat down, bending forward, whispering to Lisette, stroking her sweat-darkened hair and clammy brow. He ran a thumb across the thin scar that scored her chin, marvelling at how translucent it now seemed, and felt his own body shudder in time with hers. There were times when he resented the stubborn Frenchwoman for placing her duty to the queen above her love for him, and frequently imagined that he would do himself a service by cutting her out of his life. And yet now, at this very instant, he would gladly have absorbed the fever to the detriment of his own body, if it would save her.

A bulky ginger cat prowled nearby, weaving between table legs and under the straw pallets, senses hunt-sharp. Chambers moved to the mantelpiece and took down a small box. He made some clicking noises and the cat came slinking up to him, rubbing its fluffy flanks against the doctor's chubby ankles.

'I'm puzzled,' Chambers said, as he grasped several chunks of what appeared to be dried meat from the box. 'It's not often you see such a fair Gaul.'

'Her mother was German,' Stryker explained, watching as Chambers tossed the meat to the flagstones. The cat let out an excited buzzing sound and pounced on the food.

'Hence the golden locks and azure eyes.'

'Indeed. What is that?'

Chambers put the lid back on the box and returned it to the mantel. 'Salted herring. Harold cannot get enough of the stuff.' He shot Stryker a serious look. 'Who is she, Captain?'

'I cannot tell you more than this,' Stryker replied, genuinely sorry to dissemble with the man who had kept Lisette alive this long. 'She is a loyal servant of the Crown.'

Chambers nodded, and turned to Barkworth. 'Will you fetch us some victuals, Simeon?'

The dwarf shook his head. 'I'm not to leave, Doctor.'

Chambers sighed theatrically. 'The kitchens are but yards away, Simeon. It won't take you five minutes.' Barkworth did not move, and Chambers glowered. 'God help you should you require my ministrations one day, for I fear they'll be sore ineffective.'

Barkworth gritted his teeth, but the threat was enough and he went quickly from the room.

'Now that he's gone,' Chambers said, turning back to Stryker, an earnest expression clouding his usually happy countenance. 'Are we to be attacked?'

'I would not wager against it,' Stryker said seriously. 'Though your earl does not believe so.'

'Oh, he does. But he must make like he has no care so that he cannot be accused of abandoning the city while he hides in the Close. He is simply stricken with fear.'

'Stricken with more besides,' Forrester added.

Chambers's face was rueful. 'Gout, aye. A terrible affliction, and it has him gripped. Too much good living. You might wish to think on it too, sir.'

Forrester's jaw gaped in affront. 'God bestowed a manly big-boned frame on the men of my family, sir. It would be a sin to deny it. And you are hardly in a position to cast aspersions.'

Chambers ran his palms across his own midriff. 'Ha! Perhaps you are right, Captain Forrester. I suffer the same excess of manliness! It is merely something of which the likes of you and I must be wary, lest we end up like the unfortunate baron.' His voice dropped suddenly, its tone clandestine. 'But that is not the greatest problem we face.'

'Doctor?' Stryker urged, equally as softly.

'The Earl of Chesterfield is a coward. He wishes to hide in the Close and remain as inconspicuous as possible. I fear if we are attacked he will give up both town and cathedral for the sake of his own worthless hide.'

'Do not let that puny firebrand hear you, Doctor,' Skellen said, glancing at the doorway. 'You'll be swingin' from the battlements by nightfall.'

Chambers smiled, taking up a vacant stool. 'I must be careful of some ears, Sergeant, you are right. But not Barkworth's. He is loyal to the death, and would defend his master like Stanhope's bloody mastiffs, but he is sensible.'

'Then why ask him to leave?' Stryker said.

'Just because he has sense, it does not mean he would enjoy hearing my opinion. I would rather avoid the argument.'

'Then he does not agree?' Forrester asked.

Chambers blew out his cheeks. 'Deep down he knows I am right. How could he not? He has eyes in his head,

149

and he is an experienced campaigner. But Stanhope is his master, and that is what matters most to him.'

'Bloody zealot,' said Skellen.

Chambers shook his head. 'If you offend his sense of loyalty he'll rail at you, for certain, but he is no zealot. Far from it.'

'Could've fooled me,' Skellen grumbled.

Chambers's eyes narrowed in amusement as he stood to clamp his spectacles on to his face. The ginger cat, having finished gulping down its herring, sprang with silent agility on to the newly vacant stool, curling down upon its surface to enjoy the warmth left behind by Chambers's considerable backside.

The man with the belly canker moaned in the background, his lamentations echoing softly off the stone walls.

'How long does he have?' Stryker asked.

'Your guess is as good as mine, Captain.' Chambers stood in thought for a moment, chewing the inside of his mouth. Eventually he reached back to grasp the stool, tipping the drowsy cat from it as he did so. He dragged it nearer to Stryker and sat again, leaning in. 'I confess, I struggle to believe Lichfield will be assaulted. We are small compared with some of the other towns in the region. And Cathedral Close is strong. Will the rebels really be inclined to attack us here? There must surely be more significant – and less formidable – targets to pick.'

Stryker fixed him with a hard stare. If the man wanted to know the truth of the situation, then he would speak plain. 'Let me spell it out for you, Doctor Chambers. At present, your rebel holds London, most of the lands to the south-east of the capital, the eastern counties and Derbyshire.'

Chambers rolled his eyes. 'Please, Captain, I do not require schooling like some slow-witted child. They have their heartlands, we have ours. The King holds the west country, Wales and much of the north down as far as Nottinghamshire.'

Stryker dipped his head. 'As you so rightly state, the north heralds our cause, and the Welsh are more loyal to King Charles than any of their English cousins. What a force they would make were they to combine their strength. But they cannot, for they find themselves divided. Separated by a narrow tract of land. A corridor that splits the King's territories in two. An area where no side yet reigns supreme.'

'The Midlands,' Chambers said.

'You have it, sir.'

'Or that part of it,' Forrester added as he came to stand at the physician's shoulder, 'west of Derby and Nottingham counties. It is the Holy Grail for our worthy sovereign, Doctor Chambers. And if it is his Holy Grail, then it must surely be Parliament's.'

'And perched at its centre lies this very city, Doctor,' Stryker picked up the point again. 'Lichfield may not be the grandest place in all England, but it guards the high road from Leeds to Bristol. The main communication route between Charles's strongest provinces. Mark this well, Doctor Chambers. I fear your little town will not remain anonymous for long.'

Skellen grunted. The men turned to him.

'And you'll be a fuckin' busy man then, Doc.'

Stryker did not leave Lisette's bedside. He sat with her, watching the trembling shoulders and twitching eyelids, hour after hour, mood as grey as the day. When night drew in, blackening the infirmary to a dank sepulchre, he burned candles so that he might yet study Lisette's ashen features, hoping against hope that they would betray signs of renewed life.

Chambers advised – however carefully chosen his words might have been – that Lisette would probably die. He warned that she had been in the fever's stranglehold too long, that even the hardiest constitution must eventually wilt, that the wound would begin to fester once more and the pain would increase, and that she would slip away. Stryker ignored him, suppressed his own feelings of gut-wrenching helplessness, trickled cold beads of water across and beyond her thin, purple lips and changed her sheets. At times she would seem to improve, as though lucidity was returning, but the sudden animation simply preceded the fever-stoked ravings that made her seem fit for Bedlam. Stryker did not understand most of what she said, for the words were muttered, fast-paced French, and he contented himself with wiping the sweat from her brow.

The short winter days passed slowly, achingly, as though time itself dragged. A dawn of rich pink greeted Stryker as he woke on the third morning. When he had splashed freezing water on to his bestubbled face, he observed the now familiar routine of dabbing the cooling liquid across Lisette's burning cheeks, then went to stand at the nearest window.

The walls of Cathedral Close rose high and forbidding beyond, but he could hear the sounds of life emanate from Lichfield's busy streets, and he thought of how vulnerable the townsfolk must feel with no defences of their own.

High above the walls a black smudge glided with effortless grace. Stryker watched it bank left and right on the breeze, its ample body and broad wings silhouetted against the pinkness of the clouds behind.

'Our buzzard,' Simeon Barkworth's constricted voice carried to him from somewhere nearby. 'It circles the town every so often.'

Stryker turned to look at him. 'I thought it was a kite.'

'A kite's wings are splayed at the ends, like so,' Barkworth said, placing the jug he had been holding on the ground, and stretching out his gnarled fingers to mimic the way the bird's feathers fanned out at the tips of its great wings. 'Your buzzard's a bulkier beast, and its wings curve upwards when it soars.'

Stryker peered back at the sky. He saw that the bird's wings were indeed bowed up in the shape of a U.

'I spent a lot of time watching them on campaign,' Barkworth offered in explanation. 'Little else to do between fights.'

Stryker smiled to himself. 'That is soldiering, Master Barkworth. A man could die by the blade in one instant, and through boredom the next.'

'You ever see the highlanders?'

Stryker met Barkworth's gaze levelly. 'I did, sir. Frightened me to me very guts.'

Barkworth could not stifle his grin, yellow eyes bright with pride. 'We were the most fearsome brigade ever to fight those Pope's-turds. They were hard days.' He stooped to collect the jug and offered it to Stryker. 'Ale?'

Stryker took it gratefully. 'Thank you.'

Barkworth took the vessel back and took his own swig.

'Where did you fight?' he said when he had wiped thin lips with the grey wool of his coat sleeve.

'Everywhere. Captain Forrester and I were with Skaithlocke's company.'

Barkworth dipped his head. 'A good body o' men.'

'We were.'

'Was that where you were wounded?' Barkworth ventured tentatively.

Stryker's instant reaction was to tell the diminutive man to keep his damned impertinent tongue inside his mouth, for he did not enjoy discussing the subject, but something about the grizzled highlander's demeanour garnered respect. 'Aye,' he conceded.

'Cannon? I saw many a man wounded or killed when his own ordnance blew up.'

If only that were so, Stryker thought. 'It was the result of a disagreement,' he said, 'with a fellow officer.' He saw Barkworth's face contort in surprise, and added, 'He paid dear for it.'

'I am heartened to hear it,' Barkworth said seriously.

'And what of your—injury? You said it was a noose. You were hanged?'

The Scot absently lifted a hand to his neck and rubbed the ruined skin. 'After the defeat at Nördlingen I was separated from my company. Lost amongst the human shambles.' He took a long draught of the ale, as if to steady himself against the unwanted memory. 'Didn't know where the bloody hell I was. I wandered for a while, thinking I'd surely run into a Spanish or Italian patrol before long and they'd string me up.'

Stryker was puzzled. 'You said before that no Papist noose did that.'

Barkworth gave a small snort that might have been a chuckle were it not entirely devoid of mirth. 'It wasn't. The soldiers I met were ours. Germans.'

'Puritans.'

'Puritans,' Barkworth confirmed. 'They had been smashed during the battle. They were dejected and bloodied and beaten. And they needed something – *someone* – to blame.' He opened his arms expansively. 'Look at me, Captain. What better explanation for God's abandonment of an army than its employment of unnatural forces.'

Stryker understood. Men infused with religious zeal fought under God's banner and with His blessing. It often proved impossible, then, for such men to fathom the reason for a defeat. 'They took you for a warlock.'

Barkworth nodded slowly, clearly still racked by the memory. 'Or some Romish witch's familiar. I never did comprehend the charge, for I could not understand their language. All I know is that I was hoisted by my neck from a stout branch and left there to dance.'

Stryker stared at him, taking in the devastated skin of a near wrung neck. 'Then how—?'

'Locals,' Barkworth replied, anticipating the question. 'Villagers from a nearby hamlet. They'd been watching from the trees. They heard the charges and undertook to cut me down as soon as the executioners had ridden away.' He met Stryker's eye. 'You know the joke of it? Those gentlefolk were Papists. They saved my life.'

The men were silent for a while. Stryker drank from the jug, glancing every so often at Lisette's shivering form.

'You're the first person since Maggy to hear my tale, Captain Stryker,' Barkworth said eventually.

Stryker understood the intimation. 'Thank you for trusting me. And you can trust my men.' He pointed to Lisette. 'We are here only for her.'

Barkworth nodded. 'I cannot follow all three of you. Besides, you're brothers of the blade, sir, and it isn't often I get to meet the like in this town.' His gaze was suddenly sharp. 'But if there is any trouble, I'll kill the lot of you.'

NEAR SHIPSTON-ON-STOUR, WARWICKSHIRE,
27 FEBRUARY 1643

'Aren't they rare beauties?' fire-worker Jonathan Blaze said enthusiastically.

They had dismounted at the top of a grassy ridge. Far below, on a road running diagonally away from their position, was a great ambling column of men, iron and scores of horses. Royalists, they had decided, by the red scarves at the officers' waists. An artillery train; half-a-dozen smaller cannon, falcons or falconets to Burton's inexperienced eye, followed by a brace of enormous black cylinders that looked as threatening as they were lumbering.

Blaze was watching those larger pieces, the bright glint in his blue eyes betraying his life's passion, and Burton followed his gaze. 'They're certainly big, sir.'

'Big?' Blaze spluttered. 'You infantrymen truly are the worst kind of cretins! They're utterly magnificent!' Finally on the move after more than a week waiting for the inclement weather to ease, they had covered the last few miles quickly, and Blaze was brimming with cheer. 'Magnificent!'

'Culverins,' Jesper Rontry, Blaze's softly spoken assistant, said.

'Yes, thank you, Jes,' Blaze replied waspishly, 'I am quite capable of speaking for myself.'

Rontry cast his eyes back to the meandering train, embarrassment colouring his cheeks, as a host of low chortles sounded behind them. Burton's harquebusiers were sitting beside their mounts, gulping down stale liquid from their water skins and chatting aimlessly about the women of Cirencester and how they might compare to those in Kenilworth.

'As Master Rontry says,' Blaze went on, entirely ignorant of his assistant's discomfiture, 'they are culverins. Well, one is. The one on the far side is a demi-culverin.' He proffered Burton a sparkling grin. 'The bigger of the two will lob a fifteen-pound shot more than two and a half thousand yards, and still have enough bite to take a chunk out of a castle wall.'

'I have to admit, sir, my experience of siege pieces is limited,' Burton said.

'Have you seen them operate on open ground?' Blaze asked. 'In battle, Lieutenant?'

Burton nodded. 'A great barrage of noise and not a deal else. They terrified me at Kineton, for it was my first real fight, but the shots were poorly aimed, by our own side as well as the enemy. I think more damage was done to a fellow's ears than his flesh.'

'And that's where I come in.'

'Sir?'

'It takes an expert to fire one of those beauties, Burton. We've not seen war here this past generation, so there are none who can wield a piece like those two monsters to any proper effect.'

'It is why the King has so many Frenchies in his employ,' Burton replied.

'Right enough. But ordnance requires more than simple experience,' Blaze said, his excitement at seeing the artillery train tempered now by talk of his life's work. 'The likes of La Roche, Montgarnier and St Martin are all authorities in ordnance, but they are foreign men, and there is much to be lost in translation. It is a matter of the perfect trajectory, the right amount of powder, exemplary timing and the art of instructing a team.' He watched the train's slow progress for a short while, before glancing up at Burton. 'Look at that culverin, Lieutenant. That beast takes eight crew and nine horses simply to move it from one place to the next. It requires four gunners and six assistants – mattrosses, we call them – just to get the thing working! Artillery is a complex and costly business. All that detail, all that organization. Not easy for a man who don't have the native tongue, *eh*? But one that does—' He stared hard into Burton's face. 'Well, remember Edgehill.'

Burton thought back to the fair-meadow between the villages of Radway and Kineton. The Battle of Edgehill had been fought there. It had been opened by artillery, which caused little damage, but the sight and sound of cannon balls pulverizing the earth all around them had wrought havoc with morale. He shuddered. 'I remember it.'

'A man that can bring all the elements together can turn that terror to real carnage.'

'You believe you can bring cannon to bear on the field?' Burton said, unable to keep the incredulity from his voice. 'To make a real difference?'

'He has done it many times on the Continent, Lieutenant,' Rontry said now, pride inflecting his voice.

'That I have,' Blaze declared. 'Give me a big gun to fire and a decent crew to fire it, and Parliament's forces shall not stand, I promise you that.'

Robert Greville, second Baron Brooke and newly appointed Parliamentarian General for the Midland Counties, swung a high-booted leg over his mount's back and slid nimbly from the saddle. He took off his wide-brimmed hat, running gloved fingers through sweat-matted hair, before placing it back atop his narrow head as he squinted into the western horizon. 'See the smoke, Major Aylworth?'

'I do, sir,' the nearby officer replied. He was one of half a dozen that had reined in and dismounted, and he followed his general's keen gaze.

Brooke's sharp eyes took in the thin trails of wood smoke meandering skyward. 'A good town, Walter. Godly, loyal and brave.'

His subordinate glanced down from the mass of dark streaks that dominated the pale light of a setting winter sun, and studied the black lines of a map held tight between thumb and forefinger. 'Birmingham, sir?'

Brooke nodded, taking a moment to smooth down the tip of his sharply pointed beard. 'The very same. Declared for Parliament soon as the King raised his standard.'

'A foul day, sir,' Aylworth said, fishing out a wad of dark tobacco hidden in his boot. 'In every sense of the word. Rained heavy, did it not?'

'It did, it did. An ill omen if ever there was one. The king's men should have packed up and gone home that very night.'

The major lifted his head, staring back towards the smoke funnels, trying to discern the chimneys from whence they rose. 'The town's in for a rough time, my lord.'

'Aye, I believe Prince Robber will fall upon them before long,' Brooke agreed grimly. He rifled in one of his saddle-bags, fishing out a small flask of water and taking a long draft. 'But they shall fight him off, Walter,' he said as he rammed the stopper home and returned the vessel to the saddle. 'Have no fear.'

Lord Brooke turned away from the western horizon to cast eyes across the column of men marching past. 'If they have half the heart of our lads, they'll stand firm.'

Major Aylworth began packing his clay pipe with the tight ball of fragrant leaf. 'True enough, sir. They're grow-ing more formidable with every action. Not many can have seen what we have seen. Edgehill Fight and now Stratford. Veterans already!'

'Do not forget Brentford,' Brooke added, shuddering as he remembered the rout when his barricade had finally fallen. Many of his men had taken their chances with the Thames, preferring to face the great river than Prince Rupert's vengeful cavalry.

'Aye, Brentford too,' Aylworth agreed sombrely. 'Though one must admit the shine's dulled since we raised them back in the summer.'

'War takes its toll, Walter,' Brooke replied, still eyeing the purple uniforms, noting how ragged some had become. 'But I wanted a regiment of fighters, not dandies. So long as those muskets are blackened from battle, rather than neglect, I am satisfied.'

The major smiled wryly. 'And what of the shortened pikes?'

'He that cuts short his pike, cuts short his life,' Brooke said sourly, his eyes resting on several of the pole-arms that bobbed a foot or two lower than the rest. 'I cannot keep the fools from trimming. It has been a bitter winter, and they would have their fires ablaze. But nor will I weep for them when it comes to the press. Praise God, events at Stratford did not require such a course.' Brooke had challenged the Royalist force of Colonel Wagstaffe just two days earlier for control of the strategically crucial town of Stratford-upon-Avon.

Aylworth managed to light his tobacco and sucked rapidly on the clay stem. 'I feared,' he said, speech clipped through pursed lips, 'we'd be obliged to engage them.'

Brooke did not take his eyes from the marching column. 'I prayed our guns would scare them off. Hallelujah they did.' Wagstaffe's men, facing Lord Brooke's tough veterans across the Welcombe Hills a mile outside Stratford, had cut and run after the first sharp volley from their fearsome artillery.

'I was adopted, Walter,' said Brooke unexpectedly, as he studied the men at his command.

'Sir,' Major Aylworth said absently.

'I am of Greville blood, of course. Was my uncle Fulke adopted me. He childless and me orphaned. But adopted nevertheless. Do you not see?' He looked at Aylworth, who was sucking the pipe stem enthusiastically, sending plumes of smoke into the air. 'There are no coincidences, Major. No accidents by which our fates twist from one path to the next. It is all by God's design. And His design placed me with land and title that, by rights, might not have been mine. I am His tool. An implement of His work. Put on His earth to oppose Satan's own Romish church and its worshippers.'

'Sir?' Aylworth said, peering at him through the tobacco smoke.

'I was born to fight for Parliament,' Brooke went on, raising his voice above the jangle and clatter of the artillery crews as they trundled noisily past. He watched them labour through the shin-deep filth, his new piece, Black Bess, in front, while a handful of smaller drakes were drawn in the demi-culverin's wake. '*Born* to it,' he said when the noise subsided.

Aylworth nodded, the others stifled smiles, and Brooke rolled his eyes, exasperated with the general lack of zeal, but aware he had told the story more times than was perhaps necessary. 'Let us resume,' he said when the ordnance had finally moved beyond them. Those gun crews were the last element of his grand column, and he paced across to his waiting horse, leaping up into the saddle. 'We make excellent progress,' he called to the group cantering at his flanks and in his wake. The road was better than he had expected, its muddy surface not nearly as swamplike as many of the nation's thoroughfares. 'All to the good. The men need rest as soon as we might find it. Stratford was a fast victory, thank the Lord, but they're weary as old dogs.'

The group kicked their animals into action and ploughed through the churned road behind the regiment. 'The county is ours, praise God. We may now turn to Staffordshire, as Parliament orders,' Brooke called across to another officer who cantered at his side. 'How fairs Stanhope, Lieutenant?'

The man caught his eye from behind the iron nosepiece of his Dutch pot. 'Word from the city tells us Chesterfield cowers behind the cathedral's walls, my lord.' He grinned maliciously. 'Cowers and devours.'

Brooke did not share the amusement. 'The very epitome of Cavalier greed and sloth.' He gave the lieutenant a hard look. 'Chesterfield has a stomach for the finer things. But do the townsfolk have a stomach for him?'

The man shook his iron-clad head. 'Some, sir. But most of that ilk hide in the cathedral too. The larger part will offer us faith and friendship.'

At this Brooke allowed the faintest flicker of a smile. He urged his horse to quicken its step. 'Then next to Lichfield, gentlemen.'

CHAPTER 8

At midday Forrester and Skellen returned from a foray into Lichfield's tense streets in search of supplies.

'Strange morning,' Forrester said, as he snatched off his wide-brimmed hat and tossed it on to an empty palliasse. He spent a moment ruffling his damp hair, thinning as it was, and strode to the hearth. A small cauldron hung above the smouldering embers, and he began stirring the contents with a thick wooden ladle.

'How so?' Stryker said absently, watching his fellow officer take up three bowls and as many spoons from the mantelpiece.

Forrester decanted the cauldron's piping broth into the bowls and handed one each to Stryker and Skellen. The latter raised the corner of his upper lip in distaste. 'Winter veg; by the looks of it,' Forrester explained, 'with the gristle of some unidentifiable creature.' He went to the palliasse that held his hat and perched on its edge. 'As I was saying, it was a strange morning. Firstly, it seems our friend's left town.'

Stryker looked at Lisette's pale face and lost any vestige of appetite. He set the broth on the floor. 'Who?'

'Menjam,' Forrester said, trying to ignore Skellen's

ravenous slurping. Evidently, the sergeant had overcome his initial aversion to the food.

Sparks of clarity began to force their way through the fog as the name jarred in Stryker's mind and an image of the rat-faced traveller came to him. 'Gone where?'

Forrester swallowed back a mouthful of broth. 'I know not. Skellen and I went to the city at dawn.' He rubbed a chubby hand across tired eyes. 'We came across Richard Gunn.'

'Menjam's cousin?'

'The very same. He said Menjam had gone.'

Stryker turned back to Lisette. So Menjam had left Lichfield. Was that such a crime? He felt a pang of anger towards Forrester; for his gossiping and his concern over such triviality when Lisette lay so close to death. It was all he could do to keep from saying as much.

Forrester evidently read his friend's mind, for he leaned forward suddenly, urgency tainting his tone. 'Gunn was coy. Evasive, even. He let slip his cousin had taken leave that night. The night we arrived. Does that not seem strange? I asked him the same.'

Stryker turned back, his interest piqued again. 'And?'

'He retreated. Stammered and tripped on his tongue. As though he'd said too much. He was not supposed to tell us – tell *anyone* – Menjam had gone.'

Stryker rubbed dirty nails along his rough chin, wondering what this meant. 'I did not trust him. Not from the very first time we met. He asked too many questions; was too jaunty for a man who might have been dead on that road, had we not appeared.'

Forrester took a few more mouthfuls from his bowl, then looked at Stryker. 'You are right.'

'An enemy agent, do you think?' It irked Stryker to imagine that he might have saved such a man.

'Perhaps,' Forrester pondered. 'He was reformist in his views, that much was clear. An agent, though? Doesn't seem the type, somehow. Too small.'

'Small?' Stryker scoffed. 'Lisette is small, but you'd not wish to cross her, I'd wager.'

'Or that bloody ranting midget,' Skellen offered dourly.

'Christ, no!' Forrester was forced to concede. 'But he and Lisette are fierce. It is in their characters. Menjam was a rodent. A weasel.'

'I wonder,' Stryker said. Something stirred in his mind. A memory of the filthy road up from Lechlade, and an ambush that resulted in three dead men. 'I might have spared the third . . .'

'Beg your pardon?' Forrester replied.

Stryker gnawed his bottom lip as he deliberated. 'The night we encountered Master Menjam. You and Will had already shot the first two brigands, but I might have spared the third. I was not given the chance.'

'I do not recollect.'

'It was Menjam. He lay there, between the footpad and I, for all the world a beaten man. And then he kicked him, Forry. From nowhere, Menjam stuck his boot into the thief's stones as though he were breaking through an oak door.' Frown lines carved their way into Stryker's forehead as he looked up. 'And they called him a traitor.'

'You're saying Menjam instigated that final fight? A risky strategy. It nearly got him killed.'

'Aye, but a strategy worth pursuing if he needed that third man dead.'

Forrester's brow raised and he blew out his cheeks.

'And secondly?' Stryker went on. 'You said Menjam's disappearance was the first strange thing you'd encountered this morning.'

A heavy knock at the infirmary door startled the three men, and they peered down the length of the room to where a tall, soberly dressed figure approached.

'Perfect timing,' Forrester said. He turned back to Stryker. 'There's something afoot in the town. I can feel it in my very marrow.'

Stryker looked past Forrester to study the newcomer. To his surprise he recognized Sir Richard Dyott.

When he reached them, Dyott offered a brief nod and glanced from Lisette to Stryker. 'How does she fare, Captain?'

'She lives yet,' was all Stryker could think to say.

'Then I thank God for it, though I do not know who she is.'

Stryker ignored the insinuation. 'What can I do for you, Sir Richard?'

Dyott's long fingers rose to worry at the waxed point of his dark beard. 'I asked Captain Forrester if I might come.'

Stryker threw Forrester a quizzical glance.

'As I say,' Forrester said, placing the empty wooden bowl on the stone floor and reaching to pick up his hat, 'there is something ominous afoot. Suffice it to say, our recent sojourn into town will be our last.'

'Oh?'

'The common folk are becoming resentful of the earl's isolation, for that isolation is increasingly construed as abandonment.' Forrester set down the hat and stretched chubby hands behind him, leaning back, letting his arms take the weight. 'At first we were confident that two

167

able-looking men, armed and wary as we were, would attract no more hostility than a narrow-eyed glance or suspicious whisper.'

Stryker met his friend's blue gaze. 'So what has changed?'

Forrester frowned as he searched for the right expression. 'A new bravery is taking hold. Their whispers are now shouts. Once furtive glances have become angry, brazen stares. In short; the buggers ain't scared of us.'

'It's true,' Skellen added, his deep-set eyes remarkable by their glimmering concern. 'They didn't like King's men much when first we arrived, but now they're all rebel-minded and up for a proper brabble.'

'Which is why I am here,' Sir Richard Dyott spoke now. He stepped forward, face suddenly earnest. 'I have heard Lord Brooke has marched into the county. I fear he may set his sights upon Lichfield.'

'I'd say he will,' Stryker replied.

'And that is why you must speak with Baron Stanhope.'

Stryker almost laughed. 'Me? To what end?'

'He must see that trouble is on the horizon. Parliament's sway in the town grows every day the earl shuts his gates to the people. They want protection. Protection he refuses to provide. So what will they do if the enemy comes?'

'They'll do whatever it takes to survive.'

'They will, Captain. And if the earl will not look to their interests, then they will throw in their lot with Parliament. And we here will find ourselves a lone island in a sea of enemies.'

'Can you not petition the earl?' Stryker asked.

Dyott gave a slight shrug. 'I have petitioned him every day since my return from Coventry. You witnessed one such attempt yourselves. My words fall on deaf ears.'

'Then why would my words fair any better?'

'They may not,' Dyott replied honestly, 'but you are a man from the King's army. You have seen the war beyond our little town, and he might deign to listen to you. It is worth the attempt, is it not?'

FALCON TAVERN, HUNTINGDON, 28 FEBRUARY 1643

Zacharie Girns sat at one of the tavern's low tables, turning the silver half-groat between thumb and forefinger, watching the midday light dance across the king's face and garnished shield in turn. He glanced up at a sound outside, immediately alert to danger, and peered through the adjacent window, but relaxed when he saw young Tom Slater pacing across the courtyard beyond. He turned his attention back to the coin, feeling the bile rise in his throat as the king's face stared back at him. Even this small, humble artefact grated at his soul. 'The king's image placed on coinage of the realm.'

Lieutenant Trim was standing nearby, clumsily attempting to darn his spare pair of breeches. He tore squinting eyes away from the needle and thread. 'Sir?'

'I said the King's image. It is graven, Josiah.'

Trim raised his brow. 'You would have Christ, perhaps? Christ with His cross on one side, Parliament on the reverse?'

Girns slapped the coin on to the table, the sound making Trim visibly start. 'Have you learned nothing, man? The King places his face on every object he might, in hope that we might worship him as we worship the Almighty. But to mint even the humblest penny with an

169

image of Christ. That is all the worse. It is nothing short of idolatry. And why do we fight, if not to purge England of such sin?'

'Amen to that,' a new voice echoed from the direction of the doorway.

Girns did not acknowledge Slater, his attention still fixed on the coin. 'But I like your thought of the Parliament. Yes. Perhaps a small inscription upon the reverse. God's Justice, or similar.'

'A hard fight before that happens,' Slater said.

Girns looked up. 'Do not lose faith, Tom. Not for an instant.' Finally he seemed to notice the thin, finger-length tube in Slater's hand. 'What have you there?'

The corporal grinned. 'News, sir. From our man.'

As if a lightning bolt had struck Girns's boots, he shot up from the stool, virtually leaping across the room to snatch the vellum scroll from Slater's grimy fingers. 'Did I not tell you?' he said feverishly as he unravelled the parchment as quickly as he might. 'Our patience has been rewarded, as I knew it would.'

The younger men looked on as Girns placed the message on the table before him and snatched up the hat that had been perched on his lap. He rummaged inside, fiddling with the seam of its velvet lining, eventually producing a folded piece of parchment. He set down the hat again, opened the parchment, and flattened it out on the table beside the piece brought by Slater.

'Sir?' Trim said inquisitively.

'This,' Girns said, tapping the unfurled scroll with his fingers, 'is a coded message. And this,' he made the same motion on the scrap that had been inside his hat, 'is the key to unlocking its contents.'

Girns's green eyes darted left and right between the two sets of blotchy scrawl, taking in every morsel, absorbing the impact of each word as he deciphered it.

Trim and Slater stood like statues, breath baited, neither wishing to interrupt.

Their patience paid dividends as Girns finally looked up, meeting each man's eye in turn. 'We have him.'

'Blaze?' Slater asked, though he already knew the answer.

'Blaze,' Girns repeated slowly, the word rolling off his tongue with exquisite relish. 'He is bound for Kenilworth.'

'Kenilworth?' Slater echoed, his nose wrinkling, 'What for?'

'Kenilworth has a castle.'

'Hardly important though, is it?' Slater continued.

'Do not be so surprised, Corporal. Oxford is safe for the time being, the north will not be busy until the Popish harlot returns – pray God she is drowned in the North Sea – which leaves the Midlands. They are hotly contested at present, and vital to the fortunes of both sides. We must take all the strongholds; Lichfield, Stafford, Kenilworth, all of them, if we are to take the Midlands.'

'And Kenilworth has high walls and big guns,' offered Trim.

'Precisely, Lieutenant. If the right men work their artillery, they will be a difficult canker to cut from the land.' He gnawed a fingernail. 'Yes indeed. Blaze goes thither to bolster the walls with his skill in ordnance.'

Slater snorted his derision. 'In my experience, artillery makes a deal o' noise and bluster, but little else.'

'Because the men who take aim are incompetent half-wits, Tom,' Girns replied. 'Now, imagine an expert behind one of those giant pieces. A demi-cannon or such. Imagine it pouring its venom straight into our ranks.' He looked at Slater. 'Noise and bluster for certain, Tom, but murder too.'

'It'd be hellish,' Trim offered.

'Hellish. So we will stop him,' Girns was beginning to hiss, such was his welling enthusiasm, his green eyes twinkling bright.

'But Kenilworth's a long way, sir,' Trim said tentatively. 'Would it not be more expedient to send word to—'

'Enough!' Girns's fist crashed into the tabletop with frightening force. He fixed Trim with a glare that seemed to singe the air between them. 'This is *my* task. *My* quarry. Jonathan Blaze is *mine* to kill. You can never understand. Mine is a higher purpose.' He straightened suddenly, turning to Slater. 'Fetch the horses.'

'Sir,' Slater blurted.

With that, Major Zacharie Girns stalked from the tavern with a vigour he had not felt since sending a musket-ball into Lazarus Blaze's spine. Their man had betrayed the older sibling, and now Girns would strike. 'Thank you, Jesus,' he whispered.

LICHFIELD, STAFFORDSHIRE, 28 FEBRUARY 1643

'He's what?'

'Bathing, sir.'

Forrester's indignant expression was matched by the rising colour in his fleshy cheeks. 'Bathing? God's ankles, man, but we must speak with him at once!'

'Hold, Forry,' Stryker intervened.

172

The sentry stood a little straighter as Stryker came near, puffing up his chest like a cockerel. 'Like I say, sir, you cannot pass. Not till the earl is ready to receive you.'

Stryker considered forcing the matter, but that would only end in bloodshed and a fight he could not hope to win. He turned questioningly to Dyott.

'The earl is particular about his ablutions, Captain,' Dyott answered apologetically. 'He may be a while longer, I fear.'

Stryker fixed his grey stare upon the leading sentry. 'Tell the earl I wish to speak with him. It is a matter of utmost urgency.'

'I will, sir, I will.'

Stryker turned on his heel, annoyed at being dragged from Lisette's bedside for nothing, and began to stride back down the corridor that would return him to her.

'Stryker,' Forrester's voice called behind him.

Stryker turned. 'What is it?'

'It is a fresh afternoon, old man. Let us view the city.'

Stryker could not keep the surprise from his voice. 'Only this morning you told me it was too dangerous for us now.'

Forrester shook his head. '*View* the city, Stryker. Not walk its treacherous streets.'

Stryker began to decline, but Forrester cut him off, his tone strained, beseeching. 'Please, Stryker. You have sat inside for days now. Chambers looks to her. Won't you at least join us while we await Chesterfield's summons?'

Stryker, Forrester and Skellen stood on the viewing platform atop the cathedral's central spire and gazed down upon Lichfield. The short day was almost over and the sky around them was the dark grey of rain-soaked slate, thunder grumbling across the distant hills beyond.

The city's great conduits, Bridge Street and Dam Street, stretched away beyond the Minster and the Bishop's Pools. Crowded at their flanks were the shops and homes of Lichfield's citizens, those folk caught in the maelstrom of a war with no enemy.

'You wouldn't know,' Forrester said quietly.

'Sir?' replied Skellen, leaning back from the stone edge.

'That war rages beyond this place. They go about their routines, scuttling this way and that like ants in a nest.'

Stryker studied the civilisation far below. The people did indeed seem to scurry from this high vantage. And more besides. Cattle, horses, street-sellers and carts all fought for space on the dirty streets. Bustling bodies moved to and fro, weaving left and right in the dusky air that would, he knew, be ripe with the aroma of straw and horse shit. He felt a pang of sympathy for the folk. Despite the prevailing antipathy towards their king, he did not wish destruction upon them. He had seen all too often what war did to places like this, and the thought that Europe's atrocities would be replicated here brought a twisting sickness to his stomach.

Stryker looked away, catching Forrester's eye. 'I am sorry for this. All of it.'

Forrester recognized the morose shadow in his friend's gaze and slid, back hard against the stone parapet, on to his haunches. 'Suddenly I am compelled to sit.'

Stryker and Skellen watched him for a moment before following suit.

Forrester took off his hat, placing it carefully at his side, and rubbed his eyes with a tired hand. 'What I wouldn't give for a full pipe and a warm wench.'

'I can help you wi' one o' those, sir.' Skellen unslung his snapsack and began rummaging through its contents.

'Please tell me you've a willing wench hidden away, Sergeant.'

''Fraid not, sir,' Skellen replied, brow creased in concentration as he gazed into the dark interior of the bag. The others looked on as he first took a spare shoe from the snapsack, placing it next to his hat. Then came a sewing kit and a small leather drinking flask, followed by a pouch that clinked and jangled with spare musket-balls. Eventually another, smaller pouch appeared and the sinewy sergeant held it up with a brown-toothed grin of triumph. 'Got 'im!'

'Is that what I think it is, William?' Forrester asked eagerly.

'Fancy a wad o' decent Chezpeake sotweed, sir?'

Forrester's eyes glimmered, and he quickly produced a clay pipe from the folds of his coat. 'Need I answer?'

Stryker, so detached and morose in recent days, could not help but share Forrester's infectious enthusiasm, and retrieved his own well-worn pipe while Skellen fished in the snapsack again. Eventually the tall man produced a tinderbox and an old, gnawed pipe and began to pack the bowl with the coarse tobacco. When the pipe held the requisite amount, he clamped the end of its stem between his teeth and handed the pouch to Forrester and Stryker in turn. While the officers packed their respective bowls, Skellen took the steel, flint and char cloth from the tinder-box and struck up some sparks until the cloth glowed with orange tongues of flame. With impressive dexterity, he dipped a sulphur splint into the fire and it roared into life.

'Jesu, but this'll be a welcome breath, eh?' Forrester exclaimed through lips pursed around the clay stem. 'I do declare the drinking of smoke to be God's own remedy for tired lungs!'

Skellen had his pipe lit now, and had handed the rapidly burning sulphur splint to Forrester. 'Welcome to it, sir,' he said happily as the sotweed rose above the pipe bowl's rim amid the attentions of the charring light, his face obscured in belching smoke. 'We'll all be rottin' soon.'

'How delightfully cheerful of you, William,' Forrester chimed between deep puffs of the acrid vapour.

Charring light waning, Skellen was already tamping down the surface of his tobacco with a small cylindrical chunk of wood in preparation for the inevitable need to reignite. 'If that bloody bed-presser gets his way, leastwise.'

At this, Stryker looked up sharply, his narrow face and quicksilver-grey eye appearing positively demonic amid the smoke wreaths. 'Keep some respect in that lofty head of yours, Skellen.'

Skellen concentrated on relighting his pipe. 'Right you are, sir. Keep me opinions to meself, sir.'

The silence that followed should have suited Stryker, such was his mood, but he was nothing if not aware of his sergeant's displays of outward disinterestedness that so often veiled startling insight. It would be foolish to let the matter rest.

'That ill-advised description of the earl aside, what was your point?'

Skellen sucked contentedly at the clay stem, letting plumes of smoke pump from his nostrils to fill the air between and above them. 'Only that Chessy-field ain't up

176

for a fight, is he? He should be fortifying this place. Building defences, making it difficult for the rebels to dig him out. Or he should high-tail it away from here, into Wales or down to Oxford. Instead he hides. Takes baths to avoid the likes of you, if you pardon the expression. Cowers behind these walls as if they're protection enough. All the while prayin' they'll pass him over for bigger fish.'

'Go on.'

'My point, sir, is that Brooke'll see this place as a big enough fish for his supper. The talk in town says his purple-cocks are on the rampage. He wants the whole bleedin' shire under his boot. Wants the old church smashed away. And that means he'll want to take this grand pile o' stone.' He shrugged and drew on his pipe again. 'It's his crazy belly, like Cap'n Forrester says.'

'His what?'

Forrester beamed. 'Casus Belli.'

'Just so,' Skellen said. 'The earl's in this fight 'cause he'll be in trouble with the King if he ain't loyal. But Lord Brooke's in it to change the world. And that means he won't leave Lichfield alone. He can't. This fancy church'll be temptation enough for 'im. So we'll 'ave to sit here like tethered goats waiting for the Roundheads to come slaughter us.'

Stryker looked at both men in turn. 'As I said, I'm sorry you've been dragged into this. You can always leave, Will.'

Skellen simply snorted his derision. 'You need me to look after you when Brooke comes.'

Stryker felt guilt thump at his guts, because he knew Skellen was probably right, and that the enemy – far from wishing to avoid laying siege to Cathedral Close – would see its capture as a prime target. And he knew that he,

Forrester and Skellen should ride away from this cursed town with their skins intact. But Lisette was here.

'I won't leave her. Not till she is all well.'

'We know that, Stryker,' Forrester said from deep within the smoke cloud. 'And we shan't leave you. So here we all are.'

Footfalls echoed suddenly, emanating up from the spiral staircase beneath them, growing louder with each second.

'Captain!' A voice carried to them in the wake of the footsteps. 'Captain!'

Simeon Barkworth appeared from the depths and sprang up on to the platform as the three men stood to greet him, tapping their pipes on the edge of the parapet so that the blackened tobacco was swept away by the breeze.

Barkworth's face was taut, his yellow eyes wide, bright. He could not hold himself still, but shifted his weight from foot to foot, excitedly.

'What news, man?' Stryker snapped impatiently.

The fiery Scot proffered him with a crooked-toothed grin. 'She wakes, sir.'

Stryker was already dashing down the first of the shallow steps as Barkworth's constricted tones echoed behind him. 'Your woman, Captain. She wakes!'

NEAR ROUGHLEY, STAFFORDSHIRE,
28 FEBRUARY 1643

'Thither, m'lord.'

The speaker, a terrified shepherd-boy, barely into his teens and struggling to keep control of his bowels, muttered through a mouth full of rotten gums. He was staring up at a soldier, as though the gigantic, yellow-coated visage was nothing short of a denizen of hell.

Major Henning Edberg had dismounted, handing his sleekly dark horse's reins to a frizzy-haired subordinate, and now loomed over the shepherd like some prehistoric obelisk.

'That way, you say?' Edberg held out a gloved fist, extending a finger to the north and east, where three colossal stone spires rose above the tree-lined horizon like black daggers in the dusk.

The lad's skull shivered suddenly in what Edberg took to be affirmation. 'Aye. A one-eyed man and three fedaries. One tall 'un, one short 'un and one run to fat.'

'To where?' Edberg snapped irritably. 'What town is this?'

The shepherd followed the pointing hand. 'Lichfield, m'lord.'

'Lich-field,' Edberg repeated slowly as he struggled to negotiate a language not his own. He considered himself competent with the English tongue, but some of the country's infernal placenames remained stubbornly difficult to master. 'Who holds it?'

The shepherd offered an expression of wide eyes and slack jaw that spoke only of ignorance. Edberg glared at him, serving only to increase the boy's trembling, and rounded on the dragoon that had taken hold of his mount. 'Who holds Lichfield?'

'King, sir,' the dragoon answered hurriedly. 'Last I heard.'

Edberg turned back to the shepherd. 'You hear different?'

The boy shook his head mutely, eyes flicking from the big foreigner to the twenty or so yellow-coated soldiers that stared pitilessly down at him from malevolent-looking beasts.

Edberg's eyes narrowed to suspicious slits. 'You seen soldiers march that way?'

'No, m'lord, I swears!' the shepherd-boy replied desperately, bleating like one of his flock. 'Not since them what you described.'

Edberg and his diminished troop had made dire progress across the empty fields of Staffordshire. Those fields would have been lush, verdant pastures in days gone by, but now, with no one to tend them, they had given all they could yield. The land, Edberg thought, was falling daily into the war-ravaged abyss that had swallowed the rest of northern Europe.

The young man, awed into quivering supplication by the strange-sounding officer's terse manner and fearsome physique, had quickly confirmed the presence of his quarry. In truth, the major had not expected to hear that Stryker travelled with a third companion, for the information given by Colonel Crow was that there were only two in his renegade band, but the presence of another in the group did not affect Edberg's task.

'No rebel armies have come to take this town from us,' Edberg said to the trooper with the wiry hair.

The trooper thought for a moment. 'Not from this direction, leastwise,' he conceded.

Edberg jerked his chin imperiously towards the shepherd. 'He would have heard if an army had been in the region. From any direction.'

The subordinate nodded agreement. 'Less he's lying, sir.'

Edberg's ice-blue gaze bore down implacably upon the shepherd. 'If you lie to me, boy, I will return.'

'I speak true, m'lord, by me papa's grave,' the lad replied as quickly and as heartfelt as he might, stepping backwards involuntarily as he spoke.

Major Henning Edberg turned away, stalking across the wet ground to clamber up into a saddle as black as the horse beneath it. He raked the beast's flanks, spurring it into sudden, muscular energy, and it churned the mud excitedly, flinging clods of muck into the air, leaving the shepherd to duck away in their wake. Edberg heard his score of dragoons close behind and allowed himself a rare smile. For the rats were indeed in Lichfield. And soon his terriers would have them cornered.

LICHFIELD, STAFFORDSHIRE, 28 FEBRUARY 1643

Lisette Gaillard was already sitting up when Stryker entered the infirmary. She must have read the racking mixture of concern and relief on his face, for she cast him a withering glance as she sipped at the contents of a pewter goblet.

Stryker wanted to run the length of the large room, but his men were at his heels, and Chambers was standing over her palliasse, so he forced himself to maintain a steady, calm pace, the rhythm of which was entirely at odds with the beating of his heart.

'Madam,' he said quietly when he was at her side. He took off his hat, instinctively tidying the black tendrils of hair that fell beside his cheeks.

'Captain,' she replied equally as softly.

They stared at one another for what seemed like an age.

Chambers cleared his throat with unnecessary volume. 'Well now, I must see to the hearth. Urge her to rest,' he added under his breath as he strode past Stryker.

Stryker nodded absently and sat on the edge of the bed, feeling the packed straw shift and sink with his weight. She was magnificent in the night-darkened room, her hair shimmering in the flame light, wan skin almost translucent. But Stryker knew that such delicate beauty, however alluring, was also the outward manifestation of an exhausted, damaged body. Lisette was far from recovered. He placed a hand tenderly on her good shoulder. 'You must lie back, Lisette. The doctor—'

A spark flashed across Lisette's sapphire eyes and she shrugged him off. 'I'll sit, *merci*. The doctor can try to convince me otherwise if he wishes his eye blackened.'

Stryker's narrow face split in a wide smile. Lisette had returned to him.

CHAPTER 9

'The man I escorted was named Blaze. Now he's dead.'

It was mid morning, and, after a night of deep sleep, Lisette had finally woken, squeezing Stryker's hand as he dozed in a chair beside her. After enjoying several impressive gulps of small beer and a large chunk of gritty bread, she had seemed well enough to talk, and Stryker decided that it was time to find some answers.

'Blaze?' William Skellen said. Stryker had asked him and Forrester to join them, feeling the pair deserved an explanation as much as he. 'The petardier?'

'Yes,' replied Stryker, his mind working to fathom the significance. He looked at Lisette. 'We have just encountered Master Blaze. He is not dead, I assure you, but in Oxford.'

'Lucky him,' Skellen said dourly.

'Lazarus,' Lisette replied, ignoring the sergeant. 'My charge's name was Lazarus Blaze.' She frowned suddenly as an idea entered her mind. 'But he was in correspondence with his brother. Always scribbling letters to him. A man named Jonathan.'

'Aye, that was him,' Stryker agreed. 'Jonathan Blaze.'

'Jonathan may well thrive, *mon amour*, but I can assure you Lazarus is entirely dead. I saw him fall. Watched his blood spray the trees.'

So that answered Rupert's question, Stryker thought. He leaned close, reading the pain in her expression. 'What happened, Lisette?'

'I was escorting him from Devizes to Stafford,' Lisette began. 'Blaze was a fire-worker and an engineer; a good one.'

'Like his brother,' Skellen grunted.

Lisette's brow rose with interest. 'A family business, then.' She turned back to Stryker. 'Prince Rupert employs me while my queen awaits a change in the weather.'

Stryker blew a chest full of air out through his nose.

Lisette tilted her head to one side, studying him with interest. 'Do not be jealous, *mon amour*,' she said coquettishly.

'And I imagine the rebel blockades don't aid her cause a great deal,' Forrester offered quickly, uncomfortable amidst the lovers' spat.

Lisette's upper lip rose in unconcealed disgust. 'Blockades,' she sneered. 'She will punch her way through their pathetic efforts. The Generalissima will set sail as soon as this cursed country's gales abate.'

'Generalissima?' Stryker asked sourly, rediscovering his irritation at the shadowy world Lisette inhabited. A world ruled by that arch schemer, Queen Henrietta Maria. 'That's how she styles herself now?'

Lisette fixed him with a caustic stare. 'She has built an army, Stryker. With it she will cut a swathe through Parliament's cobbled militias. But for now she offers me, so that at least she may help her husband's cause.'

'And what were you supposed to do?'

'The Prince is anxious to keep hold of the Midland towns,' she explained. 'Derbyshire supports the rebellion. Birmingham is a den of traitors, too. It is only a matter of time before they move against our strongholds in the region.'

'Stafford.'

She nodded. 'An expert fire-worker could make the place impregnable.'

'What happened?'

'We were ambushed, Stryker! Is that not obvious?' Her shoulders slumped slightly, the fire leaving as soon as it had come, though Stryker guessed it was born more from exhaustion than regret for her outburst. 'I am sorry, *mon amour*.'

Lisette's eyes became glassy, searching the distance to retrieve fever-warped memories. The room fell silent for what seemed to be an eternity. Eventually she looked up. 'We'd been tracked for some days by a group of horsemen. Three of the bastards. I had been able to ensure safe passage for much of the journey, using little-known routes and arranging decoys.' She looked at Stryker, her face a mask of regret. 'I thought we would make it, Stryker, I really did.'

'Go on,' Stryker prompted.

'We were making for Lichfield.'

Stryker frowned. 'The Close? The earl does not know you.'

She spluttered the beginnings of a venomous chuckle, though it turned quickly into a racking cough. 'No. The Prince would never trust Chesterfield. The man is incompetent.'

Stryker leaned closer. 'Voice down, woman,' he hissed, 'you are in his domain!'

She pulled a face that told him she was unconcerned. 'Rupert has a man in the town. One of our horses had stumbled during the day. It was becoming lame. We could not afford to stop at an inn, for fear our three shadows would reappear. I decided it would be better to pay the Prince's agent a visit. He would see us safely on our way with supplies and a fresh horse.'

'But you did not reach Lichfield,' Forrester said. 'Not with Blaze, anyway.'

'They appeared before dawn; it was a rainy day in January,' replied Lisette. 'It was dark. I couldn't see them in the tree line. They used firelocks of some kind, so I did not spy them till it was too late.'

'Professionals, then?' Forrester asked. The matchlock musket was a more robust weapon than its flintlock cousin, better suited to the rigours and trials of campaigning, and most regiments favoured it. But firelocks had their uses. Often they were employed by men guarding powder magazines, when the lack of a naked flame proved far safer, but in many cases they were the preferred tool for covert operations. Those that might be jeopardized by a telltale glow in the dark. 'Assassins?'

Lisette gazed into the distance. 'They killed our driver, and the coach crashed into the forest. I was thrown across the cabin. It was chaos. Cracking wood and flying splinters.' She lifted a hand to her bandaged shoulder. 'Received this for my troubles.' Her eyes were suddenly bright again, and her richly accented words thick with relish. 'But I shot one of their men, Stryker. Right in the face.'

Stryker ignored Forrester's small shudder. 'And then?'

'We ran into the trees, but one of them was a good shot. Hit Master Blaze. I escaped.' She shook her head at the memory. 'I ran and I ran. At dawn's light I saw spires.'

'The cathedral.'

'*Oui*,' Lisette said, her voice dropped to a whisper. 'I was bleeding so much. I thought I would die.'

Stryker thought for a moment. 'Did they not give chase?'

'They were not interested in me, Stryker. Their task was complete when Lazarus Blaze fell.' She saw his doubt and went on. 'They were not common highwaymen, *mon amour*. They had followed us too long, through the foulest of weather. Brigands after cheap plunder would have abandoned the chase long before that black night. And to track us along such a winding route took rare skill. So did the killing shot, for that matter. No, they were intent on dispatching Blaze, and he alone. What I do not understand is how they found us in the first place. How they knew we'd set out from Devizes.'

'An informant,' Stryker said bluntly.

Lisette looked at him, eyes shimmering. 'I want to kill that bastard.'

'The informant or the killer?'

'Both.' She thought for a moment. 'Where did you say Lazarus's brother is?'

'He will be at Oxford by now, if the roads are passable.'

'Then my enemy will be in his wake. I must go there. I must find him.' She lurched forward, making to stand, but swooned at the sudden movement and crashed back on to the palliasse.

'Wait, Lisette,' Stryker pleaded, as the Frenchwoman's stream of oaths began to subside. 'You are not yet strong enough to travel. And how can you be sure of this assassin's intent?'

She sighed heavily, as though forced to explain the situation to a dullard. 'Because he was after Lazarus Blaze. Not me, not our driver. Lazarus alone. Think on it, *mon amour*. He targeted Blaze for his skill. His knowledge. The rebels wished to prevent the application of that knowledge.'

'They succeeded,' Skellen grunted.

'In part, Sergeant,' she replied. 'But Jonathan Blaze wields that same expertise. He poses the same threat. If Parliament set out to eliminate Lazarus before he could join the Stafford garrison . . .'

Forrester continued the thought, 'Then they'll harbour similar ambitions for Jonathan before he can bolster some other fortress.'

'*Oui*,' Lisette said, certainty lending steel to her voice. 'Why kill one and leave the other?'

'Of course, our assassin friend may not be in receipt of information regarding the elder brother,' Forrester said brightly.

'You feel certain of that?' Lisette replied.

Forrester's sweaty jowls shook. 'No.'

'So I ride to Oxford before this Jonathan takes his leave.'

Stryker placed a hand on her good shoulder, keeping her still with ease. 'You cannot, Lisette. You are too weak. I'd wager you do not yet have the strength to control a horse. How might you take on this team of killers?'

She threw him a glance of exasperation. 'I am the Queen's best agent, Stryker.'

'Aye,' he conceded, 'but you are not yourself. Not yet. And these men you face are clearly no common brawlers.'

As soon as the words left his mouth, Stryker regretted them. His single eye met Lisette's blue gaze, and he knew she had knocked with her feisty talk and he had opened the door.

She smiled sweetly. 'You will go.'

'Lisette, I—'

'This assassin must be stopped,' she interrupted, not allowing Stryker time to gather his thoughts. 'If the Roundheads are willing to put their best men to the task of seeing Lazarus Blaze dead, then it makes sense that Jonathan is destined for a similar fate. And if that is so, then we must surely put our best men to the task of keeping him alive.'

Stryker put a calloused hand to her pale cheek. 'I came here to find you, Lisette. You are here. You are alive. That is enough.' He wondered, then, if he should detail the exact nature of his current circumstances, but thought better of it. She was weak enough as it was, without the added worry for Stryker's new-found fugitive status.

Lisette inspected her fingernails for a while. When she looked up at him, her eyes did not carry their usual fire, but were distant and glazed with sadness. 'Lazarus Blaze was in my care, under my protection, when he died,' she said softly. 'I am alive now, and I thank the Holy Mother for it, but I will die of shame if Jonathan Blaze is murdered too. Please, *mon amour*, I am begging you. *You* must go. *You* must find him. Protect him.'

'He was a conceited bastard,' Stryker offered in a last, futile retort.

Lisette punched his chest playfully. 'You are a child sometimes.'

She began to fall forwards, and at first Stryker thought she was collapsing into unconsciousness, but, when he caught her in his arms, she tilted back her head to kiss him.

'Will you not do this?' she said when their lips finally parted, keeping her mouth close so that he could feel the warm breath on his face. 'For me?'

Stryker gritted his teeth hard. He was angry with himself. Angry because, for all his prowess in battle, for all the accolades he had won with lead and steel, and for all the danger he had faced without so much as a second thought, he knew that, in the face of Lisette Gaillard, he was as weak as an August breeze.

'I'm not certain you've thought this through, Stryker,' Captain Lancelot Forrester said as they paced quickly along one of the dingy corridors that bisected the Bishop's Palace. 'With all due respect, sir,' he added quickly.

They were on their way to petition Philip Stanhope, the Earl of Chesterfield and commander of the king's Lichfield garrison. With Lisette clearly on the road to recovery, Stryker had decided that it was time to honour the promise he had made to Sir Richard Dyott. With a large force on the march from Warwickshire, it was only a matter of time before their attention turned to Lichfield. Time to prepare the town's defences was rapidly dwindling.

'Not now, Forry,' Stryker said mildly. 'We can discuss it later.'

'As you wish,' Forrester murmured unhappily. He and Skellen were striding at Stryker's flanks. 'I'm simply a tad concerned at the thought of gallivanting down to Oxford in search of our petardier when in all likelihood we'll be arrested as outlaws before we so much as lay eyes upon him.'

Stryker stopped abruptly and fixed his eye on Forrester's concerned face. 'I said, we'll talk about this later,' he snapped. Forrester nodded mutely, but it was disappointment that clouded his expression rather than fear, and Stryker immediately felt ashamed. 'I—I am—'

Forrester shook his head quickly and offered a weak smile. 'No, sir. I should not question you.'

'Christ, Forry, can a man not apologize?' Stryker said in exasperation. 'You are right. I have not thought it through at all. But I—she—'

Forrester held up a hand. 'Say no more, Stryker. We all have a common vice, do we not? It is what makes us men.'

Stryker began to walk on again. It was pathetic, he knew. But that did not change the fact that Lisette wanted his help, and he would rather die than turn his back. Somehow he would find a way to save Jonathan Blaze.

'I am tired of this discussion, sir,' the Earl of Chesterfield squawked. 'I do not believe Parliament will send anyone to Lichfield. It is too small a morsel. And I do not have enough men to defend the city if the enemy were to come. No, Captain, we will hold the Close for the protection of those loyal to the Crown, and let the rebels pass us by.'

Stryker stood in the same spot where he had first met the earl and his court. Once again, Stanhope was slouched in his large chair, gout-crippled leg thrust out in front. The earl's retinue were present once again, and Stryker wondered whether they ever left him alone. 'The enemy will come, sir. Lichfield may be small, but it is strategically crucial. Please, my lord, I urge you to make provision for an assault.'

Chesterfield rolled his eyes. 'Then what the devil would you have me do?'

'Make the roads stronger, my lord,' Stryker replied. He was careful to keep his voice respectful but firm. 'It is important Lichfield does not fall. You must make the routes into the city difficult to break.'

'Preposterous!' Chesterfield spat. 'You have seen my force, yes? Know the number I have, yes? To man the perimeter would spread 'em too damned thin.'

'I do not urge you to man the entire perimeter, my lord. A large attacking force would have to come through one of the major high roads. Of which there are four, are there not?'

The earl was unconvinced. 'How will that aid our cause, sir?'

'Prince Rupert leads his flying army to the south of here, my lord. It is large and formidable. Parliament must gather its strength to face him or he will lay waste to their towns. They cannot spare anything more than a regiment or two to engage Lichfield.'

Chesterfield tilted his head back and brayed. 'My God, man, but a regiment or two would destroy our little garrison, were we to engage them. Have you lost your wits?'

'No, my lord,' Stryker replied calmly. 'I simply make the point that such a force, though too large to engage in the field, could be well bloodied by determined snipers, if they are funnelled through the old town gates.'

'Those gates are long crumbled, Captain.'

'Aye, my lord, but the roads are still narrow where they once stood.' He cast his mind back to the day he, Forrester, Skellen and Menjam had entered the town, forced as they were to pass through the constricted part of highway that once bisected the medieval walls. 'Any rebel army would be forced to squeeze through them. If we have so much as a score of muskets trained on those narrow points, we'll make the enemy think twice. It might even turn them back altogether. If we stay here in the Close, they will swarm into the city unhindered. And then we shall have no chance of escape. No chance of victory. And, crucially, no supplies.'

The Earl of Chesterfield stared at Stryker for several moments. He clicked fat fingers suddenly, and the two mastiffs – Toad and Copper – came bounding to his side. As he stroked their sleek heads he chewed the inside of his mouth in thought. Eventually he looked up and nodded. 'Thermopylae.'

Stryker frowned. 'Sir?'

'We will do as you suggest, Captain.'

Stryker caught the eye of a tall, brown-haired man standing half a dozen paces behind the earl. It was Sir Richard Dyott, and his grin was fuelled with a mixture of triumph and relief. Stryker made to smile back, but his eye was drawn to another movement, one at Chesterfield's feet. The dogs were suddenly sniffing the air, their ears pricked up sharply. Stryker watched the animals for a heartbeat, wondering what might have startled them. A second later, the great oaken door swung open and a burly sentry came running into the chamber. Each stride was a jangling cacophony of metal, and all eyes turned at the disturbance.

Chesterfield craned his large head to see beyond Stryker. 'What is the meaning of this!'

The sentry bowed briefly. 'I am sorry, my lord.'

'Well? What is it, man? Spit it out!'

'Horsemen, my lord. King's men. They say they must be granted entrance as a matter of urgency.'

Chesterfield's eyes narrowed suspiciously. 'A rebel trick, perhaps. They have credentials, yes?'

'They do, sir.'

'What regiment?'

'Yellowcoats, my lord. Colonel Crow's dragoons.'

Forrester and Skellen were at Stryker's heels as they strode through the palace's hefty outer doorway and into the wan light beyond. The palace was in the north-east corner of the Close, and between that grand group of buildings and the south-west gate sat the vast cathedral. They paced quickly into the open courtyard, so that the cathedral was on their right, and made their way to the as yet invisible gate.

'What the bloody hell are we going to do?' Forrester said rapidly.

Stryker kept his gaze in front, always wary of a vengeful tide of blade-wielding dragoons rounding the cathedral's corner. 'I don't know. We are captured, Forry.'

'Zounds, those bloody Potts brothers have a case to answer,' Forrester rasped bitterly.

Stryker stopped in his tracks, fixing his friend with a hard stare. 'That's just it. They cannot answer. They're dead.'

Forrester was indignant. 'And they deserved their fate!'

'The fact remains I killed them. I was found guilty of the act, and I fled my punishment. I have no defence.'

'And it was I set you free,' Forrester said, his voice suddenly hollow.

'Aye, and I thank you for that. I would not have found Lisette without you. But we are out of time.'

The sound of hoofbeats on cobbles, like an avalanche of boulders down a hillside, reached them in roaring crescendo, and they turned their attention back in the direction of the south-west. The gate itself was still hidden from view behind the squat bulk of the cathedral, but they did not need to move another step. The first of the troop rounded the corner, cantering in a steady stream, blades sheathed but backs straight. The poise of men with purpose. At their head rode a young cornet, his colour of yellow and blue fluttering bright above him.

'Is it?' Forrester asked quickly.

'Aye, they're Crow's men. It is his colour.'

'Perchance it is coincidence,' Forrester said, though it was clear the optimism did not sit naturally in his voice. 'Crow's troop may simply be sent here as reinforcements.'

'Why send horsemen to garrison a fort?' said Skellen.

Forrester's grimace was answer enough.

'Besides,' Stryker said, 'it's not his full troop. There might be twenty there. Twenty-five, no more. This is a force with a particular task.'

Forrester began to step backwards. 'I know what that goddamned task is.'

Stryker turned, grasped a fistful of Forrester's buff-coat and held him firm. 'We will not run.'

A flash of panic streaked across Forrester's reddening cheeks, and he resisted his friend's grip. 'I have no wish to be lynched, Stryker,' he hissed desperately, and a hand fell instinctively to his sword-hilt. 'Silent bravery will see you swing. We must fight our way out!'

'And where would you have us go?' Stryker replied levelly.

'We're trapped in this fucking place,' Skellen said in his unflappable tone.

Forrester's resistance faltered, his shoulders sagging, defiance deflating like a set of broken bellows. He nodded, almost imperceptibly, and moved to Stryker's side in silent resignation.

The yellowcoated dragoons swarmed towards them. A big man, blond moustaches visible behind the steel face bars of his helmet, was beside his cornet, bellowing orders at the men in his wake. When his gaze fell upon Stryker, he drew his sword, levelling the blade in the officer's direction, its point guiding the dragoons to their target.

'I know him,' Stryker said quietly.

The dragoons came on, parting left and right as they drew close, sweeping around the three men – three fugitives – in a wide, impenetrable circle of hooves and steel.

Flaming torches and fat beeswax candles lit the Great Hall as dusk lengthened the shadows all around them. The Earl of Chesterfield's court seemed to be more crowded than ever, and Stryker, standing once again before the earl's creaking seat, supposed it was a reaction to the news of his impending arrest.

'He is a fugitive, my lord. A criminal.' The speaker was the large, fair-whiskered man who had ridden at the head of the dragoons. 'I am come to arrest him.' He was a man of powerful frame and confident manner, despite the fact that his followers had been forbidden from entering the Great Hall. The earl had not wished a score of armed strangers in his midst, so they were left to tend their horses out in the Close, while their leader was allowed to explain himself.

Chesterfield puffed out his cheeks in astonishment, a gesture he had made a dozen times since the yellowcoats' arrival. 'So you say, Major.' He looked at Stryker. 'This is true?'

'Aye, my lord.'

'As are his two men,' the accuser went on. 'Stryker killed two of my comrades back in Cirencester. One an officer.'

Stryker turned on the dragoon. 'In self-defence.'

The big man ignored him, keeping his eyes fixed on the earl. 'There was a fracas, my lord, but this man overstepped the mark. He and his sergeant were charged with two counts of murder.'

'Jesu, Edberg, what is wrong with you?' Stryker hissed.

The big Swede finally met Stryker's gaze, sucking his moustaches nonchalantly. 'Colonel Crow pays my shillings. I follow his orders.' He looked at the earl again. 'Captain Stryker and Sergeant Skellen were found guilty, my lord.'

Chesterfield's eyes widened. 'Guilty? By whom?'

'Prince Rupert of the Rhine, my lord. General of Horse. But they escaped prison,' he turned to point at Forrester, standing with Skellen some half-dozen paces behind Stryker, 'with the aid of this man.'

Chesterfield stared at each man in turn. As his eyes flicked from one face to the next, his fleshy cheeks visibly reddened, anger beginning to well up like a fountain. 'You—you come here, yes?' he eventually said to Stryker, fury barely controlled. 'To my garrison, yes? And you are outside the law? Common criminals. Murderers!'

'I am sent to Lichfield on behalf of my commander, Colonel Artemas Crow,' Edberg continued in the lingering silence that followed the earl's enraged outburst, 'to bring the fugitives to justice. I work on highest authority. The Prince himself.'

'This is absurd!' All eyes went to where Forrester was standing, unable to contain himself any longer. 'Captain Stryker acted in honourable self-defence in the face of two base fellows intent upon stealing his horse in the chaos after the town's fall. Colonel Crow's anger, and his thirst for retribution, far outweighs the initial crime. He has some personal vendetta against the Captain, I swear it!'

With sudden ferocity, Edberg rounded on him. 'Speak more and I'll cut out your fat tongue!'

Forrester was not cowed. 'Make your most valiant attempt, sir, do. We'll see who is left able to chatter.'

The major's stare seemed to bore through Forrester, but the captain held his nerve and his gaze. Eventually Edberg turned back to address the earl. 'The General of Horse ordered me to bring these men back – or see them dead – my lord. That is what I must do.'

'Be my guest, bull-witted dullard,' Forrester sniped again.

Edberg visibly bristled. He took a step towards Forrester.

'Enough!' Chesterfield blurted, exasperated and furious in equal measure. He gave a rapid nod to his guards, the only armed men allowed in the room, and two of them paced forwards threateningly. 'Another word from either of you and you shall both lose your tongues!'

More silence followed. When Chesterfield had taken several deep breaths, he spoke again, calmer this time. He clicked his fingers at the dragoon. 'Edberg, approach and show me your papers.'

Edberg did as he was ordered. 'It is mere formality, my lord. You will see they are complete.'

Chesterfield ran beady eyes over the paper. 'So it would appear.' He looked up, meeting Edberg's expectant stare. 'But a formality it is not, Major. Far from it. You see, your quarry here possesses a similar parchment, beseeching I lend assistance to its bearer without delay or hindrance.'

Edberg was unmoved. 'A forgery, my lord.'

Sir Richard Dyott had come to the earl's side. 'Then it was a good forgery,' he said smoothly, 'for it carried Prince Rupert's personal seal.'

Chesterfield nodded slowly. 'It did, Sir Richard. That it did.' He looked at Edberg, who was beginning to tug at the matted ends of his moustache. 'Sir Richard is a lawyer by profession, Major. I trust him entirely in such matters.'

Edberg looked sideways at Stryker. 'You would have him remain at large, my lord?' His voice sounded tense for the first time.

Silence followed. The courtiers were alert with anticipation, Stryker held his breath, and the Earl of Chesterfield seemed to study the eaves as if searching for inspiration. It seemed like hours before the latter spoke. 'No, Major Edberg. I would not. Captain Stryker and his men will return to the infirmary, and there they will remain under guard until I have sent word to Prince Rupert. I will let him resolve this.'

KENILWORTH, WARWICKSHIRE, I MARCH 1643

Major Zacharie Girns, in his room on the upper floor of the Two Virgins tavern, knelt beside the window and prayed. He had been awake since dawn, watching and

199

waiting for his prey to come to him, always confident that the information would prove accurate. But now, as the afternoon began to drag into evening, the first cracks of doubt were beginning to open in his hitherto granite-hewn self-assurance. So he had decided to pray until God rectified matters, as Girns knew He would.

Girns heard them before he saw them. The jangle of bridles, the clomp of hooves, the chatter of men who did not suspect a threat this chilly morning. Girns clambered to his feet, though he stayed low against the windowsill to remain unseen, and peered right, studying the darkening High Street. There, perhaps a hundred paces along the sodden road, was the group he had been expecting.

A rapid knock at his door precipitated the arrival of Trim and Slater. 'Sir!' one blurted excitedly as they bounded into the room like excited hounds before a hunt.

Girns did not turn. 'I know.' He watched the slow-moving procession for a few moments, counting them as they resolved from the gloom, ensuring none had gone ahead to scout the route. 'All present and as anticipated.' Finally he faced his men. 'Fetch your weapons. Let us get to work.'

Lieutenant Andrew Burton rode at the small column's head. Bruce, his chestnut gelding, loped steadily, and he whispered soothing words of encouragement into the beast's pricked ear, adding a mutter of thanks to God for guiding his father's hand in the horse's purchase. Bruce's easy strength and sturdy character had proven a true blessing since Burton had lost most of the strength in his right arm. A more skittish animal would have been impossible to control with just one hand on the reins.

'We are here?' Jonathan Blaze, master fire-worker and, as far as Burton was concerned, expert irritant, yelped from somewhere to the rear.

Burton twisted back to catch his eye. 'Indeed, sir. Kenilworth it is.' He looked along the High Street to read the small wooden sign that was placed at the roadside. 'The Two Virgins,' he said, raising his voice for all to hear. 'I would water the horses a while before we push on to the castle.'

Blaze spurred his mount from the back of the party to draw up beside Burton. 'Christ, but I'm exhausted! I wouldn't mind a drop of ale either.'

'The respite is for the horses, Master Blaze,' Burton said patiently. 'But you're perfectly entitled to sup while we wait.'

'Good news, then,' Blaze said. He glanced back at Rontry, who had not followed his master from the rearward position. 'Must I not keep up my strength, Jes, eh? If I'm to win this war for His Majesty.'

Jesper Rontry offered a weak smile. 'Absolutely.'

'Quite right!' Blaze bellowed in ebullience. 'Quite right!' He looked at Burton wolfishly. 'And you will join me for a drink, Lieutenant?'

Burton shook his head. 'Drink has done me great harm of late.' He frowned suddenly. 'Will you return to your place, sir?' It was phrased as a question, for Burton knew better than to offend Blaze's inflated sense of self-importance, but he kept his tone deliberately firm.

Blaze's open face contorted. 'I seem to spend my life humouring you, Lieutenant. It is becoming tiresome, to say the very least.'

'You know it is for your safety,' Burton said, repeating the explanation for what seemed like the hundredth time.

'Yes, yes, I know,' Blaze retorted with a wearied wave of the hand, as though he were swatting away a horsefly.

'You and Mister Rontry must stay behind the six of us,' Burton went on unperturbed, indicating the five armed horsemen at his flanks, 'and in front of the rearguard.' That rearguard was made up of two of Burton's best charges. They were positioned to guard against any attack from behind the group.

'He's right, sir,' Rontry called. 'Come, ride by me.'

'Have it your way,' Blaze sighed, and slowed his horse so that the vanguard could trot past.

'You see their leader?' Girns said, pointing out the party's foremost rider. 'He has one arm in a sling.'

'Aye,' Tom Slater murmured to Girns's right.

Girns was at the long upper chamber's central window. There was another, smaller window to his left, and one to the right. From here they would conduct their task.

'When I throw,' Girns said quietly, 'you fire.'

'Simple,' said Slater.

Girns looked across at the man crouched to his left. 'Are you ready to do your duty, Josiah?'

Lieutenant Josiah Trim was to fire through the left-hand window. He glanced down at the oncoming riders, back to Girns, then down at the riders. 'Aye, sir.'

'Then all is well.' Girns ran a hand over the pocked, pulpy skin of his forehead and closed his emerald eyes. He prayed, quickly and fervently, before fixing Slater and Trim with the most poisonous stare he could muster. 'I want Blaze alive. Do not fail me in that.'

The men nodded silently and went to work. Each had

three flintlock muskets at their feet, and they set about loading the weapons in turn.

Girns had already primed his muskets, and instead bent to retrieve a leather sack from which he pulled a spherical object the size of his fist. It was a ball of iron, like a miniature cannon ball, and from its smooth edge protruded a length of match-cord.

A series of clicks left and right told Girns that his companions had moved their weapons to the half-cock position. They were ready. He rose to his feet, still bowing low so his head would not be seen from ground level, and looked out upon Kenilworth's sleepy High Street, realizing that the lateness of his quarry's arrival was clearly a boon from God. Dusk had sent the town to their homes, leaving the streets empty and quiet. The party were immediately below them now; six soldiers out front, Jonathan Blaze and his servant in the centre, and two more soldiers protecting the rear.

Girns nodded briefly to Slater and Trim, and stooped to collect a candle from the floorboards nearby. It was already lit, tremulous in the cold breeze, and he lifted it gently, reverently, before holding the tip of its orange flame to the end of the iron ball's dangling match.

The men out on the road chattered, Slater grinned maliciously, Trim swallowed hard.

And Major Zacharie Girns stood. 'God be with us,' he said, and tossed the grenade out of the window.

The explosion was deafening.

Lieutenant Andrew Burton had not seen the bomb, but, as red-hot shards of metal lashed about them in a short but deadly radius, he knew exactly what it was. The wicked device had come from somewhere above them, meeting the mud just behind Bruce's hind quarters with a wet smack.

He was surprised in that first moment to find that he was unhurt, and wrenched hard on Bruce's reins, wheeling him round with all the strength his only useful arm could muster, desperate and terrified in equal measure to lay eyes upon the havoc he knew the grenade would have unleashed.

The tableau was worse than he feared. Smoke swirled, choked, blinded. Burton could hear screams, could see faces, but they would vanish as quickly as they appeared. Each scream would become muffled, replaced by another from another point within the melee.

'To me! To me!' he bawled, praying his voice would be heard above the ensuing anarchy, but knowing it was a vain hope.

It must have been just seconds, he knew, but the roiling smoke seemed to conceal the horror for hours. He urged Bruce forwards, aiming to plunge into the darkness to seek survivors and offer help, but the horse would not move. Burton kicked again, snarling curses at the big gelding's timidity, until the beast let out a stifled whimper. It was the most pitiful sound Burton had ever heard, and he knew the horse was wounded. From high in the saddle he could not see where the injury had been sustained, but Bruce's breaths were faltering already. Rasping, as though drawn through water. And his gait was increasingly unsteady.

Burton blinked savagely, unwilling to let the tears prick at his eyes while there was work to be done. He leapt down on to the muddy street and drew his sword. The cold breeze grew in strength suddenly, and all at once Burton's group reappeared from the smoke cloud.

Burton's jaw dropped. Four of his five leading horsemen were down, shards of metal having eviscerated their bodies with frightening ease. The fifth man had dismounted, but he simply gazed at the carnage as though in a daze. Blaze and Rontry were further back. They were on foot, too, but both unharmed, cowering behind their mounts, and beyond them the two rearguard horsemen were circling defensively, eyes scanning all around them for the next attack.

And then, as though shaken from a nightmare, Burton's mind finally sharpened. He knew exactly from where the attack had originated. He looked up, eyes raking across the trio of windows along the upper floor of the Two Virgins. It was then that stabs of bright flame flashed down at them.

'Muskets!' Burton screamed. 'Down! Down!' He saw Bruce had fallen now, his life all but ebbed away save the occasional jerking hoof, and Burton dived behind the sagging chestnut bulk.

Lieutenant Josiah Trim had one job. He was to kill any of the front six soldiers that might have survived the grenade's impact.

He took up his musket, pulling back the cock to its final, deadly position. He watched the smoke clear, saw that two men still lived amid the panic.

'Jesus, Lord, guide me,' he whispered as he picked the first of his targets. He had joined Girns in order to rid the world of the malignant forces of Popery and a corrupt king. But now that it came to murder, his mind was as confused as the men on the road.

Trim sighted the dismounted horseman along his flint-lock's dark barrel.

'Lord God. Almighty God. Forgive me. Forgive me. Forgive me.'

He could hear Slater's shots crack through the air now, and knew he would have to follow suit. He fired.

Down on the road, Burton was frantically trying to gauge the situation. He desperately needed to keep what little force he had alive, for he needed to defend Blaze. 'Get down!' Burton screamed again at the dazed soldier as another musket shot coughed from the tavern's upper floor. The man did go down, but it was with a great gushing hole in his forehead.

'Help me!' Blaze was screaming from over to Burton's left. He sheathed his blade and made to scramble across the mud to where the fire-worker was still hidden behind his horse, but more fire spat at them and he was forced to remain in position.

A quick glance beyond Blaze told him that both his final two men had been killed, their bodies face down on the street. 'Jesu,' Burton hissed, for he knew now that his mission had failed. He knew he would die.

Lieutenant Josiah Trim took up his second gun. He had killed. Murdered. But that place in heaven for which he had yearned seemed somehow distant now. As though the act had only served to move him further away from God.

He peered over the sill, cocked the musket and took aim. It was so easy. Too easy. The target was there, unarmed, cowering behind the carcass of his fallen horse. There was no way the man could load a musket, for one arm was tightly bound in a blood-spattered sling. He was a sitting duck.

Trim took aim, desperately trying to steady quivering hands. The Royalist officer was so close. There were no obstacles between the line of Trim's sleek barrel and his enemy's flushed face. He pulled the musket's stock close so that its kick would be borne by his taut shoulder muscles, whispered another prayer, and pulled the trigger.

Major Zacharie Girns had known the grenade would make an indelible mark on this operation, but even he had been impressed with its efficacy. He had cut the match perfectly, allowing the optimum time before the flame made contact with the iron ball's gunpowder-packed innards, and all he and his fellow assassins needed to do was wait.

The explosion had been designed to take out the six men protecting Blaze's front, and that was exactly what it had done. He had been careful to use the correct amount of powder, for he needed Blaze alive, and could not afford shards of iron to rip him apart as it had done those first half-dozen. Trim was to dispatch any survivors from that foremost group in the initial confusion, while Slater would take care of the pair at the party's rear.

'Fuck me!' Slater squealed with delight from the depths of the smoke-filled room. 'Fuck me! We got 'em, Major! We got the buggers!'

Girns felt himself bristle at the younger man's profanity, but there was no time to dwell on it now. 'Are they dead? All of them?'

'Aye, sir, and good riddance too!' Slater replied gleefully.

Trim remained silent. He simply stared down at the bodies that now scattered the road below.

'Let us take our prize, gentlemen,' Girns said calmly, taking up one of his weapons and running out on to the candlelit landing. Trim and Slater followed.

CHAPTER 10

The alarm was raised at first light.

Inside the infirmary the cries and shouts sounded muffled, illusory. Precise words, pitched high and querulous out in the courtyard, were hard to discern, the reason for the Close's sudden panic impossible to ascertain. And yet Stryker instantly understood. He rose from the edge of Lisette's bed, moving to the rectangular window, and gazed out upon the grey walls beyond. Nothing here. No one running. No one bellowing orders. And yet, from somewhere to the south, from the direction of the cathedral, the alarm went on.

'What is it, *mon amour?*'

Stryker glanced back at Lisette, searching for the words that would tell her he could no longer carry out the promise he had made. It had been a difficult enough night, having been forced to finally explain to her the nature of his flight from Cirencester, but he could, at the very least, give his word that he would escape this gaol as he had the one before. But now it was clear that such assurance was no more than a dream.

'Time for a fight,' Sergeant Skellen replied for him from somewhere deeper in the room.

Lisette looked from Skellen to Stryker. 'Trapped?'

Stryker nodded. 'Aye.'

It was all he needed to say, for there could be only one explanation. Lord Brooke had arrived in Lichfield.

Doctor Gregory Chambers looked up from the emaciated form of the canker-ridden patient a few beds away. His heavy frame sidled towards them. 'We are to be captured?'

Forrester was on his feet as well now and he nodded morosely. 'If our enemy brings a large enough force. And we're stuck in this hole. Unarmed and useless, like rabbits in a bear pit.'

The knock at the infirmary's door startled them all. Surely even veterans like Brooke's regiment would not have moved so swiftly? Instinctively, they braced themselves for a struggle, Skellen and Forrester striding towards the door, stools hefted like clubs, while Stryker moved to stand in front of Lisette's palliasse.

It was with great surprise, then, that they recognized Sir Richard Dyott. He did not stand on ceremony and paced directly into the room, followed by a man of remarkably similar features who carried one of the longest firearms Stryker had ever seen. Dyott noted the quizzical stares and nodded towards his companion. 'My brother, John. His fowling piece has seen employment only in the pursuit of ducks, but it will have to do.'

Stryker looked the weapon up and down, impressed by the sight of a barrel that must have stretched to all of seven feet long. 'Do for what?'

'Brooke is in the town,' Dyott said breathlessly. 'He passes through the old walls as we speak. They march this way.'

'How many?' Forrester asked.

'I do not yet know.'

'What do you wish me to do?' Stryker asked.

'To fight, Captain!' Dyott rasped. 'It is as you said last night. We must bloody his nose, lest Lichfield be known as a town of cowards! For that we need you!'

'Chesterfield—' Stryker began attempting to fathom how Dyott made it past the guards stationed outside.

'Will agree!' Dyott interrupted quickly, striding between and beyond Skellen and Forrester. 'He will have to. We will make him.'

'He did not listen to you before,' Stryker replied.

'But he listened to you,' Dyott said, and he lurched forward, taking hold of Stryker's coat, and dragged him towards the door, 'before the—*incident*—with Major Edberg. But now we are in desperate straits. The earl will listen again. Besides, I have a man who has the earl's ear like no other.'

They were out in the corridor now. 'Who?'

'Me.'

Stryker looked down into the amber gaze of Simeon Barkworth.

'That's it, my lads!' bellowed Robert Greville, second Baron Brooke and Parliamentarian General for the Midland Counties. 'Onwards! They'll not stand! Upon my honour, they'll not!'

Brooke felt as though he were a cauldron. God's fire burned white beneath him, building his confidence with every prayer, every victory, bubbling up, frenzied and inexorable, spilling over the brim. He sat astride his horse, feeling like some Roman emperor of old, watching his purple-coated troops march through the old barr in Lichfield's ancient defences. Twelve hundred men to capture this little town. It would be perfect. They would take the cathedral, the very symbol of all Brooke loathed, and then turn towards the great Royalist stronghold of Stafford itself.

Brooke's second-in-command reined in at his right hand. 'What news, Edward?'

Lieutenant-Colonel Edward Peyto nodded curtly. 'I have enough men inside the city to begin the assault, sir.'

'Then to your task, Colonel.' Brooke looked back to the road outside Lichfield. The slower elements of his regiment were coming up now. The baggage, supply wagons, farriers and ordnance. When he looked back into the lieutenant-colonel's face, he read concern. 'What is it, Mister Peyto?'

'I fear the malignants will simply scurry back to their Close and shut the door.'

Brooke's confidence was unyielding. He stared back at the ordnance as it trundled along the road. At the very rear of the column was a huge cannon; dark, vast and breathtaking to behold. 'Take the town, Mister Peyto, and worry not. If they shut their gates, Black Bess will come a-knocking.'

Barkworth seemed to walk on the tips of his toes, such was his evident excitement. 'Let them come,' he was hissing in that coarse tone. 'Let them see how we greet the bastardly gullions.'

The group – save Chambers, who had stayed with Lisette and his other charges – strode passed the Great Hall, and out into the grey dawn. The earl, Barkworth had informed them, was already outside in the courtyard, coordinating the defence.

'Fanning the flames of panic,' Dyott added sourly.

Barkworth chose to ignore the barb for once. 'Leave him to me. I am his military adviser.'

'What in God's name are they about, sir?' Philip Stanhope, Earl of Chesterfield and commander of the king's Lichfield garrison, bawled as he laid eyes on Stryker and his men.

Chesterfield was at the centre of a score of well-dressed men, none of whom seemed to know what to do in the face of the impending attack. The earl himself was red-faced and breathing heavily. He leant forwards on a stout staff, letting the knotted wood take his considerable weight.

Stryker approached the group at Barkworth's heels. They seemed like a gaggle of headless cockerels to him, so many men with more knowledge of plumage than war. 'My lord, I—'

'Get him back in there!' Chesterfield snapped across Stryker's words. 'I said lock him up, Barkworth! I will not have a man under such a charge at liberty in my Close.'

Barkworth stepped forward. 'We need him, my lord. He is the most experienced man in this garrison.'

'And he might very well be a murderer!' Chesterfield squawked, wincing with the pain in his gouty leg.

'Believe me, my lord,' Barkworth replied calmly, surprising Stryker with his tact, given the little man's generally scorching disposition, 'it is men like that you require in times such as this.' He glanced beyond the panting earl to throw a withering look at the milling courtiers. '*They* will not save Lichfield for you.'

The Earl of Chesterfield turned back and took in the sight of his well-upholstered retinue. His shoulders sagged.

That was enough for Barkworth. 'Do what you must, Captain Stryker. The men are yours.'

'How many fighting men do we have?' Stryker snapped.

'Three hundred at most, Captain,' Sir Richard Dyott answered. He pointed towards the men surrounding the earl. 'These few and their retainers.'

'There won't be time to mobilize them all before Brooke reaches the Close,' Barkworth said.

'We're not waiting for him to come,' said Stryker.

'Sir?'

'We must seize the initiative. If Brooke has only sent a small vanguard into the town, then we must repel it while we can. Make him think twice before making another attack. Muster as many men and muskets as you can. And Edberg's dragoons. Anyone with a gun.'

It was then that twenty or so yellowcoated men came pouring from one of the cathedral's low side doors, a big, moustachioed officer at their head. 'Christ,' Stryker muttered.

'My lord! My lord!' Major Henning Edberg was shouting as he drew ever closer. 'What is happening?' His eyes fell upon Stryker and smouldered. 'And why is this man free?'

Chesterfield looked from the Swede to Stryker and finally found his voice. 'He—you can't—'

Stryker rounded on him. 'You did not protect the town, my lord, and now it may fall. But do not abandon its citizens without first showing the rebels a fight. I will lead your men, if you let me.'

'It is a matter of morale, my lord,' Barkworth agreed. 'Many of these men have kin in the town. They must be given the chance to defend them.'

At last, the light of understanding shone in the earl's small eyes. 'Very well.' He ignored Edberg's furious expression and looked at Stryker. 'Take whom you will, Captain.'

'Get the women and children into the cathedral, my lord,' Stryker instructed, then strode past Chesterfield, fixing his grey eye on as many of the courtiers' gazes as he could. 'You each brought men? Gather them now. Bring them down to the south gate.' He turned to the dragoon commander, whose stare was so acerbic Stryker thought it might almost burn the air between them. 'You too, Major.'

Stryker waited until he had a force of perhaps ninety strong. Many more could be mustered in time, but time was the one thing he had so little of.

Deciding Brooke needed to be engaged sooner rather than later, and with his musket and sword duly returned, Stryker led the defenders out through the south gate, across the causeway rising above the Minster Pool and on to Dam Street, the long road that ran all the way to the south of the town. He did not look back, knowing instinctively that Skellen and Forrester were with him, and hearing the thundering boots of dozens more. If the enemy truly had a large force, this show of defiance would be little more than a futile gesture. But while Stryker did not know the odds he faced, he would try his damnedest to do his duty.

One of the earl's men was running up from the direction of St Mary's church. Stryker recognized him as one of the sentries guarding the old barr at the southern perimeter.

'Make your report,' Stryker said as the man reached them.

The sentry doubled forward in exhaustion as soon as he stopped his unwelcome exertion. 'Roundheads—sir,' he panted through gasped breaths.

'Where?' Stryker snapped impatiently. 'Where, man?'

The sentry kept hands clutched to his knees, but craned his neck up to look into Stryker's concerned face. 'Everywhere! From—south—sir. Like—a swarm. They come up here,' he pointed along Dam Street as it stretched away behind him. 'And up—Bridge Street. All roads, sir. Purple'uns.'

'It's Brooke, right enough,' Forrester said.

'Hundreds—sir!' the sentry added, desperate to convey the town's plight. 'Praps thousands!'

And then Stryker knew the day was lost, for this was no curious party of scouts, nor tentative vanguard, but Brooke's full force, and they were clearly not here for mere forage or reconnaissance, but to execute a mandate to drive the Royalists from Lichfield.

Stryker patted the sentry on his heaving back. 'Thank you,' he said briefly, stepping round him and beckoning for the others to follow. The large group paced quickly southwards along Dam Street, sending panicked towns-folk scattering in all directions like so many mice.

'Now yer for it!' a black-hooded woman screeched from an upstairs window. 'Pym's brave boys'll skin you Romish bastards, as you deserve!'

'Shut it, Rosy!' another woman howled back from one of the houses opposite. Stryker stared up to see her

216

leaning precariously out between painted shutters. 'These are Charlie's rightfuls!' The woman leaned yet further out of the window so that her plump face could be seen by the earl's men. 'Skewer them fuckin' Banbury-men, good sirs. Chase the buggers off! God 'n Saint Chad be with you!'

More shouts accompanied the defenders' march. Men and women lurched from upper rooms to wave fists and decry Chesterfield's soldiers, or whoop and squawk their allegiance.

'My father once planted an avenue of hornbeam leading up to our family home,' Forrester said, his words matter-of-fact but his tone strained. 'I hated walking up that long road as a child, for the rooks would pack those bloody trees and mock our every step with their confounded cawing.' He shuddered. 'That noise.' He paused suddenly, pointing a chubby finger up at an open window immediately above them. 'Still your tongue, woman, or I'll still it for you!'

'Easy, Forry,' Stryker said calmly. 'Let them shout what they will. They are frightened fools.'

Forrester turned silently back to the road, his face grim.

With the bellowed words of scorn and encouragement ringing in their ears, the soldiers crossed the marketplace and reached the squat stone edifice of St Mary's church. It stood in the centre of the town, dominating the junction between Dam Street, Bore Street and Sadler Street, and it was here that Stryker paused. He turned to the assembled throng. Chesterfield's officers were mostly amateurs who had hoped to pass this war safely barricaded behind the high ramparts of Cathedral Close. But events had conspired against them, and Stryker could see that they were as frightened as their men. 'Whichever way they advance,' he called, meeting as many anxious gazes as he could, 'they'll have to pass by here. So it is here we shall make our stand.'

A nervous tension seemed to hold the soldiers in thrall. They stared back at Stryker, unsure of what to do next. They were on the wrong side of the earl's great walls, and the wrong side of his deep moats.

Skellen did not await an order. He grunted something unintelligible, and set about loading his musket. For a heartbeat Lichfield's beleaguered Royalists stood inert and dumbstruck, watching him entranced.

As he checked the length of the match against the closed priming pan, ensuring it would ignite successfully when called upon, the long-limbed sergeant glanced up, eyes sepulchre-black in their deep sockets. 'Shut yer beslubberin' ale-pipes and get your guns primed!' he bellowed with sudden, terrifying savagery, making several men start in alarm. 'Gapin' like Lot's bloody goodwife'll get you shot! If not by the enemy, then by *me*!'

And then there was a flutter of movement within the throng as a man bearing a fearsome-looking fowling piece shook himself into action and reached for a powder flask. Stryker recognized him as John Dyott, brother of Sir Richard, and he offered a small nod of recognition. A couple more followed his lead, then ten more, then a score. Before long the entire mass of men were making their weapons ready for combat, and Stryker was thanking God for William Skellen.

A small man hefting a musket as tall as himself stepped forward. 'What now?' he asked in a coarse, half-throttled tone.

'Master Barkworth. You'll take these men,' Stryker said, indicating the thirty or so soldiers immediately to Barkworth's rear, 'and cover Sadler. I want that street bristling with muskets.'

Barkworth nodded, dour determination etching deep valleys across his face, yellow eyes brighter and more feral than Stryker had seen them. He well understood, for that same battle excitement was washing over him too: the terror and the risk, and the base need to shed blood for a cause.

The men Stryker had pointed out began to group in Barkworth's wake, following him to their defensive positions, and Stryker turned quickly to Skellen. 'Bore Street, Will.'

The sergeant spun immediately away. 'You lot!' he called to a swathe of the remaining men. 'Let's have you!' No one argued.

'The rest stay with me,' Stryker ordered. He caught Forrester's gaze. 'Take some across the street, Forry. We need all angles covered.'

'Sir,' Forrester responded.

And then, like spectres materializing at the town's southern limit, men in purple uniforms began to appear. At first there were three, then fifteen, then fifty. By the time Stryker had arranged his men around the nearest homes and shops of Dam Street, the invaders were too numerous to count. It was a column of men in Lord Brooke's distinctive purple coats, urged on by bawling halberdiers and bristling with musketry and steel. A vast square of purple taffeta swayed in the breeze above their metal-clad heads bearing the arms of England and seven stars in the field. It was a standard that told of a hardy, experienced force. One that had come to claim Lichfield for Parliament.

The attackers were on the very fringe of musket range, but Lichfield's Royalist garrison could not wait. They needed to delay the swelling tide of Roundheads. If not kill them, then make it plain that further advance would bring lead to their bodies. Stryker did not order any man to fire, but fire they did. It was sporadic, erratic, each man loading and firing in his own time, but the effect was profound and immediate. The oncoming column seemed to slow, then its front rank took a step backwards. The men around St Mary's cheered and Brooke's purplecoats hesitated and his sergeants snarled.

But the garrison's joy was to be short-lived, for, just when their desperate defence seemed destined for miraculous success, the Parliamentarian force changed tack. The foremost ranks broke into small groups, perhaps half a dozen in each, and burst from the column suddenly, darting ten or twenty paces up the road. One such group stopped to level their muskets, and let fly a small volley that ripped its way up the street. The defenders ducked low, or flattened themselves against houses and within doorways, but the range was still too great, and the bullets hurtled uselessly above their heads. But as the Royalists came out into plain view again in order to offer shots in reply, another of the smaller attacking groups opened up their own minor volley. A third joined them, and then a fourth. Most of the balls sailed past the defenders, peppering the church's austere stonework at their backs, but the range was gradually closing, and one of Chesterfield's men clattered to the ground to Stryker's left with a heavy sigh.

'There's too many,' another man whimpered queru-lously. 'By the Virgin's piss, there's too many.'

Stryker threw him a vicious look. 'Hold! Hold I say, or you'll meet a swifter end than you expect.'

The man clamped his jaw shut and forced himself to stand firm, though his hands shook so violently Stryker wondered whether he would even be able to bring his musket to bear.

Brooke's strategy was clear now. His companies were advancing in small packs, giving light volley fire like skir-mishers. The lord did not want a cumbersome column that would be easy for the defenders to pick off, a mass of bodies offering guaranteed success to even the most ill-aimed of shots. He had deployed his men into fast-moving groups, giving fire alternately so that the Royalist garrison was granted no respite to load and aim their weapons. It was a good strategy. One that, allied with vast numerical superiority, would see him bring a swift end to this fight. For a moment Stryker considered abandoning the defence, for there was no chance of repelling such a large, deter-mined force, but he would be damned if he'd let Brooke have things all his own way. If only for courageous men like Barkworth, Stryker would not have it said that Lichfield was surrendered without so much as an altercation.

The high crack of a carbine volley came sharp and deafening from the far side of St Mary's and Stryker was given renewed hope, for it announced the arrival of Edberg's troop into the fray. He could not see the yellow-coated dragoons, but knew they would be dismounted for this fight, and hoped their combined fire would stem the enemy's flow along Bridge Street.

Stryker's men on Dam Street were firing as rapidly as they might, their shots rarely finding success at this range, but serving to delay Brooke's inexorable progress. A crackle of musketry came back at them, and Stryker dodged behind an abandoned cart. Up ahead, at the far end of Dam Street, scores of purple-coated musketeers came on rapidly, pairs breaking away intermittently to check the flanking houses for snipers.

Stryker knew there were none, and he cursed the earl's inertia.

'Shoot 'em! Shoot the bastards!' Skellen's snarling tones carried to him from the entrance to Bore Street. The fact that his pitch was even remotely shrill was cause for grave concern. Clearly, the swarming enemy were as numerous along that road as they were on this.

In a moment of supreme shock, he felt a pressure at his temple and, lifting his free hand to feel for the anticipated wound, his fingertips met with skin that was made slithery with moisture. Stryker crouched low behind the cart as he checked his hand for the expected slick of blood that would soon be pulsing freely down his face, but instead he saw only a completely transparent liquid. He touched his head again, realising that there was no pain, and this time his fingers came away covered in small white specks. He stood, peering into the cart, and, for the first time, noticed it was piled with small, wizened apples. A volley from down the street crashed into the area around him again, and several of the fruit were destroyed in an instant, pulverized into specks of white flesh by hot musket-balls. He ducked once more, wiping more apple pulp from his head and cheeks.

Crouching still, Stryker loaded and primed his musket, threaded the long barrel between two of the cart's wheel spokes, picked a target and sent forth its vicious missile. A stout man, gleaming partizan in hand, was snatched backwards, twitching where he lay.

He loaded again, squinted through the thick cloud of throat-burning smoke now roiling about his head, and picked another target. The intended victim bent low to grasp something he had dropped, and the movement saved his life. Stryker cursed silently as the ball holed a water trough some yards beyond its mark.

More shots rang out, some from the outward-facing defenders ranged around St Mary's and the entrances to Bore, Sadler and Dam Streets, others from Brooke's men, their sheer weight of numbers ensuring progress was inevitable, despite the hail of lead that greeted each step. Windows shattered, a scrawny dog lay whimpering pathetically at the side of the road, blood cascading down its hind quarters where an errant ball had entered.

Still the Parliamentarians came, and for the first time Stryker noticed the frequency of defensive fire was beginning to wane. Chesterfield's amateurs were tiring, their fire increasingly desultory. Individual muskets continued to cough, cracks echoing loudly in the narrow streets, but their collective sound was more like the rattle of hail on a still lake than the thunderous crescendo of a coordinated volley.

'We'll have to fall back!' Forrester called from the other side of Dam Street.

Stryker peered across to where his friend was standing, back pressed against the door of a timber-framed house. 'Not yet!'

Forrester's face was lurid puce against his black hat and fair fringe. 'Jesu, Stryker, there are too many! You'll have us all dead with your stubbornness!' He shook his head angrily, loaded his musket, looked up again and grinned.

Stryker grinned back, loaded, and shot a purplecoat in the chest.

'God and Parliament!' came the cry from the oncoming attackers. It resounded about the buildings, echoing all the way up Dam Street to the little church that had become the makeshift defensive hub, and its sheer volume, competing admirably with the sporadic gunfire, gave away the true nature of their numbers.

'They won't stand!' a curiously hoarse voice reached Stryker's ears. 'The craven zealots won't stand before us, sir!'

He turned. It was Barkworth, the small man having joined him behind the apple-cart. 'Make your report.'

Barkworth's eyes seemed to shine like gemstones, as though the action had breathed new life into him. 'My lads cover Sadler Street, Captain. But there's plenty of the bastards.'

Stryker was not surprised, for he had foreseen Brooke would deploy his men along all the main roads through Lichfield, rendering defence near impossible, forcing Chesterfield's men to spread themselves too thinly to be effective. 'Perhaps it is time to give ground.'

Barkworth's jaw dropped. 'Nay, Captain Stryker, do not utter it,' he had to shout above the terrified braying of an ancient-looking palfrey, left tied to a wooden post near St Mary's south-west corner. 'The devils shan't stand for long.'

Stryker was amazed. 'I thought you spoke of our men, Master Barkworth!' He jerked his head back towards the oncoming Parliamentarians. 'Just count them, sir! The enemy could be unarmed to a man and they'd still win this fight.' He turned away from Barkworth's look of fury and flinched as a musket-ball careened above the cart and into the stone of the church just behind them. His heart sank, for the men in purple were too close now, the Royalists' best efforts seemingly having no effect. He cupped a hand and bellowed across the road to where Forrester maintained his volley fire. 'Forry! Forry! Retreat! If we stay, they'll surround us!'

'Thank Christ you've seen sense!' Forrester barked back, immediately corralling the nearest men so that they might follow him back towards the church and Cathedral Close beyond.

Stryker turned away, looking to the men within his own earshot, but found his path blocked by an indignant Simeon Barkworth.

'What is the meaning of this?' Barkworth snarled.

'You say they come up Sadler Street, sir. My sergeant fights them along Bore Street. And look,' he pointed at the tide of men he and Forrester had been attempting to quell. 'They are on Dam Street also. There are too many, from too many directions. We'll be cut off and cut down if we do not retire to the Close in short order.'

Barkworth's face looked as though it might implode, his veins rising from the skin at his temples. 'To hell with your yellow bloody cowardice, sir! We'll cut these Banbury-men a new set of arseholes, and feed their innards to our dogs!'

Stryker did not have time for delay. He took Barkworth by a scrawny shoulder and thrust him aside. 'I do believe you have lost your wits, sir.'

'I'm not afraid!' Barkworth bawled behind him. 'I'll cut these stoneless bastards to shreds, so help me! They'll not stand! They'll not fucking stand!'

Stryker was at once staggered and repelled by the little man's bravado, but something about Barkworth compelled him to see that the crazed fellow lived. He turned back, taking a fistful of the back of Barkworth's collar, and hauled him towards the safety of the Close.

'I'll die here!' Barkworth screamed.

'I do not doubt it,' Stryker replied, feeling certain the Scottish firebrand's immeasurable courage and lust for violence would indeed make an end of him. 'But not today.'

BRIDLINGTON, YORKSHIRE, 2 MARCH 1643

The wind howled. Great gusts, swirling, freezing and relentless, lashed inland from the North Sea coast like an army of screaming banshees, besieging those fortunate enough to seek solace within warm cloaks, and punishing those who were not.

A small man – pinched, rodent-like face the colour of rose petals in the cold – trudged slowly through the make-shift camp. His eyes, black and gleaming, like coals in contrast to his grey hair, twitched left and right, studying the narrow alleys between off-white tents. His gaze raked across the groups of soldiers huddled around the belea-guered flames of wind-harried fires, always assessing, always evaluating, ever alert to potential danger. Yet here, at least, he felt relatively safe. Safe as he ever could. Here he was surrounded by friends, like-minded individuals who would die for the cause as readily as he.

'Colonel Black, sir.'

The small man looked up to see a figure step into his path. He smiled a greeting, pleased to hear his real name uttered after so long existing under a different guise. And though he would never say it, the way in which his rank was uttered with such deference was particularly agreeable. It might only have been a nominal title, but that did not stop it sounding fine to his ears.

'Where is she?'

The man who had hailed Black stepped aside, stretching out a hand to show the way. 'In the town. Follow me, sir, if you would.'

Colonel Abel Black – known sometimes as Abel Menjam – nodded curtly. 'Lead on, Major Roberts.'

'They walked in silence for a time, Black's eyes twitching ceaselessly. 'She is safe?'

Major Roberts glanced back. 'The Generalissima is safe and strong as ever, Colonel.'

'But your crossing—'

'Was difficult, to say the least.' Roberts halted at the approach of a grime-faced man bearing a partizan and a sour countenance. 'Corporal?'

'Beggin' your pardon, sirs, but I've come direct from Her She-Majesty,' the corporal said, bowing low in the face of the high-ranking glares. 'She—er—wants to know when we can be off, sir.'

Roberts let out a long-suffering sigh. 'We are on our way to the Queen now. I will speak with her.' The corporal nodded, evidently relieved he did not have to deal with the sovereign's wife himself, and moved quickly from their path.

'She is eager to leave?' Black asked as they resumed their walk.

Roberts nodded. 'She wishes to seek shelter with the Earl of Newcastle at York.'

'And you do not?' Black replied, sensing the unease in the major's tone.

'There is a sizeable party of rebels at Hull. As soon as our army moves from here, we will be intercepted. I urge her simply to delay our departure until we can be sure we will not be attacked.'

Black was amused, for he could well imagine the difficulty Roberts must have had in persuading the queen to stay in Bridlington. 'I take it the Generalissima was less than receptive to your caution, Major?'

Roberts laughed at that. 'By God, she was not!'

Black shrugged. 'She is eager to win the war for her husband.'

Roberts looked him squarely in the eye. 'And I am eager to keep her safe.'

'And for that you have my utmost respect, Major, truly. Then what of your voyage?'

'As I said, it was difficult. We were turned back twice by blockade and gale. But she is stubborn.'

'That she is.'

'And she would not be dissuaded by enemy or element.'

They had reached the centre of the sprawling encampment, the roofs of the town's low timber-framed structures poking above the awnings in the distance. Black listened intently as they walked, though he had already heard the tale of how Queen Henrietta Maria and her convoy of much needed supplies and munitions – bankrolled by the great and good of Europe – had finally reached England after several abortive attempts. His contacts in Lichfield, and in Derby, Sheffield and York, had all relayed the story, and with that news, Black had travelled north, into the Royalist territory of

Yorkshire, and, finally, to the camp of Her She-Majesty, Generalissima, Henrietta Maria.

'Roundheads in the north had the ports covered, ready to chase us back into the sea,' Roberts continued, 'and that big navy o' theirs snaked up and down the east coast.' He grinned suddenly, with pride and more than a hint of relief. 'But here we are. Made landfall at Bridlington Bay some eight days back. Five rebel men-o'-war bombarded the town when they realized we'd slipped their treacherous net.'

'I heard tell they near met with success.'

Roberts nodded, his face serious. 'Her Majesty's lodgings were struck by cannon fire, aye.'

Black whistled softly. 'Dear God.'

'But she was unhurt, Colonel. The Lord's protection was upon her.'

'That and a deep ditch.'

Roberts's smile was rueful. 'You have it, sir, aye. The Israelites were sent manna, we were sent a ditch! The Queen and her retinue fled there, just outside the town, till the bombardment stopped. Thankfully, our Dutch escort was still in the bay and threatened to engage the rebel fleet lest they hold their fire. Now we camp outside the town for our own safety. Vice-Admiral Batten is a dogged old palliard, and may yet return.'

'How long does Her Majesty intend to stay in the north?'

'As short a time as possible, Colonel,' Roberts replied. 'She would march south, rendezvous with the King.'

Abel Black frowned. 'She will be disappointed, then.'

Roberts raised his eyebrows. 'She expects her nephew to have cut through the rebel strongholds by now.'

Black gave a regretful grimace. 'She expects too much,' as was so often the case, he thought. 'Prince Rupert fights hard in the Midlands, and will undoubtedly take it in, perhaps, a few months, but Parliament is strong in the region.'

Roberts seemed unsettled. 'You are certain?'

Black nodded. 'I have come from there, Major. The Queen may yet lead her army to Oxford, but not until summer. Prince Rupert must clear the road first.'

'I will let you break the news to her, sir. She is already displeased with me for keeping her in Bridlington.'

'I thought you might afford me that pleasure, Major Roberts.'

'We are here, sir.'

It was the largest tent in the sprawling encampment, sitting centrally amid the teeming humanity of an army on campaign. A fat spider sitting in a complex web of grimy awnings and flickering fires, bustling camp followers washing clothes in troughs of icy water, and men shouting and drinking and sharpening blades. Hardly a fitting home for the Queen of England, but it would not, Black knew, deprive Henrietta of sleep. She was beautiful, in her own sharp-featured way, and valued things of equal beauty, be they silken garments, exquisite jewels or the opulent furnishings to which her privileged lifestyle had made her accustomed. And yet, Black thought, as he approached the tent's humble entrance, the queen had proven herself uniquely and admirably resolute. She may have been chased from Whitehall by the rising Parliamentarian tide, and she might have fled the country almost exactly a year previously, but that time in exile had served to harden her resolve. She had pawned those magnificent jewels, and swallowed her pride to beg help from royal kin in France and Spain. She had faced hardships hitherto unknown in her advantaged life, and now she had returned with an iron determination, a newly flourishing loyalty to her husband and king, and with an army at her back. The sentries at the tent's entrance moved aside for the face they knew well, and, with quickening pulse, Colonel Abel Black went inside.

'Your Majesty.'

Queen Henrietta Maria was perched on a sturdy, high-backed chair set towards the rear of the tent. She wore a simple dress beneath a fur-trimmed cloak that shielded her from the worst of the bitter March air, yet in Black's eyes she was like a goddess. Straight-spined, beautiful and imperious. Everything a queen should be. That was why he had served her for so many years. He bowed as low as his back would allow.

'Stand, Abel, stand,' Henrietta said, her voice friendly. 'Fare you well?'

Black straightened up. 'Well enough, Majesty.'

'Oh?' the queen said, her almond-shaped eyes falling upon the gash at his forehead. It had healed well in the days since the attack, but the line of congealed scarlet was still livid against the pale hue of his wispy hair.

Black touched a hand to the wound. 'This? Nothing, Majesty. A mere scratch compared with your own tribulations.'

'You always were a modest thing, Colonel,' the queen chided gently. She rose from her chair and walked to a small chest of swirling walnut that sat nearby, its four drawers adorned with a pattern of delicate apple blossoms, skilfully crafted in mother-of-pearl. 'It is colonel, I take it? Or do you carry some other fanciful rank now? Captain-General perhaps?'

Black knew better than to note the queen's own colourful use of military titles. 'Colonel will do, Majesty.'

She smiled warmly. 'As you wish, *Colonel*. After all, I would not begin to question how one of my chief intelligencers conducts his business.' From the walnut chest Henrietta took a small leather pouch. She moved quickly to where Black stood, handing it to him. It jangled metallically. 'You have served me well for half a lifetime, Abel, and I would afford you any title you wish. Save King, naturally.'

Abel Black weighed the pouch in his hand, feeling the satisfying burden of coin, and bowed. '*Naturellement, Majesté.*' When he met her gaze again he saw the glint of iron that made the daughter of the old King of France so formidable. He decided to nip the anticipated tirade in the bud. 'I agree with Major Roberts.'

Black's words caught the queen off guard and she seemed momentarily taken aback.

'With respect, Majesty,' Black added smoothly.

'It does not surprise me,' Henrietta said eventually. 'You always were as coddling as Roberts.'

'When it comes to your safety, Majesty, yes,' Black replied.

The queen wrinkled her nose in distaste. 'Captain Hotham—'

'Of Hull?'

'The same. He came here three days hence to exchange prisoners.' She gazed at the tent's ceiling, watching it quiver in the North Sea wind as she reflected on the event. 'He was—def—def—'

'Defiant?' Black offered. Even with her fluent grasp of English, some words remained elusive.

The queen shook her head, angry at herself for the slip. '*Non*! Opposite of that, Abel. Quite the opposite! *Deferment*?'

Black frowned. 'Deferent?'

'*Oui*!' Queen Henrietta clapped gloved hands in delight and relief. 'He was deferent. So much so that I thought he might declare fealty to me then and there.'

Black understood. 'And that is why you wish to move to York quickly?'

She nodded her head, its dark ringlets trembling at her cheeks. 'Aye, Colonel. Hotham will not attack us, I am certain. His loyalty to Parliament wavers at best.'

'Then I will go to Hull, Majesty. Treat with Hotham. Make him see the righteousness of our cause.'

She nodded. 'Just so. Just so.' Suddenly the brown gaze was enquiring again. 'But tell me of this wound, Abel, do. You are an old friend and I shan't have you dismiss such things as mere trivialities.'

Black sighed as though the gash was of no consequence. 'I was ambushed by men sent by the Parliament.'

'Careless of you, Abel.'

'Aye, Your Majesty, that it was. I had spent some weeks in London, as you instructed, coordinating our resistance efforts. I was discovered.'

The queen raised her brow in surprise.

Black felt his cheeks burn. 'A former associate recognized me on Lombard Street. He knew me as a king's man.'

'And he a rebel?'

'You have it. Denounced me there and then. In the middle of the street!' He shuddered at the horrific recollection. 'I

233

was fortunate to escape with my skin intact. I resolved to go to the safe house at Lichfield, and when I left the capital I believed I had done so undetected. I was wrong. They had sent a team of dragooners in my wake. The devils caught up with me on the road north.'

Henrietta Maria was enthralled, and she wound a sleek ringlet of hair around one of her fingers as she listened. 'How did you escape your ambushers?'

It was then that Abel Black halted his tale, for the surreal night was difficult enough to remember, let alone recount. 'The most curious event, Majesty. I was rescued. Quite by chance. Some fellows burst from the darkness in my moment of need.'

'Perhaps they were angels?'

Black tilted his head to the side. 'Perhaps. Though I had not imagined the heavenly host to be so skilfully murderous, nor so foul-mouthed.'

The corners of her thin lips twitched. 'They were for our cause?'

'Aye, Majesty, they were. Though they did not seem to be on king's business, but rather they were searching for someone, from what I could glean. A girl.'

Her face darkened. 'But you kept your own business private, I trust?'

'To be certain, Majesty. I travelled with them so far as my agent's home, and then we parted.'

'And the rebels?'

'All dead,' Black replied confidently.

Queen Henrietta Maria nodded, her mood lightening again. 'Then all is well. And praise God for the timely intervention of your bloodthirsty angels. Did they give you their names?'

'No, Majesty. Aliases only. They were guarded, as was I.'

'A shame. I should have liked to reward them.'

'Alas,' Black shook his small head. 'The only genuine name I heard whispered was that of the woman they sought. Undoubtedly one of their favourite callets. Strange name to hear in Staffordshire, though, I'll admit. *Lisette*, I think it was.'

CHAPTER 11

A storm smouldered on the horizon, clouds melding and parting in inky confusion.

High up on the square viewing platform of the cathedral's central tower, spire soaring into the air above their heads, three men gazed out upon the town, watching with grim interest as the purple-coated regiment of Lord Brooke decamped in Lichfield's streets and houses.

'To think,' Captain Lancelot Forrester said, his voice bleak as the March wind, 'I could have stayed with the army. Stayed in Oxford. Found a cosy corner of some fuggy tavern, with a cup of spiced claret in hand and a big-bosomed wench on my lap. But instead I find myself here. With the pair of you. About to be flayed alive by a rabid pack of Roundheads. Again.'

Stryker, Forrester and Skellen had fallen back to the Close with the rest of the Royalist garrison as the Parliamentarians swarmed up Dam Street. They had climbed the spiral staircase of the tallest of the three towers to watch their enemy tighten its grip on the town, and now, as the early morning air carried the metallic aroma of impending rain to their nostrils, they could do nothing but consider their predicament with a growing sense of dread.

'Does seem you've made some bad choices, sir,' Skellen replied.

'I must be positively addled.'

Stryker remained silent as he watched the tiny figures scuttle busily beyond the high walls. Brooke had advanced through a town markedly devoid of traffic as far as the south side of the Close, and from there, it seemed, he would launch whatever offensive he had planned. Now his men had exchanged muskets for spades, and, just out of musket range, were busily digging earthworks in preparation for a siege.

'Let me see if I have this true.'

It was Forrester's voice that broke into his reverie, and Stryker looked at him. 'Go on.'

'We are stuck here, in this fortified church, holding a town that – for the most part – don't even want us.'

Stryker grimaced in reply to the stark summation. He looked up at the brooding clouds. The buzzard was there again, hunting on the freshening breeze, and he watched it glide silently over the town, wings curved upwards as Barkworth had told him. It soared and banked without a care, save the pursuit of some small field-dwelling creature, and Stryker found himself yearning to share just a fraction of its freedom.

'And our esteemed leader,' Forrester went on morosely, 'is a craven, gouty old pachyderm, lacking in any warlike quality or military experience, who can bring no more than three hundred, largely rather green, men to arms.'

'And we face the Lord Brooke,' Skellen said sourly.

'A man hearsay tells us to be young, forthright and courageous,' said Forrester, counting the Roundhead general's ominously impressive qualities on each of his fingers. 'He has a force of, what, twelve or thirteen hundred men? Most of 'em veterans we three have already faced in this new war, and who, one must concede, fought impressively last autumn against horrifying odds.'

Skellen scratched his chin. 'And they're all Puritans. They'll be itchin' to pull this place down around our ears.'

'Indeed. And they have that fuckin' monstrosity in their train, so it shouldn't prove too taxing.'

Stryker and Skellen followed Forrester's pointing hand to a place deep within Lichfield's heart. It was there that, after several moments of scrutiny, they finally laid eyes upon a huge, black cylinder. It was propped on wheels and was being drawn northwards along Dam Street by a half-dozen labouring nags, wending its inexorable way towards the Close.

'Christ, they have a demi-culverin,' Stryker said quietly. 'A castle-killer,' Skellen droned. 'Now we're for it.'

The cannon finally came to rest far nearer to the Close than Stryker had expected. The three watched mutely as Brooke's artillery crews manoeuvred the vast gun to the point where Dam Street met the raised causeway across Minster Pool. The range was no more than a hundred paces, making the sturdy gate an ominously easy target for even the most inexperienced gunner.

'They'll be firing point-blank,' Skellen said tonelessly. 'That gate'll be kindling afore luncheon.'

Stryker heard the first cracks of shots being fired by Lichfield's defenders. He leant over the platform's parapet and took in the scene below. Perched on the rickety scaf-folding that ran along the inside of the high boundary walls, Chesterfield's men were beginning to offer sporadic musketry. The action took little effect, for the Roundheads had sent a party of infantry ahead of the long siege piece to erect a barricade of wagons, hay bales, grain sacks and barrels in order to protect the men tasked with operating the demi-culverin. But at least the garrison was offering some level of defiance.

High up on the watchtower, Stryker and his men began to load their muskets, preparing to add more fire to the desultory efforts of Chesterfield's force. The wind was up now, rushing at so great a height, making any level of accuracy impossible, but, as they watched the cannon's dark barrel move in a great arc to find its optimum trajectory, they realized that there was simply no other option.

Footsteps sounded on the staircase below them, as more men came up from the cathedral's inner sanctum to stare down at the enemy's preparations. Sir Richard Dyott was in the lead, accompanied by a pair of well-dressed men who were evidently two of the garrison's senior officers. When he stepped on to the stone platform, he immediately moved to the battlement to take in the extent of the force ranged against them.

'My God,' Dyott whispered. He looked up at Stryker, who had gone to stand at his side. 'Will they breach the gate?'

Stryker nodded. 'For certain. If they're given enough time.'

'Then how must we deny them that commodity?' one of the officers asked.

Skellen gave his distinctive snort and nestled his musket against his shoulder. 'Shoot the buggers.'

*

The bombardment of the south gate began with an almighty explosion that rent the air and vibrated through the very fabric of the cathedral. A fleeting tongue of orange licked from the mouth of the demi-culverin, and it jetted smoke in a swelling cloud that obscured both gun and gunners.

Stryker did not see ball meet gate, but knew the opening salvo had been a success, for a shower of splintered timber and rubble burst forth, raining down on the Minster Pool like giant hailstones.

The soldiers manning the walls were not in any danger, but they instinctively shrank back. And the Parliamentarians cheered.

Protected as they were by their makeshift shelter, the gun crew adjusted the demi-culverin's elevation without hindrance and began the process of reloading. Feeling the pressure of holding the only position that allowed a man to fire over the barricade, Stryker leant against the stone ledge so that its cold top pressed hard against his waist, and hefted his musket. He trained the barrel on a purple-coat wielding the long lighting stick and squeezed the trigger. Through the wreath of powder smoke he saw the gunner flinch and knew the shot had flown close, but it was difficult to take account of such a swirling wind.

Another explosion came, spitting fire and iron at the king's garrison, its heavy sound putting Stryker in mind of the opening bombardment at Edgehill. Men ducked down again. The gates of Lichfield's Cathedral Close shuddered.

The wind dropped. Skellen's musket was primed and ready, and he tested the air with a wet fingertip, raising an eyebrow at his captain as he did so.

'Quickly!' Stryker urged.

The longarm was butted against his shoulder before the word was beyond his lips, and, as the sergeant eased back his trigger, one of the gun crew crumpled as though his very bones had vanished from his flesh.

Like a nest of dormice suddenly discovered by a hungry cat, Brooke's artillerymen scurried away, desperate to be out of musket range. And the smoking cannon was left still and silent, at least until the wind gathered pace once more. Now it was the Royalists' turn to cheer.

Lord Brooke looked towards the door of the Sadler Street home he had made his headquarters. 'What is it, Thomas?'

Captain Thomas Fitch stood beneath the lintel, gazing up at the cloudy sky. 'Bird of prey, sir. Buzzard or kite or some such. Couldn't help wonder if it held some portent for us, my lord.'

Brooke was seated at a low table, considering a trencher of bread and cheese. He closed his eyes. 'Lord, forgive that comment.' He opened them to meet Fitch's sludge-green stare. 'Do not let superstition cloud your mind, Thomas,' he chided. 'It is the Devil's game.'

The captain looked shame-faced. 'I'm sorry, my lord. I am merely nervous. These are high walls. A tough nut to crack with so many fresh troops.'

Brooke's hand rose to twist at the point of his neat beard. 'What would you have me do? We lost many men last season. Praise God Parliament saw fit to furnish our humble regiment with so many reinforcements.' He took a small chunk of bread from the trencher and popped it on his tongue, chewing slowly. 'Take heart, Captain,' he said after swallowing down the bread. 'We have plenty of veterans left. You and I included. And we have righteous-ness on our side. Never forget that unalienable truth. It is a righteousness that defines us, breathes life and morality into our cause. It is why we fight. And *that* place . . .'

Fitch strode into the room, the door swinging shut at his armour-plated back. 'That place, sir?'

'Lichfield's vile cathedral.' His words were spoken as though they dissolved the flesh of his tongue. 'High Church, Thomas. It is but a stone's throw from outright Popery. Outright idolatry. Outright superstition. Such creeping evil cannot be allowed to work its way back into our country. It was why I left for the New World. Why Sayebrooke was founded.'

'But you returned.'

'I returned because men such as me finally have a voice. The Parliament sits again, after all these years, and we can save England at last. God is on our side, Thomas! Can you not feel it?' Brooke thrust the chair backwards and stood. 'And it is why we will prevail here. Now come! Join me. Let us inspect Black Bess's progress.'

The pair walked out into Sadler Street, purple-coated soldiers doffing caps and removing helmets as they passed. Brooke was resplendent in his own tunic beneath a newly oiled buff-coat of bright yellow, a steel gauntlet on his left arm and plate armour across back and breast. In his right hand he held a highly polished helmet with neck guard and five long bars to protect the face.

Fitch looked at the helmet. 'Will you not don it, sir? For safety's sake.'

'Lord, no!' Brooke scoffed. 'We are perfectly safe here, Thomas. Let the men see their general. It is good for morale.'

'Here, sir,' Fitch said, indicating a narrow alleyway midway along Sadler Street.

Brooke led the way through the gloomy conduit and out into the expansive marketplace. Handfuls of figures had begun to appear at the entrances to homes and businesses, huddled close and nervous, but too intrigued by the cannon fire to stay indoors. 'How are the townsmen disposed to us?'

'Well, in the main,' Fitch responded.

'In the main? There are plenty in their number would take up arms against us?'

'Not arms, sir. Those who'd wish us violence are within the cathedral's walls.'

'And those without?' Brooke asked dubiously. 'There are a good number who would, at the very least, harbour enmity for our cause, even if they do not act upon it?'

'The men and women in there,' Fitch said, pointing towards the soaring mass of the cathedral as they reached a row of houses on the north-east side of the marketplace, 'have kin out here. It is a truly divided city.'

Brooke sighed. 'It is a truly divided country, Thomas.'

They moved quickly along the row of houses, safe in the knowledge that the buildings blocked any view of their progress from the Close's snipers, until they were hailed by a sergeant waving a long halberd. 'This way, my lord,' the man said gruffly in the accent of Birmingham. He was shorter than most, and almost as wide as he was tall, his purple uniform stretched to splitting point across his bull-like frame, and he virtually waddled into the nearest house.

The house had once been someone's home, but now it appeared more like a guardroom, such was the number of Brooke's soldiers stationed within.

'This is our route on to Dam Street,' Captain Fitch said to Brooke as they reached an unassuming back room with a low door that opened on to the road beyond. 'Black Bess sits yonder. But please do not leave the house, my lord. The street is within musket range.'

Brooke paced to the door, but remained beneath the protection of its low porch. Immediately he laid eyes upon the empty stretch of road that was Dam Street. To his right lay the buildings of the city, while to his left he saw the burgeoning earthworks, hurriedly dug by his beloved purplecoats. Further forward, and ringed by its pile of wood and sacking, was the gun position of Brooke's formidable demi-culverin, Black Bess. To his surprise and delight, the gunners were all there, gathered around the weapon like a swarm of bees at a honey pot.

Brooke turned to the sergeant. 'The enemy have ceased fire?'

'The wind's up an' whistlin' again, General, sir. They couldn't hit a bullock from ten yards.'

'Then we might resume the bombardment?'

And Black Bess opened fire.

'Lord, but she's magnificent!' Brooke yelped in delight amid the silence that followed the gun's deafening cough. 'She'll have us through that stubborn gate in no time at all! I must see her work up close. Come, Captain Fitch!'

'General!' Fitch snapped, rather more aggressively than he had intended. 'With respect, my lord, you must not step on to the road.'

'Poppycock!' Brooke scoffed, moving further out from the safety of the porch.

'The men up in the tower can see our lines well, General!'

Brooke rounded on Fitch. 'Then let the malignant fools stare. May they shout their Romish prattle down upon our heads.' He brandished a sudden grin. 'And we in turn shall pray for their souls, eh?'

Fitch was not mollified. 'They will do more than *shout* at our heads, my lord.'

Brooke took a step back into the house so that he was entirely out of view from the Close. 'Dear Thomas, you do worry so. They'll spew their muskets, certainly, but to what end? The men on their walls cannot see beyond our barricades, and those up in the clouds could not hope to shoot true with the wind swirling so. At that height, they may throw dried peas at us, for all the good they'll do.' He turned back towards the street. 'Come!'

'Sir,' was all Fitch could say. He had protested to the limit of his rank. Any further obstinacy would be seen as insubordination.

Another shot went crashing from the cannon, engendering whoops of encouragement from the purplecoats nearby. For a terrible moment Fitch thought his commander might step straight out to take a view of the devastation Black Bess had wrought, but, to the captain's limitless relief, the General of the Midland Counties let forth a dramatic sigh of acquiescence. 'So be it, Thomas. You really are an old maid sometimes, but if it'll salve your nerves,' he put on the gleaming steel helmet, so far clutched in a gloved hand, 'I shall at least wear this.'

Sergeant William Skellen and Captain Lancelot Forrester were on the viewing platform facing south, elbows propped on the stone ledge. They turned at the footfalls, nodding a brief welcome to the newcomers before returning to their study of the town.

'That one were a good'un, sir,' Skellen said. 'Spanked the framework o' the drawbridge. Another one and it'll be out of action.'

Stryker nodded. 'Felt it down in the infirmary.' He went to stand between them, leaning forward too, his expert eye taking in the scene.

'I trust she thrives?' Forrester asked.

'She does, thank you, Forry. Almost well enough to travel.'

'I hope you appreciate the irony, old man.'

Dyott had returned with Stryker. For his part, the Steward of Lichfield had been reporting on the progress of Brooke's rapidly forming siege works. 'It is impossible,' he said sullenly. 'The men at the walls cannot penetrate their earthworks.'

'And us up 'ere,' Skellen added, 'can't even piss straight, let alone shoot.'

Stryker turned on Skellen, preparing to bawl at him for such talk in Dyott's presence, but he bit his tongue when he saw the sergeant's expression.

'Hark at that,' Skellen said, never taking his eyes from a point far below on Dam Street. 'Looks like King bloody Arthur's joined the Roun'eads.'

Stryker followed his gaze. 'I wonder.'

Now Skellen looked up. 'Sir?'

'Do we have a glass up here?' Stryker asked Dyott. 'A spyglass. I need a better view.'

To Stryker's mild surprise, Dyott reached down at his waist, to where a narrow tube of leather-bound metal hung from a hook at his belt. 'Here.'

Stryker took the telescope. 'A fine piece, Sir Richard.'

Forrester's eyes were wide as cartwheels. 'Lipershey, if I'm not mistaken.'

Dyott beamed. 'Indeed, Captain Forrester. A Hans Lipershey original. My purse was a deal lighter after its purchase, I can tell you.'

Forrester whistled softly. 'My compliments.'

Stryker lifted the glass, opening his solitary eye as wide as he could. The muscles of the adjacent empty socket mimicked the gesture, the tight swirling mass of thick tissue resisting stubbornly, pulling at the point where bad skin met good at forehead and cheek. It was a sensation to which he had long become accustomed, but that did not make it comfortable. Rather, it served only to remind him of the toll a life of soldiering had taken.

'Why do you fight?' Dyott said at his left ear, as if reading Stryker's thoughts.

Stryker kept his focus on the burgeoning siege works in the town. 'We're at war.'

'At war with ourselves, Captain.' Dyott replied. 'It is not the French or the Scots you eye down the pike shaft, but Englishmen just like yourself. My reason is clear. I am a privileged man, and I stand to lose a great deal under a new regime that would seek to threaten society. Forcibly deprive my children of their rightful inheritance. But you are not . . .'

'Rich enough?' Stryker said, though without real bitterness. He swept the glass from the busy purple-coated diggers immediately south of the Close towards the open ground of the marketplace and the streets beyond. Timber-framed homes, painted gables and thatched roofs rushed across his vision in a great blur until he reached the little church of St Mary, where more soldiers teemed. He watched them for a second, wondering if that building was to be the hub of the siege works, before scanning the long tract of paving that was Dam Street.

'Not simply that, sir,' Dyott replied. 'Men such as I fight for their estates, while for others it is a matter of faith, or perhaps some deep-seated loyalty to the old order of things. But you do not seem to fit any mould.'

Stryker removed the telescope from his eye and looked at Dyott. 'I fight because it is what I know. What I've always done. But you are right, I have no great zeal. My loyalties are local. To my men first, to my colonel second, and then, if he is lucky, to my king. I do not hate the Roundheads, any more or less than I hate you or your earl or Doctor Chambers. But on the battlefield they are my enemy.'

'Why?'

'Because their job is to get in my way.'

'And yours?' said Dyott.

'My job, Sir Richard,' Stryker lifted the telescope once again and resumed his search of Dam Street, 'is to move them.'

After several moments Stryker found his target; the place and the person Skellen had indicated. He held the glass still, studying a man in purple cassock, fine, mirror-shining armour and a distinctive five-barred helmet. A helmet Stryker knew to be owned by a particular Parliamentarian officer.

'I envy you,' Dyott was saying. 'An uncomplicated existence is to be cherished.'

'Perhaps it is,' Stryker replied, handing back the telescope, 'but my existence is about to become a might tangled, Sir Richard.'

Dyott looked puzzled. 'How so?'

'I'm going to kill a lord.'

All three pairs of eyes were on him now. 'You're what?' Dyott spluttered.

'In fact,' Stryker said, 'your brother is. Where is John?'

'Er—he is—er—down on the walls,' Dyott managed to blurt.

'Fetch him, if you would, Sir Richard. And bid him bring his duck killer.'

'Captain?'

Stryker turned back to face the town and gazed down at the man Skellen's keen eyes had spotted at the entrance to an otherwise unassuming property. 'It may not be King Arthur pays us a visit, but it is Lord Brooke.'

Forrester was watching the small, plate-clad figure. 'But he is not within range, old man.'

'Not for you or I, Forry. But a decent shot with a well-kept fowling piece might have a fair throw of the dice, wouldn't you say?'

'St Chad's Day!' Robert Greville, Lord Brooke, was hovering at the edge of the cover afforded by the porch. He looked back into the house. 'Is that not the most apt date imaginable, Captain? We'll knock down their damned cathedral on the very day their patron is honoured! A perfect sign from God!'

Captain Thomas Fitch was not so ebullient. 'The malignants will be able to see you from the tower, General.'

Brooke glowered. 'My men are out there digging earthworks and firing our cannon. The least I can do is show them I face the same risks as they.'

Fitch frowned but stayed silent, moving forwards to stand with Brooke. Out on the edge of Minster Pool, where Dam Street ended and the causeway across the moat began, the infantrymen were making impressive progress. They were out in the open, and flinched with every shot fired from the Close, but, Fitch had to concede, none of the sporadic defensive fire was finding flesh. His confidence began to grow.

'Damned if I can see,' Lord Brooke growled irritably.

'Sir?'

'I can see Bess and her crew right enough, and a joy they are to behold, but I want to lay eyes upon the very gate she pounds.' At that, he leaned forwards so that his torso was clear of the porch, giving himself a clear view of the Cathedral Close's south gate and the damage his ordnance was inflicting.

John Dyott had joined Stryker on the central tower's viewing platform. The rest of the group had moved some distance down the spiral staircase so as to allow Sir Richard's brother room to wield his vast fowling piece.

'Now,' Stryker said, 'I want you to take aim at that man.' He pointed down on to Dam Street. 'The one in plate and helmet. See him?'

John Dyott remained silent, gazing down at the city stretching away beneath him.

Stryker was staggered by the man's discourteousness and bit back a barbed comment. 'I said, do you see him, sir?'

Dyott knelt and chose a lead ball from the small pile of ammunition he had placed on the stone at his feet.

'God's teeth, man!' Stryker snapped, unused to this kind of insult.

'Captain Stryker!' The voice was Sir Richard's. He had come to the top of the staircase. 'I am sorry. I thought you were aware of my brother's affliction.'

Stryker looked at him. 'Affliction?'

'Dear John is quite deaf, Captain. Deaf and dumb from birth.'

Stryker stared back at the man who was already taking aim with the huge weapon. 'Stone me. My apologies, Sir Richard. I did not know. But he is a good shot?'

'The very best. Why he—'

Stryker did not hear Sir Richard's words, for the man who could neither speak nor hear had opened fire.

Captain Thomas Fitch shrank back from the fine shower of sticky liquid that sprayed his face. He frantically wiped his eyes clear, wondering where on earth his general had gone, and dashed forwards into the porch area.

'My lord! General!' Fitch cried, hoping Brooke had not stridden out into the open. But then he saw the booted feet to the left of the doorway, and he peered round the frame to see a pair of inert legs. Fitch moved further out with growing trepidation, only to see the armoured torso and then, horrifyingly, the head crowned with an exquisitely crafted helmet.

It was only then that Fitch looked down at his hands. They were covered in blood, and he suddenly understood that that was the substance he had wiped from his eyes.

'My God,' he said to no one. 'Dear God.'

Fitch scrambled out on to Dam Street, unconcerned with the men in the Close, and knelt beside the prostrate body. 'Help here!' he bellowed back into the house. 'Help here, damn your eyes!'

Men came running. They joined the captain, helped him drag Lord Brooke back into the safety of the house. Only then did Fitch turn his general over.

'A sign from God,' Captain Thomas Fitch murmured. And then he began to weep. For Robert Greville, second Baron Brooke, was dead; a wide, ragged hole of glistening scarlet where his left eye had been.

'For Saint Chad!' Philip Stanhope, Earl of Chesterfield, bellowed into the crisp morning sky. 'God and Saint Chad!'

The news of Brooke's sudden and shocking demise had already spread throughout the garrison by the time Stryker's feet touched terra firma. Now he was out in the courtyard, listening to the cheers of Chesterfield's newly invigorated men. The earl himself was at the centre of the throng, wrapped tight in a fur-trimmed cloak, shadowed discreetly by the ever-watchful Barkworth, and lofting his walking stick as though it were the king's own standard. And why not, Stryker thought? The garrison needed an infusion of confidence, and if Chesterfield could achieve such a hitherto difficult task by reminding them that their enemy had died on the very day dedicated to Lichfield's patron saint, then all to the good.

He strode past the crowing group, pleased to be at some liberty again, and made for the infirmary.

'Watch yourself, Captain,' a voice called sharply to him from the shadows between two nearby wagons.

Stryker held his stride and a hand went to his sword-hilt, ready to draw the weapon at a moment's notice. He could not yet see the man who had hailed him, but the accent was one with which he was all too familiar. 'I always do, Major.'

Like a wherry boat resolving from a Thames morning mist, the stark features of Henning Edberg gradually appeared as he stepped into the light. 'You think you have evaded justice?'

Stryker shook his head. 'No. You're still here, aren't you? The charge still stands. Chesterfield merely sees more use in keeping me free than locking me up. While the rebels are at his door, leastwise.' He remembered the earl's curt acceptance of his skills in those breathless moments after that first skirmish in Lichfield's streets. Chesterfield's glances were narrow, his voice reticent, for he remained suspicious of a man on such a heinous charge, but the bloody action had convinced the earl that the presence of Stryker and his men was infinitely more of a help than a hindrance. Stryker also remembered the Swedish dragoon's outrage as he was told that the matter would be dealt with as soon as Parliament's forces had turned tail back to Warwickshire. 'You and I can settle our differences once this—' he waved a hand above his head, indicating the entire Close, 'is finished.'

'I would settle this now,' Edberg growled, his face set in a sour grimace, and he stepped forward so that Stryker wondered if he were about to launch an attack.

Stryker held his ground. 'You would duel here, in the open, with so many to bear witness? Christ, Edberg, are you entirely frantic? The Close is a prison, whether I am in chains or not. I cannot take my leave. You have me captured, sir.' And then his voice trailed off, for something in Edberg's eyes had unsettled him. There was a fury there, the blood-fury Stryker himself felt when in the heat of battle, at that moment when he scented a kill.

And then, just as Stryker moved to unsheathe his sword, Edberg stepped back, plunging into the shadows again, leaving Stryker standing alone, questions swirling about his mind.

'This woman is a rare marvel, Captain,' Doctor Gregory Chambers greeted him in the perpetually gloomy room.

'She fares well, then?'

'Well?' Chambers grinned. 'Near better than most in this God-forsaken fort!' He clapped Stryker on the shoulder suddenly. 'I hear you stuck a ball through Banbury Brooke's eye! Well done, sir. Well done indeed!'

Stryker shook his head. 'The feat is not mine to claim, Doctor. Sir Richard's brother must take the credit.'

'Ah, stands to reason,' Chambers said. 'Dumb Dyott is an impressive shot. Always was.'

Stryker felt heat burn at his cheeks suddenly. 'Dumb Dyott?'

'Oh, worry not, sir,' Chambers blurted quickly, evidently reading threat in the officer's stare, 'the term is not made in offence, but endearment, I assure you. Honest John is known as Dumb Dyott in Lichfield. He and his goodwife Katherine were both deaf and dumb from birth.'

Stryker had not realized his expression was so readable, and felt instantly embarrassed, wondering if the doctor could tell that such nicknames, bestowed for a man's physical misfortunes, bore him a particular pain. He stared at his boots. 'May I see her?'

Chambers moved aside. 'Naturally, Captain.'

'You do not understand,' Stryker said, as he sat in his usual place at Lisette's side. It was mid afternoon, and he had spent the four or so hours since Brooke's death watching her sleep. There seemed little point in staying at the walls, for the enemy cannon fire had ceased at a stroke on the death of their general. Now Lichfield's beleaguered Royalist garrison simply waited for the purplecoats to make their next move.

'No, *mon amour*, you do not bloody understand!' Lisette was sitting, cushions propped at her back, colour finally returning to her cheeks. She was still weak, and Stryker could tell that the pain in her shoulder fringed on the unbearable, though she would never admit it. But, mercifully, the fever was long gone. She glared at Stryker. 'I must reach Jonathan Blaze.'

Stryker rubbed his eye with a powder-blackened palm. 'Lisette, please, listen to me. You are not strong enough yet. Besides, we are trapped here. Brooke besieges the cathedral.'

'Brooke is gone,' she said defiantly.

'But his regiment is not. They have stopped the bombardment, yes, but only while they deal with the loss of their general. His death does not spell the end of the siege.'

'And you say they attack from the south? From the town?'

He nodded. 'Aye.'

'Then why can we not go north?'

Stryker stared at her, thoughts a whirl. 'I do not know,' he said eventually.

'Captain! Captain!' The shout came from the infirmary's doorway. It was an unusual-sounding voice, but one Stryker had come to know well.

He turned. 'Barkworth?'

'They're attacking again, sir!'

'Then get up on the walls,' Stryker responded tartly. 'Start shooting.'

Barkworth's head shook vigorously, and Stryker saw that his face – a face scarred and weathered from a lifetime of fighting – was etched with concern. Perhaps even fear.

Stryker stood. 'What is it?'

'Come to the walls, sir, please!'

Stryker climbed the ladder to the wooden rail that ran along the inside face of the Close's wall, providing a shallow platform from which the defenders could pour their fire. As he ascended, he peered down at the south gate, noting that stout lengths of timber had been nailed to the cannon-weakened structure to bolster it in advance of a further bombardment. He was satisfied to see Chesterfield had not been idle during the respite afforded in the wake of Brooke's death.

But that respite had not ended. There were no more booming artillery salvos, no splintering of wood or crumbling of stone. So what, then, was this new attack of which Barkworth spoke?

'My God,' Stryker said aloud as he risked a glance over the parapet.

Down in the town, near to the point in Dam Street where Lord Brooke had fallen, a crowd was gathering. They were civilians by their clothes, but this was clearly not the simple coming together of curious townsfolk wishing to view the siege works. It was a mass of bodies, tethered together by long chains. Hostages, cajoled and harried from behind by the blades and muskets of purple-coated soldiers.

The men at the walls, Stryker among them, looked on in horror as the crowd began to move. They walked slowly, faces chalk-white, reluctance marking each pace, all the while prodded onwards at sword-point.

'Jesu, Edith!' a man some yards to Stryker's right wailed. 'It is my Edith! And little Rose!'

Stryker followed the man's pointing finger to a pair of citizens at the front of the oncoming crowd. He realized that those faces were that of women – or, rather, a woman and a little girl – and he realized with chilled blood that these must be the enraged man's wife and daughter.

'It is our kin!' another was screaming. He balled his fist, shaking it in impotent fury at the purple-coated men who remained at the rear of the advancing throng. 'You'll burn in hell's flames for this, you craven bastards! Burn in hell, I say!'

Along Dam Street they came, the rebel column and their unwilling human shield, until they had reached the causeway that would lead them to the south gate. With each step the captives' cries grew louder. They tried to turn back, but the chains and the weapons and the snarling Parliamentarians kept them moving forwards.

The attackers were progressing towards the gate unhindered, and would be smashing their way through with ram or petard in a matter of minutes. Stryker knew something had to be done, and he looked left and right in search of the Earl of Chesterfield, but, though he could hear the earl's cries of furious derision well enough, he could not see him for the sheer volume of bodies that had climbed up on to the battlements. The platform was crammed with soldiers, all screaming obscenities at the rebels but unwilling to loose a shot lest they put a ball through their womenfolk and children.

Stryker licked the tip of his index finger, holding it aloft. 'Wind's died.'

'Don't!' Barkworth's voice reached him, and Stryker looked down at the small Scot who had taken up position at his side.

'Don't?' Stryker echoed.

'Do not fire upon them, sir. You say you fought in Germany? Then you'll know that too many innocents died in those sieges because neither side spared a thought for the poor bastards.' Barkworth's face was grey with disquiet. 'Do not bring that barbarity here, sir.'

Forrester, Skellen and John Dyott were still in the watchtower when Stryker and Barkworth appeared from the narrow staircase behind them.

'And Brooke was a damned Puritan!' Forrester exclaimed as Stryker went to the ledge next to him. 'You'd think all those high bloody morals would set a man against employing women and children as a living siege work!'

'You're probably right, Forry,' Stryker replied as he looked down upon the streets. Those thoroughfares were busy now, for the townsfolk had appeared in their droves from hitherto barred and shuttered homes, to pour scorn upon the purplecoats. 'But Brooke's gone. Whoever's taken charge clearly does not share the baron's sense of honour.'

Forrester glared down upon the oncoming horde with a rare expression of fury. His usually rose-coloured cheeks were a deep scarlet, and his round, perpetually amused eyes seemed narrower now, as though that which they beheld had sucked the joy from them. 'What can we do?'

'You want us to shoot,' Skellen said suddenly. His face was calm, expressionless, though Stryker detected a strained undertone in his voice. 'Don't you, sir?'

'The wind's dropped,' Stryker said simply.

All eyes were on him now. 'You cannot mean it, old man,' Forrester began. 'We cannot risk hitting one of the civilians. We'd be bloody lynched. It's prepost—'

'Jesu, Forry, will you just do as I damn-well tell you?' Stryker snarled with abrupt ferocity. Forrester's jaw froze where it was, the word left unfinished on his tongue, and Stryker glared at the others on the platform. Barkworth had already said his piece and kept silent, though his face was tense, while Dyott, evidently reading the words as they formed on Stryker's lips, stared at him wide-eyed, a single tear tracing its way down his cheek.

Stryker turned back to the town below them. 'Look!' he pointed to a place just beyond the Close's outer wall. 'They're on the damned causeway. Just yards from the bloody gate. If we don't act now, the rebels will be through and then we're really in trouble. We've killed their general, for Christ's sake! You think they'll let us leave unharmed?'

'I s'pose we've a better chance of success from up 'ere,' Skellen said, and took up his already loaded musket. 'Just have to be a bit careful.'

There was no preamble. No discussion or carefully baited breath. The tall sergeant simply took aim and fired. Out on the causeway a man in purple uniform gave a sharp, terrible cry and fell to the ground, stone dead.

Stryker patted Skellen on the back and loaded his own weapon. The others followed suit.

Down below it was chaos. The men at the Close's high walls were all turning, craning their heads up to see who had had the audacity to fire a shot so near to their tethered kin. A great wail of horror and desperation rose up from the captive crowd outside, driven onwards like a flock of terrified sheep. At their flanks and backs the rebel soldiers jabbed at them all the more aggressively as they realized their strategy was not working entirely as planned. A few gave replying fire up at the tower, but they could not hope to hit the unseen figures.

Stryker eased back his trigger and another purplecoat fell, hands clutched to a kneecap that seemed to pump blood like a fountain. Dyott picked a target with his monstrous iron fowling piece and the result was a twitching Parliamentarian body far below. Forrester's shot found a sergeant's chest, knocking him backwards as though he had been hit by a battering ram, his halberd clattering at the feet of his prisoners.

'Again!' Stryker barked.

Skellen's musket had been reloaded, and he closed an eye as he carefully sighted a man down its barrel. Another purplecoat fell.

Stryker was ready next. He leant over the stone ledge, feeling the old comfort of the wooden stock against his shoulder. He scanned the crowd, desperate to choose a target far enough away from the women and children to ensure that even a poorly aimed shot would not find innocent flesh. It was then that he saw a man dressed differently to the rest. He had the same coat and breeches of purple, but the ensemble was interwoven with silver thread. His falling band collar was a lacy affair, and, now that they were so near the gate, Stryker could even see his sword's impressively ornate hilt and pommel.

Stryker had no idea who the man was, but took him to be the attackers' commanding officer. The well-dressed soldier was positioned behind a middle-aged woman who seemed to pray aloud while she stroked the heads of two terrified children clutched tight to her skirts. He bellowed orders left and right, unconcerned for himself, protected as he was by his walking shield.

Stryker wanted him. He wanted to put a ball in the officer. But it was all too close to risk. The woman was in the way. He'd likely hit her or, worse, the children. But the fury was welling in him now. He had chosen the man he would kill. The barrel wavered out in front of him, hovering around the tethered woman's stoic face, waiting to let its lead fly as soon as she moved out of the way. Stryker watched and waited, holding his breath, his finger curled in preparation around the musket's smooth trigger.

At his flanks, Dyott, Barkworth and Forrester all fired, and more Parliamentarians fell. One of their victims was a musketeer some five or six paces away from the woman blocking Stryker's aim. She instinctively ducked. The officer behind her did not. Stryker shot him in the face.

A great cheer went up then, confusing Stryker at first, for he thought it had come from the attackers, but he soon realized that it was the men on the walls who were celebrating. He knew then that the man he hit must surely have been a senior figure.

As if to confirm the suspicion, the attack began to stall. With impossibly high casualties, a human shield as yet untouched and a sudden lack of positive orders, the

Roundhead drovers were rapidly losing the will to force their screaming livestock any further. Far from providing safe passage to the gate, the slow-moving prisoners had simply ensured that the soldiers were easy targets for the snipers up in the tower.

Whether in response to a new order or simply a collective instinct, Stryker could not tell, but the purplecoats suddenly broke from cover and surged the final few paces towards the Close. It was a final gesture of defiance in the wake of a plan that lacked either honour or success, and Stryker wondered how they planned to make it through the newly bolstered gate. But came they did, more and more, scuttling like crabs, bent low and weaving side to side so as to avoid being caught by the terrifyingly effective snipers high up above.

But it was not the snipers whom they should have feared, for now that they had abandoned the civilian screen they were easy pickings for the earl's men at the walls. Stryker watched implacably as the men below him on the wooden platform let loose a ragged volley that rippled in a great wave across their vengeful ranks.

It was too much for the attackers. A white flag appeared from somewhere – perhaps, Stryker wondered, a piece of shirt taken from one of his early victims – and a helmeted man was waving it frantically. The earl's defenders, so impotent for such a long time, were not inclined to curtail their fury, and more shots spat down from the Close, claiming half a dozen casualties. Eventually, however, the earl and his officers managed to regain control of their unforgiving charges. And all was silent.

CHAPTER 12

'We must look to the north wall, yes?' the Earl of Chesterfield said as the garrison's most senior figures sat around a large table in the Great Hall. Candles burned bright on the stout walls, alleviating the gloom of a night devoid of moonlight or the shimmer of stars, their light smothered by the thick blanket of cloud that hung over the city. It was well past midnight, but the earl had called a council of war in the wake of such an eventful day.

'They have only been concerned with the south thus far, my lord,' one of the assembled officers said in reply. He held a delicate kerchief over his nose to stifle the stench of tallow. The supply of beeswax candles, like so much else in the ill-prepared garrison, had been quickly exhausted.

Sir Richard Dyott was present at the assembly, and he leant forward impatiently. 'But that is surely because they do not know the lie of the land hereabouts.'

Next to Dyott sat a tall, lean man with a clean-shaven chin and a single, grey eye. 'The north wall is really so vulnerable?'

Dyott nodded. 'It is, Captain Stryker. There are no pools that side of the Close, for the ground is too sloped, and our walls there are no higher than seven or eight feet.'

263

'No trouble for a determined assault,' Stryker replied. Once the Parliamentarian attackers had dragged their dead and wounded away from the south gate, releasing the unscathed captives amid jeers and taunts from the high walls, he had returned to the infirmary to check on Lisette. Satisfied that she was recovering well, he had returned to the palace to take up his new-found place as adviser to the earl. It was a strange situation, for many of the council remained wary of him and his companions, but the earl, encouraged by Dyott and Barkworth, had decided to trust him for the moment at least.

Dyott jerked his chin towards the man positioned the other side of Stryker. 'A lofty fellow like Sergeant Skellen, there, could vault it, like as not. It is only a matter of time before the local Parliament men tell their new commander.'

'Thank God they have not thought of it thus far,' the earl said. 'I wonder if their cowardly enterprise with our kin has set a few minds against them, yes?'

Stryker thought the earl might well be right. The advance against the south gate had ended in nothing but blood and humiliation for the purplecoats, and must surely have made enemies of many in the town who might otherwise have offered sympathy. But they could certainly not rely on such a hope. There would doubtless remain plenty of support for the rebels, and one of those folk must surely recommend an attack from the north before long.

'Perhaps we might station Major Edberg's dragoons out by the north wall?' Stryker suggested. 'He would, at least, be in a position to quickly harry any that might come over.'

Edberg was sat, stone still and glowering, at the far end

of the table. He threw Stryker a baleful gaze. 'I do not take orders from criminals.'

Stryker opened his mouth to offer a stinging retort, but Chesterfield thumped his chubby fist on to the table's polished surface. 'Enough of this, Major! Your charge is taken seriously, sir, but the safety of this garrison is paramount.'

'My lord, I do not question your judgement,' Edberg replied, his voice lacking any conviction, 'but my orders were to apprehend the captain.'

'That's as may be, sir,' said the earl, 'but Stryker is a proven expert in warfare, one of only a handful at my disposal. He remains a free man while Lichfield is in danger. And look around you, Major. He can hardly take his leave of this place!'

Edberg tensed at the chorus of sycophantic chortles, but knew there was no benefit in arguing further. His menacing gaze twitched from Chesterfield to Stryker, fury barely restrained. 'North wall, then.'

Shots rang out. They were distant, somewhere outside in the darkness, and the council of war was immediately at an end. Men stood quickly, moving towards the door and the courtyard beyond.

Stryker wondered at first whether Dumb Dyott was still up in the tower, putting his punt gun to good use once more, but there was no way he could pick out targets on such a black night, and Stryker, like the others, began to wonder whether another assault was underway.

The officers, mingling now with their men, who had been roused from fitful sleep by the gunfire, ran quickly across the Close and clambered up the groaning ladders to the walls. They peered out, squinting into the blackness, eager to identify the threat. Sure enough, the night was punctuated by flashes of orange, but those shots were delivered deep within the town in the direction of the south-west.

'Look there!' a voice near Stryker cried out, and he turned with the others to see more flashes, accompanied by more crackling musketry, away to the north-west.

At once it became clear. A force had circled around Lichfield and launched a two-pronged attack against the Roundhead occupiers. Now, in the smallest hours of early morning, battle raged.

'It is king's men!' another voice burst forth excitedly from the mass of bodies on the viewing platform. 'A relief force! We are saved!'

As the Earl of Chesterfield boomed a great huzza, and his garrison cheered until they were hoarse, Stryker turned away from the bright gunshots and bounded down the wooden ladder. When he reached ground level, a hand grasped his shoulder, spinning him round.

'What news?' It was Lancelot Forrester. He and Skellen had been unable to get on to the platform due to the sheer weight of numbers already vying for space, and his eyes were like great spheres in the gloom.

Stryker glanced up at the figures on the walls. 'Someone is attacking Brooke's men.'

Forrester grinned, his teeth shining even whiter than his eyes. 'Thank Christ for that!'

'Go to the kitchens,' Stryker said, already walking away.

'Hungry, sir?' a bemused Skellen called at his officer's back as the pair followed in his wake.

'No. You're fetching supplies and I'm fetching Lisette,' Stryker said hurriedly over his shoulder, 'then we're getting the hell out of this bloody place.'

The trio parted, and Stryker paced quickly along the corridor that would take him to the infirmary and Lisette Gaillard. He thought of her, of taking her out of this House of God that had become a prison, and felt new buoyancy. They had been trapped here by both sides – Roundhead guns without, and Edberg's accusations within – but the distraction caused by the battle raging in the city had suddenly, incredibly, made escape seem tantalisingly achievable.

Stryker's step quickened at the thought. They would take Lisette from her bed – carry her if needs be – and make their way to the north wall. While Chesterfield's garrison were transfixed upon the fight, Stryker and his companions would find a way to flee. He had considered the incredible revelation of the north wall's vulnerability with the mind of a defender, taking the fact that they were so easily scaled as a terrible blow, but, now that this new diversion had presented itself, his thoughts were turning to flight. As he saw the infirmary door up ahead, he allowed a small smile. Freedom was finally within his grasp.

In his reverie, Stryker's instincts were not as sharp as they might have otherwise been, and he failed to notice the figure that stepped into his path until it was too late.

'Alone at last,' Major Henning Edberg said quietly, the tip of his sword nestled beneath Stryker's chin.

NEAR RADBOURN, WARWICKSHIRE, 3 MARCH 1643

Lieutenant Andrew Burton swore viciously as his leather sling snagged on a jagged branch. He freed it with his good hand, trying to still his heaving chest so that he might listen to the night's sounds, but nothing resonated above his own blood as it rushed within his skull.

'Where are you?' he whispered, eyes darting left and right, probing the forest's dark interior for a flicker of movement or the telltale glow of a firearm's match. Nothing.

Burton leaned back on the trunk of the tree that had waylaid him, desperate to catch his breath. For the first time he noticed the cold creeping up his legs, and he realized that his boots and breeches were damp, having absorbed moisture from ground left sodden by thawing snow. Thank God it had not rained, he thought, for his waterproof buff-coat had been jettisoned many hours earlier, a casualty of the need to travel light.

A high-pitched screech snapped the silence somewhere away to his right, and every muscle in Burton's lean frame tensed. He waited for movement to register. Still nothing. Probably a fox, he thought.

He stepped out from the tree, the snapping of twigs beneath his boots sounding excruciatingly cacophonous in the still night, and began to run again. It had been so long, so many hours of running and hiding since that fateful ambush outside an innocuous-looking tavern in Kenilworth. Blaze was dead. They were all dead. He had failed.

A noise some distance behind Burton made him turn. He saw a flicker, nothing definite, but a movement of grey amid the dark oaken boughs, and it made him quicken his step. He stumbled. A branch, a pothole, a rock. He could not tell, such was the blackness shrouding his progress. He hit the earth, good arm breaking his fall amid twigs and ice-cold mulch. No sound yet. Just his own, heaving, agonizing breaths.

Burton hauled himself to his feet. His hunter was gaining once again. He could sense it with every heightened nerve in his body. His useless shoulder ached in the tight leather strap. He gritted his teeth, ignoring the sensation for the trivial distraction it was. His breath steamed out with every laboured lungful, white and hectic in the air about his head. He concentrated on the ground, staring, studying, scrutinizing the narrow animal track lest he falter again. He would push on through the night, as he had the night before, and find a place to hide during daylight, moving ever south and east in search of Oxford and safety.

Now there were sounds. Burton slowed slightly. Turned.

The shot flew high and wide. Burton ducked instinctively, his foot slipped on a patch of wet leaves. He swore again, breaking into a sprint. It was a man, alone and on foot, that ran in his wake. The same man who had tracked him since the ambush. The man he had considered bested until, like a bloodhound after a scent, he would reappear some way behind, tenacious and hungry for the kill. Each time, though, the distance between predator and prey had been great enough for the latter to safely find a place to hide, or simply change direction and throw his pursuer into confusion as he battled to pick up the lost trail. But this time the man had him within pistol shot. He was simply too close to evade.

Perhaps before his injury Burton might have fancied his chances against a single assailant who had evidently abandoned his mount when he plunged into the dense wood after his quarry. But, though the shattered shoulder bone had not become infected, its muscles had never fully regained their strength. They had simply withered so that he could barely move his right hand and could certainly not lift the arm beyond a few degrees. Exhausted, unarmed and crippled, Lieutenant Burton knew his chances of survival were slim.

He ran on, slipping, sliding, chest heaving, heart likely to explode against his ribs. He would not give up. The bullet meant to kill him outside the Two Virgins had whistled several feet above his head, and such a poor shot, Burton told himself, can only have been a sign from God that he was supposed to live. At the very least, he had been given a short reprieve, and he would be damned if he'd give up his life without a fight. That, thought Burton, was the very least Captain Stryker would expect of him.

Lieutenant Josiah Trim thrust the spent pistol back into the holster at his waist. He was a God-fearing man and would not curse, though he sorely felt like it. His horse, a good one, had been left, tethered and ripe for theft, at the edge of the forest, for the dense labyrinth of branch and root was too treacherous for even the trustiest steed.

The soldier some sixty paces up ahead seemed more like a slippery eel than a man. He was only young, Trim had recognized that from the close view he had received during the ambush, but that belied a character that was clearly both resourceful and resolute. Trim had been given a day to track down and dispose of the only man to have escaped the carnage wrought at the Two Virgins, and it had seemed an especially easy task when, during that first night, he had come across the Royalist's lame mount abandoned at the side of the road. But his quarry had proven as adept at evasion on foot as he was at fleeing on horseback, and the day's grace Major Girns had allowed was now stretching into two, such was the difficulty Trim had had in keeping the trail warm. He was angry and he was humiliated.

He upped his pace as best he could. Leaping exposed roots, kicking away thickets of brown bracken, he did not take his focus from the grey form of the Royalist up ahead. It was a moonless night, made even darker by the thick canopy of leaf and branch above, but as long as he kept up this pace, the distant figure would gradually resolve from the gloom. He drew a second pistol.

Burton scrambled through the blackness. The hunter was gaining rapidly, for his fresh legs were powering through the cloying earth in a way Burton could never hope to match with his numb limbs. He hoped and prayed that his pursuer had exhausted his only weapon already, but somehow he doubted such optimism, and he weaved in and out of stout trunks, desperate to make himself a moving target for the next shot.

He toppled over the brow of the escarpment before he even knew it was there. The ground simply vanished from beneath him as Burton made to plant his right foot on the wet earth, and he pitched forwards, toppling into what felt like oblivion. For a moment he wondered if this was the journey to the next life. Perhaps, he wondered, a pistol ball had finally found its mark and he was already floating into a black abyss. But then he saw trees to his left and right, racing, spiralling, plummeting past him in a blur of greens and browns, and he realized he was falling.

Burton hit the ground hard. He tumbled in ragged cartwheels for what seemed like an hour, knees, head, back, elbows bouncing against the ground in turns. When he finally came to rest, he clutched a hand to his stomach, certain his guts had been impaled by the flapping sword at his waist, but thankfully the scabbard had protected him from anything more than a sickening bruise.

He stood gingerly, feeling each aching part of his torso for a break or cut, but finding nothing of note. His mind was slow, as though the heavy clouds had covered his wits as well as the moon and stars, and it took several moments for the memory of recent days to regain, image by image, some semblance of clarity. He remembered Blaze and Rontry, their faces terrified as shots, pouring down from on high, had enfiladed the small convoy. He remembered seeking shelter behind poor Bruce, heard again the sharp report of a single musket shot that flew so close to his head. And then the memory of a scrambled, frenzied escape came back to him in a horrific flood. The dazed, half-lame horse he had taken from the scene, the feeling that vengeful enemies would run him to ground at any moment.

And then he remembered this night. The race through the woods. The shot at his back. The man he had first seen on the black line of the horizon, who had expertly tracked him to this place.

Burton tilted back his head, eyes climbing the escarpment all the way back to the high crest. And there, at the very top, stood a figure.

'Thank you, Lord,' Lieutenant Josiah Trim prayed aloud as he reached the ridge. How he had thought to slow his chase at the moment when the ground sloped sharply away was nothing short of a miracle. His quarry had clearly not been so blessed, for Trim had caught a brief glimpse of the man at the foot of the small hill. That man vanished into shadow again, but, Trim thought as he jogged carefully down the steep gradient, to have fallen all the way down would have left the fellow stunned, if not seriously wounded.

Trim held out the pistol in front of him, ready to pull the trigger immediately now that the range was more reasonable. He scanned the darkness, the trees and bushes on either side of the slope's foot, hoping to catch a glimpse of the Cavalier fugitive and thus to finally bring an end to this awful, bloody enterprise. He had not wanted to kill. Captain Cromwell had recommended him to Girns only as a tracker, but the zeal that drove his new master was both frightening and infectious. Trim did not wish to disappoint the major – or anger him – and found himself agreeing to join the Kenilworth ambush. But that first killing he had committed seemed to stab like a vast dagger at his heart and soul. When it came to letting his second shot fly, Trim had panicked, lost his nerve, and lost his aim. The humiliation burned in him. At least now he would make amends.

A rustling sound carried to Trim's keen ear. He spun to where it originated, a patch of mouldering bracken some ten paces away, and levelled the gun. 'Come out, sir!'

A second noise, louder this time, rang out from the trees further to his left, startling him, and Trim turned nimbly to face the possible threat. He was face down in the damp forest soil before he could blink, a great, irresistible force pressing against his back and head. The gun fired into the ground at his side, his mouth and nostrils filled with suffocating mud. Trim tried to fight back. He bucked and writhed and squirmed against the weight, but he was dazed and weakened from that first collision, and each second of denied air saw his strength wane further, as if it were being sapped directly into the ground by some unknown force.

Andrew Burton near pissed his breeches when his unsheathed blade had brushed some of the bracken within which he was concealed. To his horror, the noise had carried to the Roundhead gunman, and that man's reflexes were proven impressively sharp when Burton saw the pistol levelled almost precisely in line with his face.

So Burton had tossed the sword away, hoping that his pursuer would not see its path of flight, only hear when it came to rest. As soon as the man's eyes darted sideways to assess that new sound, Burton had burst forth from the bracken like an avenging angel, clattering into the Parliamentarian with all his weight, all the force and fury he could muster, knocking the man to the floor and the breath from his lungs.

It was not easy to keep the stunned body beneath his own, not least because Burton could only bring one arm to bear, but he was bigger and more powerful than the man who had hitherto been his hunter, and he dug his knees between his enemy's shoulder blades and clamped his effective hand on the back of the jerking skull.

Burton's reactions were instinctive, thinking only of avoiding a pistol ball in the face, and he had certainly not planned to choke the Roundhead soldier to death. But as the thrashing became weaker, and the resistance gradually dissolved into a series of pathetic twitches, the lieutenant realized that was exactly what he had achieved.

Burton waited, unwilling to relent until he could be sure of the outcome. He pressed down on the back of the man's head, driving the face into the soaking mud, grinding nose, eyes, chin ever downwards with his last ounce of strength. After what must have been several minutes, he sat back, hands shaking with shock and relief. It was over.

LICHFIELD, STAFFORDSHIRE, 3 MARCH 1643

'They'll join me any moment.'

The thick bristles of Major Henning Edberg's moustache twitched upwards as his lip rose in an unpleasant smirk. 'Your lackeys?' He shook his head. 'Not before I am done, Captain.'

Stryker's hands were raised, palms open and vertical, his eye darting between the poised blade and its malevolent master. 'You would murder me here? In the Close?'

'Self-defence,' Edberg said, evidently sensing the surprise in Stryker's voice. 'You came at me, but were bested by the superior swordsman.'

'But why?'

'It is my duty,' Edberg replied casually.

Stryker almost laughed. 'To arrest me, perhaps, but why is it your bloody duty to see me dead, Major? I do not believe the Prince ordered such a course.'

Edberg's face was set hard, though Stryker saw a spark of amusement in the blue eyes. 'The *Prince*,' he spat on the floor between them. 'Irrelevant.'

Stryker was taken aback. 'Irrelevant? It was he ordered my imprisonment!'

'And he wants you returned, for sure,' Edberg replied, 'but not dead.'

'Then what—' A thought came to Stryker then, and the question remained stillborn on his lips. 'Crow.'

'*Colonel* Crow,' Edberg corrected, 'gives me my orders, not that fucking Bohemian popinjay. And the colonel says you are a devil. He wants your hide for a new scabbard.'

So, Stryker thought, Crow had gone above Rupert's head in this, dispatching Edberg on the pretence of recapturing the fugitives, but all the while expecting their deaths. 'Forrester and Skellen will likely arrive together, Edberg. The two will be a tougher proposition than I alone.'

'Colonel Crow gives not a cat's arse for them, Stryker. Only you.'

'I do not understand,' Stryker began, but Edberg jerked the blade forwards suddenly, so that he could feel the cold steel just below his chin.

'You will die and I will receive praise for disposing of a dangerous criminal. But before then . . .' The tall Swede's gaze moved away from Stryker, and the captain realized that he was staring at the infirmary door, some ten paces further along the corridor. Edberg looked back to his captive and winked, 'I shall take a far more pleasurable reward.'

'I am no man's reward, you hog-stinking bloody Viking,' Lisette Gaillard's voice rang loud in the enclosed space.

The noise startled Stryker, for he could not see where the Frenchwoman stood, and the sound had not come from the direction of the infirmary. But Henning Edberg seemed even more surprised. The big dragoon's eyes, like bright globes of glass in the gloom, were expanding in circumference, widening with shock and horror. Stryker watched as his frame seemed to stiffen and his jaw quivered as he gritted his teeth.

'Lower your sword, sir,' Lisette's confident voice ordered. 'Unless you wish to be gut-shot here and now.'

Stryker looked on as the stunned Edberg reluctantly dropped the long blade, letting it clatter on to the stone floor at his feet. 'Romish bitch.'

Like a ghostly apparition, Lisette emerged from behind Edberg. She was deathly pale, the white smock she wore only serving to increase the wraithlike appearance, but the dag in her hand was primed and steady. 'I have been called worse,' she said, moving round to stand beside the Englishman.

Edberg seemed to be weighing up his chances. His venom-filled gaze raked across Lisette and Stryker in turn, studying for weaknesses. Eventually his eyes met the gun's black barrel. They rested there for a heartbeat, eventually ascertaining that it was steady as rock. 'Shoot then, whore.'

Lisette raised the dag so that the shot would pulverize the dragoon's face.

'No,' Stryker said, raising a hand to take hold of Lisette's arm. 'Not like this.'

Lisette shot him a withering glance. '*Merde*, Stryker, he would have run you through. Let me kill the bastard.'

Stryker shook his head. 'Killing is what caused this mess in the first place.' For a moment the Frenchwoman did not move as she decided whether or not to obey. 'I insist,' Stryker added, applying pressure to her forearm.

Edberg stooped to pick up his sword as the weapon was lowered. Wordlessly, but with an audible outbreath, he backed away quickly, slipping into the shadows of the palace complex.

Lisette glared angrily at Stryker, muttered something rancorous in her native tongue, and promptly collapsed into his arms.

The new dawn did not herald a lifting of the siege. The night's action, it transpired, was a fleeting attack made by a local force of Cavaliers.

'Blind Hastings,' the earl's man, Simeon Barkworth, explained as Stryker, Forrester and Skellen met him in the central tower. The little Scot's face flushed suddenly and he looked out on to the streets and houses. 'I—that is to say—'

'That is to say,' Forrester interrupted, shooting Stryker a playful wink, 'that he resembles our good captain?'

Barkworth could not bear to meet any of their gazes. 'I am sorry. A poor choice of words. It is simply what people call him.'

'No matter,' Stryker said, remembering his accidental betrayal of emotion at hearing John Dyott's common name and promising himself to lock such feeling deep down this time. 'Is he like me?'

'Colonel Hastings lost an eye at the war's outset, sir, yes. Wears a patch now.'

'What of him?' Skellen said impatiently.

'He leads a troop of horse in the region,' Barkworth said, ignoring Skellen's curt tone. 'Spends his time harrying Roundheads wherever he might find them. The skirmish last night was his work.'

'But he did not win?' Stryker asked.

Barkworth winced. 'Hastings is not famed for standing firm, sir. He lives by his wits, hits the enemy hard and retires to fight another day. His purpose was to inflict casualties, not liberate the Close.'

'Then we are no nearer an end,' said Stryker, gazing out on Lichfield's streets. He raked his gaze from right to left, starting at the Bishop's Pool, crossing the marketplace and Sadler Street behind it, then to Dam Street. There was plenty of commotion, for the townsfolk were forced to continue their ordinary lives while the besiegers settled to their task, but there was also the busy comings and goings of soldiers. St Mary's, the cathedral's smaller cousin, seemed a hive of activity, purple-coated soldiers moving in and out, issuing orders, performing musket and pike evolutions. But this morning it was not simply men in uniforms of purple and buff leather that scurried like ants. There were other men now, most clothed in coats of grey. Reinforcements, Barkworth explained, had come with Brooke's replacement.

'Sir John Gell,' Barkworth said. 'He was a great enemy of my earl and his father before him. It was the bastard Gell who chased us from Bretby Park.'

Stryker looked at the little man. 'I'd wager you would not have abandoned the house,' he said wryly.

'Perhaps not,' Barkworth conceded. 'But it was not my order to give.' He gazed down at the drilling Parliamentarians. 'Gell is a real bastard. A bully of a man. A vicious piece of lamb's puke with the morals of a gong scourer and the pretensions of a gentry cove. He is more Cavalier than the men you'll find with the King in Oxford. If you see him, straight-backed and proud on his horse, and covered in gilt plate and silver lace . . .'

'Shoot the bugger?' Skellen said.

Barkworth nodded. 'Shoot the bugger.'

'Christ,' Stryker said, staring out on the town but thinking of Lisette. Of how she had risked her own health to save him from Edberg.

'Thank God you gave her that bloody pistol, eh?' Forrester said, as if reading Stryker's thoughts.

Stryker nodded. 'After Brooke's death, Edberg accosted me in the courtyard. There was something in his manner – something more dangerous than before. It made me think to give her a pistol.'

'Just as well,' Skellen said. His voice dropped suddenly so that Barkworth could not hear. 'But we're still stuck in this bloody place.'

The night's exertions had taken a heavy toll on Lisette and now, with Chambers as attentive as ever, she was back asleep in the infirmary. This time, though, there was a pair of sentries at the door, ordered there by Barkworth.

'I am sorry I could not do more,' said the Scot. 'Just as the earl requires the three of you at his disposal, he requires Edberg and his yellowcoats. He will ignore what transpires between you for the good of the garrison.' Barkworth fell silent for perhaps a minute, before finally looking up at Stryker. 'Sir,' he said, his voice more sheepish than usual, 'I have not had chance to thank you.'

Stryker looked away from the city to meet Barkworth's sallow eyes, and thought of his vicious thrashing as he had dragged the enraged Scot away from the fight on Dam Street. 'I saved you from your own stupidity.'

'Aye,' Barkworth murmured, cheeks red as he stared at the ground between them. 'Thank you, anyway. And it was a pleasure fighting beside real soldiers again.' He looked at Skellen. 'Even this long streak o' piss.'

Skellen snorted. 'You ain't half bad neither,' he said turning his attention to the north-east, 'for a stumpy lump o' Scotch cow dung.'

Barkworth grinned and made to return the compliment, but immediately saw that Skellen was interested in something in the distance. 'What is it?'

Skellen did not look round. 'Movement.' He pointed to a little church that rose from the fields beyond a vast body of water known as Stowe Pool. 'A lot of movement. Out there.'

All eyes followed the sergeant's lead. Brooke's lads had garrisoned the church, but now their usual drilling was being augmented by teams of men carrying ladders to a point beside the church where they were depositing them in one large pile.

'They're preparing a storming party,' Forrester voiced what all the others were thinking.

'But they've already gone for us once, even hid behind women and chil'en, and got their arses tanned,' Skellen replied.

'They're not going to scale the south wall,' Stryker said quietly.

'Aye, sir, you're in the right of it,' Barkworth agreed in his croaking tone. 'It is as we feared. They've discovered the nature of our north wall. We must go tell the earl at once. Sir?'

Stryker was still staring down at Stowe church. Between that smaller building and the great cathedral there ran a single lane. After several seconds he turned to Barkworth. 'That road,' he said, indicating the lane and Stowe church beyond with an outstretched finger, 'is barely visible beneath the trees.'

'Aye, sir,' Barkworth confirmed. 'Gaia Lane is no more than an ancient track. It is sunk between high banks and overhung by thick branches.'

'Then let us visit your earl. I believe we have our plan.'

Stryker ordered Sergeant Skellen to stay in the lofty vantage point, tasked with keeping an eye on the happenings at Stowe church, while the rest went to engage the earl.

Barkworth, the nimblest of the three, scurried down the steep spiral stairs like a rat down a drain, and was already explaining what they had seen to Stanhope by the time Stryker and Forrester had emerged from the cathedral.

To Stryker's relief, Chesterfield's jowls were wobbling in a vigorous nod. He went to approach the earl to finalize the plan, but was brought to a sudden halt by a great cry of alarm from the defenders at the walls.

'Jesu, what now?' Stryker hissed, as he climbed the ladders once again.

To his horror and surprise the Parliamentarians were advancing on the south gate once again. And once again they were cowering behind a mob of wailing women and children.

'Have they not learned a single bloody thing?' Forrester exclaimed. He was standing at Stryker's side, mouth agape.

Stryker turned inwards, watching a group of musketeers make their way into the cathedral. They were doubtless en route to the central tower to play the role of snipers, just as he and the others had done during that first assault. He hoped those men could shoot well enough.

'My lord, please!' The voice belonged to Simeon Barkworth. The Scot was standing below the platform next to the Earl of Chesterfield, both peering through knots in the planks of the wooden gate as the action unfolded.

'I will not risk civilian lives, Simeon!' Chesterfield was saying.

Barkworth turned to his earl, arms gesticulating manically. 'But it is not as before, sir. They're moving quicker. Look, sir, there are no chains.'

Stryker peered back over the parapet and realized that the little man was right. This was not the painfully slow progress that had marked the previous day's failed assault. The captives were unchained and moved at a rapid pace over the causeway, prodded onwards by the blades of snarling rebels. The enemy had clearly learned that to linger was to be shot.

'They mean to burn the drawbridge, my lord!' Barkworth was saying now, his voice urgent, beseeching.

It was then that Stryker saw the fiery iron pots carried by some of the rebels, flames licking hungrily over the tops of the dark vessels, and realized that they were brim full of blazing tar. 'Jesu,' he said, turning back to the nearest ladder and clambering down as fast as he could manage.

'Let me out there, my lord!' Barkworth was saying when Stryker reached him and the earl.

'Are you mad, sir?' Chesterfield exclaimed. 'I'll not drop the damned drawbridge!'

The attackers were at the gates now. One or two had been picked off by the snipers in the tower, but enough – perhaps thirty or forty – had made it to the great gate and its sturdy drawbridge. They were so close that the men above them could not lean far enough over the battlements to shoot down at them with any efficacy. The captives now cowered either side of the drawbridge, backs flush against the stone wall, weeping and screaming and praying, while the Roundheads stooped at the drawbridge's base, setting their tar pots beside the timbers.

'It is only a matter of time before the planks ignite!' Stryker said, stepping between the earl and his personal guard. 'If you do not drop it, my lord, the rebels will burn it to ashes, and then they will be through for certain. Let us attempt to preserve the Close, sir, at the very least.'

Stryker did not know whether it was a sudden understanding of the situation that stirred the earl to action, or whether it was the aggressiveness of his tone, but Chesterfield unexpectedly turned to the men manning the drawbridge. 'Drop the bridge! Drop the bridge!' He turned to Stryker. 'Lay into them, Captain, yes?' His fat hand grasped Stryker's sleeve in an impressively strong grip. 'If you fail in this, I will hold you personally responsible, sir.'

Stryker glanced at the hand, then up at Chesterfield's dark eyes. 'If I fail in this, I'll be dead, my lord.'

He turned away. There were, he estimated, perhaps threescore of the earl's men immediately at his disposal, the rest still crowded on the walls, firing down impotently at the invaders vertically below. He sucked air into his lungs and, as a great creak hailed the lowering of the drawbridge, bellowed into the cold air. 'To me! To me! Out, out, out!'

The drawbridge smashed down on to the causeway, accompanied by the rapidly stunted cries of rebel soldiers caught beneath its terrible weight.

Stryker was first out, followed closely by Simeon Barkworth. He knew Forrester would be there amid the dozens that came in their wake, but could not see him.

It all happened so quickly that only a few of the defenders had stopped to load their muskets, so it was with swords drawn that Stryker's improvised band of marauders met the first of the Parliament men.

Stryker almost ran on to a waiting blade, such was the speed at which he bounded towards the causeway. A stocky sergeant had levelled the tuck at his throat, and in his eagerness Stryker only just managed to duck below it. But duck he did, and his own weapon was stabbing at the man's guts. The sergeant's buff-coat was evidently of good quality, for the steel failed to penetrate, but the sheer weight of the blow forced him to double over and Stryker kicked him in the face.

The next man came on, but Stryker parried his sword-strike and twisted away from the reverse swing, only to barge into another enemy. The pair fell to the ground amid crashing metal and snarled oaths. Stryker had dropped his sword, but managed to free a hand from the tangle of limbs and drew a dagger from his boot. He stabbed the Roundhead twice in the face. The first blow glanced off the bridge of the man's nose, scouring a great gash along his cheek. The second plunged into his eye, and the man fell suddenly limp.

Stryker scrambled to his feet just as the Parliamentarian whose blow he had initially parried came back to finish the job. Stryker, armed only with his dagger, stood his ground, even as the oncoming man grinned maliciously.

'Nice try, you bat-fowling bastard!' Barkworth's voice roared from behind the Parliamentarian, and the man fell, bloodied steel protruding from his throat.

Stryker nodded his thanks and stooped to retrieve his sword. Straightening, he looked left and right for more enemies to face, but, as rapidly as it had begun, the fight fizzled out and Parliament's attackers fled back towards the town.

The causeway was littered with the carnage of the skirmish. Iron pots of tar were kicked unceremoniously into the Minster Pool, and the wounded purplecoats were skewered where they lay. The sound of violence was replaced by weeping and, as one, the Lichfield men remembered their captive families, still huddled in terrified groups against the walls.

Stryker pointed his sword at the white-faced civilians. 'Get them inside! Now!' He cast his gaze around the triumphant Royalists, still basking in the glory of the small victory. 'No rest, lads! There is more work for us to do yet!' He looked at Barkworth, noticing the way the little man's eyes shone like a cat's on a moonlit night. 'We must to Gaia Lane at once. They will be looking to the north wall while our attention is fixed here.'

CHAPTER 13

Stryker, Forrester and Barkworth were leading more than a hundred garrison men across the expanse of the Close's yard when they were intercepted.

'Well?' Stryker snapped.

'Wagon's ready, sir,' Sergeant William Skellen announced casually as he fell into step beside his officer. 'They piled all them ladders on it while you was busy brabblin'.'

'How many?'

'Praps fifty troopers at a pinch, sir,' Skellen said, a glint in his hooded eye.

Stryker nodded. 'Let's get over that damned wall before they reach us then, eh?'

Skellen snorted. 'Old Chessy-field's lettin' us take the bastards on then, sir?'

'Do not be so surprised, Sergeant,' Barkworth growled, ever ready to leap to his master's defence, 'he is not the pissabreech you take him for.'

Skellen glanced down at the Scot and his mouth split into a brown-toothed grin. 'Don't know about that, friend, but I know you certainly ain't.' He slapped Barkworth hard between the shoulders. 'Let's have at 'em, eh?'

Barkworth shot him a grin of his own.

Brothers of the Blade, Stryker thought. They were to be found in the unlikeliest of places.

The wall was manned by Major Edberg's yellowcoats, and they parted like the Red Sea to allow the task force through. Edberg was nowhere to be seen, but Stryker knew he would be there, staring, assessing. But there was no time to think of him. Stryker picked the tallest man, Skellen, to clamber over first. He threaded his fingers together, making a step for Skellen's boot, and gave the sergeant a leg up, heaving him on to the wall's apex. For all his great height, a lifetime's campaigning had made Skellen as supple as any man, and he straddled the wall with ease, swinging his trailing leg over swiftly and landing on the opposite side in near silence.

'He's like some gigantic cat,' Barkworth said, impressed with Skellen's agility.

'Lazy as a bloody cat as well,' Forrester responded dryly.

'Next,' a disembodied voice carried to them. 'And I've an ache in me back, so no blubber-guts!'

The men at the walls grinned, and Stryker was thankful for a sergeant who always knew how to diffuse the tension.

Stryker cupped his hands again, helping the next man over the wall. He could hear Skellen speaking to him as the sergeant helped bring the soldier down. He stooped again, beckoning another to make the ascent, Forrester and half a dozen others following suit. Each man safely across the stone barrier turned to help their comrades across, and the Royalist force was quickly assembled on the narrow lane that ran flush against the north wall.

Forrester was last across, and he scowled at the groaning of the men who helped him down. 'It is muscle!' he bleated indignantly. 'Muscle, damn your impudence!'

A ripple of laughter swept across the throng. Stryker raised his hands for quiet. 'Take a moment to make ready your muskets,' he said, addressing the entire group. 'We have the advantage of numbers, but they are experienced fighting men and will be difficult to overcome at close quarters. If we come at them with shot first, there will be little need for steel.' He looked into the faces of Lichfield's defenders and saw a mixture of apprehension and fatigue. These were not veterans of Europe. Not the kind of men used to death and depredation. But they had proved themselves hardy during this long day of turmoil, and he felt a surprising pride in each one. 'You must trust me in this! Look to Sergeant Skellen and Captain Forrester for your lead. Watch your own Master Barkworth, too. Do as they do, and we will overcome, you have my word.'

When muskets were loaded and matches lit, Stryker led his makeshift troop at a rapid trot north-eastwards along Gaia Lane. They ran in the direction of Stowe church, knowing they risked meeting the Roundhead storming party at any time, but praying that they would find a suitable place for an ambush before such a clash took place.

The lane started as a narrow track but widened as it went, all the while sinking into the fields either side, so that, eventually, the men's progress was flanked by steep, forested banks. The afternoon light grew weaker by the moment, and it almost seemed like night had fallen, such was the dense coverage from the overhanging canopy.

After around a hundred paces, Stryker waved left and right, signalling for the force to split. Stryker led half the group to the right, while Forrester commanded those who went left. Both parties climbed their respective bank, wading through the tangled roots and bushes near the foot of the slope, becoming entirely immersed in the dense trees higher up.

Stryker's fifty or so men dropped to a kneeling position as soon as they were satisfied with the cover provided by bush and trunk, and threaded the musket barrels through the foliage so that their leaden packages could be brought to bear on the rutted track below. He knew the same actions would be simultaneously carried out on the opposite bank.

He checked his match one more time, careful that the priming pan was closed so as to avoid prematurely firing the weapon. The length was good, and, as the cold seeped from the wet mud to creep up the fabric at his knees, he blew on the glowing tip, keeping its stored venom alive.

The Royalists did not have to wait long. Voices carried to them from further along Gaia Lane, voices joined in short order by the squelching of boots, the sound carrying to them with eerie clarity as it echoed between the steep banks. And then, after what seemed to Stryker like hours but was probably only a matter of minutes, the front ranks of the Parliamentarian force came into view. They marched with steady purpose, backs straight and muskets shouldered. As Skellen had estimated, there were just short of fifty troopers in all, and in their wake trundled a large cart, piled high with the ladders the sergeant had spotted stored on the land adjacent to Stowe church.

'Jesu,' Stryker hissed when he saw the cart's driver. He was not armed or protected by steel and buff-hide, but clothed in a simple russet smock. This was no soldier, but a common man, the owner of the vehicle and the pair of horses that drew it. His face was pale as a summer cloud, and it was clear that the armed men sat at his rear were tasked with ensuring he did not try to escape. It was too late to issue new orders to Chesterfield's waiting men, and Stryker silently prayed that they would not mistake the carter – present only under extreme duress – as a legitimate target.

The soldiers and their lumbering wagon came ever closer, wide wheels bouncing in and out of potholes and over roots, horses whickering, scabbards and bandoliers clinking, boots trudging.

Stryker had decreed that no man was to fire before him, his shot being the signal to launch the ambush, and he waited until the very last moment. Only when the seven or eight ranks had marched past his position did he pull the trigger. And the world erupted.

The Parliamentarians did not stand a chance. Musketballs rained down from the banks of Gaia Lane as though part of some great biblical judgement. Stryker's men came with fire and brimstone upon the screaming inhabitants of a bridleway that had become the focus of God's judgement. It seemed as though every rebel was hit, some falling stone dead in that first volley, others winged in arm or leg, spun around and dumped into the mud by unseen assailants.

Stryker stood, reversed his musket, and descended into the roadway, jabbing the wooden stock into the first face – that of a kneeling rebel – he encountered. The man crumpled, blood and bits of teeth spraying up Stryker's fingers and sleeves, and Stryker stepped over him, seeking out more enemies.

The rest of the Royalist party were with him now, having followed him down from the right-hand bank or streamed down in Forrester's wake from the slope opposite. They overwhelmed the bewildered Roundheads, strode amongst them, stabbed with blades and battered with muskets.

Stryker reloaded his long-arm quickly, scanning a scene of such carnage that it shocked even him. He peered some distance along the lane, and was pleased to see the carter's back, the man sprinting away down the road in terrified flight.

The sight of the man reminded him of the wagon, and he looked back to the ladder-piled vehicle. An enemy soldier, ragged trail of blood glistening at his temple, had jumped up into the carter's place and was scrabbling around for the reins. Stryker nestled his musket in the strong muscles of his shoulder, took careful aim, and fired the shot. The man rose into the air with sudden violence, snatched back off the seat as the ball took him square in the chest. He crashed into the myriad of rungs behind, the cracking and splintering wood providing strange accompaniment to his final, short-lived scream.

The sounds of battle quickly died. Those rebel soldiers left in the melee were cut down without quarter, while the handful still unhurt scrambled away from the scene, running pell-mell back in the direction of Stowe church. Clanging steel and igniting gunpowder and snarled oaths were replaced by the sickening, despairing moans of grievously wounded men. Stryker spun on his heels, surveying the destruction. To his amazement, not a single man under his command had received anything greater than a flesh wound. By contrast, the Parliamentarian troopers had been utterly annihilated.

'Skellen,' Stryker called.

His sergeant, unflustered and indestructible as ever, emerged from the mass of tired but exultant men. 'Sir.'

Stryker used the still-smoking barrel of his musket to point at the wagon. 'Unhitch the nags and burn those bloody ladders.' He turned full circle so as to catch the eye of as many of Lichfield's garrison as possible. 'Well done, lads! Well done indeed! Now, let's get this place cleared and go home!'

Nightfall brought with it respite, for the Parliamentarian besiegers launched no more assaults in the rainy darkness.

'They chirp like a nest full o' chicks,' William Skellen complained as he joined Stryker and Forrester in the infirmary.

'Leave them to their joy, Sergeant,' Forrester chided gently. 'They're surrounded, and beleaguered, but they've beaten the rebels back time and again. They've even killed the enemy general, no less! Our friends believe those small victories, and Saint Chad's boundless blessings, have knocked the fight out of the Parliament men.'

Skellen gave his derisive snort. 'The bastards ain't attacking 'cause it's pissin' down with rain. What good's powder when it's damp as a gander's arse?'

Stryker looked up from where he dabbed a damp cloth at Lisette's brow. 'And they'll be looking outwards tonight in case Hastings pays them another visit.'

Skellen grimaced, drew his sword, and sat down heavily on the end of a palliasse. He rummaged in his snapsack for a whetstone and began honing the steel, but his movements did not carry their usual smooth efficiency.

Stryker watched his old comrade carefully. 'You'll slice off your fingers if you keep jerking that bloody stone.'

Skellen paused and looked up. 'Sir?'

'What is it, Sergeant?'

'The earl sent out a party, 'bout an hour ago.'

'Oh? Where?'

'Back up on Gaia Lane.' Skellen leaned forward, his tight-skinned face and dark eye sockets appearing all the more demonic in the infirmary's gloom. 'To retrieve the ironwork from all them ladders we torched. If Chessy-field's willin' to risk his precious men collecting up scrap like a bunch of bloody magpies, we're runnin' proper low on supplies.' Stryker took a moment to consider the implication, but Skellen went on relentlessly, determined to air his grievances. 'And I've just heard we're down to the last o' that swine-feed bread.' He shook his head angrily. 'This siege has been goin', what, two days? And we're about to starve! He's made no provision at all. None!'

'Let us make our escape tonight . . .' A new voice broke the ensuing silence, its tone soft and exotic.

Stryker looked down at Lisette Gaillard. He smiled, but shook his head. 'We cannot.'

'Why not?' Lisette said indignantly. 'We would have been away from this godforsaken hole last night were it not for Edberg waylaying us.'

'It was not Edberg waylaid us, Lisette. You swooned after being on your feet for only moments.'

She scowled petulantly. 'I went for a long walk. Of course I was tired.'

'It was a short walk,' Stryker retorted, finality edging his voice. 'You are simply not well enough to travel. And

294

besides, we had but one opportunity to get over the wall while Sir Henry Hastings drew all eyes to him.'

'You said he might attack again tonight,' Lisette said hopefully.

Stryker nodded. 'Aye, but now Edberg watches the north wall. We could never cross through with his yellow-coats swarming at its foot.'

'What of the earl?' Lisette asked, unwilling to let the argument go. 'He trusts you now. Tell him you have an urgent message for the King. You must take your leave tonight!'

Forrester chortled ruefully. 'A message to be delivered by all four of us?'

Lisette glared at Forrester, and he suddenly found the need to study his boots.

'Chesterfield grants us liberty within Cathedral Close,' Stryker said, diffusing the tension, 'because it suits him to have use of our swords. But he does not trust us.'

'Fortunately,' Forrester added, 'he does not trust Edberg either.'

'Aye, but he'll nevertheless hand us straight back to the Prince if we survive this siege.'

'So the fact remains,' Lisette said. 'We must escape.'

NEAR PRESCOTE, OXFORDSHIRE, 4 MARCH 1643

Lieutenant Andrew Burton forced his weary body onwards. Not wishing to trust his fortunes to the open highway, he had traced the west bank of the River Cherwell southwards through the blackest depths of the night and all of the next day, never stopping, ever watchful for more men tracking his footsteps.

The previous night he had reached a point where the deep waterway swept away to the west in a great arc. After several hours searching for a way across, he had chanced upon a little ford of piled pebbles, and spent the rest of the time before dawn trudging through the high grass of untilled fields awaiting, as his reasonable knowledge of geography told him, the time when the river would rejoin him on the north–south trajectory.

Sure enough, around mid morning he had seen a glistening silver snake on the horizon. A surge of relief flowed through his veins, and he quickened his pace as best his tired limbs would allow, for the Cherwell was his key to survival. It would show him the way south, to the next Royalist safe haven, Banbury. Of course, having made his crossing, he was now on the eastern bank – the wrong bank – but he and the regiment had spent a brief spell in Banbury following Kineton Fight and he remembered that a stone bridge joined east and west at the nearby village of Cropredy. There, Burton told himself, was where he would get back over to the Banbury side. After resting at Banbury, he would push on to Oxford, and the closer he came to the king's new capital, the nearer he knew he was to safety.

Now, as the winter sun set at its wan afternoon zenith, a grumble of hooves reached him. It was low and pulsating, like distant rolling thunder, and he dismissed it at first as the rushing sound of the thaw-swollen waterway. But the thunder grew, slowly but steadily, and it was punctuated by voices, lightning bolts striking fear into Burton's heart.

He had been tracing the path of an ancient animal track through some dense woodland, rather than strolling out in the open, and he was able to duck behind a mesh of branches before any horseman came into sight. He prayed that these newcomers would not be Parliament men, all the while inwardly scolding himself for staying quite so close to the river. The great natural guide would suddenly become a great natural barrier at his back, should he be discovered.

The lieutenant stayed frozen in place, ignoring the cold and the perpetual ache at his shoulder. He allowed himself only sparrow-like breaths, sharp and shallow, his mouth parched to the point of pain.

Could these be the soldiers who had sent the man to track him?

Burton's heart hammered loud and clear so that the pulse in his skull almost matched the noise of the horses.

He had not possessed the strength to bury the man's body. What if they had discovered it, face still pressed into the mud?

After four or five tense minutes, Burton finally laid eyes on the horsemen. Crouching and concealed as he was, his view was limited, and he could only catch fleeting glimpses of riders and beasts as they cantered along a wider track running parallel to the one he had followed, some fifty paces away.

Burton was exhausted, and his eyes stung and streamed, bathing everything in a surreal blur, but he could see that it was a half-troop, perhaps some forty-five men. They were definitely Roundheads, for flickers of orange carried to him from ribbons and sashes at arm and chest, and all were swathed in the pale yellow of new buff-leather coats, with flared skirts and thinner, flexible sleeves. These were new recruits, he reckoned, freshly raised and bankrolled by some benevolent – and wealthy – patron. The image was further bolstered by the gleaming plate each rider wore at back and breast, and by the helmets adorned with flexible lobster-tails to protect the owner's neck.

Burton felt a pang of relief. They were an impressive force, well equipped and eager-looking, but, above all, they were part of a fledgling troop. And that made affiliation with the professional killers who had ambushed Burton and his men with such devastating efficacy extremely unlikely.

Burton stayed low. The troop might not have been searching for him specifically, but he would still be captured as an enemy of Parliament; or worse, if they took him for a spy.

'Go on,' Burton whispered, the leaves at his face quivering against his breath. 'Go on, you bastards. Ride away.'

The horsemen were nearly all past him now. His eyes began to sting again, racked with tiredness and the rigours of being forced open during this new alert. He raised a hand, rubbing the lids, feeling beads of moisture tumble from their corners, and, when they felt a little better, he glanced up again.

And realized the sashes and ribbons were not, in fact, orange. They were red.

LICHFIELD, STAFFORDSHIRE, 4 MARCH 1643

The Royalist garrison and their families gathered in the Great Hall of the Bishop's Palace for what victuals the womenfolk could muster. There was not a great deal to divide between hungry mouths that – since the rescue of the captives during the enemy's failed attempt to burn the drawbridge – had swelled in number to well over three hundred.

'What are we to do, my lord?' one of Chesterfield's officers, a Derbyshire man, shouted to the earl as he watched his small child nibble on a hunk of mouldering bread. Despair etched deep lines in his face and strained at each reluctantly delivered word. 'We may fight them off each time they come, sir, but how are we to put food in our bellies?'

Philip Stanhope, Earl of Chesterfield, rose awkwardly from his stool, helped on to gout-ridden feet by a pair of grunting stewards. 'We will prevail here, yes?' he said, leaning forwards on his gnarled and knotted stick, his huge stomach swaying low like a sack of turnips. 'We have held firm long enough for word to reach Oxford, yes? And Hastings has seen our plight, do not forget. A relief force will be on its way.'

'Before my daughter wastes to nothing!' the Derbyshire man snapped waspishly.

Chesterfield narrowed his beady gaze, but evidently thought better of rebuking the man for fear of instigating a mutiny. 'We will prevail, Sir Edward, you must have faith. In King Charles and in God. Tomorrow is Sunday, and we shall gather in the cathedral, come rain or shine, for prayers.'

'Prayers ain't gonna fucking feed us,' Sergeant William Skellen murmured. He, his two officers and Lisette Gaillard were in the Great Hall with the rest of the exhausted multitude.

Stryker glanced sideways at his sergeant, seeing no pleasure in the taller man's face for having been proved right in the matter of the Close's supplies. 'Voice down, Will.'

'He's right,' Lisette muttered in Stryker's ear. 'We'll be starved out of here in a few days at most. Did he not prepare at all?'

Stryker looked at her. He had given his own rations to Lisette in order to keep up her strength, and was pleased to see that she was now able to walk short distances, albeit with his help. 'He did not expect to be besieged. He thought he could go on taking anything he required from the city.'

She shook her head in amazement.

'But he may be right,' Stryker said after a time. 'About the relief force, I mean. Word will have reached our high command by now.' He forced a weak smile in response to Lisette's incredulous grimace.

The boom was as shocking as it was loud. It was cacophonous, as though the very sky was caving in over Lichfield. It was deep, rib-shaking, gut-churning. Terrifying.

The women and children within the Great Hall screamed, their men gaped at one another, slack-jawed with confusion and fear, and then they streamed out through the thick doors and into the courtyard.

Stryker hooked Lisette's arm around his shoulders and virtually carried her out into the open. There, joined by Skellen and Forrester, they stared up at the brooding clouds, at the three spires and the battlements, wondering what had caused such a noise.

'Mortar!' a man bellowed from the direction of the cathedral.

Stryker recognized him as one of the men – fearless with heights and a reliable shot – the earl regularly used as lookout-cum-sniper in the central tower. 'Come,' he said urgently, compelling Lisette towards the cathedral.

'They have a mortar-piece, my lord!' the look-out was saying breathlessly, his rapid descent having taken its toll on heaving lungs.

'Slowly, Corporal, slowly,' Chesterfield replied as steadily as his own concern would allow. 'Calm yourself. Now; where is this mortar?'

'Down in Sadler Street, in one of the gardens that runs right up to Minster Pool.'

'Can we not shoot them from the tower?' asked the earl. 'If it is against the Minster, then it is well within range, yes?'

The corporal shook his head. 'I fear not, my lord. It is well protected by earthworks. They must've dug them while it was dark.'

'Jesu,' Stryker whispered. 'The noise was the mortar firing.'

'Now we know why they didn't bother attacking again last night,' Skellen said unhelpfully.

'Where did the shot fall?' Chesterfield was asking now, having to raise his voice above the anxious murmurings of the garrison and their families.

'Well wide, my lord,' the corporal replied.

'Thank God.'

Another explosion suddenly erupted outside the walls, cutting off whatever the earl might have said next, and the inhabitants of the Close ducked down in fright, instinctively shying away from the ensuing firebomb. When no calamity befell them, it gradually dawned on the Royalists that whoever was setting the mortar's trajectory was afflicted with a sorry aim. A desultory half-cheer went up from the tired, hungry throng.

Stryker left Lisette in Forrester's care and climbed the ladder up to the platform running along the south wall.

He peered out upon the city, resting his eye on the gardens jutting out from Sadler Street and, eventually, the earth-work from which a pall of new smoke belched.

'What kind of evil is this?' a man stood to his left was saying.

Stryker turned his head to bring the young soldier into his limited field of vision. 'A mortar is a wide-mouthed thing,' he explained, realizing that many here would never have seen such a machine before, 'like a great iron toad.'

The soldier stared back at him, unable to keep his gaze from the mutilated left side of Stryker's face as he spoke. 'And they fire it at the drawbridge? It is a poor effort.'

Stryker shook his head. 'No. They do not try to smash our walls. That tactic was tried and has so far failed. They wish to burn us out.'

The soldier's gaze widened. 'Burn, sir? How the—'

'They take an iron ball, about so big,' Stryker said, setting his palms apart to demonstrate a diameter similar to that of his forearm, from elbow to wrist, 'and pack it full of black powder. There is a small hole into which they insert a length of tow, and that is lit to make a fuse. Then they sling the damn thing over high walls, for the mortar allows for a tremendously high trajectory.'

The soldier gaped at him. 'And these powder-shells explode!'

'They do. Inside the walls. It is not a weapon to destroy a castle, but to destroy the morale of those within.'

'Chad protect us,' the younger man said quietly, looking back into the Close.

'Have faith, sir,' Stryker said. 'I am sure God will save us, and dusk fast approaches so, at the very least, they will be forced to wait till morning.' At least the latter was true, he thought.

A third immense boom reverberated about the buildings of Lichfield as a mortar was brought to bear once more. Stryker ducked behind the battlements, praying the incendiary would not find its mark near the scaffolding on which he stood.

It was not an explosion he heard next, but a great splash, followed by more jeers from the Royalist side. He looked up. The shell had found a home in the Minster Pool.

NEAR BERKSWELL, WARWICKSHIRE, 4 MARCH 1643

As dusk steadily drew close, the small party of four riders, trotting slowly but steadily in single file, made their way north and east. The resumption of this journey had been a vexing decision to make, for they were without one of their number, but time could not be spared.

'What about Josiah, sir?' Tom Slater's nasal tone carried to the lead horseman from the back of the group.

Major Zacharie Girns, clad in black and with skin so pale it seemed to glow, clusters of warts sprouting like miniature cabbages at his nose and chin, twisted in his saddle to look over his shoulder. He had to lean slightly to see beyond the two riders immediately at his back. 'We have waited long enough for Lieutenant Trim. I gave him a day, and it was near two when yesterday we broke camp. I will waste no more time on him. If he wishes to dawdle in his task, then that is not our concern.'

'What if that bugger's shaken him off?'

Girns shook his head. 'Impossible. Trim was the best tracker Cromwell had to offer. Besides, I allowed him to go after that last Cavalier because it was his shot that missed.' In the aftermath of the ambush at the Two Virgins, Girns had emerged from the inn to lay eyes upon an almost perfect vista. Blaze and his servant, terrified and babbling though they were, had survived the carnage without so much as a scratch, while all their Royalist escort lay dead. Almost all. 'Trim must atone for the mistake,' he growled, remembering the sight of the Cavalier officer speeding away down the high road on one of his fallen comrades' horses. 'But you and I have our *real* quarry, so we will press on. If Trim is worth his salt, he will pick up our trail. Concern yourself only with our friends here. And keep the grenades close, in case we run into difficulty.'

Slater nodded, leaning across to pat the cloth sack that hung from his saddle. 'Got 'em here, safe and sound, Major.'

'And when shall we rest?'

It was the second rider of the four that spoke now. Girns glared at the big, blond-haired man riding some half-dozen yards behind him. 'Still your flapping mouth, sir, or I shall remove your tongue.'

Jonathan Blaze grimaced. 'But I am exhausted!'

'We ain't been travellin' long!' Tom Slater called from the back of the group.

'Long enough,' Blaze responded tartly. 'And I am unused to such privation.'

Girns ignored him. He hated the way his prisoner bleated like a stuck sheep at every perceived hardship. It was an attitude borne of a privileged life. A life where sovereigns and generals parted with vast sums of cash to

304

secure his services. Girns loathed such men, but he would suffer Blaze's infernal chatter, for this trial would see him well rewarded.

'Where are we going, Zacharie?' Blaze moaned after a time.

'You're goin' to your grave!' Slater chirped nastily. 'And it's Major Girns to you.'

'Then why do we live yet?' Blaze sniped back, his voice haughty, unwilling to be cowed by a man he clearly regarded as beneath contempt.

Girns twisted round. 'Oh you *will* die, Jonathan, do not make the mistake of thinking otherwise.'

'Sir Samuel Luke,' Slater said with relish, 'Parliament's new Scoutmaster General. He's put a juicy price on your bonce.'

'Glad to see my reputation is worthy of the attention of such a man,' Blaze replied.

Girns almost laughed. 'Even in your final hours you are arrogant as ever. Still, I will puncture that pride, just as I did Lazarus's.'

Blaze stared at him. 'Lazarus? What have you done to him, Zacharie?'

'I said, you'll address him as Major, you Rome-lovin' antick!' Slater snarled.

Girns tugged gently at his mount's reins, and the beast came to an obedient halt. 'Relent, Thomas. Master Blaze and I are very well acquainted. There is no need for formality.' Leaving Slater looking baffled, the major stared at Blaze, his green eyes twinkling. 'Oh yes, sir. Lazarus tried to flee, of course, but he was fatter than I remembered him.' He shrugged, as if that was explanation enough. 'It was a relatively simple shot, was it not, Tom?'

Slater licked his thin lips. 'Easy as shooting a boar in a basket, sir.'

Tears glistened at the corners of Blaze's eyes. 'My poor, sweet brother.'

'He was a Popish traitor!' Girns hissed suddenly, startling all but his own horse. 'He would use his knowledge of gun and powder to win this conflict for the King and his sinful lackeys. With that victory would come the insidious tide of Catholicism. It had to be stopped. *He* had to be stopped. And so, Jonathan, do you.'

Blaze simply stared in bewilderment and fear. At length he turned to the man riding behind him, but his aide, Jesper Rontry, kept his gaze firmly on the ground.

'Then why do you not put an end to this, Zacharie?' he said eventually, seeing no support would come from his terror-stricken companion. 'Leave me dead and claim your money!'

'Not yet,' Girns replied calmly. 'For it is not the scoutmaster's coin I want. We'll claim the prize, Tom,' he added sharply, noticing Slater's thin-lipped mouth open like a landed carp, 'do not worry. The money shall be yours.'

'And you, Zacharie?' Blaze asked. 'What do you want? For Christ's sake, man, where do you take me?'

Girns fixed his green gaze upon the blustering captive. 'I want your salvation.' He grinned suddenly. 'We're going home!'

CHAPTER 14

The men, women and children of Cathedral Close's dog-tired and hungry garrison gathered in the great building dedicated to St Chad. It was Sunday and, as the Earl of Chesterfield had promised, they would pray together, beseeching God for a swift and complete salvation.

The earl, his gout-afflicted gait as pronounced as ever, led the procession along the nave in silence, though the lack of chatter or humour was more the result of the congregation's condition than of any reverence to the glowering stone effigy of Lichfield's saint.

Stryker and his three companions were there. Three because, as dawn had sent its tendrils creeping across the horizon, Lisette had managed to walk unaided from her bed. She was weak, not least because of the rapidly dwindling rations, but Stryker had never met a more resilient human being, and her vitality was gradually returning.

When they were at the high altar, the procession stopped, and Chesterfield turned to face the assembly like some powerful bishop. The difference being that many in this congregation could barely muster the strength to keep their eyelids open. Men stood stoically, though they seemed to sway a little, women leant against their husbands for support and children simply sat in lethargic stillness, clinging to their mothers' skirts for comfort.

Chesterfield began with a short word of thanks for the cessation of the mortar bombardment the previous evening. With that final, wayward shot that plunged in a great foaming jet of water into the Minster Pool, the Parliamentarian commander, Sir John Gell, had evidently decided to postpone matters.

'If his boys can't hit a whole cathedral from bugger-all range,' Skellen had droned, 'then they ain't goin' to improve much in the dark, are they?'

The sergeant had been correct and, as dusk cast great shadows across the Close, so the black gun and its wicked grenadoes had fallen silent.

The folk assembled before the earl gave a weak but heartfelt cheer, which surprised Stryker at first, for the mortar would surely spring to life on the morrow, once the Sabbath was behind them. The mere thought of a day's respite – and an extra day for the urgently prayed-for relief force to arrive – was enough to boost spirits, however. It seemed to Stryker that, for every new depre-dation borne by the Royalists of Lichfield, their faith grew in equal measure. He supposed they had no other option.

'And on that sacred day, the day of Saint Chad himself,' the earl was now saying, his voice loud in the cathedral's high beams, despite its undercurrent of strain, 'we were sent a miracle. A sign. The man who would have torn up the very foundation stones of this great building was smit-ten by God. Struck down as he cast his vile gaze over Satan's work.'

A chorus of amens followed as people remembered the shocking and sudden demise of Lord Brooke, a demise that now seemed so long in the past.

'Praise Jesus Christ!' a woman at the front of the congregation shouted out.

'Praise His holy name!' a brown-coated soldier near Stryker bellowed in response. 'And praise His blessings, without which Honest John would not have done God's miraculous bidding!'

Stryker gazed around the group as more amens and huzzas rang out.

Forrester leaned in close, whispering, 'Knows how to rouse a rabble, I'll give him that.'

'Indeed, indeed,' Chesterfield cried. 'Honest John Dyott: the very hammer in God's avenging fist!' He peered out across the faces ranged before him. 'And where is this fair city's most blessed son?'

At that moment the ebullient mood, so carefully nurtured by the earl, was intruded upon by a commotion back down the nave. Voices were ringing out, urgent but indecipherable from wherever they hailed. With a great bang, the door to the central tower swung violently open.

The first man burst through into the cathedral, and Stryker saw that it was dumb John Dyott, appearing as if in response to Chesterfield's summons. At first, he wondered whether this was staged to whip up the beleaguered defenders' morale. But Dyott, usually so serene, was gesticulating wildly as he paced quickly along the aisle, and by his expression Stryker understood that serenity had long left him.

'My lord!' Another man came from the tower in Dyott's wake, racing down the nave. 'They are bringing the mortar to bear!'

Chesterfield stepped forwards involuntarily. 'Now? This very morning, yes?'

His words were lost in the ensuing panic. Men and women gabbled frantically, asking each other, the earl and God Himself how Gell could violate the Sabbath in such a craven fashion.

'Don't know what the fuss is about,' Skellen muttered close to Stryker's ear. 'I'd have been lobbin' up grenadoes since sunrise.'

Forrester looked up at the sergeant. 'This is not the Low Countries, William. They still hold notions of gentlemanly conduct sacrosanct.' He sighed. 'I fear this war will suck such genteel concepts from our people, as it did the folk of Germany.'

'Clearly Gell harbours no such scruples,' Stryker said.

'Man after me own heart,' replied Skellen.

'Mine too,' agreed Lisette.

'Philistines, the lot of you,' Forrester said as they joined the disbanded congregation. The folk assembled for a quiet Sunday of prayer and worship were pouring from the cathedral because now, as the first great boom resounded from Sadler Street, this revered building had become a place of physical danger.

A shell whizzed high in a vast arc, seemingly held at its zenith by invisible hands, before plummeting down towards the Close. The garrison families stared up at the dark sphere, not knowing which way to run. It fell at an irresistible pace, and even those who might have discerned where exactly it would strike would not have been able to move away from that place in time. It was a matter of watching, waiting and praying.

A huge, fountain-spawning splash heralded the strike, as the grenadoe fell harmlessly into the Minster Pool.

'Picking up where they left off,' Forrester said amid the sound of Royalist jeers.

Stryker nodded. 'All the better for us. It'll take them time to reset the mortar and adjust its aim.'

'When presented with gunners employing the oft practised art of guesswork,' Forrester said wryly, 'one can appreciate a man of Jonathan Blaze's talents.'

'You see?' Lisette said defiantly. 'You see why Blaze must be protected? If Gell had a man like him out there, they'd have turned this place to cinders yesterday.'

Stryker did see. 'So we must stop your assassins reaching him.'

'You promised me.'

'I did. If we get out of here, we will find Blaze and keep him alive.'

Mercifully, the Earl of Chesterfield had been pragmatic enough to move the women and children as far away from the mortar as possible. There was nowhere entirely safe, trapped as they were within the cathedral compound, but Sadler Street was to the south of the Close, so the most reasonable place to hide was as far to the north as they could get. All those not actively engaged in the defence of the makeshift fortress were promptly escorted back to the Bishop's Palace.

The mortar coughed almost exactly half an hour after its first salvo, and this time there were no jeers. The shell, trajectory altered by degrees, made it beyond the stone perimeter, exploding in a flash of blinding light and shuddering violence in the open ground between the cathedral and the former homes of clerics that hugged the south wall. Fortunately, the defenders had taken shelter at the crucial moment, and none was harmed, but faces were masked with horror as they emerged from the Close's various buildings. A great crater, deep, wide and black as night, had opened up where the incendiary had landed.

Stryker had been inside the cathedral, but, now that there was time before the next shot, he went to stand on the wall's rickety platform. He could not see the mortar itself from here, but several men were required to keep lookout lest another foot-borne attack was mounted across the causeway.

'Praise Jesus,' a man to his right whispered. Stryker turned to ask him what was so deserving of such a statement, when he recognized the soldier.

'Your family were quartered in one of the canons' homes?' he asked, nodding down at the buildings so recently sprayed with hot shards of metal.

The man nodded. 'They were, sir. But thank God my goodwife and little daughters are now safely in the palace.'

'No one is to enter the cathedral!' The earl's querulous, staccato voice carried to them from down on the ground. He was surveying the still smouldering crater, eyes wider than Stryker had thought possible. 'The next shot will surely be closer when they make their infernal adjustments.' He turned to Barkworth, who stood at his heel like a guard dog. 'Get Dyott down here, Simeon. It pains me to say it, but I want none left in there, yes?'

Barkworth nodded curtly and went to do his master's bidding.

Philip Stanhope, Earl of Chesterfield, was, in Captain Stryker's opinion, a pig-headed, short-sighted man of no military merit and, given the near starvation of the garrison, entirely devoid of the ability to plan. But despite this, Stryker had to concede that the decision to evacuate the cathedral was entirely well made.

The shell, sent up on its lingering loop only minutes after Dumb Dyott had appeared in the Close, pitched directly into the cathedral's roof, punching its way through tile and wood to rest somewhere within the great building. The people out in the Close looked on in horror as they awaited the lick of flames to take hold, but, to their great relief, none came.

'Tow must have come loose,' Barkworth said to Stryker as they stood together near the crater excavated earlier.

'Aye,' agreed Stryker, 'but they've found their range now. They'll settle into a rhythm and pound us till the church burns.'

Stryker's warning to Barkworth proved to be only half right. The Parliamentarian gunners did indeed concentrate their efforts on the cathedral, sending regular grenadoes whistling down on to the roof. But the grand symbol of Royalist defiance did not burn.

The garrison men organized themselves into teams of six or seven, each equipped with buckets of water drawn from the well and thick blankets taken from the infirmary. When the mortar belched and its shell smashed down into the cathedral's nave, those teams would mobilize, scrambling to douse the smouldering tow before it could ignite its charge.

Stryker was with one of the teams, Forrester another. Edberg had even volunteered to join one such crew, giving Stryker cause to relax somewhat with regards to Lisette's safety. Nevertheless, he ordered a disgruntled

Mademoiselle Gaillard to stay in the infirmary, and posted Skellen outside its door, just to be certain.

The bombardment continued throughout the day and, to Stryker's surprise, took very little toll on the cathedral, for the diligent water teams prevented all but two shells from exploding, and of those neither fire took hold. But it was on morale that the mortar wrought genuine damage. The hitherto redoubtable spirits of the garrison's women-folk – gathered up in the Bishop's Palace like so many hens in a coop, unable to leave, unable to help their husbands and sons, all the while listening to the mortar's fierce booms – were beginning to dissolve. Their children did not weep, for they were too tired, and they did not laugh or play, for their movements had become too sluggish from hunger. This hellish reality, accompanied all the while by the great thunderous claps from the malevolent gun, simply proved too much to bear, and, as the afternoon drew on, the women sent a delegation out into the Close to speak with the earl.

'Hold out, my lord, I beg it of you,' Simeon Barkworth's noose-throttled voice echoed with desperate urgency in the Great Hall.

With the falling of night, the earl had summoned his garrison and their families to a special council, one that would decide the future of Royalist resistance in Lichfield.

Stryker was standing at the back of the throng, Skellen, Forrester and Lisette at his flanks. They could not see Barkworth, for the little man was at the very front, and his diminutive frame was obscured by all the other bodies, but his tone was as assured and forthright as ever.

'It is your sacred duty.'

Chesterfield glared down at his Scottish steward. 'Do not presume to tell me my duty, Barkworth!' The portly earl took a deep breath and steadied himself, clearly unwilling to let anger cloud this crucial meeting. 'I would not surrender the Close,' he said, his tone softer and marked by a deep weariness, 'but we are in a desperate way, yes?' He stood facing the assembly, leaning heavily on his broad stick, and winced every now and then, his gout clearly exacerbated by recent hardships.

'But, my lord,' Barkworth replied, 'it is surely a grave sin to hand this city to the Parliament so meekly.'

Stryker felt Forrester lean close to his ear. 'He'll find himself on thin ice with such talk,' the latter whispered.

'Meekly?' The speaker was one of Chesterfield's senior officers, a man Stryker recognized as Sir John Tichaber, and his face was red with outrage. 'There has been nothing meek in our defence, Barkworth. We've fought 'em off sundry times, killed their cursed general and burned their scaling ladders. What more could the Lord ask of us, you damnable cur?'

'Now, now, gentlemen,' the earl said, raising his hands for calm, 'this is not the time . . .'

'And what of my Jenny?' One of the officers' wives spoke up now, hunger and desperation overwhelming any sense of propriety. 'Is she worth nothing?'

'Well said, madam!' Tichaber bellowed. 'If surrender is sin, then is it not a greater sin to see our wives and children starve to bare bones?'

'I am with Barkworth,' another senior man called from the crowd. 'We must hold the cathedral at any cost.'

'We have no victuals,' a fresh-faced captain piped up. 'Nothing to eat. We are ill-prepared for a siege.'

'It seems the voices for peace outweigh our brave Scot,' Forrester said at the back of the crowd.

Stryker glanced sideways at him. 'Are you surprised? They are brave men. But the earl has made no provision for a siege of any length. The decision is made for him, whether Barkworth likes it or not.'

'Just a while longer, my lord,' the little Scotsman's pleading voiced rang out again. 'Will not Hastings mount another attack? Or the relief force from Stafford?'

'Relief force?' Tichaber interjected with a grunt of mirthless laughter. 'It is nothing but rumour and false hope.'

'We have seen no relieving army, Simeon,' the earl agreed. 'Nor so much as heard tell of its existence.'

'Aye!' Tichaber growled again, sensing Barkworth was on the back foot. 'How many of my loved ones must die for this conjured report?'

The sound of a clearing throat rang out suddenly, and all eyes turned to a powerfully built man with blond hair and moustache, who stood in the very centre of the assembly.

'My lord Chesterfield,' Major Henning Edberg began, 'I have come direct from Prince Rupert, as you know well.'

'Make your point, Major, yes?' Chesterfield replied sharply.

'I would urge you keep these stout gates closed, no matter what hardship follows. The drawbridge must only drop when the rebels blow it from its very hinges. The General of Horse would demand it of you.'

'What's his angle?' Forrester muttered quietly as they listened to Tichaber and his supporters decry Edberg's opinion. 'He don't strike me as one who'd give two groats to save Lichfield.'

Stryker made to reply, but it was Lisette Gaillard who spoke first. 'It's not the garrison he wishes to save, Captain. He knows if the Close falls he may lose his chance to kill Stryker.'

Stryker nodded. 'At least in here he knows he will get another opportunity.'

Forrester's forehead creased in consternation. 'The man's skull is full of bees, I swear it.'

'So, in a strange way,' Skellen offered, 'surrender might prove a blessin' in disguise.'

Stryker considered the statement. 'Perhaps, Sergeant. We'll be trapped as we always were. But now we will be prisoners of Parliament instead of the King.'

'Life is never dull,' Forrester said with a sigh.

'At least Gell might feed us,' Skellen replied hopefully.

Forrester smiled. 'Every cloud, eh?'

'Unless he decides to execute us all,' added Lisette.

Forrester blew out his cheeks. 'You truly are a ray of sunshine, mademoiselle.'

GUNN'S BUTCHERY, LICHFIELD, 6 MARCH 1643

The small beer quenched Abel Black's thirst in a cascade of cooling amber, beads dripping from the corners of parched lips to set wet patches blooming like petals in his lap. When he could imbibe no more without pause for breath, he set the wooden pot on the table and looked at his surroundings, letting loose a rumbling belch as he did so.

A thick-set man of full beard and bald pate quickly hurried across the mouldering rushes to refill the cup from

317

a large, slopping jug. 'Glad you enjoy it, sir, truly. 'Tis Lizzie's own brew.'

Abel Black took a swig from the newly replenished cup and nodded at Richard Gunn. 'My compliments to your goodwife, Master Gunn. I have travelled a sore long way, and cannot fittingly describe how well met this refreshment is.'

Gunn grinned obsequiously and stepped backwards, clattering into the open door at his back as he did so. 'Apologies, Colonel, apologies.'

Black waved Gunn's concerns away. 'No harm, Richard. How long have we worked together now, eh? A dozen years? Not once in that time have you failed to play your part of doting kinsman with the utmost sincerity. Why, sometimes I wonder if you truly are my much-loved cousin.' He smiled. He genuinely liked the butcher and his family.

Gunn seemed to relax a little, his bunched shoulders loosening ever so slightly at the compliment. 'Kind in you to say it, Colonel. We are true and loyal subjects, as you know, and are only too happy to play our parts for the King, God keep him safe.'

Black gave a short bark of laughter. 'And the way you embraced me in the street, Richard.'

'Sir?'

'My last visit here. I was with three men, if you remember. You met me out near the market cross, embracing me as though I were the prodigal son.'

Gunn's face clouded with worry. 'I—I found myself carried away with the moment, sir. I am sorry to have overstepped the mark on that occasion.'

Black stood suddenly, making Gunn start in alarm. 'On the contrary, Richard! Would not Abel Menjam's beloved cousin embrace him at first sight? I think he would, sir, and considered your little—touch—to be a work of genius. My companions most certainly believed, and they were a suspicious bunch to put it lightly, so I am certain the rest of the town will have swallowed the tale, as ever.'

'A relief, Colonel.'

'For certain,' Black agreed. 'These Midland counties are so divided, I must take utmost care with my identity at every turn.'

'I am always glad to be of service, sir.'

Black patted Gunn's broad shoulder. 'I know it, and thank God for it.' The colonel moved away, walking to a small window that looked north on to the city. His dark gaze, beady and twitching, flickered left and right, studying the faces of soldiers and common folk alike for signs of danger. Content that his cover did not seem to be at immediate risk, he turned his attention to the cathedral, which rose like a leviathan in the distance. From the central tower, he could see a flag fluttering in the cold wind. 'Chesterfield surrenders, then?'

'Alas, Colonel, it is true. The red standard of the King was lowered before dawn, to be replaced by that white monstrosity. Talks have been concluded, and the garrison are to be ejected any hour now. It is the talk of the town.'

Black turned, his reactions rapier-fast. 'It is rank cowardice.'

Gunn stepped back a pace. 'Aye, sir.'

'Still,' Black said, his voice calmer now, 'Rupert harries the land hereabouts. It is but a matter of time before his gaze falls upon Lichfield, and then the rebels will reap their just rewards.' He walked back into the room, taking up his seat at the table once again. 'Now, Richard, I must look to matters of work.'

Gunn dipped his head obediently. 'Of course, sir. I am sorry to have bothered you.'

'No, sir, that is not what I meant.' Black indicated the adjacent seat. 'Come. Sit.' When Gunn had taken up his place at the table, Black fixed his tiny eyes, like little pebbles of jet, directly upon Gunn. 'My trio of companions.'

Gunn nodded. 'Their leader was missing an eye.'

'The very same. Now tell me, and think hard upon it, Richard. Where did they go?'

Gunn frowned. 'Go, sir?'

'Aye, go. Where did they go after I left them at the George and Dragon? They were seeking someone out. It did not matter at the time, but the sands, so to speak, have shifted. Now I must find them.'

'Why, Colonel,' Gunn exclaimed, relieved and delighted to be able to offer help, 'they are in the Close, sir.'

'The Close?' Black leaned forward. 'The Cathedral Close?'

'Indeed, sir,' Gunn confirmed. 'Upon Lizzie's own life, Colonel, that is where they went.'

CATHEDRAL CLOSE, LICHFIELD, 6 MARCH 1643

The Earl of Chesterfield had had no real alternative but to accept the terms offered by Sir John Gell. These were simply that the Close was to surrender forthwith, upon which event free quarter would be given to its Royalist inhabitants. To decline the terms would have been to prolong the siege, prolong the starvation and, most crucial of all, give the vengeful Parliament men license to sack the Close when eventually they broke through.

So it was with heavy and nervous hearts that the garrison of Lichfield greeted their conquerors. They were gathered at the south gate as the great wooden drawbridge crashed down for the final time, and watched, silent and apprehensive, as the purple ranks of Brooke and the greycoats of Gell marched across the causeway and into the Close. They halted in formation, a great block of men, steel and muskets arrayed in formidable depth before their new captives.

Stryker and his three companions were there, gathered close together at the back of the garrison families.

'Impressive entrance,' Skellen said.

'One must hand it to their commander,' Forrester replied quietly. 'It's an excellent show of force. If he means to cow the earl, I imagine he'll be successful.'

Just then a tall man strode through the gate at the side of the troop. He was very well dressed, his moustache immaculately trimmed and his dark hair voluminous, cascading extravagantly across his shoulders in tight, bouncing curls.

'Look at his coat and gloves,' Forrester said. 'See the silver lace? It is Gell, right enough.'

Sir John Gell paced purposefully to the front of the grimy assembly. He came to a halt before the Earl of Chesterfield, and the pair regarded each other for several seconds before Gell lifted a hand. For a moment it seemed as though he would strike the earl, and Stryker noticed Barkworth – as ever at Chesterfield's right hand – tense, ready to leap to his plump master's defence.

But Gell merely pinched the bridge of his long nose with thumb and forefinger. 'God's blood, my Lord Chesterfield, but you stink like a sow!'

Chesterfield gritted his teeth, his flabby cheeks rising to a crimson colour. 'Still your viperous tongue, Sir John, or—'

Gell beamed malevolently, relishing his old rival's helpless anger. 'Or what, my lord?' He glanced down at Barkworth. 'Or you shall set your dwarf upon me? What shall he do, may I ask? Gnaw at my ankles? Kick at my knees?'

The Parliamentarian soldiers at Gell's back chortled at their master's jest, while the earl and his steward could do nothing in their humiliation but glower and ball their fists impotently.

'Surprised little Simeon kept his reins steady then,' Skellen muttered.

'Must have been a close-run thing,' Forrester agreed.

'I have promised free quarter to every man, woman and child within these walls,' Sir John Gell was saying now, his voice loud enough for all to hear. 'Whether I see fit to honour that promise depends on your ability to behave.'

There was a murmur from the crowd then, one of anger and of fear. Gell simply stood, face split in a delighted smile, seemingly enjoying the consternation his words were creating. His narrow gaze flickered from one face to the next, studying the expressions, ever calculating.

'How dare you!' the Earl of Chesterfield finally blurted. 'You would renege on a gentleman's agreement, sir, yes?'

Gell twisted the point of his moustache, his face betraying a great deal of amusement. 'I will renege – or honour

– as I see fit, Stanhope, you great bullock. You and your people are traitors to this nation, and deserving of nothing more than contempt.'

'What of the rules of war, sir?' Chesterfield snapped indignantly.

Gell's upper lip crinkled in a sneer. 'Rules? This is not a fox hunt, my lord. I am master in Lichfield now, and any rules there might be are conjured and altered at my whim alone.' He looked away from the earl to catch as many glances as possible, and raised his voice again. 'So, as I have said, you must all behave like good children. I am your father, here to correct you as appropriate. Do not give me cause for punishment.' It was then that he turned to look back at the open gate and towards the causeway beyond. There, behind the purple and grey coats, helmeted heads, and powder-stained faces, was a large contraption of dark wood. It was a platform, set on wheels so that it might be drawn from the city on ropes, and, at its top, were two thick timbers that came together in a right angle.

'You have no honour, yes?' Chesterfield snarled, as the portable gallows were hauled through the gates and into the Close.

'I am a loyal servant of Parliament, my lord,' Gell responded, as though that was enough explanation.

The Royalists fell silent.

Gell removed his buff-gloves, tugging at each fingertip with deliberate slowness so as to prolong the discomfort of the Royalists anxiously awaiting his next decree.

At the back of the crowd, Sergeant Skellen made a clicking sound in his long throat. 'Bastard's enjoyin' this.'

'Barkworth said he was a bully,' Stryker responded in a whisper. 'He's playing games, making the earl's supporters fear him. He relishes their fright.'

'That is good!' Gell called out again. 'Very good indeed. Well done, one and all, your behaviour is every bit as genteel and praiseworthy as I'd hoped.' He stepped across the front of the dirty, exhausted garrison, meeting the gaze of man, woman and child alike. 'And your reward will be your lives.' Gell spread his arms wide, proffering his prisoners the most wolfish of grins. 'Am I not the most benevolent father imaginable?'

'Then you will honour the terms, yes?' Chesterfield asked tentatively.

Gell rounded on the defeated lord. 'Keep still your chubby tongue, you raggedy blackguard! Do not speak to me of honour, for you and your like cannot know what it damn-well means!'

Chesterfield stepped back, browbeaten by the sudden outburst and by the knowledge that he was completely at Gell's mercy.

Gell looked back to the crowd. 'You may leave here with your lives, so long as you leave this very morning and without your weapons!' He gave an almost courtly bow, clearly enjoying his new-found power. 'Now lay down your arms, gentlemen, if you'd be so kind . . .' He paused. 'Always remembering a child can dance at the end of a rope as well as any soldier.'

The threat to their children well and truly understood, a clattering wave rippled through the prisoners as swords, pole-arms, muskets and dirks were thrown to the cold earth.

Stryker noticed his companions hesitate. 'Do as he says. We have no hope of escape from here.' Skellen and

Forrester duly obliged and, with a sharp glance from Stryker, Lisette threw down her pistol.

Stryker rammed his blade into the earth between his boots, leaving the hilt to quiver in the gentle breeze. The red garnet, set deep into the pommel, winked up at him, as if mocking him for its loss.

'That's it, my good friends!' Gell was shouting now. He had gone to sit on the edge of the scaffold, as though he wanted them always to remember his name in conjunction with the terrifying object. 'And you can all be on your merry way. Be you pikeman, musketeer, cavalryman or dragoon, I care not. Walk freely from this town and do not look back.'

The crowd began to shift forwards as the folk of Chesterfield's hungry garrison prepared to take their leave.

'Except the good earl, here,' Gell added. The Royalists and their families stared at him. 'He is my prisoner, to be removed from Lichfield as soon as possible, though I am uncertain as to whether we might find a wagon sturdy enough to convey him!'

Chesterfield turned to Gell. 'Where will I be taken, Sir John?'

'London, my lord,' Gell replied coldly. 'You, your son Ferdinando, and your senior knights. You pursued this action. Defied Parliament. So you will spend your days in the Tower. You'll be taken thither to whatever fate God and His Parliament have in store for you.' He patted the gallows on which he still perched. 'Thank Christ for your lot, my lord. Things might have been a deal worse. Besides, Sir Thomas Lunsford controls the Tower. He is a man of imagination. Perhaps his rack'll cure you of that infernal manner of yours.'

'Manner, sir?'

'Yes, yes, yes, yes, yes!' Gell snapped, and, seeing Chesterfield's bewilderment, brayed with laughter. Attention turned back to those he had promised to release, he cast a hand extravagantly at the gate. 'Go, my children! Peace be with you all.'

The relieved Royalists stepped past the Parliamentarian soldiers already gathering up the surrendered weaponry, while a group of Gell's Derbyshire greycoats worked to fasten irons at the wrists of the earl and the other men their colonel had identified.

Stryker, Lisette, Forrester and Skellen were shuffling along at the back of the desperate crowd. 'Can't believe it,' the sergeant grunted. 'Just lettin' us go like that.'

'A stroke of rare luck,' Forrester agreed.

'So keep your eyes down,' Stryker hissed, 'and your head bowed, and we might just get out of here.'

'And we can go after Jonathan Blaze?' Lisette said hopefully.

'Not you, Lisette,' Stryker replied, 'you are still not well enough for such a mission. But I will find him for you.'

Folk were passing rapidly on to the causeway now. Sir Richard Dyott and his brother, Brooke's killer, John, and their families. Simeon Barkworth was there too, looking for all the world like a lost puppy as his earl was led away to an uncertain fate.

'Hold!' The voice was that of Sir John Gell. 'Hold that man, damn your crow-bitten eyes!'

Head bowed and eye firmly fixed on his toes, Stryker could not tell who it was Gell had identified, but a knot formed in the pit of his stomach as instinct told him something had gone wrong. They were so nearly there, so close to the causeway and the freedom beyond. Stryker could see the archway of the gate and the flattened drawbridge that led to Dam Street. So nearly there. *Hurry, hurry, hurry!*

A grey-coated corporal stepped into his path. He was a skinny man, the uniform far too large for his little frame, as though he wore a tent awning on his shoulders, but the musket in his hands was authority enough. He levelled the barrel at Stryker's chest.

'Bring him here,' Gell barked. 'And those others with him. The tall one, the fat one and the girl.'

The corporal jerked the musket in Gell's direction, and the four of them did as they were told. As Stryker made his way away from the main group, he looked up at Gell, noticing that the Parliamentarian commander was speaking to a man. A man in a yellow coat, with a thick yellow moustache and long golden hair. 'Is that so?' Gell was saying.

Stryker swore quietly.

Major Henning Edberg stepped away from Gell, offered Stryker a curt nod, and turned on his heels. At the gate his troop of grinning dragoons waited. They had been stripped of weapons and deprived of their horses, but they would walk out of Lichfield free to rejoin the Royalist army, and for that they were happy men.

Stryker instinctively knew what was about to come, but that did not make the realization any easier to bear. He stood before Gell, looking up into the Parliamentarian's calculating eyes. 'Sir?'

'The major tells me you're spies,' Gell said flatly. 'He claims you are all spies in the pay of Rupert of the Rhine.'

Stryker inwardly scolded himself for a fool. He should have seen this coming. Should have sought out and silenced Edberg – at the end of a blade if necessary – as soon as the council of war, or rather council of peace, had adjourned with the earl's acquiescence in the face of so many suing for surrender. 'He lies,' was all Stryker could say, the words sounding feeble as they rolled off his tongue.

Gell sighed. 'Well, you were hardly bound to admit the charge, were you?' He caught the eye of one of his men. 'Search them!'

'How can I prove our innocence, sir?' Stryker pleaded, as calloused hands patted him roughly from head to toe.

'I suppose you can't,' Gell said with a simple shrug. He caught Lisette's eye then, falling briefly silent while his own gaze raked her up and down. 'What is wrong with the woman? She is whiter than Chesterfield's flag.'

'She had a fever, sir,' Stryker explained. 'She is still not recovered.'

Gell made a grunting sound somewhere deep in his chest, and jumped down from the platform. 'I'll do the honours, Corporal.'

The man about to check Lisette scowled in reluctance, but knew better than to argue. He stepped away from the Frenchwoman.

The leering Gell paced slowly across to the prisoners, pausing only to jerk Stryker's ornate sword from the cold earth. He held it for a moment, weighing it, revering its craftsmanship and balance, before wordlessly thrusting it into his quickly vacated scabbard.

Stryker watched with a building fury as Gell drew close to Lisette. He leant in, whispering something in her ear, his black locks, longer even than hers, mingling with her golden tresses. He ran his hands down her arms, under her armpits, snaking them along her flanks, past the swell of her breasts and down to her hips. She leant back, recoiling from his touch, nose wrinkled as though he carried the stench of a pigsty, but unwilling to appear intimidated.

Stryker was a professional, a man used to hardships and difficulties, and he had grown adept at controlling himself under acute duress. Yet now, unarmed and surrounded by hundreds of Parliamentarian soldiers wielding muskets and blades, he felt that control disintegrating. He took a deep breath, preparing to spring forwards and tear the throat from Sir John Gell's neck, utterly unconcerned with the consequences.

And then the face of the man searching him suddenly sparked in triumph. 'Got somethin', Colonel!'

And Stryker froze. Because the greycoat was brandishing the parchment he had carried since their escape from Cirencester.

Gell strode across to his subordinate and took the parchment, reading it quickly before letting out a small, satisfied chuckle. 'The major lies, does he?' He held up the paper. 'I think we have our proof, sir!'

Stryker searched for an argument to refute the claims, but he could find nothing, and he knew then that all was lost. Sir John Gell might have been Lord Brooke's replacement, but he was no honourable Puritan hero. As Stryker looked into those almost blank eyes, he saw no scruples.

'We work for the Prince, Sir John,' Stryker said weakly, 'but we are no spies.'

'Perhaps you are, and perhaps you are not,' Gell said, his gaze hard and cold as ice, 'but you understand, I cannot run the risk of allowing you to leave.' He glanced up at the scaffold looming above them. 'Or live.'

CHAPTER 15

It was an hour past midnight, and the cold seemed to penetrate the body's very core. Stryker, Lisette, Forrester and Skellen were back in the infirmary, but this time the bland room had been turned into a prison, with guards standing both inside and outside the single door and another pacing outside along the wall with its trio of empty windows.

'Can they not spare us a mere twig or two for the hearth?' Forrester complained as he sat on one of the palliasses, wrapped in as many spare sheets as he could find, he now looked like an Egyptian mummy.

'They mean to stretch our necks at dawn, Forry,' Stryker replied. 'You imagine a man such as Gell would spare fuel for the walking dead?'

Forrester gnawed his bottom lip. 'I suppose not.'

'Least they donated a candle,' Skellen said, gesturing to the single tallow stem perched in a steel holder on the wall at the door end of the room. Its light was dim at best, and Gell had been careful to keep the only source of flame well away from his prisoners, but its light was certainly not unwelcome.

'I wonder if Gregory is well,' Lisette Gaillard spoke now. She was sat close to Stryker, his arm wrapped across her slender shoulders to share his warmth.

'Gregory?' Stryker asked, brow raised pointedly.

'He saved my life, Stryker,' she chided. 'Tended me for weeks.'

He smiled. 'A jest, Lisette. A jest only. Chambers is a good man.'

'An angry man,' Forrester added. 'The guard told me they'd stuck him in one of those poky hovels down near the drawbridge.' Chambers had been kept on as part of Sir John Gell's new garrison, for his skills were invaluable, regardless of which side's wounds he tended, but, for the time being, he had been ordered to leave his little domain. His other patients had been moved, too, and now, amid much grumbling from the doctor, there was an impromptu infirmary in one of the canons' houses built into the south wall.

'Makes sense,' Skellen said. 'This is an easy enough hole to keep blocked up.'

Stryker nodded. 'And it's only for the night.' There had been many tasks to see to during the previous evening – provisions to be arranged and billets to be secured for the men – so Gell had postponed the execution until the following morning. 'Barkworth told me Sir John has a penchant for a good hanging, so I'm not surprised he'd like to give us his full attention.'

'I'm not averse to watchin' a decent rope-dance myself,' Skellen said darkly. 'Used to see 'em down at the docks as a child. Always gave me an appetite.'

Forrester shuddered. 'You really are a vile specimen, Sergeant.'

'Do me best, Cap'n. Only hangings, mind. Saw some Spaniard's execution over in 'olland once. Didn't like that one little bit.'

'I'm certain I shall regret asking,' Forrester replied, 'but what did you dislike?'

'They lopped off the poor bastard's privy member, showed it him, then lopped off his head. Parboiled it in brine to keep it nice.'

'His privy member?'

'No, his head,' Skellen replied. 'Till the crows stripped him clean.'

'Naturally.'

'Can't say I'm lookin' forward to me own hangin', though.'

Forrester gave a snort of mirthless laughter. 'Don't imagine seeing one's own piss drip from one's boots has the same level of spectator enjoyment.' The red-cheeked officer, still weighty of frame, though perhaps slightly less so after the rationing of recent days, stood suddenly, fishing within his doublet. 'I have a tiny confession to make.' Without another word he produced a small pouch, dangling it out at arm's length.

Skellen's hooded eyes glinted. 'Is that what I think it is?'

Forrester winked. 'If you think it is common sotweed, then no, Sergeant, it ain't.' He loosed the pouch string and pinched a tiny amount of the contents within, rubbing his thumb and forefinger together, sprinkling the dark substance back again. 'This, William, is finest verinshe, shipped direct from New Granada. 'Tis the Lord's own leaf.'

Stryker's single eye narrowed. 'I thought you said you'd run out.'

'Of the plebeian muck the two of you tend to prefer, yes. This, however, I was keeping back for a special occasion.' He took his pipe from another pocket stitched into the lining of his coat. 'I think one's final night in the land of the living is special enough, don't you?' He turned towards the door, squinting to see the figures at the far end of the room. 'You there, kind sir!'

One of the pair of sentries stared back. 'Problem?'

Forrester brandished his most charming smile. 'Not the least of it, my good man! I merely wish to garner your assistance.'

The guard took two or three tentative paces towards Forrester. 'Oh?'

Forrester held up his clay pipe. 'Would you spare a light for a condemned man?'

The sentry nodded, set down his long-arm and took the flickering candle from its stand. He held out the flame to the prisoners, though his companion was careful to keep his own musket trained squarely on Forrester's chest. Skellen scrambled quickly to his feet and went to where the aromatic leaf was being packed in the clay bowl, eager not to miss his turn with the pipe.

Back at the palliasse near the hearth, Stryker and Lisette stayed huddled closely, neither wishing to break the embrace.

Lisette leaned up to speak into Stryker's ear. 'I saw your face,' she said softly, her breath warm against his skin.

'My face?'

'When that bastard touched me.'

Stryker thought back to Gell's appearance in the Close, surprised at himself for his near suicidal attack on Gell. 'He searched you well.'

She kissed his neck, sending a jolt of desire through him. 'Can you blame him, *mon amour*?'

Stryker nudged her gently with his elbow. 'Conceit, Lisette. You'd make a terrible Puritan.' She laughed at that, and he looked down at her, his face suddenly serious. 'I am sorry.'

'Sorry?' Lisette replied.

Stryker found he could not hold her gaze, and he glanced up to watch his comrades take turns on the pipe that now belched smoke to the ceiling. 'That I could not save you.'

She leant up to kiss him again, soft lips feeling cold against his cheek. 'You risked the wrath of Prince Rupert to save me, *mon amour*.' She smiled then, the expression impish in the dim and distant candle glow. 'Besides, I could not expect an amateur to succeed in such a task.'

Stryker smiled back. 'If the roles were reversed?'

She nudged him with her elbow. 'Then we would all be sipping fine wine in Paris by now! Roaming where we may, free as birds!'

Stryker chuckled ruefully. 'I believe you. Speaking of birds, can you hear that damned tweeting out there?'

Lisette remained silent for a moment, bemusement etching her face. 'I can.' She looked up at Stryker. 'But why does it sing at this hour?'

Out in the narrow space of ground between the infirmary and the north wall, Musketeer John Bunce listened appreciatively to the soft birdsong. It was tuneful, lilting and soothing to his ears.

Bunce had not been told why he had been stationed here, only that it was his job to guard the windows that sat midway up the infirmary's wall. It was a tawdry commission, one marked by boredom and coldness, but he enjoyed it nonetheless. Bunce had been one of Brooke's original besiegers. He had fought Wagstaffe's cowardly Cavaliers at the fall of Stratford, had been in the vanquished assault on the drawbridge, where the tar-filled pots had done nothing more than fizzle to their deaths in the Minster Pool, and had battled Blind Hastings's harquebusiers in the streets of Lichfield. The action in this little city had been hard, bloody and, until Chesterfield's eventual surrender, utterly fruitless, so to be given the task of strolling up and down for a few hours was one to be relished.

Bunce looked down at his musket's firing mechanism, marvelling at its design. It was a flintlock and he had never held one before this night. Gell wanted him armed and ready at all times, but understood that to keep a match-cord glowing through the night was both tedious and costly, so the colonel had arranged for the guards to borrow flintlocks from the men guarding the ordnance.

Bunce looked up suddenly. There it was again. Birdsong.

He paused his stride, listening to the beautiful tune, admiring its clear simplicity. It was dark, and he could not see from whence the sound came, so he closed his eyes, attempting to pinpoint the sound in the blackness.

There, perhaps ten yards away, at the foot of the north wall.

Musketeer John Bunce moved forwards slowly, silently. He had no wish to startle the bird, but wondered if it might be injured. Perhaps it had suffered a broken wing, or been mauled by the ginger tomcat he had seen prowling about earlier. He closed in on the sound, hoping perhaps to corner the animal and take it back to his new quarters.

When he was four or five paces away, the song abruptly ceased. Bunce frowned, leaning forward into the shadows.

The first he saw of the dagger was its dark hilt protruding from the flesh below his chin. He tried to call out, but only hot, sticky liquid came bubbling into his mouth. He tried to back away, but his limbs refused to obey. His hands failed him then, and the musket dropped to the ground. It was then that he saw a face. Pale-skinned, small and sharp-featured, like that of a rodent. The black eyes were tiny, like little pebbles of coal, and in their glimmering reflection he watched his own face droop as he collapsed to the ground.

'Did you hear that?' Lisette whispered. 'A thud, out beyond the window. Something falling.'

Stryker nodded.

The Frenchwoman looked towards the guards. They were still standing with Skellen and Forrester, paying no attention to this end of the infirmary. 'The birdsong has stopped.'

Stryker glanced behind and above them at the window-sill. 'Probably nothing. That damned cat wondering what's become of Doctor Chambers.'

Lisette followed his gaze, then quickly looked back into the room so as not to arouse the guards' suspicions. 'Clumsy cat.'

But Stryker did not turn back. Instead, his gaze remained transfixed upon the window, and the face that now appeared like a pale spectre from the depths of the night. It was a face he had never thought to see again, and certainly not here, at this desperate moment. 'Jesu,' he whispered.

337

Lisette was careful not to turn round. 'What is it?'

Stryker looked down at her. 'Abel Menjam.'

'Neither a borrower nor a lender be!' Captain Lancelot Forrester declared, one hand thumped flat against his chest, the other thrust out in the manner of the great players. 'The beloved bard wrote it in his *Hamlet*, the part I was fortunate enough to reproduce at the Swine and Swan near Lincoln's Inn a couple of years back. He knew what he was about, did Shakespeare.'

The musketeer still hogged the pipe, so fragrant and satisfying was the rare verinshe, and he stared hard at Forrester through the fug.

'But,' Forrester added quickly, 'seeing as you're the one with a gun at his side, I am perfectly content to ignore the bard and be a lender. This one time.'

'Thought you might be,' grunted the musketeer.

'Here!' a voice called from the far end of the room. 'You there! I need help!'

Forrester, Skellen and the two guards looked round to see Stryker standing over Lisette's lifeless form.

'What is it, old man?' Forrester called back.

'Christ, Forry, not you!' Stryker snapped. 'She has swooned. She must have water!'

Forrester turned to the man with the pipe. 'You have our water skins. Will you relinquish but one?'

The musketeer glanced across at the pile of snapsacks by the door, inside which would be the precious skins. He seemed to consider going to them, but looked down at the glowing pipe bowl. 'Needs tamping.' He looked back to his comrade at the door. 'You go.'

The second musketeer shook his head. 'Why me?'

338

''Cause I fuckin' said so, Woolly!'

The second man sighed in annoyance but acquiesced all the same. He went to the snapsacks, fishing in one after the other until he had found a reasonably full drinking vessel. He paced past his colleague, and the two prisoners still awaiting their turn with the verinshe, and strode down the length of the long room.

'Here,' he said when finally he reached Stryker. He held out the bulging skin. 'But be quick about it. Colonel Gell's ordered you deprived o' drink an' vittles.'

'Thank you,' Stryker said, but made no move to take the flask.

The dagger made a dull thud as it struck the guard's chest. It had spun in a quicksilver blur from one of the three windows and the soldier had no time to react before it punched through woollen coat and linen shirt. He made no sound, for the blade must have punctured his lung, the air escaping out from the wound in a heavy, almost tired sigh.

At the door, the musketeer with Forrester's pipe was busy taking a great chestful of the grey smoke. He saw his mate speak with Stryker, but his view was obscured by the cloud swirling at his head. By the time he realized his comrade had fallen and danger registered in his mind, it was simply too late. Forrester was blissfully unaware of what was going on, but Skellen had seen the musketeer drop silently to his knees and knew that something was afoot. He hammered a fist straight into the guard's cheek, sending the man sprawling on the flagstones. The man tried to get up, arms flailing in the direction of his musket, but it was too far away, and Skellen kicked him in the face. The blow threw him backwards and he landed heavily, the back of his skull meeting the floor with a wet smack. He did not move again.

Stryker was last through the window, climbing on one of the beds to provide the extra height required to haul himself over the stone sill. Grabbing hands met him on the other side, helping him down into the alley, and, before he had found his bearings, they were on the move.

'I'm only glad they weren't wearing buff,' their rescuer said happily. 'The dagger would not have made it through if they had, and then where would we be?'

Stryker grasped the shrewish man's shoulder, more roughly than was deserving of a man who had risked all to liberate them. 'You throw daggers? Christ, Menjam, you're no bloody corn merchant.'

'That's for bleedin' sure,' Skellen muttered in the darkness.

'And how the hell did you get up there?' Stryker said, glancing back at the window that was positioned in the infirmary's stone wall. A man of Skellen's height might have looked through it, but not the diminutive Menjam.

The little man grinned broadly, baring the sharp, rodent-like teeth Stryker remembered well, and nodded to a place at the base. 'I had help.'

The newly rescued prisoners followed the newcomer's gaze. There, obscured by the night's pitch depths, they laid eyes upon an object. It appeared to be a large, black sack.

'It's a body,' Skellen said.

Stryker stared at the object for a few more seconds before the shape of a man began to resolve. He seemed to be sitting with his back against the wall, but he was slumped forwards, head lolling, as though sound asleep.

'A necessary evil,' their rescuer said simply. 'Unavoidable in the current circumstances. Made an excellent ladder, though. Come,' he began to walk again, short legs moving rapidly along the passage between the infirmary and the north wall, 'there's a place up ahead where the battlements have crumbled somewhat. We'll be over it in a trice.'

Stryker stooped to draw the dead musketeer's sword, before following the man they had first known as a humble corn seller to the wall. A pyramid of rotting timbers and bits of rubble had been piled on the inside, making a reasonable ramp, which they climbed quickly.

And then they were over and standing in Jayes Lane, the path that bordered the Close to the north. Abel Menjam indicated a narrow track that ran away northwards between dense trees. 'The horses are just along there. Now come, we must move quickly before you are missed.'

Stryker and Skellen each took one of Lisette's arms and the group ran along the track. After no more than fifty yards, the soft whickering of horses carried to them from a place within the tree line.

'Who are you?' Stryker said, as they waded through the tangled foliage at the side of the lane.

The little man turned. 'My name is Abel Black, and I have come to rescue you.'

BROCTON, STAFFORDSHIRE, 7 MARCH 1643

The first light of day was pallid and weak. It broke through the forest canopy in grey shards, turning the trees into distorted, demonic claws.

Four silent figures moved among those claws, their outlines glinting like wraiths gliding in the half-light. Their progress was slow, halting at every rustle and squawk from the depths of the labyrinthine wood.

Major Zacharie Girns picked his way between ancient boughs and wizened branches, a hundred grasping hands of a hundred skeletal giants. *Not far now*, he told himself. He glanced over his shoulder, making certain Blaze, Rontry and Slater were with him. In twenty paces or so, the extent of the wooded kingdom would be reached and they would break out on to the clearing beyond.

But there, in that clearing, they would be exposed. Their dark cowls gleaming silver beneath the clear dawn sky. And in that there was danger. They had seen a troop of enemy cavalry in the area the previous evening, and Girns could not be sure that the malignants had left the village and its surrounds. A pang of indecision stabbed him; a torrent of concern and self-preservation that was almost irrepressible. But repressed it must be. The reward would be worth the risk.

Girns looked back again, signalling that the group should make their move. The prisoners hesitated briefly, but Slater shoved the bigger of the two, Jonathan Blaze, hard in the back. And then they were running. They burst from the protection of the last trees and out on to the open ground. The clear grey sky seemed to burn, as if to highlight the scuttling bodies in deliberate persecution. But Girns kept going, kept running, holding breath, tensing muscles, praying, praying, praying.

No shouts of alarm went up. Not scraping of swords or rumbling of hooves. Silence.

Up ahead were walls of stone, grey and stoical against the breaking morning, and Girns's spirits soared, for their destination had been reached. To the right and left were more stones, markers for the bones of folk long dead, waist high and rounded at the summit. They appeared like gigantic teeth, jutting random and crooked from the earth, and Girns indicated that the group should duck behind the biggest to recapture their breath.

The building was no more than ten paces away now, and, other than their own laboured breathing, nothing could be heard. Gradually doubt evaporated. Yes, thought Zacharie Girns, he would be rewarded mightily. For it was not silver or gold that awaited the success of this mission, but a place at God's right hand.

Girns offered a silent prayer of thanks and stood, making for the small oaken door set half a yard below ground level. It was as he remembered, just as it had been all those years ago. This place that preyed so heavily on his mind, the place so dear to his heart.

They had travelled north and east, careful not to encounter soldiers from either faction, and, sure enough, as the previous night had begun to give way to dawn, Girns had pointed out a right turn in the road, leading them on to a track bisecting dense woodland that, his childhood memories promised, opened on to cleared land. It was a cemetery and, at its centre, they would find a chapel. Having tethered the horses to some oak trunks in the forest's depths, the four had proceeded on foot.

Girns descended the two stone slabs, their surfaces smooth from the footfalls of generations, taking him down to the chapel's brick-floored porch and the little door at its far end. He reached out to turn the loop of dark iron, but the latch would not lift. The door was locked.

'What now?' Slater hissed.

Girns ignored him. Instead he knelt to the side of the door and ran his gloved hands along the space between the red bricks and a line of grey flagstones that skirted the door's threshold. In seconds he had found a point where the gap between brick and stone was slightly wider than elsewhere, and he forced his fingers into the crack, curling them under the flagstone's rough edge. And then he heaved.

'The good Lord,' Girns said through gritted teeth, as he levered the flagstone out of its snug position, 'will provide.'

Slater stepped closer, peering down at the patch of earth suddenly exposed to the light. Something gleamed there, at the very centre, and his wispy-haired top lip curled upwards, exposing a mouthful of rotting teeth. 'A key.'

'Well, get it quickly then, fool,' Girns uttered in a voice betraying the strain of the heavy stone.

Slater did as he was told, darting forwards and snatching up the fat length of rust-plagued iron. Girns let the flagstone drop loudly back to earth and straightened up, holding out his palm, into which Slater placed the precious object.

The door was unlocked in a flash, and Girns moved inside the little building, pleased that the large rectangular window above the altar allowed the blossoming dawn's wan bounty to pour in, bathing the limewashed walls in a dull glow. The place looked as though it had been long abandoned. A thick layer of dust and cobwebs covered everything from the little pulpit and railed altar at the building's north end, to the half-dozen pews that sat on either side of the short nave, to the high wooden roof beams. At the southern end, in the corner nearest the door, there was a great stack of hay where once the place had been employed as a stable, though now the material was dusty and ancient.

'What is this place?' Tom Slater asked, removing his cloak and closing the door firmly behind them.

'This is Girns Chapel,' the major replied, his voice low, reverent. 'Built by our family three centuries ago. It is long since abandoned. Long forgotten. And far enough from the village that we will not be disturbed.'

Slater gazed around the little structure, unfastening the ties of his buff-coat after the long, sweat-inducing ride. 'So what now?'

'Now?' Girns replied, turning the key in the iron lock. He turned to face the room, casting a look of pure acidity at Blaze. 'Now this Romish blood-sucker will recant his ways.'

'Recant?' Slater said dubiously. 'I thought we was going to slit his gizzard.'

'We shall, Thomas, if he does not recant.'

Girns drew his sword, the sudden metallic rasp causing the others to flinch, and strode along the short nave to the wooden cross that formed the chapel's altar. Without word or warning, the tall major leant across the rail and swung the blade in a great arc, face tight with determination, arms moving with practised speed and power. The sword connected with the wood at the point where vertical and horizontal piece connected. It scythed diagonally through the cross as though it were pure water, cleaving the top away with such force that the blade did not stop until it met with the floor, sending a shower of sparks in all directions.

Girns stared at the altar that was now just a sharpened stake thrusting out from the flagstones. 'Graven images will be torn down, praise God,' he rasped, his breathing suddenly laboured.

'Jesu, Zacharie,' Blaze whispered.

'You mean to tell me all this 'as been to turn this bugger Puritan?' Slater said, his voice a mix of incredulity and rising vexation.

Girns turned slowly. 'Be still, Tom,' he ordered, sheathing the blade, 'and take care of your vile language. Is there a higher purpose than to bring a man to God? Especially one so talented.'

'Jesus fucking Christ, Major,' Slater hissed, anger finally outweighing respect for the sallow-faced officer, 'we ain't goin' for Luke's reward, are we?'

Girns rounded on his skinny subordinate, lurching forwards to clasp a bunch of Slater's collar in a gloved fist. 'That is the last time you curse or blaspheme in my presence, Thomas.' He released his grip suddenly, sending Slater sprawling on the straw at his feet. 'If Blaze recants and joins our righteous cause, he may live. If not, we will shoot him dead and claim Sir Samuel Luke's generous incentive.'

'I shall not—' Blaze began, though the bluster was punctured from his voice as he beheld the threat in Girns's face.

'You will recognize the righteousness of our fight,' Girns hissed with sudden fury, 'and sovereignty of the Parliament, or, by God, it will be the worse for you!'

Blaze's blue eyes met the green of his captor, and, for several seconds, they simply stared. 'What has happened to you, Zacharie?' the former said eventually.

'Do not think I will hesitate to—'

'That is not what we agreed,' another voice sounded from the corner of the room.

All eyes turned to where Jesper Rontry stood.

'Jes?' Blaze said quietly. 'It is not what *who* agreed?'

Rontry looked up at his master then, eyes sorrowful. 'I have been with you for years, sir. Ever at your side. Ever servile. Ever attentive. And what do you give me in return?'

Blaze stared at him, eyes wide with disbelief. 'I—'

'Nothing,' Rontry went on remorselessly. 'You gave me nothing. Not a word of kindness or affection.'

Blaze could not keep his mouth from lolling open. His face flushed and it seemed for a moment as though he might faint. At length the big man steadied himself, but when he spoke his voice was barely audible. 'You betrayed me?'

'He did.' Girns spoke for the servant. 'You *and* Lazarus.'

Blaze did not move. 'Is this true?'

Jesper Rontry scratched at his bald pate. He cleared his throat and adjusted his stance. And then he nodded.

'Sweet Lord,' Blaze murmured.

'Rontry and I have been in communication for some time,' Girns explained, triumph running like a vein of granite through his words. 'His information has proven invaluable.'

Blaze could not tear his gaze away from Rontry. 'You warned him of our journey to Kenilworth?'

Rontry remained silent, so Girns spoke for him again. 'And Lazarus's journey to Stafford.'

347

'My God,' Blaze whispered. 'Such betrayal for—for the want of a kind word or two?'

Rontry peered back at Blaze through tear-filled eyes. 'A kind word? Still you do not understand. It was – it *is* – so much more than that.'

'I knew Lazarus would never recant his Popery,' Girns intervened, 'nor fight against his king, so I was forced to dispatch him before he damaged the rebellion. But you are different. You would betray your king and your faith to save your own skin.' He gave a small grunt of laughter. 'Ironic, is it not, that your innate cowardice might be the route to your salvation?'

'You presume too much,' Blaze replied.

'I thought he was going to die,' muttered Rontry, studying the ground again. 'That was the agreement. Blaze's death and a share of the money.'

'Not necessarily,' Girns replied, keeping his own eyes squarely on Blaze.

'Why not?' Slater spat the words. He had risen to his feet now and was advancing quickly.

Girns spun around, drawing his sword again when he saw the fury on Slater's face.

'Why the fucking hell not, Major?' Slater went on regardless. 'We were to kill the bastard and get the money. Why spare him now?'

Girns suddenly lunged.

The steel plunged deep into the soft flesh of Slater's stomach, and the young man pitched forward, hands clasped at his destroyed guts, blood pumping freely between his fingers.

'I told you not to swear again, Slater.' Girns drew a pistol with his free hand, levelling it at Blaze. 'It is loaded.

Do not think to do anything rash. To be gut-shot is a painful way to die.'

'Why?' The speaker was Thomas Slater. He was curled on the flagstones beside the vast pile of dirty hay, lying in his own blood as it pooled around him in an expanding lake of scarlet. 'I don't understand any of this.'

Girns opened his mouth to speak, but Slater let out a deep moan. His face was as grey as the dawn outside, and his lips drew back in a ghoulish mask as agony racked his reed-thin body. And then he was still.

'You never told him?' Blaze said, staring down in horror at the newly made cadaver.

Girns looked up and shook his head.

'Told him what?' said Rontry from his shadowy corner.

Blaze stared at his treacherous servant. 'This is not about money, Jes. Nor revenge. It never was.'

NEAR APPLEBY MAGNA, DERBYSHIRE, 7 MARCH 1643

'The horses were kindly provided by Richard Gunn,' Abel Black chirped from atop his grey mount.

They were riding east, because Gell, Black reckoned, would assume they'd have headed either south to Oxford or north to Stafford. East, he said, would throw the rebels off the scent.

'Richard Gunn the butcher?' Forrester asked in surprise.

'Let me guess,' Stryker said, cantering at Black's left side, so that he could keep him on his sighted flank. 'He's not a real butcher?'

Black gave his high-pitched laugh. 'Oh, he is a butcher, Captain, as God is my witness. But he also works for me.'

'Is he really your cousin?'

Black shook his head. 'Alas, no. A good man, though. We keep up the facade because it suits my purposes.'

'Which are?'

'To move freely around the country, of course. I have such people all over England and Wales. And France too, for that matter.'

'You are a spy?' Lisette asked.

Black looked across at the Frenchwoman. 'Of sorts, my dear. I have served the Queen ever since she married our good King. My coat fastens over a number of duties. My nominal rank is Colonel, but I am sometime servant, sometime cook, sometime personal guard, soldier, sailor, messenger and, on occasion, spy.'

'I do not know you,' Lisette said incredulously.

'Nor I you,' Black replied. 'The Queen strives to build a more mature intelligence service than the amateurish fumblings directed by Luke and Hudson. She would return to the days of Walsingham. The first step on that road cannot be taken while all intelligencers are known to one another.'

'Then how did you find us?' Stryker asked abruptly. They had spent the hours before daybreak explaining their own business: Lisette's ill-fated mission with Blaze and her near mortal wound; Stryker's search for her and the subsequent siege, although Stryker had left out the killings at Cirencester, and also the fact that a vengeful dragoon had been sent to kill him. 'Why were you even looking for us?'

Black's small, twitching eyes flickered to meet the face of each person in turn. 'It was pure accident, I freely admit. I mentioned our previous encounter to the Queen.'

'Wait!' Lisette interrupted, her voice shrill with excitement. 'Her Majesty is in England?'

Black beamed. 'That she is, mademoiselle. Landed in Yorkshire at the end of last month.'

'Praise the Holy Mother,' Lisette whispered, closing her eyes.

'You mentioned our encounter?' Stryker prompted impatiently.

'Ah yes!' Black replied, his attention returning from Lisette's reverie. 'I recounted the ambush on the Lechlade Road, and that you kind fellows rescued me.'

'But that does not explain your presence here,' Forrester said. 'We were using false names.'

'Of course you were. I knew it as soon as we met. So I listened close, hoping to discover your real names and intentions. Eventually I heard you say you were looking for someone named Lisette. It meant nothing to me, but, seeing as you uttered it furtively, suggesting that Lisette, alone, was not an alias, I thought to mention it to Her Majesty.'

'And she knew it was me,' Lisette said.

Black shook his head. 'Not for certain. But how many Lisettes are there in England? And the Queen knew you had been deployed in the Midlands by Prince Rupert, and had already read in his despatches that he had—mislaid you.' He looked across at Stryker. 'When I described your—features—it confirmed who you were, Captain, for you are known to the Queen. Your association with Mademoiselle Gaillard is also known, so, of course, it proved to the Queen that the Lisette you sought would be *our* Lisette. That knowledge alone, though fascinating, did not cause us any great concern, but then we heard

Lichfield was under siege.' He gave a modest flap of the hand. 'The Queen wished Lisette kept safe, and I owed you my life. We both had an interest in effecting a rescue. So here I am.'

'Why not send a regiment?' Stryker asked dubiously. 'The Queen had an army with her when last I heard.'

'Tell me her convoy did not fall foul of the North Sea gales,' said Forrester.

Black shook his head vigorously. 'No, not a bit of it. The entire convoy made the crossing successfully, thank God, though not without a few little trials. But the Queen would rendezvous with the Earl of Newcastle at York. They will march south together. Besides, you have spent your fair share of time in Lichfield. You know that one man with knowledge of the city's geography has a better chance of getting across the wall than an entire army operating in ignorance. I left Bridlington immediately, hoping and praying I would reach the city before Lord Brooke broke through.'

'Brooke's dead,' Stryker said.

'I know. A fact that will suit his replacement.'

'Oh?'

'Sir John Gell is a seeker of renown, Captain Stryker. Cold, brutal and desperate for glory, he will doubtless let it be known that the fall of Lichfield is down to him.' Black looked ahead at the distant hills. The dawn sun was creeping above them, like an extra, shimmering, hillock, and he was forced to squint as he gauged the terrain. 'And that will be useful for our flight, for such a determined cultivator of publicity will not wish it known that he let four Cavalier prisoners escape from right under his nose. He'll pretend it never happened.'

'Which means we can stop ridin' into this sun?' Skellen asked.

'You have it, Sergeant,' Black exclaimed. 'I believe we have ridden this way long enough. It is time we parted.'

'We?' Stryker echoed the word.

'Of course,' Black said casually. 'The Generalissima would recall Mademoiselle Gaillard forthwith.' He twisted, saddle creaking, to meet Lisette's quizzical gaze. 'She thinks a great deal of you, and, after your evident tribulations suffered under Rupert's command, she no longer trusts her nephew to—wield—you correctly.'

'I—' Lisette began in a voice full of desperation, 'I cannot.'

'And you, Captain,' Black went on, ignoring the French woman's stuttering reticence, 'will wish to head south, I suspect. The Queen told me you are Mowbray's, yes?'

'Aye, sir,' Stryker said, not wishing to mention the fact that a return to his regiment would probably see him back in prison; or worse.

'Well, it would seem most prudent for you to go direct to Oxford. If Mowbray's Foot aren't there, then you will at least discover where they can be found. And you'll be needing new weapons and kit, too. All of which can be found in the King's blossoming new capital.'

Stryker nodded his acquiescence, but Lisette was not so easily commanded. 'I cannot,' she was saying, louder this time. 'I must make for Oxford also.' She stared from Black to Stryker. 'I must find Jonathan Blaze. Make amends.'

'Blaze is not your responsibility,' Colonel Black said firmly. 'The Generalissima requires your presence at York, so York is where you shall go.'

She looked again at Stryker, her blue eyes wide, pleading. Stryker tugged at his horse's reins and the animal dropped back so that it was in step with Lisette's. 'You cannot argue. It is the Queen's order,' he said, then leaned across suddenly to whisper, 'but you heard the colonel. *I* am to go to Oxford.'

Lisette stared at him for a heartbeat, the flash of understanding registering in her eyes. 'But you are hunted men, Stryker,' she said, equally as quietly. 'Oxford is the lion's den.'

'Edberg thinks we are dead, or will be by dawn. We can't go strolling into Oxford, admittedly, but nor will they be actively looking for us.'

Lisette leaned over, kissing him hard, her tongue lambent and exhilarating against his. When she straightened up, she whispered, '*Merci, mon amour.*'

CHAPTER 16

It was night, and the chapel was dark and cold and dank. Jonathan Blaze watched the beetle with a level of focus he might previously have thought impossible. He followed its progress over the tiny grains of dust and ragged strands of mouldering hay, studied its rapid legs, felt every miniature hill and valley it was forced to negotiate. He watched the scuttling creature with this intensity, because it took him away from the disused chapel, far away from the smell of mildew and soil, piss and blood.

But every so often he had no choice but to immerse himself in the terrible, agonizing present. Every time he went to urinate and the bruises at his stomach and ribs made it feel as though he passed shards of jagged glass. Every time he licked dry lips and the sear of broken teeth jarred at his mind and soul. And every time he went to grasp something with hands that were now nothing but raw, fingerless stumps. Zacharie Girns, a man he had never thought to see again, had brought him to a place built for heaven, and shown him hell itself.

He glanced across at the inert lump of flesh that had once been Thomas Slater. The cadaver lay where it had fallen, the stink of blood and putrefying flesh hanging ripe in the locked building. Soon, Blaze knew, there would be a second body. The thought had terrified him at first, but now, after two days of torment, he longed for the release death would bring.

Blaze prayed silently, though he felt there were no more ways he could verbalize the plea. God was simply not listening. He wept.

OXFORD, 11 MARCH 1643

The clerk was hunched over his cluttered desk in the New Inn Hall office. He rubbed his hands together to force some cold into the long, blue-knuckled fingers, and picked up his quill. He squinted at the square of vellum laid out before him, scratching the quill in deliberate motions, careful not to waste both ink and material with a sloppy mistake.

A knock at the door startled him. 'Jesu!' he hissed, dabbing his already blackened sleeve on the vellum, battling in vain to blot the black specks that had shot out across it as his hand jerked in alarm.

The door swung open and the unwanted visitor strode into the room.

'Yes?' the clerk snapped irritably, not deigning to look up.

'My apologies, sir, but this is the office of Uriah Redpith, is it not?'

The clerk sniffed back mucus from his long red nose. 'What do you want?'

The stranger took the non-committal response as confirmation and took a step closer to the desk. 'To my shame, Master Redpith, I am utterly lost.'

Uriah Redpith set down his quill and leant against the high back of his chair. 'And?'

The stranger gave a slight shrug. 'And people say you know the new capital like the very lines of your palm, sir.'

Redpith sighed heavily. He was annoyed at the intrusion, and wished for nothing more than to be left to forge on with his mounting pile of regimental accounts, but Oxford, he knew from experience, was a sprawling maze to the uninitiated. The labyrinthine roads and alleyways winding in and out of myriad large university buildings – all now commandeered for the war effort – could be a difficult place to navigate.

'And you are?'

'John Twine,' the stranger said. 'I've come from Worcester to serve His Majesty's cause.'

'Good, good,' Redpith said with a dismissive wave of the hand. 'Which regiment?'

Twine lifted chubby hands. 'No, sir. I am not the fighting type, God forgive me.'

Redpith studied the man more closely. He was of average height, but large of frame. A man too used to good living, and most certainly, in Redpith's opinion, not the fighting type. He looked back down at his desk, attempting to find a new piece of vellum on which to repeat the spoiled work. 'A clerk, then?'

Twine bobbed his head of thinning, sandy-coloured hair. 'Indeed, sir, like yourself. I am bound for service with the fire-worker, Jonathan Blaze.'

Redpith looked up sharply. 'Blaze?'

Twine smiled. 'He sent for me, for I once scribed for him in Holland. You know the name, sir?'

357

'Of course, Mister Twine, I am chief clerk here. The generals can't even piss without me knowing. Besides, Jonathan Blaze was famed in this land even before his untimely demise.' Twine's rosy face drooped suddenly, and Redpith inwardly chided himself for taking satisfaction in the shock he had caused. The boredom of a clerk's life could turn a man to mean pleasures. 'My apologies,' he added, 'I did not intend any upset.'

'No, no,' Twine replied quickly, 'none caused, sir, I assure you. It is a shock, that is all. A rare shock. My time on his staff was enjoyable, so to hear that he is now dead is a blow. I'm sure you can imagine.'

Redpith nodded. 'Not least because you are now bereft of work.'

'Yes, yes, of course, sir,' Twine replied absently.

'Still,' Redpith said as he rifled through a pile of parchment that perched at the desk's edge, 'I'm certain we can find a suitable position. Money, men and munitions, Mister Twine. The very cogs of war.'

'Sir?'

'Who must grease those cogs but clerks, sir? War is an evil business, Mister Twine, but, by God, it creates employment like nothing else!'

'What happened?'

Redpith frowned. 'Happened?'

'To Master Blaze, sir. How did he die?'

'Ambush,' Redpith replied. 'Shot to bits on his way to a posting in the Midlands, so I hear. Bad business, undoubtedly, but such things happen in a time of conflict. Be a clerk, sir,' he said, brightening suddenly, 'it is damned boring, but damned safe!'

Twine smiled weakly. 'Quite right.'

358

'*Ah ha*!' Redpith exclaimed happily, his eyes snaking across one particular scroll. 'I have something perfect for you. Prince Rupert requires a scribe.'

Twine's brow lifted in surprise. 'Prince Rupert is in Oxford, sir?'

'Indeed he is. Gloucester and Bristol would not open their gates to him, despite first wooing the treacherous felons and then threatening them, so he led his flying column back here.'

'He'll doubtless return,' Twine said.

'Be certain of it,' Redpith agreed. 'But how does such a post suit?'

'Perfectly, sir, thank you. But may I ask one more thing?'

Redpith's eyes narrowed suspiciously. 'Oh?'

'Were all in Fire-worker Blaze's party killed? I was a great friend of his servant, Jesper Rontry, and—'

'All save one,' Redpith interrupted. 'One man escaped with his life and found his way here. It is how we heard of the ambush in the first place.'

'Tell me it was Rontry,' Twine said, his voice desperate with hope.

'Alas no,' Redpith replied, staring down at the parchments to hide his discomfort. 'The sole survivor was a soldier.'

John Twine stepped gingerly through the wood on the outskirts of Oxford. He knew where he was headed, and might have walked with confidence had it been noon, but it was now evening, and, as the dusk air cooled, shadows lengthened into twisted parodies of the trees from whence they sprang. It was an eerie place of dark, forbidding shapes and treacherous root-rutted ground. Not a place to be out for a stroll, especially when hefting a bulging sack full of precious objects.

Eventually he saw what he was looking for. A small clearing some twenty paces up ahead, a place where ancient elms had surrounded and killed the earth's foliage with their sun-blotting canopy. He upped his pace, careful to keep an eye on the narrow track for potholes and debris, but eager to make it to the clearing.

Another shadow appeared; one that moved like a gliding demon through the bracken and branches with astonishing stealth. The clerk froze, for he saw the blade that moved with it. In an instant the shadow was on the path, travelling quickly towards him, the sword levelled with intent.

The demon's features began to resolve as it reached Twine. Tall, thin of face, broad at shoulder, with long raven-black hair tied at the nape of his neck, a single eye, the colour of his sword, on one side of his face and a deep, mottled, hideous scar on the other.

'Heavens above, old man, but you're fearsome as a dose o' the pestis.'

The demon frowned. 'Christ, Forry, I could've skewered you.'

Captain Lancelot Forrester shrugged in the darkness. 'I couldn't remember whether it was an owl's hoot or a fox's bark.'

Stryker shook his head in exasperation. 'You obtained the items?'

Forrester squeezed the sack so that its contents jangled. 'Blades, cloaks and buff-leather. All spirited away from the Astronomy School.'

'They will not be missed?'

'Missed?' Forrester's brow shot up. 'Unlikely. They're using the university buildings as barracks, offices and storage depots. They build drawbridges, of all things, in the Rhetoric School. Law and Logic are now granaries, and Magdalen Grove's a bloody artillery park. I assure you, Stryker, a clerk with a bag of kit is just one more faceless ant scurrying about. It's a vast and ever-growing colony. And besides, I played the part of Clerk Twine to perfection. Even the great Ned Allen would've been proud of the performance.'

'Well done,' Stryker acknowledged. 'What else did you discover?'

Forrester tilted his head to the side. 'May we discuss it beside the fire? This bloody bag weighs a ton, and I'm so cold even my arse feels numb.'

Stryker turned away. 'Follow me.'

'I've good news and bad,' Forrester said as he strode into the warm light of the small fire at the centre of the little camp. He swung the sack down from his shoulder, letting it land with a muffled crash at his feet.

'Go on,' Stryker said, thrusting the sword into the soft earth and sitting on ground kept reasonably dry by a thick ceiling of foliage above them. Skellen was already seated, long legs crossed, stabbing at the flaring embers with a long stick.

'Blaze is dead,' Forrester said, as he fished in the sack, drawing out three sleeveless buff-coats, three voluminous cloaks and three long, leather belts. 'Ambushed, like his brother. I'm sorry, Stryker, but they already got to him.'

Stryker looked at his friend across the flickering flames. 'You're certain?'

Forrester tossed the garments to sergeant and captain and kept a belt, cloak and buff-coat for himself. Then he thrust a hand back into the sack to produce a pair of gleaming, newly forged swords and a trio of scabbards. He threw one blade and sheath in the direction of Skellen and dropped the other at his own feet. The spare scabbard went to Stryker. 'I spoke with Uriah Redpith himself.'

'Chief clerk,' Skellen grunted. He was standing now, checking the fit of the new buff-coat and buckling the belt across his torso, from right shoulder to left hip.

'The very same. There was one survivor, and he some-how extricated himself from the ambush and managed to meet up with a passing Royalist troop. They were on their way here, so here is where he's ended up.'

Stryker lifted a hand to rub his tired eye, wondering how on earth he would break the news to Lisette. 'Jesu, we were too late.'

'Much too late, old man,' Forrester agreed, fitting his scabbard at his hip and sheathing the new blade. Suddenly he smiled. 'But as I said, Stryker, I had some good news as well.'

A sound of rustling carried to them suddenly from the periphery of the clearing. All three heads swivelled to face the direction of the noise.

There was a figure, a man, out in the gathering gloom. Stryker stood, jerking his blade from the soil, already aware that if this were an arrest party, then they stood no hope of fighting their way through. He heard the scrape of steel to his right and glanced across to see that Will Skellen was similarly armed and prepared for a skirmish. His heart pounded, senses keen and halberd sharp. No sound came from his other flank, and he turned, wondering why Forrester had failed to unsheathe his own blade. To his bewilderment, the captain was grinning like an April Fool.

'Stone me backwards, Captain,' an unexpectedly familiar voice carried to them from the direction of the dark apparition. 'It's bloody good to see you.'

And Stryker lowered his sword as Lieutenant Andrew Burton stepped out into the clearing.

NEAR TADCASTER, YORKSHIRE, 13 MARCH 1643

Abel Black and Lisette Gaillard galloped northwards. They had taken a somewhat circuitous route from Lichfield to Yorkshire, prompted by the strong Parliamentarian presence in the Midland shires, but now, as soft diagonal sheets of rain fell at their backs, they began to feel safe. The north was a hotbed of Royalist sympathy, and at York itself they would find the combined forces of the Earl of Newcastle and Her She-Majesty Generalissima Queen Henrietta Maria.

'How much further?' Lisette called across to Black, who rode his grey mare at her left side.

Black returned the glance. 'Hardly a trice! Tadcaster is next on our route, after that we find York!'

Lisette looked back to the road ahead. It was muddy and was gradually worsening with every minute of rain, but their steeds were steady beasts and could cope with the terrain if handled with strength and care. And strength was something that was rapidly returning to Lisette Gaillard. She had recovered well enough in Lichfield under the care of Stryker and the expertise of

Chambers, but now that Black had taken her on to England's high roads, fresh air filling her lungs and a good supply of food in her snapsack, that recovery had gathered pace. She was not yet fully well, and her shoulder hurt with every jarring hoofbeat, but a new energy fizzed like a grenadoe's fuse within her veins.

She kicked at her bay horse's flanks, urging it on, desperate to be with the queen again. It had been far too long. That prospect, though, was tinged with gnawing regret. A lean face, at once feral and distinguished, mutilated and handsome, appeared in her mind's eye. Once again she was apart from the man she loved. The man who had risked all to find her. The man who, even now, was seeking out Jonathan Blaze simply because she had asked it of him. 'Look!' Abel Black's voice smashed through Lisette's reverie like a shell from Sir John Gell's mortar.

The image of Stryker's face vanished and she followed Black's outstretched hand, her eyes eventually settling on a point some two hundred yards ahead. It was a lone rider moving slowly north along the highway. Lisette watched him for several moments, noting that the horseman wore simple black doublet and breeches. A sword jutted out from his side, but he had no armour or buff-leather of any kind. She looked across at the colonel. 'Not a soldier.'

Black shook his head. 'But he may have news.'

'Let's see.'

They gained ground rapidly, and, though he remained in the saddle, it was soon apparent that the rider's mount was lame. He twisted round upon hearing their approach, eyes widening as he saw them bear down on his position, and began to frantically kick at his horse.

'Why does he run?' Lisette called, raising her voice above the squelching of the hooves.

Black frowned in puzzlement. 'Something to hide, methinks. Hold, sir!' he bellowed suddenly. 'We mean no harm!'

But the rider seemed to become more frantic than before. His head jerked left and right as he searched for a way off the road, but the thoroughfare was enclosed by thick hedgerows, and he quickly realized there was nowhere to go. He turned the horse as the pair drew within twenty paces.

'Good day to you, sir,' Black hailed the horseman.

Close up now, Lisette could see that the man was not much older than a child. His face was not only clean-shaven, but fresh-skinned and unblemished. His hair was a mass of tight red curls, and his slender neck betrayed a frame that had not yet thickened with muscle. He might have been only fifteen or sixteen years old, and yet there was something disturbing in his demeanour.

'G—good day, sir,' the lad replied, offering the colonel a curt nod.

Lisette studied him as he and Black exchanged pleasantries, noticing that his brown eyes never rested in one place. They did not twitch in practised watchfulness, like Black's, but almost convulsed. It was fear, Lisette realized. All-consuming fear.

Abel Black slid down from his saddle, boots sinking into the cloying mud. 'Where are you bound, sir? Perhaps we might travel together awhile?'

Lisette watched the rider nod quickly in response to the older man's suggestion, and wondered why he should agree to such a thing without discovering the identity of the two strangers. And then she saw it, the glimmer of metal in the rider's hand, and she realized that he had somehow grasped hold of a pistol from a holster at his saddle. Perhaps the foul weather had obscured their view, or perhaps the rider's tender years had made them blind to the danger he presented, but either way, Lisette understood, danger there certainly was.

'Gun!' Lisette shrieked in the hope that Black would react, for she had no weapon of her own, but the young man was already raising his arm.

Black saw the danger now, but it was too little, too late, and the rider's pistol flashed bright in the drizzle-hazed air. There was a dull fizzing sound, and for a moment Lisette dared hope that the powder had become damp, but then the charge ignited properly, the pistol spat its ball clear, and Abel Black was thrown from his feet as though kicked by a cart-horse.

Lisette swung a leg across her saddle, desperate to get down on to the road, but the panicked rider matched her by turns, and they were both standing ankle-deep in the mud at precisely the same moment. Lisette quickly scanned the scene, searching for a weapon to snatch up, but Black's prone form was too far away, wide eyes staring sightlessly up at the hoary sky, a film of rain glistening on his skin.

The red-headed horseman levelled his pistol again, pulling back the trigger with a spindly white finger. The flint snapped down, no shot came, and it was only then that the trembling killer remembered he had already discharged the weapon. But Lisette was already scrambling across the increasingly slick turf to find Black's pistol.

The rider threw his spent firearm into the hedge and drew his sword.

Lisette was on all fours now, crouched over Abel Black's still body, scrabbling in the folds of his coat for the pistol she knew he had.

'I—I didn't want—I didn't want to do that!' the young man blurted, almost in tears. He lurched forwards, swinging the steel down in a great arc that might have cleaved the Frenchwoman's skull in two.

Lisette rolled away, landing on her back in a shallow ditch at the road's edge. She scrambled up and sprang into a crouch, just as her assailant was preparing to lunge again. 'Who are you?'

The young man gritted his teeth. 'Just a messenger!' he cried as raindrops dripped from his curls to run down pallid cheeks, mixing with his tears. 'A messenger!'

He lunged again, but Lisette was far too quick for him and sprang nimbly out of the sword's range. 'For whom?'

'The Parliament!' The messenger was sobbing now. 'I was told to deliver the papers to Tadcaster and not engage with anyone en route. Not anyone!'

Lisette felt the unusual sensation of sympathy as she looked at this rain-soaked excuse of a fighter. The boy was too young, too naive, too raw for this task, and, though he had killed Abel Black, she knew it had been out of sheer terror at the prospect of failure. It was such a shame, for that rash decision would cost him dearly.

'Why Tadcaster?' she said, still bent low, ready to spring out of harm's way when the boy had summoned his next volley of courage. 'What is there?'

'Our new garrison,' the messenger replied, keeping his sword-tip in line with the petite woman with golden hair and granite gaze. 'Town fell some weeks back.'

Well that was one useful piece of information, Lisette thought. They had believed Tadcaster to be a friendly town, and were thinking to ride through it to collect supplies and change horses on their way to York. Now she knew better.

The horseman took a deep breath.

Lisette saw his movement and leapt to her right.

The lad lunged with all the strength he could muster, screaming a war cry that was shrill as a spring starling, and rammed the blade forwards. But Lisette was long gone, and her would-be killer flailed at thin air before tripping in the ditch and crashing headlong into the hedge.

He screamed, in pain and in fear, and Lisette was behind him while he still tried to free his torn flesh from the razor-like barbs that snagged his face in a dozen places.

Lisette took aim at his back with her pistol. But as she heard him whimper and wail and cry out for his mother, something within prevented her from pulling the trigger. She stared at the floundering, thrashing, pathetic boy, and felt only pity.

'Time to sleep,' Lisette said eventually, reversing the pistol so that she held it by its sleek barrel.

The boy heard her advance but, still stuck in the hedge's sharp talons, could not turn to face his fate. 'No! Please no!' he cried, his voice muffled in the clawing foliage.

'Do not worry, *jeune garçon*, you will wake.' She hit him hard across the back of the skull. 'But you'll feel like your horse sat on you.' The lad went limp.

'You're hardly the most elusive chap to locate, Lieutenant,' Lancelot Forrester shouted as the drizzle and wind whipped around the group. They had purchased a replacement horse for Burton as soon as the decision was taken to travel north, and now, though the weather made travel interminably difficult, they pushed on as best they could. 'As soon as old Redpith told me you were at liberty in Oxford awaiting orders, I knew to check all the taphouses!'

Burton smiled shyly. 'My habit proves to be somewhat of a blessing for once.' He hooked the reins over his weaker fist and patted his mount's hard neck in encouragement. 'Shame I could not be reunited with Bruce. He was a good companion to me. Knew how to respond to an awkward master such as I.'

'They become accustomed to a man's foibles,' Forrester said, indicating Burton's strapped arm with a nod.

Burton smiled. 'I meant before my injury, sir. I never was the most natural horseman.'

'You did well enough,' Forrester replied.

Burton pursed his lips. 'Well, now I must start afresh on this new bloody nag. Poor old Bruce. It broke my heart to see him shot stone dead from right under me.'

Stryker looked at the younger man. 'Your father purchased him for you?'

'He did, sir. And now he's dead and gone like all the others in my charge.'

'Not for certain,' said Stryker sternly. 'We've been over this ground, Lieutenant. You saw the cavalrymen killed.'

'That I did, sir.'

'And you lost Bruce, of course.'

Burton nodded mutely.

'But you did *not* see either Blaze or his servant take shot or blade?'

'I did not, sir,' agreed Burton, recounting his experience for what felt like the dozenth time, 'but it was inevitable. They came at us from nowhere. Firing from up in the tavern as we passed. Hammered us before we could but hide.' He looked at Stryker, guilt etching deep lines into his young features. 'I've failed you, sir.'

Stryker looked back to the road, shaking his head stubbornly. 'But you did not *see* it. So we will go back to Kenilworth. Back to that damned tavern, and make sure Blaze really was killed.' It was folly, Stryker knew. All borne of a desperate need to help Lisette, to find the man she sought and assuage the guilt she faced. 'Well, we might as well 'ave a bleedin' look,' Sergeant Skellen said casually. He was incongruous in the extreme, atop a horse far too small for a man of his stature.

'Absolutely, William,' Forrester chimed brightly. 'We're on the run from our own side, so either we trek up to Kenilworth on this damned foolish errand, or we stay hidden like a troop o' bloody footpads in the forest. The one thing we want to do is rejoin the regiment, and that's the only road positively blocked.' He looked at Stryker. 'We've got bugger all else to do, sir.'

'The Two Virgins it is, then,' Stryker said.

'I wouldn't mind a nice couple o' virgins right now,' Skellen remarked.

'And you say they were professionals?' Stryker asked the lieutenant, ignoring his sergeant.

'Undoubtedly, sir. Not simply in the execution of the ambush, but in the way one of the bastards tracked me.'

Burton stared off into the middle distance. 'I may not be as stealthy as I used to be, but I was first on horseback, then on foot through forests and marshland, and then I followed the Cherwell, and the bugger just kept coming. He was not only relentless, but knew his business very very well.'

Stryker thought back to Lisette's recollections of the night Lazarus had died. They had been ruthless, she said, and deadly efficient. 'It's the same team.'

'Sir?'

'The men who came after you had already been at work. They killed Blaze's younger brother back in January.'

Burton's eyes widened. 'What does this mean, sir?'

Stryker stared at the road ahead and kept his mouth shut. Because it meant that Jonathan Blaze was almost certainly dead.

NEAR TADCASTER, YORKSHIRE, 13 MARCH 1643

'To the Parliamentary commander at Tadcaster,' Lisette Gaillard read aloud, squinting at the parchment as the rain began to make the ink rapidly illegible.

It had taken all Lisette's strength to drag both bodies under the hedgerow. One would eventually come round, but, she thought, the least the flame-haired youth deserved was to wake beneath the corpse of the man he had killed.

After moving the bodies, she had chased the spare horses away, unwilling to allow the beasts to draw the attention of anyone else who might be foolish enough to travel in the inclement conditions. And then she had studied the contents of the unconscious rider's leather bag, the one carrying his message for the new Roundhead garrison at Tadcaster.

'Protect York road,' Lisette said quietly, her blue eyes studying the black scrawl. 'Stafford,' she said, scanning the words for the next salient morsel of information. 'Immediate assault. Sir William Brereton. Nantwich.'

Lisette rolled the paper back into a tube, hastily crammed it back into the leather bag and slung it across her shoulder. She strode to the one remaining horse and hauled herself up into the saddle, glancing back down at the place in the hedgerow where she had left the injured boy and the body of the man who had saved her from hanging at Lichfield. She blew Colonel Abel Black a kiss. She would report his bravery and skill to the queen, if she survived the coming days.

And then Lisette Gaillard tugged on the horse's reins so that it turned its back on the north. For Lisette was no longer bound for York. She would go south and west. To Stafford.

BROCTON, STAFFORDSHIRE, 14 MARCH 1643

As the chapel door creaked slowly open, the light positively scorched his eyes.

Blaze shrank back into the great pile of filthy hay into which he had burrowed for warmth, curled tightly like a stillborn foetus, and prayed for the light to dim again. Prayed for the man to leave.

'How are we this morning?' The voice of Major Zacharie Girns came from the doorway. Blaze cowered further in his burrow. 'You know it's been near a week, Jonathan, and still you persist with this foolishness.'

'And you thought I would recant as though it meant nothing,' Blaze mumbled through the remains of fist-pulped lips.

Girns strode into the room, wrinkling his nose at the smell. 'I confess I expected you to join us rather more readily. Satan truly works within you.'

'Satan?' Blaze replied, though to utter the word was agony. 'It is not I who commits murders, Zacharie. Nor was it poor Lazarus.'

Girns chuckled derisively. 'We were men of like mind once, you and I. But it was not I betrayed the true faith for that of Rome. You and Lazarus chose the false prophet and his insidious lies. I am giving you the chance to repent. You should thank me for it.'

Blaze lifted one of the blackened stumps that had once been hands. '*Thank* you?'

'You will live, Jonathan,' Girns replied casually. 'The wounds were well cauterized.'

'I will live? You slice away my fingers and that is all you can say?'

'Your demons are stubborn adversaries. The Lord has required severe tactics to drive them from your body.'

Blaze wanted to laugh, but the pain was too great. 'And what do your masters think, Zacharie? Of this torture?' Out of the corner of his eye, Blaze saw Jesper Rontry. His former servant had stepped into the chapel at Girns's heel. 'And what do you think, Jes?'

'Now you want my opinion.' Rontry's face was white as apple blossom, and his balding head was speckled in sweat beads. 'I wanted you dead, sir. Gone, swiftly and finally. But I did not want this.'

Girns rounded on him. 'But your wants are irrelevant, little man.'

'Jesper is of the old religion, too,' Blaze said. 'Why let him live, while you subject me to such horrors?'

'Because he is unimportant,' Girns said bluntly. 'You are not.'

'His masters do not know,' Rontry blurted suddenly. 'Luke, the rebel scoutmaster general, sanctioned your deaths. He does not know the major has taken you alive, nor does he know he plans to let you live if you convert.'

'You are the best ordnance chief in the land,' Girns said, 'I do not deny it. Parliament would welcome you with open arms.'

Tears began to well at the corners of Blaze's blackened eyes. 'Then I will join their rebellion, Zacharie, I do not know how many times I must say it!'

Girns shook his head. 'It is not enough. I would save your mortal soul. If you do not relinquish the Papacy, then you are better off dead.' He took a step forwards, a small knife appearing in his hand.

'No!' Blaze shrieked as he caught sight of the glinting blade.

'Please, Major,' Rontry was saying. 'End this now, I beg of you. He cannot stand any more agonies. I cannot bear to watch it.'

'The Lord does not test us any more than we can bear. The demons will flee when the time is right, and Blaze will be spared.' He grinned, eyes like bright emeralds, and stooped to take hold of the fire-worker's lank hair. He wrenched hard, turning Blaze's head to the side, and lowered the knife's finely honed point so that it hovered just below his captive's right ear lobe. 'And we shall pray together, Jonathan. Imagine it! Pray together and fight together. Oh, the King will not know which way to run!'

374

He moved the knife then, sawing it back and forth in powerful, jerking movements.

Jonathan Blaze screamed.

KENILWORTH, WARWICKSHIRE, 15 MARCH 1643

'It were all so damned quick,' the tapster of the Two Virgins told Stryker. 'Like the fastest lightning storm you ever saw. Clouds and flashes and screams. And then it were over. Whose were they, sir? The men that died, I mean.'

Stryker and his three men had reached Kenilworth as rain lashed mercilessly down. The buff-coats pilfered by Forrester at Oxford, freshly made and impregnated with urine-coloured fish-oil, had been worth their weight in gold, for they had kept torsos warm and dry beneath the protection of their new cloaks, but it was still a great relief to step into the hearth-warmed tavern.

'King's,' Stryker said.

The tapster nodded, his face blank, careful not to give away any allegiance.

Stryker did not blame him. 'The shooters. From where did they attack?' he asked as the tapster hastily poured their beers into four worn wooden pots.

The tapster, a squat man with puffy eyes and fat lips that made him appear slightly amphibian, pointed directly above him. 'Up there, sir, in the lodgings. They'd been there three nights. Quiet as church mice, sir. Well, till that mornin', o' course.'

'How many?' Forrester asked.

The tapster thought for a moment. 'Three, sir.'

Stryker glanced at Burton, then back to the tapster. 'Just three?'

'Aye, sir. Only saw three men. S'pose they might have had some join 'em without me noticin', but it were three what paid their way.'

'And how many were left for dead?' When the tapster paused to think, Stryker leaned in close, fixing the stubby man with a stare.

The tapster swallowed hard. 'Seven by my reckonin', sir.'

The four soldiers exchanged glances, and Burton opened his mouth to address the witness, but Stryker's hand was suddenly at his forearm, the pressure firm.

'You are sure of the number?' Forrester said earnestly.

The tapster nodded, but looked over his shoulder. 'Gwen!' he bellowed towards the door immediately at his back. 'It was seven dead'uns, weren't it?'

'Course it was, you pork-brained antick!' a female's voice squawked from an upstairs room. 'Hard to forget, seein' as we had to bury 'em!'

The tapster turned back to face his customers. 'Seven it is. They're out in the forest now, mind. More beer?'

Forrester slid his cup across the wooden surface of the bar, but Stryker shook his head. 'No, thank you.'

The four went outside to collect the horses, pleasantly surprised to discover that it had stopped raining.

'Impressive job,' Skellen said bluntly. 'For three men to batter so many.'

'They had a grenade, remember,' Stryker replied.

'That'd help,' Skellen said.

'They're alive!' Burton exclaimed as he swept his sword in and out of its scabbard, checking the rain had not caused the steel to stick. 'The escort was eight soldiers, including me.'

Stryker nodded. 'It doesn't mean they're alive now, Lieutenant. But at least we know they weren't killed at the scene. Well done, by the way. I didn't want you asking him questions, in case you said something rash. We are still outside the king's law, do not forget.'

'And now so are you, Mister Burton, sir,' Skellen said pointedly.

'If Blaze lives, then I'll find him,' Burton replied, 'regardless of whether I must ride with outlaws to do it.'

Forrester clapped the lieutenant on the back. 'That's the spirit, Andrew! Your father would be so proud!'

'Cavorting with criminals?' replied Burton. 'I doubt that very much.'

'But where must we ride to?' Skellen said as he checked his horse's saddle was fixed securely.

'Excuse the interruption, sirs,' said a new voice. It was the tapster, who had come to stand at the open doorway. He pointed at Skellen. 'I couldn't 'elp but overhear what yon fedary just said.'

'Flapping ears have a habit of getting cut off,' Stryker said dangerously. In his experience, a man with no friends must assume all others to be enemies.

The thick-lidded eyes widened in alarm, and the tapster nodded quickly. 'Just that last word's all I heard, sir, upon me life.'

'Then speak plain.'

'He asked where you'll ride next, sir. Well, I heard 'em, see?'

Burton took a step towards the tapster. 'Who? Who did you hear?'

The tapster retreated a fraction, but went on, 'Them what done the ambush you was askin' about.'

'Aye, that's right,' agreed a short, hugely obese woman who came to stand protectively at her husband's back. She might have been at his side, Stryker thought, had the two of them been able to fit in the doorway at the same time. 'The tall one, with all the warts and lily-white skin.'

'We didn't see 'em leave,' the tapster went on, 'for Gwen and I was hidin' in the back room, what with all the commotion and shootin' and such.'

'But we heard the devils chatting,' Gwen said, 'didn't we, Henry?'

'That we did. They were headed for a place I happen to be familiar with. A village quite some distance north of here.'

Stryker hauled himself up into the saddle and stared down at the tapster and his wife. 'What is the name of this place?'

'Take the north road out of Kenilworth, sirs,' the tapster continued, 'keepin' the castle on your left.'

'For Christ's sake!' Stryker snarled. 'The name!'

CHAPTER 17

The road was narrow and flanked by high, heavily wooded banks overhung by trees like willows across a stream. The depth of the road and the enmeshed canopy above made the afternoon seem darker than it was as Stryker and his small cohort pressed north. They had made sluggish progress in the two days since leaving Kenilworth, for the horses were weary and the ground sapping, and Stryker could not help but wonder if this would prove a fool's errand. But the Kenilworth tavern keepers had given them a name, so Brocton was where they would go.

Stryker squinted ahead, studying the sinister shadows at the place where the road vanished in a bend. This was the worst time to be travelling and it made him uneasy. Broad daylight made a man easy to spot, but equally allowed him to spy anyone approaching. Night-time afforded inky depths through which an experienced fellow might travel undetected. But this strange half-light offered nothing but difficulty.

'Sir?' Lieutenant Andrew Burton enquired noticing the tension in his captain's expression.

Stryker looked across at him. 'I dislike dusk.'

'It is still daytime, sir.'

Skellen, riding beside the lieutenant, craned his neck to stare up at the ceiling of foliage. 'With this cover it might as well be bloody twilight, sir.'

Burton followed the tall man's gaze. 'I suppose.'

'It strains the eyes and tricks the senses,' Stryker explained.

'I've nearly drawn my sword at three different foes thus far,' Forrester said, 'and all the buggers have transpired to be saplings!'

'Doesn't help that we're so near Birmingham,' Stryker went on. 'This is territory of the most hostile kind.'

'It was either this route or the highway further east,' Forrester replied, 'and I don't know about you men, but I'd sooner avoid another trek through Lichfield.' He glanced over at Burton. 'Count yourself fortunate to have missed that joyous adventure, Lieutenant.'

Burton feigned a look of hurt. 'My own joyous adventure proved near fatal, sir.'

'As did ours, Andrew,' Forrester retorted seriously, 'I can assure you.'

'I'm just glad you found me,' the younger man went on, 'for I need this chance to redeem myself. I must find Blaze.'

'Or his killers.'

Burton nodded. 'Or his killers, aye. Either way, I need to redeem myself.'

Forrester chuckled. 'You sound like Lisette.'

'Not sure you'll redeem yourself like this, sir,' Will Skellen said soberly. 'The Prince'll be pleased you made amends for losin' Blaze – if you'll pardon the expression, sir – but not that you managed it with us three.'

'I don't know, Sergeant,' Burton replied. 'You might find your situation improves too.'

380

Skellen dipped his head. 'Praps, sir. But did I ever tell you about the time in Germany, prob'ly ten years back, I was sent out with a bunch of Kentish boys to scout for an enemy troop we 'eard was nearby?'

'Go on.'

'A couple o' the Kent lads got caught lootin' our major's personal baggage when he went to purge his pizzle out in the woods. He caught sight of 'em on his return, but before he could lay a charge, that bloody troop jumped us.' Skellen whistled softly. 'Irishers, they were. Fighting for the Spanish. It was a rare bastard of a brabble, sir, I don't mind tellin'.'

Burton's mouth was gradually opening as the tale gripped him. 'What happened, Sergeant?'

'We drove the buggers off, sir,' said Skellen. 'And them Kentish lads, the looters, were right up there with the bravest who fought that day, as God is me witness.'

'And were they thanked?'

Skellen nodded. 'Aye, sir. They were thanked, rewarded with puffs of pipes and handshakes, and then strung up from the nearest branch next to the Irishers we'd taken.'

Burton swallowed thickly.

'If ever your condition is so dire that you consider suicide,' Forrester piped up, winking at Stryker, 'you may trust William Skellen to hand you the bloody pistol.'

'Wait!' Stryker hissed suddenly, his tone commanding immediate silence. The others shut their mouths and became utterly alert, professionalism and raw instinct taking hold. Stryker brought his mount to an immediate standstill. He waited, glaring into the shadows as the road trailed away. Listened.

There it was. The sound he'd heard the first time, but more clear. Nearer.

He turned to the others. 'You hear that?'

Forrester shook his head, Skellen frowned, but Burton slowly nodded. 'Rustling,' the lieutenant whispered. 'Twigs snapping, perhaps.'

'A fox? Badger?' Forrester said.

Stryker chewed the inside of his mouth. 'Maybe. But there's something about it—' He fell silent to listen again. More rustling, but this time it seemed to be echoing throughout the sunken road. 'It's coming from both banks,' he said finally.

Stryker looked left and right, scanning the slopes. A hand went to where his musket or carbine would normally be, and, with a quickening sense of dread, he realized that all the four of them carried were swords. Suddenly he felt utterly naked.

'Forry, Skellen,' he snapped, 'get up on those bloody banks. Find out what the hell we're dealing with.'

The two men dismounted. The gradients were too great for their horses to safely negotiate. Hurriedly each took an opposite bank and scrambled up the steep earthen roadsides. Stryker watched them go, cursing his own stupidity. In all the excitement at having been reunited with Burton, and then the exhaustion of this long journey, he had been utterly remiss in leading his men on to a bridleway so well overlooked and easily approached. He had not thought to place a man on the high ground at either side, and now they might all pay the price.

A shot cracked out then. It was fired from somewhere out in the pastures on the right, the high land into which the road was carved, and out of sight for Stryker and

Burton. Another crack followed in quick succession, and then one from the land to the left.

Almost at once a man appeared at the crest of either bank, and with unbridled relief Stryker saw that both his comrades were unscathed.

'Musketeers, Stryker!' Forrester called down. 'Hundreds of the buggers!'

'That's what I got too!' Skellen bellowed, as both men came running pell-mell down the slope, vaulting treacherous looking roots and fallen branches as they went.

'Whose are they?' shouted Burton.

Forrester clambered hastily into the saddle. 'Christ knows! They're still nigh-on a hundred paces back, but moving pretty rapidly.'

'Agreed,' Skellen said, having swung himself up on to his mount with a deal more ease than the captain. 'Can't tell if they're friend or foe.'

'At this moment, no one is our friend,' said Stryker. 'Especially if they're already shooting at us.'

'Shoot first, enquire later,' Forrester muttered. 'This place is becoming more like the Low Countries with every passing day.'

Stryker stretched out an arm to point south. 'That way!'

The four wheeled their horses round and spurred them into action, and the beasts waded their way courageously through the cloying mud. Each took turns to slip, but none lost their footing entirely, and soon they had put reasonable distance between them and the pursuing infantry.

But their relief was short-lived. Shouts sounded behind them.

Stryker twisted round, thighs burning as he clamped them to the horse's flanks. There, in the gloom, were at least twoscore of new shapes mixed with the trees on both slopes. The forms were melding in and out, then the first reached the road and turned towards its quarry. 'Cavalry!'

The others risked looks over their own shoulders, prompting a rapid chorus of curses. 'Muskets, sir!' Skellen shouted. 'Must be dragooners!'

'Good ones!' Forrester cried, impressed with the way the horses bounded down the perfidious escarpment without care for the many hazards it held.

A sickening knot formed deep in Stryker's guts. He had the terrible suspicion that it was Henning Edberg, come to complete the job he had begun at Lichfield. But it could not be him, Stryker told himself, for the Swede and his men had been stripped of their weapons and horses by Gell along with the rest of Chesterfield's garrison.

'Least they're not yellowcoats!' Forrester called breathlessly, evidently having harboured the same fear as Stryker.

A carbine coughed from somewhere behind them. Its ball whistled harmlessly past, but the warning was clear. 'We need to split up!' Stryker shouted over the sound of hooves and the bellows of the pursuers.

'There!' Burton, showing impressive horsemanship as he galloped at full speed with only one hand to hold the reins, indicated a small track up ahead with a jerk of his head.

Stryker spotted the track. It was carved into the right-hand bank, sloping gently upwards into the trees and the fields beyond. 'You and I, Lieutenant!' He threw a glance at Forrester. 'Take Skellen, Forry! Stay on the road!'

'Right you are!' Forrester bellowed. 'We'll see you in Brocton!'

Sir John Gell sat proudly atop his big horse as he led his army to war. It was a small army, he inwardly conceded, but it was, undeniably, fabulously, his. He felt like Alexander reincarnated.

He turned to look over a rain-speckled shoulder. Near on five hundred horsemen in the colours of Brooke, Gresley and Rugely led the column, their deep tracks followed by twice that number of infantry. A half-regiment of Staffordshire Moorlanders came first, bolstered by some of Brooke's former infantry, and the colonel was pleased to have them in his force, but in their wake came the real essence of Sir John Gell's army; his grey-coated Derbyshire men, seasoned, durable as granite, and ready for a fight.

They were good troops. Rogues, for certain, but the hardest fighters he had ever known. It amused Gell to imagine Brooke's pious purplecoats campaigning alongside his rough-living, filth-talking lads. They would be unhappy, to say the least. Disgusted, probably. But Brooke's men were his men now, and perhaps, he thought, they might learn something from their new commander. The late general had based his short life upon honour and prayer, and where had that got him? Dead, with a musket-ball in the eye.

'I'll not make the same mistake, by God,' said Gell quietly. He had vowed to make his life one of power and achievement over humble piety. One never knew when it would all end, and Gell would make damned sure that his legacy would be a great one.

'Sir?' a cavalry captain, riding at Gell's right hand, enquired tentatively. He was a young man, in his early twenties to Gell's eye, with close-cropped, straight hair and a high-crowned hat.

Gell shook his head. 'Never mind, Mason.'

The colonel glanced down at his new sword as it bounced against the saddle. It truly was an impressive weapon. Finely crafted, perfectly balanced, the red garnet set into the pommel seemingly winking back at him. He had never owned such a blade, and he smiled at the thought of leading the forthcoming assault with it glinting in his hand.

Christ, he thought, but the diurnals would make exquisite reading. They would report how Gell had responded to the request for support from Sir William Brereton, and that he had set out from Lichfield to uphold the Parliamentarian cause. It was perfect. The perfect story for the news-mongers to peddle. And it was precisely what Sir John had been longing for. A laudable triumph to call his own. He had taken Lichfield, certainly, but that conquest felt somehow flat. The Close was under Parliament's rule now, its Cavalier commanders taken in chains to the capital, but there had been no real fight, no scaling of the walls or swarming through a breach. To make matters worse, Lord Brooke had been killed on the most opportune day possible for Royalist propaganda. The very day dedicated to the cathedral's patron saint. 'And the goddamned malignants somehow had the better of the skirmishes.'

'Beg your pardon, sir?' Captain Mason said.

Gell looked across at him. 'I was merely pondering Chesterfield's unlikely fortune.'

'Fortune, sir? Is he not bound for the Tower?'

'But his men played merry havoc till their resolve finally crumbled,' Gell said, patting his horse's neck. 'They fought off our attempt to fire the drawbridge, and caused utter carnage down in Gaia Lane.'

'I see your point, sir,' Mason muttered.

'And most vexing of all,' Gell continued, 'those that escaped—'

'The spies, sir?'

'The spies. The men tell me they saw them at each of those actions.'

The captain frowned. 'Not surprising, sir, given the numbers Chesterfield had. I expect every able-bodied man was deemed fit to fight.'

Gell looked across at his subordinate. 'But the three spies led from the front. They orchestrated matters, organized the Royalists.' He shook his head angrily. 'And now they have slipped into the night, like dusk shadows.'

No, thought Gell, Lichfield was hardly the career-defining event for which he so yearned. He needed another. Something cleaner, grander and unhindered by the setbacks that so tainted his taking of Cathedral Close. And this next venture would be that event. One to grace the diurnals of London, Bristol and Norwich. One to be emblazoned across a thousand pamphlets and parchments, nailed to church doors and on trunks along side the nation's high roads. With this victory he would match – no, *surpass* – the fame garnered by Prince Rupert.

'Where will we rendezvous, sir?' Captain Mason asked.

Gell blinked away the daydream and met the younger man's gaze. 'To the north and east of the town. There is heath land there, ideal for our needs, and it is a place easily accessible to Brereton's advance from Nantwich.'

'It'll be a rare sight to behold,' Mason said. 'I've never seen such a muster. Not outside London, anyway.'

'Do not let the veterans hear such talk, Captain. It will be but a pimple on the arse of a sow, compared with the armies of the Continental wars.'

Mason laughed dismissively. 'I give not two beans for their arrogance, Colonel. We are not in Germany now. When we join with Colonel Brereton, our army will be the most fearsome fighting machine this side of Oxford.'

Gell's thin lips turned up at the corners. 'That it will.'

'And the town's Royalists will be ill prepared to engage us.'

'That is the hope,' agreed Gell. 'We move with speed so that our troops and Brereton's can storm the place before it knows it is threatened.'

'In the manner of Prince Robber.'

'Right enough,' Gell said. 'Rupert may be in league with the Devil, but there is much to learn from him. The few Cavaliers in their garrison will be caught with their britches down and we'll hammer them before they can form any kind of defence.'

Mason's mouth split in a wide grin. 'It will be their Cirencester.'

'Precisely. And with this victory we will finally secure the region for Parliament, and drive a wedge between the King's supporters in the north, and those in Wales and the south-west. It will change the very course of the war.'

Mason sucked in a great chestful of air and let it out slowly between gritted teeth, as though the implication was too immense to comprehend. 'To Stafford, then, sir.'

Sir John Gell urged his horse to move a little faster. 'Stafford, Captain Mason. And glory.'

Spencer Compton, Second Earl of Northampton, jumped down from his palomino gelding and immediately sank to his ankles in the field that his horsemen had churned to a morass. He pulled the leather glove from his right hand, removed his steel helmet and ran stubby fingers through the tight auburn curls that cascaded across his shoulders. 'How many do we have here, Sir Thomas?'

Sir Thomas Byron, a fair-haired, narrow-faced man in exquisite russetted armour, handed his horse's reins to a liveried servant and went to greet the earl. 'I have stationed fifty men here, my lord, light cavalry all.' He pointed a gauntleted hand eastwards. 'With another detachment of the same number in Butterbank, a mile thither.'

A third man came to join them. He was of the same middling height and wiry build as the earl, but his jaw was more pronounced and his face clean-shaven. 'We have similar forces at intervals all around Stafford's periphery, Father. I do not believe there are any rebel garrisons left in the area.'

Northampton nodded at his heir. 'Well done, James.' His eyes flicked to Byron. 'And how many prisoners have we taken?'

'That's one hundred and fourteen now, my lord,' Byron answered.

'A hundred and fourteen of the filthy rebel toads, eh?' Northampton replied. 'The castle will be fit to burst.'

'No more than they deserve.'

'Quite right, Sir Thomas.'

'And we've taken enough supplies for—' the clean-shaven man began.

Northampton looked at his son sharply. 'For?'

'For a lengthy siege, Father.'

'Lord above, James,' Northampton shook his head, 'but I do not intend on being cooped up in that damned town. Stanhope fell into that trap down in Lichfield and look what happened to him.'

'It is prudent to prepare for the worst, Father.'

'Aye, James, I accept the warning, but we came to Stafford from Banbury with a force of twelve hundred men, eleven hundred of which are cavalry. It is not an army with which one would offer stoic defiance from behind thick walls. It is one suited to taking the initiative.' He shook his head. 'No, we will ride out and destroy the enemy before they so much as spy Stafford 'pon the horizon.'

'None would question your valour, Sir James,' Byron interjected. 'A knighthood for gallantry is not easy to come by. But I agree with your father. We must smash the rebels before they can even see the town's fires.' He wiped specks of grass and mud from his breastplate. 'Prudence is wise, sir, but no substitute for a horse, a blade and a damned mad charge, eh?'

'Have we pacified the area?' Northampton suddenly asked.

'Yes, my lord,' Sir James Lord Compton responded. 'We have destroyed six rebel garrisons, taken more supplies than we need, and more prisoners than we know what to do with.'

'Get 'em sworn in on our side,' Northampton told Byron.

'I will, sir, of course.'

The Earl of Northampton gazed across the field at the excited troopers and the shackled prisoners, and at the gable ends of Coton Clanford's first little homes. 'So we have successfully secured Stafford and its surrounding villages for the King. We have now only to wait.'

Byron caught his eye. 'They will definitely come, my lord?'

'Wouldn't you, Sir Thomas?' Northampton replied quizzically. 'Gell's a self-serving bastard. He'll see Stafford as the jewel in his new territorial crown.' He glanced beyond the fair-haired knight, nodding a greeting to the cloaked newcomer who reined in beside them. 'Besides, we have reliable intelligence that says we are imminently to be attacked.' He raised his voice to call, 'Is that not right, mademoiselle?'

Lisette Gaillard drew back her hood, ignoring the open-mouthed stares she received from Byron and the earl's son. 'That is right, my lord. The message I intercepted was requesting the new commander at Tadcaster protect the roads into Chester from any advance by Newcastle's forces in York.'

'Protect, gentlemen,' Northampton went on, 'because Sir William Brereton, Parliament's man in Cheshire, marches upon Stafford.'

'Brereton marches from Nantwich,' Lisette agreed, 'and Gell from Lichfield. They are to rendezvous and storm the town.'

Sir James Lord Compton frowned, though his gaze did not move from the Frenchwoman's face. 'Rendezvous where?'

'Therein lays our problem,' the earl answered for her.

Lisette gave an apologetic wince. 'The dispatch did not say.'

Byron stepped forwards so that he was just inches from Northampton's ear. 'How can you trust this woman, my lord?' he whispered hastily.

'Because I have had dealings with her before, Sir Thomas,' Northampton replied, keeping his own voice low. 'She answers to the Queen.'

Byron's earnest gaze dropped at the mention of King Charles's beloved and formidable wife. He stared up at Lisette. 'I would admit that I doubted your word, madam. I apologize.'

'No harm, sir,' Lisette replied pleasantly.

'She is to be trusted,' Northampton said. 'I shudder to think that I might have turned back to Banbury when I found Lichfield had already fallen. The King sent me to lift the siege, to attack the rebels in the city. But Parliament's flag already flew from the cathedral when we reached it. We could not take a castle with cavalry. And then, Praise God, Mademoiselle Gaillard found me.'

'I rode first to Stafford, and was informed your force was in the area,' Lisette continued the tale.

'And she persuaded me to continue northwards and protect the town.' He looked up at the Frenchwoman. 'For that you have my thanks, mademoiselle, and the thanks of the King.'

Sir James Lord Compton jammed his helmet over his wavy black hair. 'We wait, then?'

Northampton dipped his head. 'We wait. But do not rest easy, gentlemen, for one thing is certain. The Roundheads are coming.'

The afternoon was getting old when Stryker and Burton reached the first of the houses. It had been a torrid ride. A sweating, exhausting flight in the face of the huge force of unknown dragoons, but, amid hazard-fraught terrain and frequent rain showers, they had eventually shaken off their pursuers. It was not through any skill of their own, they both knew, but simply because the dragoons had lost interest. They had broken off the chase as night fell, leaving the fugitives to turn around under cover of darkness and resume their journey north.

Now, having finally reached what they hoped was their destination, any feelings of success were tinged with the hint of failure. 'They're not here,' Burton said as they let the horses amble out from the wooded road towards the buildings.

'Skellen and Forrester will be fine, I'm sure,' Stryker lied. 'But we are here, so we shall continue.'

It was a modest hamlet, a simple group of hovels clustered around the road. Certainly not the kind of place Stryker had expected to find Blaze. He had expected to end up staring at the walls of some great fort, forbidding and impregnable, the kind of place one would expect such a high-profile captive to be held.

Stryker brought his horse to a standstill near a little dwelling of sagging roof and rotten timbers and jumped down on to the muddy road. Burton dismounted too, watching his leader approach the house and hammer a fist against the door. After a minute of standing in silence, Stryker turned to go. He was not surprised to find that people were unwilling to speak with him. England was rife with marauding, looting soldiers. Life had become dangerous and cheap, and common folk were not keen to open their homes to a stranger with a sword at his hip.

It was something of a shock, then, that the door suddenly began to creak open. Stryker turned back to face the house, only to find the black-mouthed barrel of a musket pointing directly at his chest.

'What you want?' came a voice from within the building.

Stryker squinted beyond the weapon, but could see nothing but blackness. The musket was all of five feet in length, and its muzzle only just pointed beyond the doorway, allowing its owner to stand a long way back inside the house.

'This is Brocton?' Stryker asked calmly, all the while acutely aware that he might be blown to pieces at any moment.

'No, sir. Brocton's to the north.' The sleek metal shaft jerked to its owner's left. 'That way.'

'How far?' Stryker ventured.

'Less'n a mile, sir. Now be gone!'

Stryker shook his head, careful not to make any sudden movements. 'I am searching for someone.'

'Who?' the voice sounded again.

'A tall man. Broad-framed, with hair the colour of straw.'

'Ain't seen the like,' the musket-wielder said, this time uttering enough words for Stryker to realize that the speaker was a woman. An elderly one, he judged by her coarse tone.

'He rides with three, perhaps four, other men,' Stryker said. 'Soldiers.'

'We see many soldiers, sir,' the woman said.

Stryker nodded. 'Is that why you point guns at strangers?'

'It is, sir. Playing soldier gives a man excuse to steal and rape as he pleases.' She jerked the weapon at Stryker in warning. 'And don't you think I won't use this. It is loaded and primed and in good order.'

Stryker spread his arms wide. 'I promise you, madam, my friend and I seek only this man. We mean you not a bit of harm.'

'I've nothing to tell you,' the gloom-ridden woman said, her voice becoming irritated. 'Now get back on that horse o' yours and ride away. Leave us in peace!'

'As you wish, madam,' Stryker said, backing away slowly.

'King Charles and his Parliament have brought this country nothing but hardship!' the woman shouted after him. 'They fight their wars like children at play while we common folk starve!'

'I am sorry, madam,' Stryker called back as he swung himself back into the saddle.

'Our food is stolen by their armies, and our sons lie dead in far-off fields!' the woman went on angrily. 'While the rest are left behind to contend with the demons unleashed by their foolishness!'

Stryker kicked his horse, and the beast shifted forward. Behind him he heard Burton's voice. 'Demons, madam? What kind of demons?'

'I do not know what kind, for I am no witch!' the woman shouted. 'But they are among us. I hear them wail in the night. The others think I'm mad, but I know what I hear!'

Burton wheeled his horse round to face the door, which was still ajar. 'Where? Where are these demons?'

'Out in the woods, sir, where they might practise their vile rituals without interruption. Oh, you think me insane too, I am sure, but I am not. By God I am not! I've heard 'em. And I've seen lights flicker.'

'Where, madam?' Stryker pressed. He had stayed his own horse now, interest piqued by Burton's questioning. 'Out in the trees?'

'No, sir,' the woman said, as though he were mad himself. 'They're in the old Brocton chapel. It has been haunted and godless for a generation, everyone knows that. No right-minded soul would stray near. Where else would demons feel safe to tread?'

CHAPTER 18

'It has been too long already,' the wart-infested man said quietly.

'On that we can agree,' Jonathan Blaze murmured, gazing up in resignation at a face that appeared almost transparent in the candlelight. 'Please, Zacharie, put an end to this.'

Major Zacharie Girns gazed down at the broken form before him. Blaze was a mere shadow of the proud man he had once been. A lump of damaged flesh vaguely resembling one of the greatest fire-workers ever to have lived. 'You could end this if it weren't for your arrogance.'

'Not arrogance, Zacharie,' Blaze managed to gasp. 'Faith.'

'Faith?' Girns bristled. 'You were raised a Protestant. That is the true faith. *Your* true faith. If you turn back to it now you will continue this life, with the promise of eternal life later. If you let your conceit rule your head, you will die tonight, with the promise of hell's flames to follow.'

Blaze tried to laugh, but the motion became a racking cough that sent clots of dark blood up from his damaged chest, making him splutter uncontrollably. He let the cough run its course, spitting the sticky globules on to the stone before him, and, when calm descended, looked up at Girns. 'You are right, Zacharie. I was raised Protestant. Not Puritan. We have both moved away from our roots.'

Girns sighed heavily. 'But I have moved with understanding. With scholarship. You have been working for the French and Spanish so long it has simply poisoned your mind.' The tall, pale-faced major strode across the room to take up a small wooden stool. 'It ends tonight, Jonathan, one way or the other.'

Blaze forced a macabre smile through broken teeth. 'Because I have no more fingers for you to take?'

Girns shook his head. 'Because Sir Samuel Luke expects me to return to London. He will want to hear news of your death.'

'And you will want your reward.'

'Have you listened to nothing I've said?' Girns hissed, suddenly angry. 'I was never interested in an earthly reward. Only a spiritual one. The one I would receive in heaven for bringing one of God's children back to His flock. If you will not recant – if I am forced to kill you – then I shall take Luke's coin and exchange it for men, horses and guns.' He thumped one fisted hand into the open palm of the other. 'I will use it righteously! But if I can avoid such a conclusion, then I shall.'

'Luke would be displeased.'

'He would not,' Girns said firmly. 'For with your conversion would surely come enlightenment. You would see the King's cause for what it is. An unjust fight for a corrupt monarch, reeking with the stench of Popery. And once you saw that truth, you would offer your services to the Parliament.'

'You failed, Zacharie,' Blaze said in a low voice. 'I have stomached your torture, and will rise above Rontry's betrayal. I might have betrayed my King, but I will never betray my Pope. I would rather follow Lazarus.'

Girns stood, and Blaze saw the tall man's green eyes glisten. 'Then so be it. I have tried my best, by God I have tried. You may not believe this, Jonathan, but I will miss you.'

Blaze snorted derisively. 'As you miss Lazarus?'

'I do miss him. As God is my witness, I miss him dearly.'

Major Zacharie Girns wiped a gloved finger along the underside of his left eye, and Blaze realized that the pitiless zealot had shed a solitary tear.

'You are growing weak, Zacharie.'

'No, Jonathan,' Girns replied in a voice wrought with sadness. 'I will weep as I send you to hell. But I will not shy from the task.'

Outside the chapel, at the door to the little outbuilding Girns had chosen as their billet, a small, virtually bald man was attaching sacks of food across the horses' faces. Jesper Rontry had been ordered to ride out to a nearby farm and find victuals for the men and animals, and, finally, he had found someone willing to do business. Now that he had returned, he could hear muffled conversation from inside the chapel. He shuddered. Not because he knew Girns and his victim were embarking on their nightly routine of threat and oath and torture, but because he was already becoming accustomed to the horror of it all.

It had occurred to Rontry that he could have ridden away at any point in this nightmare. Jumped into the saddle and fled for the hills. But each time his mind wavered he decided to stay. And he hated himself for that decision, for he knew it was made with a heart of greed, and of fear, and of vengeance. Luke's gold, Girns's threats and Blaze's demise. Each worthy of disgust. Each as compelling as the others.

A horse whinnied then. At first he ignored the sound, assuming it was one of the three he tended, but when it carried to his ears a second time, he realized that the plaintive beast was some distance away. Out in the trees beyond the tumble-down cemetery.

Rontry turned, staring out into the darkness. He could see nothing beyond the long untended tombstones, pale beneath the moon, jutting at awkward angles from the wet grass. Beyond the stones there was nothing. Just deep, impenetrable blackness where the dense forest began. It was from out there that the whinny had come. With a skittering heart, he left his duties and ran towards the chapel.

Stryker and Burton strode carefully between the trees, keeping their steps high and deliberate so that they would not fall foul of the treacherous roots and branches crisscrossing the narrow track.

Stryker saw the small orange glow first. He placed a hand on Burton's shoulder, and, having gained the younger man's attention, he pointed at the distant spot of light with his drawn sword. Burton gave a nod to confirm that he had seen the target, and the pair moved off.

Above them, a chill breeze gathered strength, causing the high branches above to sway, their leaves rustling gently. To Stryker's ear they whispered mockery. For his foolishness in Cirencester that had condemned them as outlaws, for his eagerness to please Lisette Gaillard, and for the temerity to approach this adder's nest without fire-arms. But he was here, he told himself, and time might be fast diminishing for Jonathan Blaze. He and Burton would strike now, while surprise was on their side and while there might just be time to save the fire-worker.

They crept on, passing broad trunks with lichen skins that shone silver in the moonlight, approaching the open ground of the cemetery encircling the little chapel. This was it, Stryker's instincts chattered in his mind. This was the place the assassins were secreted.

In moments they were at the tree line. Stryker halted, pressing his body against a thick tree, made thicker still by the bulbous tumours of bark that sprouted in manic clusters at its middle. He peered out furtively, checking for movement. The chapel was rectangular in shape, and the wall they faced was one of the two longer sides, but it had no door. There was only a narrow window, a lancet, set high in the building, through which the guttering candle-light shone. He scanned the little graveyard and its ancient markers of wood and stone. Silence. Stillness.

They broke cover, scuttling in and out of the low, regular-shaped swells of skeleton-moulded ground, always looking forwards, aiming for the chapel and whatever lay within. It seemed to take an age to cross the cemetery, but, with gushing relief, Stryker covered the last few paces without hindrance, stopping only when he was flush against the church's wall. Below the lancet, the cold stone at his back was a welcome sensation. Lieutenant Burton was with him, sword drawn, flattened against the wall a little way to Stryker's right, and Stryker felt instantly thankful to fight alongside a man who would think to remain on his sighted side at all times.

After half a dozen steadying breaths, Stryker indicated that he would move to the left, while Burton should go right. Keeping backs flush against the wall, they shuffled silently in opposite directions, snaking the length of the building's side until they each reached a corner where the longer wall met its respective gable ends.

Stryker stared back along the wall to where Burton's shadowy form stood. The lieutenant raised his blade once in parting salute, the metal glinting above his head, and then he vanished round the corner. Stryker followed his protégé's example and edged out, running his eye quickly along the gable end. There was no entrance here either, so he pressed on, cringing each time his boots scraped a pebble or snapped a twig.

The next corner brought what he was looking for. A pair of stone steps, their middles smoothed and sunken by centuries of use, led down to a small wooden doorway. The area was darker than the rest of the chapel's exterior, for its lower setting and roofed porch shrouded it from the moonlight, and it took a moment from Stryker to see that the door was ajar.

Stryker paused for the time it took his heart to beat ten times, but Burton did not appear at the other end of the building. Perhaps, Stryker wondered, the lieutenant had found a second doorway and was, even now, making his way inside.

With that thought ringing like church bells in his mind, Stryker made his move. He descended the steps in a single stride, and reached out, pressing the stout little door with the tip of his sword. It began to move slowly and, mercifully, in silence.

He stepped forward, blade poised out in front, wits battlefield keen. And then he sensed it, a shadow looming behind and above him. He began to move, cursing himself for a fool, because he knew his reaction was far too late. Next moment a blinding pain exploded at the back of his skull, the dark night flashing in pristine whiteness for a split second. He saw the world spin, felt his knees crumple, then all was black.

NEAR INGESTRE, STAFFORDSHIRE, 19 MARCH 1643

'God's belt, that was a close-run thing,' Captain Lancelot Forrester said on a heaving outbreath. He and Sergeant William Skellen had reined in amongst a dense copse on a ridge that overlooked the west bank of the River Trent. They had tethered their mounts to the wizened boughs, leaving the ties loose in case a swift exit was necessary, and had paced to the southern tree line. Now that light was bathing the land again, they would be able to spy the progress of their dogged pursuers, especially since the terrain sloped gently away from them, providing a clear view south. Amid the patchwork of copse, heathland and field they could see the vast red-brick edifice of Ingestre Hall to the south-west, and the little hamlet of Ingestre to the south-east. But, mercifully, not a horse or man was to be seen.

'Must've buggered off in the night, sir,' replied Skellen.

Forrester nodded. 'Wasn't about to make that assumption though, Sergeant. Stryker would have my innards for breakfast if I led those bloody dragooners to Brocton.' He held a hand at his brow to shield his eyes as he scanned the horizon. 'Hadn't wanted to ride as far north as here, I must admit, but at least we shook 'em off.'

'What now, sir?'

Forrester turned and began striding back into the trees. 'Back in the saddle, William. We'll head down to Brocton and see if we can't find our esteemed leader.'

Skellen followed. 'Right you are, sir.'

It was only when they were mounted and ready to kick south, that Skellen spoke again. 'What do you make o' that, sir?'

Forrester looked across at the sinewy man, and saw that the sergeant was peering northwards, his gaze fixed upon a point he evidently spied beyond the copse. The captain tried to follow the direction, and had to adjust his position in the saddle to get a clear view through to the land north of this thick cluster of trees.

He saw movement. It was a long way off, past the ridge and the waterway beyond. Far down at the village on the Trent's eastern bank. 'There's a lot of 'em,' Forrester said.

Skellen chewed the inside of his mouth. 'There's bloody hundreds, sir.'

Forrester turned to him. 'Shall we take a peek?'

No answer was necessary, and the pair spurred their horses forwards until they were at the far side of the copse. They were at the very edge of the ridge now, facing north, and had a clear view all the way down to the foot of the valley where the Trent ran deep and fast. On the other side of the river was a small village, and, sure enough, the place was teeming with life.

'Fuck me,' Skellen whispered as he took in the scene. 'There's horse, foot and cannon.' He whistled softly. 'Fuck me.'

Forrester stared mutely at the units filing westwards through the village towards the River Trent. He saw that

Skellen was right. There were several hundred cavalrymen in the vanguard, followed by tight formations of infantry that might have numbered as many as a thousand. 'It's an army,' he said eventually.

'Least we know who owns 'em this time,' Skellen said in his monotonous drone. 'Grey bastards for the most part.'

Forrester stared hard at the sergeant. 'Sir John Gell.' He turned back to the army with renewed interest, running his gaze from the rear of the column, still out to the east of the buildings, all the way to the leading cavalry troopers. Those foremost horsemen had already appeared beyond the village's western fringe, and Forrester let his eyes follow the road ahead of them until they settled upon a substantial stone bridge that carried the highway over the river. 'My God,' he said quietly.

'Sir?'

'My God,' the captain said again, louder this time. 'They're crossing the Trent.'

'Aye, sir, looks like it.'

Forrester's head snapped round, ready to bark a reproof at the sergeant, but he saw no sarcasm in Skellen's deep-set eyes. 'Where does that road lead, William?'

Skellen's bottom lip slid up so that he could suck his top lip as he cogitated. 'Don't know this area, sir. Newport, praps?'

Forrester shook his head. 'We're much further east than that, Sergeant.'

'East? What's more east than Newport?' The light of understanding suddenly shone bright in Skellen's dark gaze. 'Well I'll be a goddamned hedge-priest. That dead-eyed arsehole's going for Stafford.'

405

'Kit Marlow would be positively envious of your way with words, William,' Forrester said with a short snort of laughter.

'What do we do, sir?'

Forrester's mirth vanished as he considered the question, his lips setting in a determined line. 'We go to Stafford, forthwith. The garrison must be warned of this new attack.'

'Beg pardon, sir,' Skellen replied, 'but what of the Captain? We was meant to meet 'im and Mister Burton down at that Brocton.'

Forrester thought for a moment, leaning forward to pat his horse's thick neck as he did so. 'I think we must have a parting of the ways, Sergeant Skellen,' he said, straightening up. 'You'll want to go to Stryker, I suspect?'

Skellen sucked his bottom lip again. 'I'll do what I'm told, sir, you know that.'

BROCTON, STAFFORDSHIRE, 19 MARCH 1643

Stryker's skull felt as though it had shattered into a thousand pieces when first he opened his eye. He was lying face down in wet hay, the stink of decay all around him. He lifted a hand to the back of his head. It was as if a chicken's egg had grown out through his skin. 'Jesu,' he murmured as the pain seemed to reverberate right down to the ends of his matted hair. He closed his eye quickly, taking huge gulps of air into his lungs in a vain attempt to fight the nausea that now washed over him. He lost the battle, and vomited.

It hurt to move, but he needed to at least be away from the stinking vomit lest he repeat the experience. As gingerly as a doe negotiating a frozen lake, he pushed himself up to a sitting position. He kept his eye clamped shut, for his head pounded all the more with the new motion and his stomach lurched again, though this time nothing erupted into his throat.

'Thought they'd killed you,' a voice he thought he recognized, but could not place, suddenly lanced through the cloud of pain.

Stryker forced himself to lift his eyelid. At first he saw nothing but blurry shapes, and felt panic rise in his chest at the thought that the heavy blow had blinded him, but gradually the indistinct images began to take form. Grey was steadily giving way to splashes of colour and haze-smudged lines slowly sharpened.

Stryker was slumped in the very centre of a long room. There were walls of pale whitewashed stone all around him. To his left was the brown timber frame of a pulpit and a splintered stump of wood where an altar had once been, a large, glazed rectangular window set high above both. The centre of the room was bisected by a narrow aisle, rows of pews either side, and to his right he recognized the squat form of the doorway he had tried to enter when he had been attacked. He was inside the little chapel.

Everything in the room was bathed in the pale-yellow rays of winter light that flowed through the chancel window and its smaller cousins, the lancets Stryker had seen on his approach. It was morning, Stryker realized, the sun sitting high in the east, doing its best to illuminate the day. Finally he laid his eye upon a hunched figure slumped in the corner of the room nearest the doorway, his back pressed against the foot of a substantial mound of hay. He was leaning over a stub of candle, evidently attempting to glean what warmth he could from the pathetic flame. 'Andrew?' Stryker asked hopefully, though he knew the voice did not match that of his lieutenant.

'No,' replied the hunched man, his face and body hidden by a dirty cloak. And then an arm emerged from the folds to extend towards the opposite end of the room.

Stryker turned to the end of the chapel that was occupied by pulpit and altar. There, against the altar rail, lay another person. With a building mixture of dread and relief, Stryker recognized the man's face. He began to move towards Burton's inert body, but the pain stabbed at his head again, and he was forced to become still.

'He lives, Captain,' the first man spoke again. 'They gave him a cracked head, as they did you, but I heard them say he was only stunned. Unfortunately for you both, they stripped you of your weapons and buff-coats, so do not think to fight your way out of here.'

Stryker sat back on his haunches, noticing for the first time that he wore only boots, breeches and shirt. He looked at the hooded stranger. 'How do you know my rank?'

'Captain Stryker, isn't it?' said the figure.

A light of understanding suddenly shone in Stryker's mind. 'Blaze?' he replied, though it hurt to speak.

'It is, Captain,' Jonathan Blaze said.

Stryker stared into the gloom for several seconds. There was something amiss here. Something in the fire-worker's voice that had not been present when last they had met. It was the reason Stryker had not recognized Blaze immediately.

After three or four deep breaths, Stryker hauled himself to his feet. His guts immediately lurched, the urge to vomit almost irresistible, and his head felt as though it would explode. But he was determined to beat the unwelcome sensations and gritted his teeth as he staggered slowly across the room. When he reached the spot where Blaze still sat, hunched and ragged like a Cheapside beggar, the fire-worker looked up at him. And Stryker vomited again.

'Am I so terrible a visage?' Blaze asked gently.

'No, sir,' Stryker said when he had gathered himself. 'It is a shock to see you in such a manner, that's true, but my sickness is brewed by a pounding head.' He felt guilty for the half-lie. Jonathan Blaze had been stripped down to a shell. His clothes were torn and soiled, his face damaged almost beyond recognition. The eyes were dark and swollen, the lips split, the teeth splintered. But that was not the worst of it. Blaze's hands were nothing but stumps. No fingers protruded from his palms, only ten little stubs, congealed and scabby where they had been cauterized with fire to staunch the blood and stave off infection. All at once, Stryker forgot about his aching skull. This man had been tortured to within an inch of his life.

'Sit, Captain,' Blaze said calmly. 'I should like to hear of the outside world.'

Stryker did as he was told, not least because he suddenly understood what had changed about Blaze's voice. He was a broken man. The restless spirit, the haughtiness, the arrogance, the beaming self-assuredness that had made him what he was. It was all gone. Punched and kicked and sliced and stabbed and seared from him.

'The outside world?' echoed Stryker. 'How long have you been here?'

409

'A week,' Blaze replied, though it sounded as much like a question as an answer. 'Two, perhaps.'

'Who are these people? Why have they done this?' Stryker asked.

Blaze looked at him, the eyes Stryker remembered as dazzling blue now appearing as bruise-choked slits. 'Major Zacharie Girns. He killed my brother, Lazarus, and now he will kill me.'

'I don't understand,' Stryker said, still struggling to comprehend why Blaze had been subjected to this torture. 'They killed Lazarus outright. A musket shot to the back. Why did this Girns not do the same to you?'

'Because he wants to save my soul before I die.'

'Save your soul?' Stryker asked, unable to keep the incredulity from his tone.

'Lazarus was devout. When he and I converted to Catholicism, he did so because he truly believed.'

'And you?'

Blaze gave a stifled snort that might have been a rueful chuckle had his airways not been so badly damaged. 'Expediency.' He looked at Stryker levelly. 'We served throughout the Catholic League. It seemed prudent to share their faith.'

'They paid you more?' Stryker asked.

'Paid, trusted, respected, you name it.'

'So you and Lazarus were both converts to Catholicism. But your brother had more conviction than you?'

Blaze nodded. 'More than conviction. He was a zealot. Would have burned every Protestant to a man, if he could. Girns knew he would not be able to turn him, so he did the next best thing, as he saw it.'

'He killed him.'

'Indeed.'

'But he believed he could convert you?'

'Aye,' Blaze confirmed softly, staring off into the dim near distance. 'To the Puritan faith, and to the rebel cause.'

'But he was wrong,' Stryker said, casting his eye across Blaze's many wounds.

Blaze tried to smile. 'I am a different man to the one that left England all those years ago. If it were a simple matter of allegiance, I'd have turned my coat to stop it. Stop the pain. I thought taking my fingers would—' He trailed off, and Stryker wondered if he was crying, though he could not tell amid the swollen eye sockets. As Stryker watched, Blaze turned his head suddenly and, for the first time, Stryker noticed that the right side of his face was a torn mess of flesh and blood, glimmering in the feeble morning light. 'He took my ear,' Blaze said when his fellow captive had taken a good look. 'Sawed it off with that wicked little blade he favours.'

'Christ,' Stryker whispered, unable to take his gaze from the carnage that befouled the side of this once handsome face.

'As I say, I'd have changed sides if it were as simple as that.'

'Isn't it?'

'He was wrong about my faith.' Blaze crossed himself slowly, each movement accompanied by an anguished grimace. 'I may have converted for convenience. For greed, even. But the intervening years have been more prosperous than I ever could have imagined.'

'You attributed your success to your move to Popery?' said Stryker.

'Of course,' Blaze replied, as though Stryker were a fool. 'There is no other explanation. Lazarus and I thanked God daily for our lot. And for the foresight to give our hearts to the true faith.'

'And a good Catholic cannot fight for the rebellion,' Stryker said.

'You have it, Captain,' Blaze agreed firmly. 'A reformer may fight for the King, but there is no place for a Papist in this Puritanical revolt. To change my allegiance would have gone hand-in-glove with conversion back to Protestantism. I was not willing to make that sacrifice. Whatever the cost.'

Stryker thought about Blaze's assertion for a moment, and frowned. 'But you said Lazarus was more ardent than you.'

'At the beginning. But I am no longer a fair-weather believer. Zacharie has not seen Lazarus or me for many years. Since around the time of our conversion. His opinion of me is based upon the past.'

'*Zacharie?*' Stryker asked, confused. He leaned in close. Blaze was withholding something. 'What is this Major Girns to you, Master Blaze?'

The scrape of boots on stone sounded from the doorway suddenly. Stryker and Blaze turned. The newcomer stood like a black statue, his tall, lean frame highlighted by the morning light flooding in at his back.

'His brother,' Major Zacharie Girns said.

HOPTON HEATH, STAFFORDSHIRE, 19 MARCH 1643

Sir John Gell reined in on the crest of the ridge. He faced south and west, in the direction of a little village known as Hopton. There was a town beyond that village. A strategically pivotal town, currently under the thumb of the king and crucial to the war in the Midlands. It was less than three miles away and soon, Gell believed, it would be his. Stafford.

At Gell's back the land fell steeply away to the valley cut by the infant River Trent, to his right there were the hedge-rows of hay fields, to his left the low walls of a deer park, and at his front a great expanse of heath land.

'This might have been an apt place for a battle, Captain Mason,' Gell said, scanning the scene.

His aide, chatting to a fellow officer some yards away, kicked his horse gently so that it ambled across to his colonel's position. 'Aye, sir,' Mason agreed. 'And there's a bloody great warren full of coney holes right across this ridge. Cavalry would never charge across it, unless they were frantic-minded.'

Gell lifted a hand to twist his carefully trimmed mous-tache. 'One never knows the state of mind of a mad Cavalier, Thomas.'

'I suppose, sir.'

'Still, we shall never know how well suited this patch of earth would be to martial pursuits,' Gell said, reaching down to take a silver drinking flask from his saddlebag. 'This is a rendezvous point only. As soon as the army is assembled, we shall fall on Stafford and slaughter any malignant sees fit to oppose us.' Gell took a long draught of the liquor, grimacing involuntarily as it burned his mouth and throat. 'That's the stuff, Thomas!'

Mason looked suddenly uncomfortable. 'I would not know, sir.'

'Ha!' Gell barked. 'Sober as a Banbury-man, eh? Well, more fool you.' He rammed the stopper back on the flask and returned it to the saddlebag, before turning his head to study the northern horizon. 'What hour is it?'

'Near eleven of the clock, Sir John.'

'Brereton ought to be with us soon,' Gell muttered to himself. He glanced back at Mason. 'By Christ, he'd better, eh? Wouldn't want to give those red-scarfed bastards time to prepare for our arrival, now would we?'

BROCTON, STAFFORDSHIRE, 19 MARCH 1643

'I don't believe we've met,' the tall man said smoothly as he stepped into the chapel. His pale skin, luminous against his black hair and cloak, crinkled slightly as he offered a small, humourless smile that did not reach his eyes. There was a pistol in his right hand, and a sword-hilt poking out from beneath the cloak's folds at his waist.

'You are Major Zacharie Girns,' Stryker said icily. 'Rebel assassin.'

Girns offered a small bow. 'Then you have the advantage of me, sir.'

'Stryker.'

Girns's green eyes stared down at his new captive. 'No Christian name?'

'Stryker will do.'

Girns's gaze raked across him with the lazy watchfulness of a reptile, never panicked but always attentive. 'Cavalier,' he said after a moment's thought, 'or you would not be interested in this vile creature.'

'Not difficult to fathom,' Stryker said derisively.

'Voice of an educated man, which would make you an

officer. And a veteran of the Low Countries, to look at your scars. Major? Colonel, even?'

'Captain,' replied Stryker, deciding there was no further harm to be done by the revelation.

Girns wrinkled his nose. 'Captain? The armies are crying out for experienced campaigners. Any man with more than a day's service on the Continent is virtually guaranteed a majority.'

Stryker shrugged. 'I'm not a very good soldier.'

'Evidently. I feel almost sorry for you, Captain Stryker. The Royalists might have sent someone rather more competent, if they intended to best me.' The eyes suddenly narrowed to emerald crescents. 'How did you find us?'

Stryker met his gaze levelly. 'We were out for a stroll and stumbled across this pretty little chapel. Then some bastard hit me over the head.'

The pistol seemed to tremble in Girns's gloved hand, and Stryker thought he might have pushed the major too far. He eyed the narrow muzzle wearily as it hovered in the air like a viperous snake about to bite. 'Is it true?' he said quickly. 'That you are brothers?'

'To my eternal shame,' Blaze spoke now.

'His name, Captain, is Jonathan Girns,' the major spat with sudden venom, 'the eldest of three brothers.' Girns blew air through his nostrils in a bitter chuckle. 'The name Blaze is all vanity.'

Blaze looked up at his brother. 'Lazarus and I felt the name suited our vocation,' he argued.

'And while you were plying your trade on behalf of the Catholic League, you converted to their faith,' Stryker said. 'At first for professional expediency, but later for conscience.'

Blaze managed a wince-yielding nod. 'At the same time our youngest brother had joined a troop of dragoons fighting in the Swedish ranks.'

'And in those ranks I was blessed with an epiphany. The High Church is a study in compromise,' Girns added angrily. 'It is watered-down Protestantism; a religion founded on reform, and hung with the baubles of Popery. A church to suit all and satisfy only the godless.'

Blaze stared up at him, his expression sorrowful. 'On that, at least, we are agreed.' He turned his head to look at Stryker. 'Just as Lazarus embraced the stronger beliefs of our masters, so Zacharie embraced his.'

'I took up work with Parliament at the outbreak of war,' Girns said. 'Weeding out traitors and Papists. When I heard my brothers had returned, I knew it was a sign from God.'

Stryker looked up at his wart-faced captor in disbelief. 'To *kill* them?'

Girns's head shook, the lank tendrils of greasy black hair shining in the wan light. 'Bring them back to the true faith. Our new Scoutmaster General—'

'Sir Samuel Luke,' Stryker interrupted.

Girns dipped his head, 'Had placed a price on my brothers' heads. I sent word to Lazarus, pleading with him to meet me. But he refused. He said he would not treat with a heretic. I knew then that God would rather him burn in hell than walk free to spread Romish poison. And I knew that it was my commission from God. No one was to dispatch him but me.'

Stryker stared into Girns's face, desperately trying to gauge the pistol-wielding man before him. Was there a weakness? Could he rush the major before he pulled the trigger? Would the man hesitate to kill? But the longer he looked up at those twinkling eyes, the more he realized the answer was no on all counts. The glimmer within the emerald depths was the light of a man who had transcended mere zeal. He had the look of madness.

'So you killed Lazarus Blaze,' Stryker said, stalling for time. 'Using Luke's reward as bait to attract a team with the skills to carry out the assassination. And then you went after Jonathan.' A memory struck him then. The image of Lisette's fever ravaged face, wracked with confusion over how her attempts to protect Lazarus Blaze had been thwarted. 'But how did you know where either of them would be?'

'With my help, Captain Stryker,' the voice came from the porch behind Girns and, though Stryker could not see the speaker, he knew to whom the accent belonged.

'You?' another new voice echoed around the chapel now. It was shrill with incredulity and fury. 'It was you betrayed us at Kenilworth?'

Jesper Rontry stepped into the room and turned towards its far end to stare at Lieutenant Burton, who now sat, a hand nursing his wounded skull, against the altar rail. 'Believe me, I took no pleasure in it. I had no quarrel with you, or your men.'

'You are Puritan?' Burton asked in surprise, still blinking rapidly as he fought to gain lucidity.

Rontry shook his bald head. 'No, Lieutenant. Merely heart-broken.' He turned back and shut the door, turning the rusty key as he did so. When the lock echoed in clunking report, he threw the key to Girns and looked down at Blaze's damaged form. 'I needed you. Your affection. That was all I wanted.' His eyes glistened. 'But you treated me all the worse for it.' He let out a deep, juddering sigh that made him tremble from head to toe. 'I loved you, Master Blaze. More than I can begin to describe. But you spurned me as though I were some child, to be mocked and belittled.' A solitary tear tumbled down Rontry's cheek. 'It hurt. Hurt so much I could no longer stand it. I came to a decision.'

'That no one else should have him,' Stryker said.

Rontry gave the merest flicker of a nod.

Burton snorted in bitter laughter. 'Unrequited love. Sounds like one of Captain Forrester's plays!'

Rontry rounded on the younger man. 'Do not mock me, boy!' he snarled, before the rancour evaporated from his voice once more. 'I had to put an end to the—the pain. He had to die.'

'At this cost?' Stryker spoke now.

Rontry looked at the captain, chin trembling, eyes defiant. 'At any cost.'

Stryker was beginning to understand. 'You made contact with Parliament. And Girns replied.'

'I did not know who he was,' Rontry replied. 'Only that if I gave him Lazarus Blaze he would repay me with Jonathan.'

'Jesu,' Burton hissed. 'You conniving bastard.' He made to stand, 'I'm going to scoop out your stones with a blunt spoon, so help me God.'

Rontry drew a pistol from his waist and pointed it at Burton. 'You'll do nothing of the kind, Lieutenant.'

Girns glanced at Rontry. 'Tie them up.'

Jesper Rontry produced a pair of thick ropes and handed his weapon to Girns. Striding quickly to the altar rail, he tore the leather strap roughly from Burton's limp arm and bound both wrists together in front of his body. Satisfied with the job, he dragged the lieutenant along the short nave and thrust him down beside the other prisoners.

When Rontry turned his attention to Stryker, the captain launched upwards at him, and the smaller man recoiled in fright, but the intended violence was curtailed abruptly when Girns's pistol appeared inches from Stryker's face. Rontry, humiliated by his fearful reaction, stepped forwards and hammered a fist into the Royalist's stomach. Stryker doubled over, the wind knocked out of him, and Rontry bent to tether his wrists.

'What the bloody hell happened to him?' Burton exclaimed on seeing the cadaver that was still curled nearby at the foot of the hay stack, an island of rotting flesh amid a lake of dark crimson.

Girns handed the pistol back to his accomplice as soon as Rontry straightened up, and glanced at the cadaver. 'Corporal Slater did not share my vision.'

Burton shot Stryker a wide-eyed glance, his bravery punctured.

'Do not worry, Andrew,' Stryker whispered, still bent in a low crouch. 'If they were going to kill us, they'd have done it already.'

Girns evidently heard the hushed words, for he suddenly grinned, and this time his green eyes were full of mirth. 'On the contrary, Captain,' he said, his tone suddenly enthused. 'You are sinners. Malignant supporters of a corrupt, Pope-loving king. No better than witches.' The major's spare hand went to the folds of his cloak, eventually coming away with a small leather pouch. He lifted it to his mouth, tugging at the tie-string with his teeth, and, once its mouth gaped open, upended it so that a cloud of black powder billowed out across the great pile of hay that was stacked high against the wall.

The room fell silent as all eyes watched Girns discard the empty pouch and stride across to his brother's crouched form, kicking him hard in the face. Blaze recoiled violently, crashing into the wall behind, and Girns suddenly stooped, snatching up the little stump of tallow, its flame flickering manically at the jerking movement.

'And what must we do with witches?' Girns rasped, his voice thick with menace. He closed his eyes, tilting back his head. 'Lord, take these souls. May their sins be cleansed in your purging flames.'

And he tossed the candle into the powder-dusted hay.

CHAPTER 19

Spencer Compton, Second Earl of Northampton, felt the satisfying ache climb up his thighs as he knelt on the church's flagstones. He had placed a small cushion between his knees and the cold floor, but that provided scant protection from the unforgiving stone, and he revelled in the dull pain, for it made him feel alive.

Northampton was in the front row of the ranks of pews, as befitted his status. He gazed back at the congregation quickly, nodding to the many offering deferential bows when they caught his eye, before turning back to face the priest who stood below the high altar. It was a fabulous scene. A house built for God, filled with God's faithful servants, bathed in God's morning light as it beamed through the many broad windows and narrow lancets. It was a morning for meaningful, heart-felt prayer.

The Earl of Northampton closed his eyes and prayed hard. He prayed for God's blessings to fill every man under his command. They would soon face grave dangers if Parliament, as Lisette Gaillard had warned him, were truly intent on taking Stafford. And why would they not be, he reflected silently? It was the last major obstacle to rebel dominance in the region.

The earl felt movement at his left, and he opened an eye a fraction to see that his beloved son, James – *Sir James*, he remembered with swelling pride – had come to kneel beside him.

For a while Sir James, dressed in a sombre, if exquisitely cut, suit of black cloth and white lace, whispered silent entreaties towards St Mary's high altar with the rest of the congregation, but, after four or five minutes, the earl felt his son lean suddenly close.

'Nothing, Father,' the young man hissed through tight lips, as the priest's droning voice wafted through the pews and up into the high beams. 'Our squadrons around the town have not spied a soul worthy of concern.'

The earl did not look at his son. 'Then another day will pass without threat,' he whispered. 'It is getting late. Soon it will be noon. If they were coming today, we would have heard by now.'

Northampton's eyes snapped suddenly open at the sound of a commotion at the church's main entrance. A dozen different voices clamoured for supremacy, and, still kneeling, he twisted to see the source of the tumult, but could discern nothing beyond the bodies seated in the rows behind.

Sir James rose, face tight with anger at the disruption. 'What is the meaning of this?' he bellowed, causing more heads to turn in the direction of the nave and the entrance beyond.

The pew behind Northampton was occupied by his most senior subordinates, Sir Henry Hastings, Sir Thomas Byron and their retinues. The two commanders were also standing, the latter manhandling one of his aides out of the way so that he might go to see what was happening.

Well aware of Byron's hot temper, Northampton quickly stood. 'Hold, Sir Thomas!' he ordered at the knight's back. 'Hold, I say!'

Byron turned. 'It is beggars or Puritans, my lord,' he said sourly. 'Some malcontented faction determined to ruin our service. I'll not stand for it!'

'You will hold until I say!' Northampton snapped acidly. 'You are too quick with your blade, Sir Thomas. And while that is an undoubted quality on the field of battle, it is the kind of trait that'll see you excommunicated if it comes to the fore during devotions.'

The priest had long abandoned hope of continuing his sermon, and stood idle beside the altar, watching the service descend into chaos as the newest and most famous member of his congregation pushed his way out of the pew. Bodies shifted rapidly out of the earl's way so that he was able to step unhindered into the aisle, and he paced along the nave, Sir James, Byron and Hastings at his heels.

There were more people in the way as they reached the font, for those parishioners in the rearmost pews had quickly risen to see what the argument was about.

'Out of the way!' Sir Thomas Byron roared, and it seemed like the parting of the Red Sea, as men and women shuffled obediently left and right and a clear path to the doorway miraculously appeared.

Beneath the high Norman archway stood nine or ten of Northampton's guards. Their swords were naked, waving threateningly in the direction of whomever it was that caused such a commotion. That man was out of sight at first, though the earl could hear his voice well enough as he shouted a stream of oaths at the soldiers before him.

The earl forced his way through the tightly packed crowd of guards and onlookers. 'What is the meaning of this?' he snapped, taking in the stranger's unkempt, sweat-matted hair and bestubbled face, features that were incongruous alongside fine riding boots, buff-coat and scabbard. It seemed as though this man were half soldier and half vagabond.

'Lord Northampton, sir?' the troublemaker said.

Sir Thomas Byron was at Northampton's side in an instant, blade drawn and ready to cleave the stranger in two. 'It is Sunday, sir, a fact that makes your actions reprehensible enough, but you would scream obscenities at the church while His Grace prays? My God, I should run you through this instant, you common churl!'

'Wait, Sir Thomas,' Northampton said, raising a hand to stay Byron's imminent strike. 'Listen to his voice. This is no common churl.' He met the newcomer's blue eyes levelly. 'Are you?'

The man, still held outside the church at sword's length, shook his head. 'My name is Captain Lancelot Forrester, my lord, a loyal officer of King Charles. And a veteran of the Continental wars, like yourself.'

Northampton's eyes narrowed. 'What have you to say?'

'I have come to warn you, my lord!' the near frantic man rasped urgently through heaving lungs. 'There is an army not five miles from here. Gell's greycoats.'

Northampton's eyes widened to great spheres, while the crowd at his back, packed under the arch, straining to hear the exchange, broke into excited chatter.

'I watched them cross the Trent at Weston, my lord. The road leads here.'

'Lies, my lord!' Byron sneered suddenly. 'Our scouts would have seen the buggers, be certain of it.'

'They cannot watch every blade of grass, Sir Thomas,' Northampton replied absently as his mind processed the information. He stared at the messenger. 'How many did you see?'

'Near five hundred horse, my lord, and double that number of foot.'

Northampton scratched the black ringlets at his temple. 'Cannon?'

'Aye, my lord. I counted seven or eight drakes, and at least one bigger piece.'

'Byron is right, Father.' The voice of the earl's son came from somewhere in the crowd. 'We do not know this man. It might be a rebel trick to lure us out of the town.'

'I play no tricks, sir,' the man named Forrester said, his tone desperate and strained, 'please believe me.'

A woman's voice abruptly cut across the debate. 'He speaks the truth, my lord.'

All eyes looked beyond the dishevelled man. Behind him stood a petite woman of lithe figure and cascading tresses of golden hair. She was dressed in a tight-fitting black coat, with breeches to match, and thigh-high cavalry boots of brown leather. A pair of belts crossed her chest from which a pistol hung at her right hip and a sword from her left.

The stranger turned to her, his mouth falling open in disbelief. 'Lisette.'

Lisette winked at him and looked over his shoulder at the earl. 'No more loyal man draws breath, my lord. If he says Gell is coming, then Gell is coming.'

The muscles of Northampton's jaw rippled. 'And we already know Brereton is marching from Nantwich, thanks to Mademoiselle Gaillard.'

425

'Didn't see any other force, my lord,' Forrester said.

'Then perhaps we have time to engage Gell while he is without support.'

'Agreed,' Sir Henry Hastings had pushed his way through the throng to stand just behind the earl. 'Sally out this instant, my lord, and deal with Gell's army first. Once he is cut to shreds we may turn upon Brereton if he truly comes.'

'But the garrison is scattered in a score of billets within and without the town,' Sir James Lord Compton, Northampton's son, said earnestly. 'It will take hours to muster a force large enough to engage Gell.'

Northampton placed a hand on Sir James's shoulder. 'So be it. We have no choice in this, James. I give you two hours. Gather as many men as you can, and we will ride out together. The rebels will have to march over my corpse before I let them have this town.' He looked at Colonel-General Hastings. 'Sir Henry, you know this area better than any. If you marched a thousand men along the road from Weston, intending to join with another army before you reached Stafford's walls, where might you choose to rendezvous?'

'There's a wide swathe of heath a few miles north and east of here, my lord,' Hastings said as he ran a finger under the frayed edge of his eye patch. 'Near the village of Hopton.'

Northampton nodded. 'I think we have our target, gentlemen.' He glanced at Forrester. 'I am indebted to you, Captain. I would repay you with the respite you clearly need, but I am afraid I must prevail upon you again.'

'Furnish me with some new kit, my lord, and I'm yours to command.'

426

'All to the good.' Northampton glanced at Byron. 'Send scouts to Hopton Heath, Sir Thomas. Let us discover what Gell is about.'

BROCTON, STAFFORDSHIRE, 19 MARCH 1643

The candle flame became a raging inferno in a matter of seconds. It caught hold of the gunpowder Girns had poured across the hay in a bright, fizzing flash and, as the easy fuel burnt away, began to devour the organic matter beneath. Flames licked across the hay in an orange arc, surging rapidly along and up the stack, leaving charred remains in their wake, and smoke billowed freely into the high roof beams, darkening the room, choking the air from it with every passing moment.

Stryker was still bent low. Girns and Rontry had ignored him, assuming he was simply attempting to stay below the smoke, but he was frantically running his pinioned hands along his booted right calf. The knife he usually kept there was long gone, taken at Lichfield by Gell's men, but he had recalled something else, another object that had been all but forgotten, one that could be indescribably vital to his survival.

'Christ, Girns,' Rontry was saying as the hay crackled against the wall, 'why could we not shoot them? This is not what we agreed!'

Girns glared at him through the acrid cloud. 'Heretics burn!' he snarled. 'And I grow tired of your belly-aching, Rontry. I have no more use of you.'

The shot cracked sharply, louder and more distinct than the snapping of burning hay, and at first Stryker thought Burton or Blaze had been targeted, but, peering through the rapidly engulfing smoke, he was able to make out the lieutenant and the fire-worker, both flattened against the flagstones to evade asphyxiation. He looked towards the doorway and saw the body of Jesper Rontry slumped against the stout timbers. He faced inwards, eyes staring in lifeless surprise, an almost perfect circle of scarlet glistening at his forehead, betraying the place where the ball had entered.

'Abomination,' Stryker heard Girns say from somewhere near the door.

Stryker crawled on knees and elbows, his wrists still tied tightly together, to where his fellow captives lay. He felt for Burton through the smoke. 'This way!'

Burton looked up and began to slither across the stone floor. 'We can't escape!'

'But we can get as far away from that goddamned fire as we can!' Stryker shouted back, before being overcome by a barrage of dry, stinging coughs. He could smell the stink of roasting meat, as though someone were cooking a pig on a spit, and realized with sudden revulsion that the flames must have reached the body of Corporal Slater.

They crawled along the nave, between the dark pews, in the direction of the altar, before Burton turned back to face the carnage. 'Where's Blaze?'

Stryker followed Burton's gaze, his eye stinging as though it were assailed by a thousand hornets, but of the wounded fire-worker there was no sign. 'Jesu,' he hissed, realizing that, in his determination to save his comrade, he had neglected Blaze.

Then a scream that could curdle a mountain stream rose from the cloud. It was high-pitched, desperate, but injected with fury rather than pain, and, as Stryker and Burton twisted back to stare at the smoke, the face of Jonathan Blaze suddenly appeared. He screamed again, and, as a gust of wind came through one of the little lancets to shift the smoke, Stryker spotted Girns. The major was fumbling with the key in an attempt to unlock the low door, and did not bother to face his brother until Blaze was already at a full sprint.

Girns was a big man, but Blaze, for all the torture he had suffered these past days, was still tall, even loftier than his brother, and his frame carried a deal of weight. He bowled into Girns, head dipped like a bull in a crazed charge, catching the major in the sternum and flinging him backwards into the door. The hate-filled brothers snarled like a pair of wild beasts as they hit the ground in a tangle of thrashing limbs and bared teeth, the key tumbling through the air and into the burning hay.

The breeze had lifted some of the smoke from the nave, and Stryker and Burton were able to breathe easier. Stryker looked down at the object clutched within his right palm; the item he had finally located against his calf.

The brothers still wrestled at the foot of the door, smoke roiling around them, but Blaze was in no state to put up a real fight. He had no fingers left with which to grip, and had lost a great deal of blood. Now that the momentum of Blaze's charge was spent, Girns was quickly getting the better of the contest. Blaze had hold of Girns's slim midriff with his big arms, but the major locked Blaze's head under the crook of his elbow and raked his fingernails along the ragged area of flesh where his brother's ear had once been.

Blaze screamed, loosened his grip, and Girns wriggled free of the bear hug. He dived to his right, ending up splayed across Rontry's lifeless body, and, for a moment, a glimmer of hope flashed across Blaze's face as he antici-pated his younger brother's retreat. But then Girns turned, brandishing the pistol he had torn from Rontry's stiffen-ing fingers.

The shot rent the air, and Jonathan Blaze folded in two, as though he had taken a punch to the stomach by Samson himself.

'No!' Burton was bellowing now. The lieutenant leapt to his feet and careered along the nave.

Girns turned, prepared for this new onslaught, and kicked Burton high on the chest, sending the lieutenant sprawling away into the first row of pews. Burton flailed like a landed fish, struggling to stand with his wrists still in their fetters, and Girns drew his sword, advancing quickly.

Lisette Gaillard's silver hair pin broke through the final strands of rope at Stryker's wrists, just as Girns was rais-ing his blade for the killing blow.

'Major!' Stryker bellowed as he burst forwards.

Girns stayed his sword, looking across at Stryker in disbelief as the captain rolled at his feet, smashing them out from under him and sending him clattering to the stone floor.

Burton scrambled away, ducking behind the adjacent pew as though it were a castle parapet.

'I have put an end to my brother's Romish sin,' Girns spat as he hauled himself to his feet, his voice laced with passionate ferocity, 'and now God will guide my hand as I smite those who would foil His work.' He was not concerned with Burton now, his green gaze centred squarely upon the man who had felled him.

Stryker was on his feet again. He was near the door, and glanced around for something with which to defend himself. And then his eye rested on the inert form of Jesper Rontry. He scanned the body quickly, spotting the glint of metal at Rontry's side, and, with a tide of relief, stooped to draw the dead man's sword.

'The wind will drop!' Stryker shouted at the tall killer. 'The smoke will come back, and we'll all bloody suffocate!'

Girns shrugged casually. 'Then I will be a martyr.' He moved slowly to the right, looking to outflank his opponent. 'But before that I will cut you to shreds.'

'Be my guest.' Stryker lifted the blade so that its tip hovered in line with Girns's sallow-skinned throat.

Stryker reckoned himself a proficient swordsman. He had encountered better, those men trained by the masters of Paris and Madrid, but they were few and far between. Yet now he found himself immediately on the back foot. Girns strode forward purposefully, his face tight with controlled aggression, his poise balanced and powerful. Stryker had once seen a lion at a carnival in Vienna, and Girns's movements put him in mind of that beast. He was strong, but languid. Smooth, but predatory. And when that first lunge came, it took all of Stryker's wits to get his blade across to make the block before it skewered his heart.

But time was running out. Outside, the breeze was dying, and the smoke began to billow outwards with increasing pace and density. Before long they would all choke in the airless chapel.

Stryker went on the attack, lurching forward with a trio of sharp lunges, but his head still pounded uncontrollably, making him feel sluggish, and Girns swatted his ripostes away with scornful nonchalance.

Sensing movement behind him, Stryker risked a glanced over his shoulder to see Lieutenant Burton moving up the nave. 'Keep away, Andrew!' he ordered, seeing the look of violent determination on his subordinate's face. The young man would not think twice about helping his captain, even if his hands were still tied. 'I said keep away, damn you, or I'll kill you myself!'

'But, sir!' Burton began to protest.

'You're no use to me! Find the key! Find the fuckin' key, or we're all dead!'

Girns came forward again as Burton scampered along the outer wall, keeping well out of sword range. The major stabbed low, then swung his blade at Stryker's midriff in a backhanded slash, and finished the move with a crushing downward blow. Stryker was equal to each of the ripostes, but his hand was beginning to ache and his fingers were becoming numb.

Girns held his blade out straight, the tip cutting circles in the air before Stryker's face. Threatening, taunting.

'I can't find it!' Burton's desperate voice carried to them from within the smoke plume.

'Keep looking!' Stryker bellowed over Girns's shoulder.

Girns suddenly feinted, and Stryker flinched, causing the major to grin broadly. 'The key is irrelevant, Captain. I'll best you, and then I'll stick your young friend like a squealing little piglet.'

Stryker jumped forwards, stabbing his sword directly at Girns's face. The major stepped back, inviting Stryker on to him, and held out his own blade so that it slid along Stryker's, glancing off the Royalist's hilt and finding the web of flesh below his armpit.

Stryker grimaced and pulled away sharply. He looked down at the petals of red that blossomed on his chest. It was not a severe wound, but it hurt like hell and he forced himself to take deep, measured breaths to bring the pain under control.

'I will take you piece by piece if necessary, Captain,' Girns sneered.

They were at the doorway now, Rontry's slumped remains somewhere behind, and Stryker launched himself at Girns again, hoping to force the major into tripping on Rontry's outstretched legs. But Girns jumped nimbly backwards, clearing the obstacle with ease, and as Stryker came on, planting his foot heavily on the flagstones, he felt the ground give way beneath him. His right foot simply slid away, as if he had stepped on ice, and he glanced down to see that he had fallen foul of a patch of the dead man's blood.

As soon as Stryker hit the ground he rolled away, hearing the metallic clang of steel on stone as Girns slashed his sword into the floor where Stryker had been. Then he was up on his feet again, but now his sword was somewhere near the doorway, having jumped free of his numb grip as the hilt broke his fall, and Stryker darted out of reach of the advancing Girns. He backed away, seeing the pews come into his peripheral vision as he retreated down the nave.

Girns bore down on him, blade outstretched, eyes wide and wild. Stryker glanced over the major's shoulder, hoping against hope to see Burton emerge from the smoke, binds unfastened and key in hand. But a chorus of spluttering, gravelly coughs from within the blackening cloud told him the lieutenant was rapidly becoming overwhelmed.

The small of Stryker's back collided with something hard, and he realized that he had come up against the altar rail. Frantically now, he turned left, only to see the whitewashed fastness of the chapel's north wall. He turned right, ignoring Girns's mocking snigger, but the south wall was just as bleak, just as devoid of escape routes. At his back was the shattered altar and a pulpit that offered only to entrap him further, should he choose to ascend its short flight of steps. And in front of him was a tall man, with luminously white skin, raven-black hair and the greenest eyes he had ever seen.

Girns stepped closer, letting the blade drift lazily in to linger below Stryker's throat. Stryker stared down at the sword's poised tip. He traced the length of the red-splashed weapon, his eye taking in every notch and divot on the blade's razor edge, all the way up to the hilt at its zenith. And there, behind the hilt, sighting along the straight steel, was the emerald eye of Major Zacharie Girns. Dragoon, rebel, assassin, fratricide.

'Did you think you could stop me?' Girns said, his smoke-ravaged voice hoarse. 'Interfere with God's work? I am a hunter of men, Captain Stryker. I have hunted my brothers from the moment their ship landed on English shores, tracked them across wood and field and highway. Always found them. *Always* cornered them.'

Stryker kept his expression impassive. 'You are clearly a formidable opponent, Major.'

Girns lunged forward with sudden violence, a movement instilled with all the violence and strength and savagery he could muster.

Stryker swayed to the right, letting the sword slice past his head, cutting through a clump of hair and nicking his earlobe. But he ignored the pain, and Girns clattered into him so that their bodies were pressed tightly together, the altar rail preventing Stryker from moving backwards. Stryker wrapped an arm around the major's middle, pinning the taller man against him. He could smell the stink of the assassin's stale breath.

Girns thrashed at him, and, just as Stryker felt his grip fail, he stood on the tips of his toes and whispered, 'But there is one person you should never *ever* corner.'

And Major Zacharie Girns's wart-riddled jaw fell open. His arm, still stuck above Stryker's left shoulder, went suddenly still, and then its taut rigidity began to evaporate. Stryker heard the sword clatter to the stone floor behind, and slid out from between Girns and the wooden rail. The Parliamentarian did not react. He simply stared at the wall beyond the altar, his tall body swaying like a sapling in a stiff breeze.

Stryker went to stand next to him and, with a welt of fresh blood, jerked Lisette's long, sharpened hairpin free of Girns's slim neck.

'Me,' he said.

Stryker kicked Girns squarely in the back. The major fell forwards with a jolt, and tipped across the low rail to fall headlong on to the cross that had once formed the chapel's humble altar. But that cross had been cleaved in two by a vicious sword swipe, and was now a wicked wooden stake that passed through Girns's chest as though it were butter, bursting through into the smoky air with its new adornment of blood and tissue and bone.

Major Zacharie Girns gave one huge shudder that sent grotesque spasms throughout his entire body, and then, finally, he was still.

Stryker turned back to the chapel. Above him the roof was engulfed in flame.

STAFFORD CASTLE, 19 MARCH 1643

Sir Thomas Byron cantered into the courtyard. The castle's inner sanctum was a hive of activity as stewards scuttled this way and that, tacking up horses and fastening plate armour to their masters' chests and backs. The knight reined in at the very centre of the confusion and summoned an aide with a deft flick of the wrist. A small man, hunched and fawning, scampered across the viscous mud, grimacing each time a shoe stuck. Byron did not speak, but unfastened his helmet, yanked it off in one swift movement, and tossed it to the aide. Then he stood in his stirrups to scan the chaotic scene. His chestnut horse fidgeted uncomfortably as one of his spurs clipped its flank, but Byron brought it under control with a twitch of his thigh and a soothing word in the beast's pricked ear.

When Byron caught sight of Spencer Compton, the Earl of Northampton was standing near the door to the armoury. The bucket tops of his boots had been fully extended in order to protect his upper thighs, his coat and shirt were covered by the amber of a buff-coat, his arms were outstretched in order to allow servants access to the leather ties that would fasten back and breast plates together, and his left forearm was encased in a gleaming metal gauntlet. He, like his Cavaliers, was preparing for war.

Byron jumped down from the saddle, immediately sinking to his ankles, and strode laboriously over to where the earl stood.

'Speak to me,' said Northampton when he caught his cavalry commander's hazel eye.

Byron ran his gloved right hand through the dense thatch of fair hair that fell about his shoulders. 'Sir Henry guessed right, my lord. Gell's on Hopton Heath.'

Northampton tilted his chin upwards, like a dog sniffing the wind. 'Then let us wipe him from the earth, Sir Thomas.'

Byron felt his heart lurch in excitement. He had feared the town would be subjected to a long siege. A battle of attrition, and erosion and starvation. The type of warfare unsuited to a garrison of cavalrymen. But the Earl of Northampton was a man after his own heart. The kind of hard-riding, hard-fighting Cavalier the dour Roundheads so despised. He could not stifle a grin. 'I am with you, my lord. We'll ride straight into the rebellious scoundrels.'

'Good. I cannot think of three better men than Sir James, Sir Henry and yourself to ride with me to this fight.'

Byron bowed low. 'I thank you for your kind words, my lord.'

'I'd wager you would not doubt Mademoiselle Gaillard again, eh?' Northampton said with a sly twitch at the corner of his mouth.

'I would not,' Byron replied truthfully. 'Without her warning we might have turned back to Banbury. I shudder to think on it.'

'As do I,' the earl agreed. 'Once I secure Staffordshire for the King, I will have her to thank. Thank you, lads,' he said as his three servants stepped away, their work finished. 'Efficient as always. Bring my horse.'

Sir Thomas Byron watched in silence as the Earl of Northampton's big gelding was led out into the courtyard. Northampton pulled on his steel pot, attaching it under his chin, and pulled down the three-barred visor, before his servants moved in again to help him into the saddle.

'Join your troops, sir,' the earl said finally, when he had hold of the looped reins. 'It will not be long before we have assembled enough men for this task.'

Byron dipped his head. 'I look forward to it, my lord.'

Northampton urged his mount forwards. 'For God and King Charles!'

Within the castle keep, in one of the myriad rooms of roaring hearth and tapestry-draped walls, a slim woman, dressed entirely in black, stood by a narrow window, gazing out over the town. 'It is good to see you, Forry,' she said softly.

At the other end of the room a portly man with ruddy cheeks and thinning, sandy-coloured hair sat back in a stout chair carved of seasoned oak. 'But you would rather have seen a certain one-eyed captain.'

Lisette Gaillard turned to face him. 'Am I that transparent?'

Lancelot Forrester, dressed in the red uniform of the Earl of Northampton, interlocked his fingers across his ample stomach. 'Like a pane of glass, my dear.'

'What happened?' she said, a look of concern ghosting across her narrow face.

Forrester met her gaze. 'We went to Oxford, as you know. Asked a few questions. Discovered Blaze's group had been ambushed.'

'*Merde*,' Lisette whispered, studying the creaking floor-boards with sorrowful eyes. 'Then I truly failed.'

'Not entirely,' the captain replied. He reached across to grasp a hunk of flour-dusted bread from a trencher that had once contained Lisette's meal. 'May I?'

She nodded.

'So we rode towards Brocton,' Forrester mumbled through a bulging mouth, 'a hamlet not too far from here, as it happens. But we were harried by a troop of bloody dragoons, and forced to split up. Burton and Stryker went one way, Skellen and I the other. We agreed to meet at Brocton.'

'But then you spotted Gell's men?'

Forrester swallowed. 'On the march and headed this way. You understand I could not simply turn away and continue to Brocton.'

'Of course.'

'So Skellen went to meet Stryker, and I came here.'

She nodded. 'I suppose you stood the better chance of convincing Northampton you spoke true. You did not know I was here to corroborate, and William is not the most eloquent speaker.'

Forrester leant back in the chair and brayed. 'I'll tell him you said that! But you're right, of course. Though I think I'd have had a mutiny on my hands if I tried to stop him going to his master.'

Lisette smiled. 'You make him sound like a dog.'

'I'll tell him you said that as well.'

'I hope he is safe,' Lisette murmured.

Forrester wondered if she spoke of Blaze or Stryker, though the sudden glassiness of her eyes told him all he needed to know.

The smoke was so dense that Stryker could not see beyond the extent of his own arm as he staggered back along the nave towards the chapel door. The gunmetal-grey cloud enveloped him, swirled around his body, gnawed at his eye, scorched at his airways. He dropped to all fours and took off his blood-spattered shirt, holding it tight to his face, keeping breaths shallow, inching blindly towards the spot where he had last seen Burton.

His hands stumbled into something hard and fleshy, and he snaked his fingers across it desperately, groping for something that would identify the body. He found a limb, an arm, and quickly felt for the hands. Stumps only. Fingerless and scabby.

It was Jonathan Blaze, and, not wishing to waste his time on someone already dead, he began to move on, crawling over the now warm stone, his head becoming woozier with every moment.

'Help—me—' Blaze's voice croaked in his wake, and he realized the gut-shot fire-worker had not succumbed to his wounds yet.

The sound of coughing came from up ahead, and Stryker hesitated, a decision to make. He decided to press on, choosing his comrade above Blaze, though any elation at discovering the lieutenant alive was tempered by the knowledge that, in minutes, they would all be dead.

Stryker plunged further into the choking plume, and found Burton curled on his side, bound hands covering his face. He had been overwhelmed by the lethal cloud, and now, balled and silent, he awaited his end.

'Burton!' Stryker rasped, chest searing with the effort. 'Here!'

The lieutenant lifted his hands from his eyes and, for a moment, a spark of recognition flashed there, but he curled up again, evidently accepting his fate. Stryker lent across him and went to work on Burton's rope shackles with the hairpin. He stabbed frantically at the twisted strands, but he was too weak to break through.

'Leave it, sir,' Burton hissed weakly. 'I could not find the key.'

And Stryker fell still. He knew Burton was right. There was no point in fighting fate. The door was locked and it was too stout for him to break through now that he had been so enfeebled by the smoke, and, even if he had enough strength to get to the east end of the nave, the only window big enough to climb through was far too high to reach.

Still slumped across Burton, Stryker's mind swirled with confusion. He felt suddenly light-headed, as though his consciousness was drifting somewhere above his body. And then his eyelid became agonizingly heavy, like weights had been pinned to the lashes, and slowly, achingly, sorrowfully, he closed his eye.

Stryker heard the explosion but, in his hazy mind, it seemed like a distant clap of thunder. Suddenly a new pain cut though the stupor like the sun's rays burning away a morning mist. It was not focussed in one place, but in hundreds of smaller hurts across his legs and arms and back, as if someone had sprinkled needles across his body. And with it came movement, as he found himself flipped into the air, crashing down on to the flagstones the other side of Burton's prone form.

Dazed, he looked up, peering through the smoke, realizing that the cloud was suddenly paler, illuminated by some unseen light. And it was not swirling in the chapel's confines, but rushing madly in a single direction. The doorway.

Stryker raised himself on to hands and knees, staring in light-headed bewilderment at the stone archway that was now a great hole, the door's wooden timbers miraculously gone. And then he saw a figure. A man. Taller, even, than Blaze or Girns, but reed thin, with a small head of close-cropped hair. He stepped through the gaping doorway and into the chapel, and, though Stryker could not see his face silhouetted against the daylight at his back, he felt a jolt of euphoria surge through him.

'What the fuckin' hell 'ave you two been up to?' said Sergeant William Skellen.

'Grenade,' Skellen said as he dumped Stryker unceremoniously on to the ground outside the burning chapel.

Stryker tried to laugh at his sergeant's matter-of-fact tone, so incongruous amongst the utter carnage all around him, but the motion immediately degenerated into a spluttering cough. He hawked up as much mucus as he could from his scorched lungs, spitting the black-flecked globule on to the wet blades of grass at his feet.

Burton was coughing too, and gasping deeply between each wracking spasm, entirely unable to speak, but, mercifully, it seemed as though the fresh air was reviving him with each passing second.

'How did you get—' Stryker said, having to pause for a cavernous breath, 'a grenade?'

'Door was locked. Thick little bugger as well. I couldn't kick it in. So I looked around and found three horses in a little outbuilding yonder.' He pointed towards the brick structure Stryker had spotted the night before. 'Had a little rummage, and found a bag o' grenades. All packed and ready to go. Weren't hard to get the tow lit, there's sparks flyin' all over the shop.'

Skellen went to crouch beside Blaze, the man Stryker had ordered saved after Lieutenant Burton. 'He's in a bad way, sir.'

Stryker stood gingerly and staggered over to where Blaze lay. 'Girns shot him in the stomach.'

'Girns?'

'Never mind.' Stryker moved Blaze's broad arm to expose the wound at his gut. His ragged shirt was saturated in blood, and, at its centre, a neat hole glistened, dark and deep. Blaze groaned then. It was a low, guttural sound of pain and despair, like a bullock after gelding, and his eyes flickered open.

'Am I to die?' the fire-worker murmured.

Stryker nodded. 'Yes.'

'My brother won then.'

Skellen stared at Stryker. 'Brother?'

'I'll explain later.' Stryker frowned. 'What happened to you and Forrester?'

'Them dragooners chased us for bloody miles, sir. When we finally got shot of 'em, we were way off course. The captain went on to Stafford, and I came back to fetch you.'

Burton was sitting up now, rubbing the lump at his head. 'Stafford? Why did he go there?'

443

'On account o' Gell's army, sir,' Skellen said. 'We spied the bastards marching towards Stafford. Roun'eads are makin' a play for it. That's what it looked like to us, anyway.'

'And Captain Forrester went to warn the garrison,' Stryker said in understanding.

Skellen nodded, before glancing down at Blaze in surprise. The fire-worker's face was etched in an excruciated grimace as he tried to sit. 'Christ, sir, that ain't wise.'

Stryker hooked a bracing arm around Blaze's broad shoulders. 'Rest easy, sir, please.'

'God's blood, Captain!' Blaze snarled, trying to shrug him off. 'I have spent the past week having pieces of me cut off, and now I will die a slow death as my guts fester! Do not think to mollycoddle me now!'

Stryker let go, and Blaze slumped backwards with a yelp of pain, but, determination bright in his swollen eyes, he began to heave himself upwards again. 'They have guns at Stafford. Big ones.'

Stryker began to shake his head. 'Sir, you cannot possibly—'

'Christ, Stryker, have you not heard anything I've said?' Blaze snapped again. 'Stafford Castle has a fair array of artillery. One particular piece, so I am told, is a demi-cannon. A twenty-nine pounder.' He lifted the bloody stump that was once his left hand and jabbed it at Stryker's chest. 'You will take me to Stafford, Captain. I will die, but not yet. Give me one last chance to fire a real cannon before I depart.'

'Cannon,' Skellen muttered. 'Waste o' good iron if you ask me. Cannon never won a battle that I saw. The winners are the ones who can aim a musket and charge pikes for horse.'

Blaze looked up at the laconic sergeant, and Stryker saw a real glint in his blue eyes, the like of which he had not witnessed since their first meeting in Cirencester. 'You have never seen one fired properly,' Blaze whispered. 'Take me to Stafford. Place me in charge of that demi-cannon. I promise, you will not be disappointed.'

CHAPTER 20

HOPTON HEATH, STAFFORDSHIRE, 19 MARCH 1643

The ridge ran north-west to south-east. A diagonal crease in the terrain, its length the equivalent of twice a musket's range. To the north the land fell steeply away, a deep scar cut by the River Trent, while a long slope of heath land rolled more gently to the south. The heath and its high crest had been shorn to stubble by livestock and, just below the barren apex, at the top of the slope, a vast rabbit warren spanned its entire breadth.

'And it is here, Sir William, I propose to face them,' Sir John Gell said calmly, gently stroking his horse's mane.

Sir William Brereton, newly arrived on the expanse of heath between the Trent and the village of Hopton, shook his head animatedly. 'We agreed to storm the town, Gell.'

Gell clicked his tongue impatiently, enjoying the sour look it engendered in his co-commander. 'You are too late, Sir William. The plan was to muster on this heath and launch an attack. Storm the town while they slept.' He fixed Brereton with an equally acidic expression. 'But it is now two hours past noon. You are late. And my scouts tell me a sizeable force is assembling outside the town. Almost all cavalry.'

Brereton's brown eyes narrowed. 'Who commands them?'

'Compton,' Gell spat the word as though it were a chunk of rancid meat.

'Which one?'

'The earl and his son are both here, I am told. They must have ridden up from Banbury.'

Brereton examined his gauntlet in an attempt to appear relaxed. 'Which means Byron will be with them. He is Northampton's lapdog.'

Gell nodded. 'And they are supported by Blind Hastings. That bastardly gullion has been a thorn in my side since Lichfield.'

Brereton looked along the ridge at the troops he had brought; five hundred harquebusiers and dragoons. 'I would not relish facing Northampton's cavalry on open ground, Sir John. My troops are green by comparison.'

The corner of Gell's moustachioed lip curled upwards. 'Then you should have been more punctual. And where are your infantry?' Brereton's mouth opened and closed silently, putting Gell in mind of a fish, and the conqueror of Lichfield shook his head scornfully. 'Left 'em behind, did you?'

'The roads are bad,' Brereton began to explain. 'It was either wait upon them and fail to make our rendezvous, or leave them behind and succeed.'

'You would be well advised to watch me today, Sir William. Perhaps you will learn something.'

Leaving Brereton spluttering, Gell wheeled his horse round to view the troops he had already deployed. 'See there, Sir William,' he said, pointing first to the ridge's western periphery, where the flat plain of gorse and grass was interrupted by dense hedgerows, and then to the east, where low walls of stone rose as high as a man's waist. 'If we remain here, compel the Royalists to charge up the slope, we are well positioned. Our flanks provide ideal breastworks. I have placed drakes, dragoons and musketeers behind the hedges and walls. And here,' he pointed to the first yards of slope immediately before them, 'the terrain is pitted by coney burrows. I've never seen more hazardous terrain for cavalry. We shall place the rest of the foot here, on the crest. My brave greys in the front ranks, and those sallow bloody Moorlanders in reserve. If you'd be so kind as to deploy your horse at the flank of the main body, I'd be most grateful.'

Brereton looked at him. 'And your cavalry?'

'You will have mine too. I'll command the foot, you the horse. A thousand men each.'

Brereton studied the slope, its surface pockmarked by a vast colony of rabbits. 'It would be mad to charge a horse across this.' He looked Gell in the eye. 'So what makes you think the Cavaliers will oblige?'

Gell twisted the corner of his waxed moustache. 'Because Spencer Compton *is* mad, and so are his senior officers. Northampton will see a charge across this deadly heath as a great game. A sport akin to the hunt. His son was knighted at Kineton Fight for his own frantic charge, and Byron and Hastings—'

'Byron and Hastings,' Brereton interrupted, 'are the worst kind of swash-and-buckler men.'

Gell nodded. 'You have it, Sir William. They are a formidable force, I freely admit. If we faced them on the march we would be cut to ribbons. So we shall sit atop this ridge, in careful formation, and they won't be able to resist an assault.'

Brereton smiled for the first time since reaching the heath. 'And the warren will bring down their mounts.'

'While we shower them in a lethal crossfire from three sides.' Gell touched a spur to his horse, and it began to move along the grey-coated ranks. He twisted in the saddle and shouted over a shoulder, 'Hopton Heath affords us all the advantages, Sir William! We stay here, and wait for Northampton to blunder into our trap!'

'Sir! Colonel Gell, sir!'

Gell and Brereton peered down the slope to where a rider was cantering carefully through the treacherous warren. 'You see the difficulty they'll face?' Gell muttered smugly, before raising a hand to the approaching horse-man. 'What news, Lieutenant Wheeler?'

Wheeler reined in beside the two most senior Parliamentary officers, though he addressed Gell. 'They're coming, sir!'

Gell's round eyes became slits. 'You are certain, Lieutenant?'

Wheeler nodded rapidly, like a woodpecker chipping at bark. 'Scores, sir. They rode out from the town some minutes ago. I came here directly to warn you.'

'You did well, Wheeler,' Gell said curtly, his voice suddenly tight, before turning to the first ranks of infan-try formed up along the ridge. 'Sergeant Crane!'

A stocky man in Gell's grey uniform, with a sword at his hip and a fearsome halberd in hand, stepped forward. 'Sir!'

'The malignant horde is on its way! Time to give them our little gift!'

Gell and Brereton watched as Sergeant Crane paced from the massed ranks of pike and began bellowing orders at the men under his command. In seconds a gap opened in the lines to reveal three large iron tubes mounted on vast wheels, their mouths gaping, black and formidable.

Brereton stared at Gell. 'You have artillery.'

Gell grinned, baring sharp, yellow teeth. 'The coney warren will stop their charge, Sir William, but I do not plan to need it.'

The Earl of Northampton stood high in the saddle and stared back at the mighty throng that cantered in his wake. Scores of men and horses had gathered, a remarkable number, given the limited time with which he had given his senior officers to work, and he was proud of each and every one. The air stank of horse flesh and dung, the familiar, earthy odour filling his nostrils invigoratingly. He glanced at the nearest rider, raising his voice above the thunder of so many hooves. 'Are we ready as we hope to be?'

Sir James Lord Compton, dashing in full battle regalia and tall atop his expensive warhorse, offered a curt nod. 'We have—enough, Father.'

'Enough?' Spencer Compton, Earl of Northampton, threw his son a stern glance. 'Speak plain.'

Sir James wiped a speck of mud off his clean-shaven chin and gazed back at the deep ranks. 'Eleven hundred horse, sir, with a hundred foot in reserve.'

Northampton's bushy brow rose sharply. 'Ample to crush that base upstart!' he cried, loudly enough for the nearest cavalrymen to hear, and was rewarded with a hearty chorus of cheers.

Sir James ignored the huzzas, and kept his voice as low as he could. 'The scouts have returned, Father. It is not only Gell we face.'

450

Northampton's handsome face visibly drooped. 'We are too late?'

Sir James nodded slowly. 'Brereton has joined him.'

The earl thumped a gauntleted fist against his buff-skirted thigh. 'Christ on His Cross!'

'It will be a hard fight,' Sir James went on sombrely, 'but there is hope.'

Northampton glared at his son. 'Hope?'

'In his haste to make muster, Brereton appears to have left his infantry miles behind.'

Northampton gnawed his bottom lip. 'How many does he bring?'

'The scouts count some five hundred. All horse, though some are dragoons rather than seasoned cavalry.'

Spencer Compton, Earl of Northampton and commander of the king's forces in the Midlands, took a deep, steadying breath through his nose. 'God help us,' he murmured on the outbreath, and offered his eldest son a smile full of fondness. 'Let us show these rebels what it means to be real warriors.'

'Here, sir!' Colonel-General Sir Henry Hastings bellowed from a few yards up ahead. He tugged his horse's reins and the beast turned up a wide, tree-flanked bridle-way, Northampton, Sir James, and the rest of their earth-rumbling force in his wake.

The bridleway ended abruptly where the trees gave way to a broad expanse of gorse and grassland that sloped upwards, climbing gradually north until it ended abruptly at a ridge, before falling away to the low-lying valley along which the River Trent meandered. 'There!' Hastings called, pointing up at the ridge.

Northampton and those men at the head of his great column followed Hastings's outstretched finger, their eyes

451

falling as one upon the ridge. And there, darkening the horizon, silent and menacing, stood an army.

But Northampton did not slow his horse, for he would not sacrifice momentum. With a deft flick of his heel, he clipped sharp spurs against his mount's flanks, and the animal increased its speed. The dense ranks of cavalrymen, the cream of the Midlands gentry, surged on to the foot of the slope in his wake. To battle.

And the cannons fired.

To the south-east of Hopton Heath, on the road from Brocton, the gunfire sounded like lightning strikes, sometimes far-off, and at other times carried on a vagary of wind, earth-shakingly close.

'Demi-culverins,' said Skellen, assessing the percussive reports. 'Gell's pieces.'

The bombardment faded as the crews hurried to reload their pieces, and Burton looked across at the sergeant. 'You can tell their owner?'

Skellen remained expressionless. 'Aye, sir. Many years of experience.'

'He saw them crossing the Trent,' Stryker interjected when he saw the expression of awe on Burton's face.

Burton shot the sergeant a sour look. 'Very amusing.'

'The battle has started?' Blaze murmured through gritted teeth. He was hunched on the back of Stryker's horse, one arm hooked round the captain's midriff, the other pressed tight to the wound at his abdomen. 'It has,' confirmed Stryker. 'Forget Stafford, we follow the gunfire.'

'Or follow them,' Skellen grunted, nodding at the woodland that hugged the side of the road.

They all saw the shadows. Slithering black shapes, silhouettes of men, women and children, weaving slowly in and out of the trees on both flanks. The group watched them move, like a silent army, so many shapes appearing in the blink of an eye, then melting away just as quickly.

'Those fucking ghouls,' Skellen muttered darkly. 'Like flies on shit.'

'Destitution forces a man's hand, Sergeant,' Stryker said.

'Who are they?' Lieutenant Burton asked as he squinted into the gloom.

'They come after battle,' Skellen replied bitterly, staring into the middle distance, 'haunting the dusk, plundering the dead.'

Stryker remained silent. The looting of the dead was as much a part of battle as the fighting, but he understood Skellen's disgust. The ghouls, as Skellen put it, drifted in from town and village as night fell across a battlefield. They would pick their way through the human detritus in search of wan cadavers that could no longer protect their most precious possessions. They would pillage those corpses, or take blades to those still clinging grimly to life, rifling through pockets for anything remotely of value, and snapping already stiff fingers to relieve them of rings.

'They'll hide in the forest,' Skellen said, 'and creep out when the fighting's done.' He shuddered. Men like him did not fear battle, or the act of dying, but the thought of being one of those stripped and looted cadavers was a rare thing of terror.

'But you're in the right of it, Sergeant,' said Stryker. 'It won't be difficult to find the battlefield with that lot as our guides.'

*

Captain Lancelot Forrester thought his heart would explode, such was the fear he now felt. He swallowed hard, forcing a caustic bubble of vomit back down his throat, and gripped the reins as tight as he could. The hooves were a blur beneath him, flinging clods of mud in all directions, but he could not hear them, for their thrum was a mere fraction of the rumble that he knew would be felt all the way up to the heath's crest.

But Forrester could not see that crest, for he was one horseman in amongst so many hundred. As an infantry-man, he did not have the skill to ride with Northampton's elite harquebusiers, but the earl was astute enough to know that to lose the talents of an experienced officer would be foolish in the extreme. So Forrester had become a dragoon.

The mount he rode was slow but steady, not an oat-fed lightning bolt favoured by the cavalry, but a solid, obedi-ent beast that would not shy from gunfire. Dragoons were mounted infantry, so Forrester had a new musket slung at his back, and that gave him cause for comfort, for he hated relying on the dubious reliability of the short-arms employed by harquebusiers.

But now, in this instant, as the heavy artillery belched smoke from the ridge, he was simply one of a thousand riders. The Earl of Northampton and his son were at the front of the vast, ground-churning column, Colonel-General Hastings was out on the left with his own formidable troop, and Sir Thomas Byron headed the right flank. They thundered forwards, a cacophonous, steel-clad mass of power and speed.

Forrester could not see the lethal iron sphere, but he heard it. It whistled high and fast from the midst of the grey-coated infantry on the ridge, its cry shrill above the roaring hoofbeats of the oncoming Royalists, like the caw of a raven in an autumn gale, and Forrester instinctively ducked into his horse's neck, wincing, tensing every sinew.

And the cannon ball flew high above their heads and far beyond even the rearmost horsemen.

Forrester twisted back to see the ball smash into the wet earth. It burrowed its way into the ground, sending grass and gorse and mud flying in all directions, leaving a wide, dark smear in its wake. A tidal wave of relief washed through Forrester's veins then, as he realized the Royalist column had ridden under the arc of the ball. Their madcap sprint, its speed and recklessness, had not been the suicidal charge he had imagined, but a deliberate race to pass beyond the killing range of the rebel artillery.

When he turned back to face the slope, confidence in his commander suddenly renewed, he was startled to see the foremost riders with their arms aloft, signalling for the column to halt, and it took all his strength to wrench his eager mount to a trot.

For several moments the massed Cavaliers were in utter disarray as the more fleet-hoofed beasts overshot their slower or more compliant compatriots. The fastest horses had to be savagely kicked and cajoled back into the column, for they had no wish to break off the charge, and nor, suspected Forrester, had their masters, but Northampton was there, right at the front, stood high in his stirrups and bellowing for discipline.

The great cannon up at the top of the slope crashed another volley, but this time the Royalists paid no heed as the ball flew impotently above them. Instead they listened to their earl. He snarled orders for them to resume the

455

tight formation, threatening dire penalties for those who disobeyed. None did, and soon the column was back together, tight and bristling.

'We are safe from their ordnance, praise God!' the Earl of Northampton bellowed as he cantered across the front rank. 'But there will be no charge! No charge, I say! You wait for my mark and my mark alone!'

The earl turned his horse to face the ridge, drew his sword and thrust it up at the rebel formation's leftmost extremity. 'Look to the hedges. The rebels will have snipers there!' The blade flicked to his right, the Roundheads' left flank. 'And there too! Behind those walls!'

Captain Lancelot Forrester followed the earl's gaze and realized that he was probably right. And then a thought struck him. One that made his heart pound again and his stomach twist and his bowels begin to loosen. He swallowed hard, reached down to check that his sword slid easily in and out of its scabbard, whispered a silent prayer and awaited the inevitable order.

'Dragoons!' the Earl of Northampton cried. 'Forward!'

Stryker and his small party heard the hoofbeats and knew they were close to the killing ground. The noise gave Stryker the impulse to check his weapons, and he patted the buff-coat, pistols and sword he had taken from the outbuilding where Girns and Rontry had stayed during their time in Brocton. Happy that he was armed and prepared for a fight, he increased the group's pace as best he could, always mindful that each bump and trough in the perfidious road caused Jonathan Blaze to cry out in agony.

Eventually they reached a fork in the road, and, noticing the silhouettes in the forest were taking the right-hand option, they followed suit.

'Couldn't keep away, eh?' A croaking voice, broad with the accent of Britain's far north, rang out from behind a wide tree, sudden and heart-stopping. 'I heard you'd escaped the Close, but didn't think I'd be seeing you so soon.'

All eyes turned to the tree line, Stryker, Burton and Skellen unsheathing swords, Blaze yelping at the movement.

A man clutching a long sword stepped into their path. At his back came more men. Soldiers bearing muskets and blades.

And Stryker grinned. Not because the soldiers wore the red sashes of King Charles, but because their leader was a stocky, scarred, bald-headed dwarf, with bright yellow eyes and a huge, mottled scar that ran across the breadth of his neck.

'What are you doing here, Master Barkworth?'

Simeon Barkworth sheathed his weapon. 'Where were we to go when Gell sent us packing?' he said. 'He stripped us of anything of value, including our weapons. So we walked to Stafford.'

'All of you?'

'Aye, sir,' Barkworth replied in that hissing tone, a legacy of a noose-crushed windpipe. The Scot raised a brow. 'Your Swedish friend, too.'

'Jesu,' Stryker muttered. It was the first time he had thought on Henning Edberg since Lichfield, and the revelation that he was somewhere on Hopton Heath was a bitter blow indeed.

Barkworth shrugged. 'But he is away with the dragoons. Even now they're deployed on the heath.'

'And you?'

'I have the pickets, sir,' the little man explained. 'Protecting the earl's rear, should Gell think to sweep round the flank and attack the artillery.' He pointed to the road at his back. 'The battle is on the heath thither.'

'You have artillery?' Blaze spoke now, his weak voice suddenly pricked with a needle of excitement.

Barkworth looked at him, his amber eyes widening as he took in Blaze's damaged appearance. 'Aye—sir. Roaring Meg is being readied even now.'

Blaze leaned forward to speak directly into Stryker's ear. 'Roaring Meg, Captain. I must go to her!'

Stryker twisted in his saddle to catch Blaze's blackened eye. 'Who is she?'

Blaze's shredded lips turned up at the corners. '*She*, Stryker, is Stafford's famed demi-cannon. A fearsome beast!'

Stryker nodded in understanding and stared back down at the commander of Northampton's pickets. 'The earl leaves you out here, while the battle rages?'

Simeon Barkworth offered a rueful smile. 'He knows only what he sees, sir. A little man from a defeated garrison. We are humiliated, Captain. Fit enough for picket duty only.'

Stryker looked at Skellen. 'A waste, wouldn't you say, Sergeant?'

Skellen sniffed. 'For certain, sir. Poison dwarf should be in the front rank, where he can block a few musket-balls.'

Barkworth's feline eyes narrowed as he looked at Skellen. 'Battles are treacherous places, Sir Crannion. Be sure to watch for daggers between those lofty shoulders.'

Skellen grinned broadly. 'You couldn't reach these lofty shoulders.'

'We're here to fight, Barkworth,' Stryker interjected. 'And you're coming with us.'

The little man's features creased in a crooked-toothed smile that turned the scars on his face a pale white. 'Sir. Thank you, sir.'

'Who is your second here?'

Barkworth indicated a halberd-wielding fellow half a dozen paces to his right. 'Sergeant Meadows, sir.'

'You there!' Stryker called to the man Barkworth had pointed out. 'Meadows!'

The sergeant, tall and willowy, with a hooked nose and a face full of red freckles, strode obediently over. 'Sir?' he said, copying his superior's deference when addressing the one-eyed stranger.

'Master Barkworth has duties with me,' Stryker said curtly.

'And you are?' replied a baffled Meadows.

Stryker's face darkened. 'Someone you'd do well to avoid displeasing.'

Meadows's thin neck quivered as he swallowed nervously. 'Master Barkworth is with you, sir.'

'Good lad,' Stryker replied. 'You're in charge here now.'

Barkworth stepped forward. 'Sir?'

Stryker met the yellow gaze. 'How does the earl mean to proceed?'

Barkworth thought for a moment. 'After the dragoons have cleared the rebel flanks? He has cavalry, sir. He will lead a frontal charge.'

'Hardly a shock,' Stryker said, thinking back to Spencer Compton's exploits during the Continental wars.

Barkworth's face became taut. 'You mean to join him?'

'Gell has my sword,' Stryker replied truthfully, 'and I want it back.'

'Captain,' another voice broke across the discussion.

Stryker turned his head so that he could speak across his shoulder. 'I had not forgotten you, Master Blaze.' He looked back at Barkworth. 'This is Jonathan Blaze. The greatest expert in ordnance under the king's command.'

Barkworth eyed the fire-worker dubiously, but nodded understanding. 'Roaring Meg?'

'Roaring Meg,' echoed Stryker. 'Take us to her, if you would.'

To Stryker's surprise, Simeon Barkworth's face lit up in a smile that reached all the way to his eyes.

'You seem—pleased?' Stryker stared at the Scot nonplussed.

'I think there is something you'll wish to see, sir.'

The dragoons surged forwards, their cornets at the front, small flags high, rippling manically in the rushing wind.

Captain Lancelot Forrester was galloping at the very centre of the massed horsemen. The hoof-borne thunder was deafening, the cold air parched his mouth, the sweat dripped from beneath his pot to send stinging rivulets into his eyes. All around him were the red coats of the Earl of Northampton's regiment, bright smears of colour stark in the drab afternoon. Occasionally his eye would catch other uniforms. Browns and greens and yellows. But he paid them no heed. Today he was one of Compton's men.

The prearranged time to separate was upon them in short order. Mid-way up the slope half the dragoon column were to peel to the left, and half to the right. The fluttering cornets were raised even higher, and the riders urged their horses one way or the other, and then the large force divided, a pair of vast snakes, slithering across the grass and gorse.

Forrester was with the faction surging to the left of Hopton Heath. He peered up at the ridge. It stretched out above them, a looming spectre that was, he reckoned, of a length equivalent to two musket shots. Grey-coated pike-men and musketeers manned that ridge, darkening the sky at their backs by sheer weight of numbers, but Forrester ignored them, for those men were hemmed in by hedgerows on one side and low walls on the other. It was those flanks that interested him.

As the dragoons surged on, Forrester squinted up at the hedges that formed the Parliamentarian right flank. Already he could see their dull pastel colours were inter-spersed by the metallic glint of weaponry, and realized the enclosures beyond would fairly bristle with defenders.

The sharp reports of musketry began to split the late afternoon as the dragoons came within range. Forrester gritted his teeth and urged his mount on, for the only choice was to ride headlong at the rebel flank and smash those musketeers to oblivion. He saw the smoke plumes drift listlessly from the foremost hedgerows, giving away the shooters' positions, and picked one as his first target, praying he would reach the man beyond before a lead ball picked him clean off his horse.

When they were fifty yards from the first hedge, the ground became suddenly pitted and they were forced to slow the charge. Forrester leant across his saddle and stared at the terrain passing in a blur beneath him, and realized with horror that they had galloped headlong into the midst of a rabbit warren. He saw, with a degree of relief, that their course took them along the warren's very periphery, the burrows becoming increasingly numerous towards the centre of the heath, but the charge was still at risk of stalling.

'On! On!' the leading officers screamed, for they were too close now to abort the attack.

Forrester dug deep for a reserve of courage and spurred his horse on, praying its hooves would not fall foul of the treacherous earth, and ducking as low as he could to avoid the musket-balls flying all about like summer midges.

And then he was there, crashing into the first hedge, his sword somehow looming high in a white-knuckled grip. The musketeer he had picked out was crouched on the far side of the dense foliage, frantically blowing on his burning match tip, desperate to reinvigorate the half-hearted embers. He stared up at the blade-wielding spectre that cast a shadow across him, eyes pristine and white with terror, and then the sword swept down in an irresistible arc, cutting through the cloth of the Roundhead's montero cap and crushing the skull beneath.

Forrester ignored the shrill cry and the gleaming blood that now dripped from his sword-point, for his own life depended upon a quick assessment of the situation. To his left and right, all the way along the hedgerow, his fellow dragoons were slashing down at the first musketeers. A handful of the enemy, like his own victim, had gambled on having their weapons reloaded by the time the horsemen reached them, and that gamble had been a bad one, but most of the grey-coated defenders were already falling back to the protection of what Forrester now saw was a complex network of enclosures, stretching back across the whole depth of the ridge. Orders carried to them from those deeper defences, and it was clear that the greycoats were busily hunkering down to make ready their muskets.

'Christ,' Forrester hissed, wondering how the dragoons would penetrate the hedges. They could no more negotiate the natural breastworks than the column of harquebusiers waiting at the foot of the slope.

'Dismount!' The order, turned to a snarl by urgency, reverberated through the dragoons, and, almost as one, they began to slide quickly from their saddles. They formed two ranks, for there was not the room for men and horses to stand side by side at the hedge-face.

Forrester, in that first rank, watched his new comrades with surprise at first, but then he realized that this was the natural course to take. He was an infantryman by trade, and, amidst the heat of battle and the metallic tang of newly shed blood, it had not occurred to him that this kind of action was exactly what Northampton had expected. Dragoons were not cavalry, but mounted infantry. Soldiers afforded both the speed of hooves and the versatility of foot. They did not need to leap the obstacles to bring blades to bear, for, unlike traditional cavalrymen, they had weapons offering far greater range.

He obeyed the order and, copying the more seasoned troopers at his flanks, moved quickly behind his horse, using the big beast's bulk as protection. He unslung his musket and began to load it.

Already the Parliamentarians were giving fire, making the air all around fizz with bullets, but their aim was poor and undisciplined, made so by anxiety, and only one man and one horse were wounded in the exchange.

And then the Royalist dragoons were primed and ready, and the orders to give fire blurted from the most senior among them. Forrester heard the directive as well as any man, and he moved out from behind his mount and stepped up to the sternum-high hedge, hoisting his musket to his right shoulder.

The Earl of Northampton's dragoons fired their flint-locks in a great volley that rolled across their front rank in a massive wave. And then that front rank was reloading amid their rising smoke halos, and the rear rank fired between them. The sound was an ear-splitting crash of simultaneous explosions as hundreds of pans flashed together, but Northampton's dragoons were seasoned troops, and not a single man flinched. The Parliamentarians in the hedgerows bore a heavy toll, for their tangled breastwork of foliage, though perfect for deterring horses, was no protection against flying lead, and their units were enfiladed with horrific ease. Men were snatched back, their blood spraying on to the bushes and mixing with the exposed soil of rabbit holes.

'Mount!' the red-coated officers screamed.

The order reached Forrester as a muffle, for the two vol-leys had obliterated his hearing, but he understood well enough, and, musket still loaded, hauled himself back into the saddle. He looked across to the left, and saw that three or four of the dragoons had slashed at the hedge with their swords until a gap had opened just big enough for a horse to pass through. Forrester wrenched on his reins and had soon joined his comrades in a single file line that passed through the hole and into the en-closure beyond. One or two muskets cracked from the Parliamentarian lines in defiance, but Gell's Derbyshire men were still in total disarray after the close-packed and disciplined Royalist volley, and they had not yet gone to ground to begin an organized resistance.

The leading redcoat suddenly stood high in his stirrups, craning to see over the next hedge, and when he turned back, Forrester saw that his face was a mask of grim relish.

'Drakes!' he bellowed excitedly. 'They've goddamned drakes back there!'

Forrester understood the truth of the situation, and the crucial task the dragoons would be required to execute. The drakes were placed on the Roundhead flank for one reason alone; to shred Northampton's cavalry as they charged against Gell's main body of infantry. They would carve bloody swathes through the Royalist column, spitting a venomous cannonade into the side of the approaching Cavaliers. Unless, thought Forrester, the dragoons could stop them.

Stryker heard the demi-cannon's crew long before he saw the great iron piece.

'Get your arses movin', damn your rancid bones!' a man with the accent of Wales growled from beyond a small copse. 'Get 'er set up to sing, or we'll be usin' your bloody ballocks for target practice!'

Stryker glanced down at Barkworth, who moved on foot beside the group, little legs almost having to run to keep pace with the loping animals. 'Go on and announce our arrival. I do not wish us mistook for the enemy and shot on sight.'

Barkworth scampered ahead of the three horses and rounded the copse, and, when Stryker, Blaze, Skellen and Burton had cleared the thicket of trees, the gun crew were waiting expectantly for them.

Stryker scanned the scene as they approached. The road had reached an abrupt end beside the copse, the sunken track of viscous mud giving way to a wide expanse of heath land that sloped away to his left. He glanced down that slope, seeing the distant buildings of the village of Hopton at its very bottom, and then ran his eye back up again. The first troops were those guarding the artillery train. Infantrymen, armed with firelocks – a necessity when in close proximity to large quantities of black powder – providing an escort for the dozen or so wagons that trundled on to the heath.

Further up the slope to his right was a dense crowd of cavalry. Northampton's harquebusiers, preparing, Barkworth had told him, to take the battle to the enemy. From this low vantage point Stryker could not see the top of the ridge, for the Royalist horsemen were in his way, but he knew that distant crest would be filled with waiting ranks of infantry. Pikemen and musketeers, all hoping to cut the king's famed riders down as they launched their great charge.

But that was not his prime concern, and Stryker stared across at the party immediately at his front. It consisted of nine men – three gunners, and their half-dozen assistants – all gathered around a vast tube of dark iron, mounted on huge wheels. There were thick ropes extending from the tube's carriage, all connected to a team of stout-looking horses, perhaps, Stryker reckoned, near twenty in all. This was Roaring Meg, the biggest gun in Stafford.

The gun captain paced forward to greet them. He hefted a long poleaxe in one hand and rested the other on the hilt of his tuck. 'Porter, sir,' he addressed Stryker, 'and may I ask which of you is Master Blaze?'

Stryker clambered down from the horse and reached up to brace the man who had shared his saddle. That man, bloody and broken, with blackened stumps for hands and a great wheel of scarlet spread across the linen at his midriff, slumped sideways, allowing the tall captain to ease him down on to the wet grass.

'This,' Stryker said to the artillery commander, as Burton and Skellen dismounted, 'is Fire-worker Jonathan Blaze.'

Porter's face convulsed as he looked at Blaze's horrific form, but a stern glare from Stryker curtailed whatever remark might have been forming on the Welshman's tongue, and the gun captain simply offered a deep bow. 'It is truly an honour to meet you, sir,' Porter said when he had recovered from the initial shock. 'I—*we*—' he corrected himself with a wave at the men gathered at his back, 'are great admirers of your work. You and your brother are truly the most revered artillerymen in the kingdom.'

Blaze seemed to shiver suddenly. 'Here,' Stryker said, hooking his arm around the wounded man, 'see if you can walk.'

Blaze did as he was told, though it was difficult in the extreme. The pain at his stomach clearly seared through his entire body, and tears welled from his eyes with every movement.

'Master Blaze,' Stryker said to Porter, 'is taking charge of this piece.'

Porter's eyes widened. 'But, sir, Roaring Meg is a tricky mistress, and he does not look to be able to—'

'Still your blasted tongue, curse you!' Jonathan Blaze hissed through lips made tight by pain. 'I am a fire-worker.

467

The best! I will command this cannon, and you will see how a real artilleryman works!'

Stryker had once despised Jonathan Blaze for his arrogance. Yet now the mere flicker of that old spark made him proud of the man who remained so defiant despite such hardship and betrayal. He fixed Porter with a hard stare that he knew would carry the shimmer of silver. 'Master Blaze will command Roaring Meg, sir. You will do as he says and, by all means, discuss any grievances with me.'

Gun Captain Porter chose not to argue further. He shouldered the poleaxe, turned on his heel and strode back to the waiting team. Stryker's party followed, Skellen taking the reins of his captain's horse as well as his own, while Stryker moved painstakingly slowly as he helped Blaze across the long grass and hazardous patches of dark gorse.

'Barkworth!' Stryker called to the little Scot walking ten paces ahead.

The former personal guard to the Earl of Chesterfield turned to meet Stryker's eye. 'Sir?'

'You said there was something at the artillery position I would wish to see.'

Barkworth's face creased. 'Aye, sir, that I did!'

'Well?' Stryker snapped impatiently as Barkworth turned away. And then he halted where he stood, his legs suddenly unable to function, such was his surprise. For a small woman dressed in a tight-fitting suit of black stepped out from behind Roaring Meg's vast bulk.

'*Bonsoir, mon amour*,' said Lisette Gaillard. 'Did you miss me?'

468

CHAPTER 21

Among the hedges and enclosures of the Parliamentarian right flank, men were dying.

The ebullient redcoats had streamed through the sword-chopped gap in the first organic breastwork, and immediately galloped across the clearing to the second hedge, cutting down any defenders slow enough to be caught in the open ground.

Lancelot Forrester was at the forefront of the attacking troops, and he could see the greycoats in the next enclosure, busily forming ranks to give volley fire. These would be a more difficult proposition than the men of the first hedgerow, for they were more numerous and evidently better organized.

And then the firing began. A crashing, ear-splitting, air-trembling volley from the foremost greycoats, men kneeling immediately behind the hedge, and their musket-balls filled the atmosphere like a meteorite shower. The man to Forrester's right was taken in the chest by one of the lethal lead spheres that flattened on impact, punching out through his back in a wide spray of red mist and white shards of bone.

For a moment the attack stalled, as more dragoons were thrown backwards, and the survivors, realizing the greycoats would cut them to pieces before they so much as touched the barrier's leaves, desperately searched for a way to pass through to the space beyond. But there was already an opening in the second hedge, a gap originally made to allow shepherds to pass between the enclosures in order to tend their sheep. Today, though, it was a wide, inviting breach in an otherwise solid breastwork, and the dragoons gave an exultant cry when they spotted it.

The first horseman reached the fissure with an unintelligible war cry. It was blocked by a low gate, but those ancient timbers were dark with rot, and the dragoon urged his mount directly into the obstacle. The horse smashed through the decaying wood, as though the gate had taken a direct hit from a mortar, and he raced through to face the Roundheads on the far side. Half a dozen muskets cracked in greeting, lifting him clean away from his saddle, suspended in the air for a heartbeat by the sheer force of six shots, and then he plummeted to the long grass, staining the heath in gushing fountains of crimson.

Forrester was next through, and he winced, clenching every fibre, ducking low, fully expecting to be pummelled by flying lead. But no shots came, and, risking a glance from behind his mount's neck, he saw that the first dragoon's horse, maddened by the pain of a musket strike at its broad chest and terrified at the sudden loss of its master, had charged headlong into the waiting Parliamentarian formation. The line of musketeers, three ranks deep, was demolished at its very centre by the crazed beast, ribs and skulls and faces kicked and crushed by flailing hooves, bodies battered out of the line by the huge, unstoppable mass of muscle.

The ends of the rebel line were still intact, but they had lost their bravery in the face of the charging beast, cohesion and competence vanishing for a fraction of a second. That fraction was enough to allow the oncoming dragoons time to close with them, and, before the rebel officers could drag order from chaos, the Royalists were upon them.

Forrester's musket was primed and ready, clutched in one hand, his reins in the other, but he was moving too fast to bring it to bear with any degree of accuracy. He kicked hard, compelling his horse to gallop straight at the waiting line, glad that no pikemen were positioned within the two ranks, and turned it at the very last moment so that he was parallel with the rebels. He was so close now that he could not miss the shot, and, like a warship firing a broadside, held the musket at arm's length and pulled the trigger. He could not see if the missile had flown true, for he was past the line in moments and wheeling round for the next assault, but the range had been undeniably deadly.

By the time Forrester completed the turn, the greycoated ranks had disintegrated. They remained dangerous, for they carried swords and many still had loaded muskets, but there was no more hope of the coordinated volley fire that was so destructive against mounted troops. Forrester spotted one such musketeer taking aim at a Royalist some ten yards away, and he lobbed his own spent long-arm directly at him. The long club of wood and metal turned cartwheels in the air before crashing into the greycoat, causing him to fire wildly at the gathering clouds.

One of the rebel's comrades turned on Forrester then, firing his own weapon at the Cavalier dragoon, and

Forrester's horse loosed a shrill scream of anguish as the ball ripped into its chest. Forrester managed to slew the wailing mount to a reluctant and twitching halt, and slid from the saddle before he was thrown. Immediately his blade was drawn, held out in front, poised for the inevitable action to come.

He did not have to wait long, for two greycoats came at him, long tucks outstretched. One, bearded face grimacing beneath a grimy montero cap, stabbed high, aiming the tip of his blade at Forrester's eyes. The other, a fellow of short stature and crooked nose, crouched down, making to cleave through the Royalist's ankles. Forrester stepped forwards, knowing retreat would only embolden them. A twitch in the bearded man's shoulder told him that the first move would come from there, and he flicked his blade upwards, using nothing but his wrist, and parried the attack with ease. The riposte bought him time to deal with the ankle blow, and, blade flashing in the grey light, he swept the sword down in a short arc to meet the shorter rebel's weapon.

But two opponents were difficult enough to best for even the greatest swordsman, and Forrester was immediately on the back foot as the first man swung at him again. Again Forrester met the blade, and this time he darted forwards with a thrust of his own that caught the Roundhead at the left temple, slicing through skin and ricocheting off the skull. The man recoiled, blinded, as blood gushed from the wound to his eye, and Forrester looked to deal with his mate. But this time he was not fast enough, and the second man was able to swipe his sword inside the captain's defence. The cutting edge of the blade slammed into Forrester's leg, just above the left ankle, and he stumbled back, pain jarring all the way up the limb. Fearing the worst, Forrester shifted all his weight on to his right foot, lest the wounded left give way at a crucial moment, and he met a succession of staccato jabs from the crooked-nosed rebel with deft flicks. He was clearly the superior swordsman, but his agonized left leg had thrown him off balance and limited his ability to attack, for he could not risk a forward thrust. He had to be content with bringing the shorter man on, allowing him free rein to swing his blade freely, and counter each riposte with a sharp parry of his own.

Just when he thought he would be backed right across the clearing and trapped against the hedge behind, Forrester saw the rebel plant his foot in a gelatinous pile of red tissue that he presumed must have been the sword-loosed entrails of some unfortunate horse. In his eagerness to achieve the kill, the greycoat had not noticed the slippery mess, and Forrester whipped his blade downwards in a low feint. The Parliamentarian moved to respond, only for Forrester to flick the steel point vertically upwards. The move was not designed to be a killer, but, as the razor tip clipped the rebel's pointed chin, it caused him to lurch violently backwards, instinctively protecting his face, and, as the Royalist officer had predicted, his foot slid from under him amid the oily intestines. In moments the man with the crooked nose was on his back, staring with wide, sparkless eyes at the drab March sky.

Forrester jerked his sword free from the sucking flesh of the greycoat's throat and stared about at the carnage. Bodies lay strewn in all directions, twisted, folded, grinning, like so many macabre dolls. Some wore the red of the Earl of Northampton, but the vast majority were swathed in the grey uniform of Sir John Gell, and Forrester knew that this second enclosure had fallen. And then he saw the drakes, four of them, miniature cannon designed to macerate flesh rather than break stone. They were at the corner of the enclosure, beyond the point where the musketeers had formed ranks, and he shuddered at the thought that their vicious attentions might have been turned upon the invading dragoons. It was only after several moments, as the fog of battle began to drift clear of his mind, that Forrester remembered the little artillery pieces were not pointed directly down the slope. They were angled away, to his right, in effect towards the centre of the heath.

'Christ almighty,' Forrester said aloud.

Sporadic musketry still crackled from deeper into the ridge, where a third enclosure harboured a new rebel force, augmented by those fugitives fortunate enough to escape the first two fights, but already the earl's dragoons were streaming through a gap in the next hedge, this one larger than before, bringing with them steel and lead and death.

Forrester looked back to where his horse had been shot. The beast was still there, but now it had slumped to its knees, blood rushing from the wound in a gushing fountain, wisps of steam drifting off the warm liquid as it met with the late afternoon air. Forrester shook his head sadly and made to join the latest assault, now as a fully-fledged infantryman, but a deep pain flashed up his shin in stark reminder of the wound he had himself sustained. He looked down, fearing the worst but seeing nothing other than a slight scar along the buff leather of his riding boots. The blade, though power-ful enough to cause a great deal of pain, had not been sharp enough to penetrate the tough boots, and Forrester privately

474

thanked God that he had not been forced to don the standard issue infantry shoes worn by Northampton's dragoon companies.

He decided to look for a new horse, one made riderless by the skirmish, but, before a suitable replacement could be spotted, a new order carried to him on the breeze. 'Form up! King's men, form up!'

Forrester hailed one of the senior officers, a bull-necked fellow with sore-looking lips and hollow cheeks. 'What now, Major Setter?'

Setter looked at him. 'The flanks are clear, and we have captured their ordnance. So we shall resume battle formation and hold this flank.'

Forrester glanced back in the direction of the slope, though the hedgerows blocked his view of the Royalist army. 'What does Northampton plan to do?'

'Plan?' Major Setter peered at Forrester as though he were an escaped Bedlamite. 'He will charge, sir.'

Spencer Compton, Earl of Northampton and supreme commander of the king's forces at Hopton Heath, was restless. He had a strong compliment of Cavaliers, many of them veterans of the European campaigns and all experts in horseback warfare. But they were not a force to be cooped up behind walls, surrounded by besiegers. They were useful for one thing, and one thing only: attack.

Northampton looked up at the ridge. 'Show the signal, damn you,' he muttered.

'My lord?' a nearby aide said in reply.

The earl shook his head. 'The signal, Watkins. They must wave that cursed flag before I will move.'

'The dragoons, my lord?'

Northampton scowled at Watkins. 'Of course the bloody dragoons!'

'May we not ride out now, my lord?' another man, a colonel by status and dandy by dress, enquired from somewhere in the rank behind.

The earl rounded on him. 'No, sir, we may not. If Gell has a shred of sense, he'll have prepared those flanks properly, which means we'll be carved to pieces from three sides, and we won't even reach his main force.'

The colonel lifted a lace kerchief to his thin mouth, dabbing daintily at the corners. 'My lord.'

'I would charge the base rogues as soon as you, God's blood I would,' Northampton went on, calmer now, 'but first the flanks must be cleared.'

He gazed back up at the ridge. At the grey coats swarming on that crest, at the glinting of leaf-shaped pike-heads and the glow of smouldering match-cords. The clouds at the rebels' back were darkening with every moment, and he knew the day was steadily drawing to a close. That thought terrified him, for nightfall would put paid to his attack more readily than any crashing volley or stubborn block of pike. He needed to attack soon, for time was running out.

Then he saw the flags. Red squares of taffeta held high. One above the hedgerows of the ridge's left-hand extremity, and one above the stone walls on the right.

The Earl of Northampton turned to his nearest officers. 'We have the flanks, gentlemen! Praise God, we have the flanks!'

A great huzza swept up from the Royalist column, swords were drawn, horses whinnied and reared.

The earl turned quickly to his aide. 'Send word to the gunners, Watkins.'

Watkins frowned. 'Yes, my lord. But—'

'But? But?'

'They'll not hit a thing from that range.'

Northampton nodded. 'But that demi-cannon'll strike the rebellious buggers with the very fear of the Lord! Do you wish Gell's men to be presenting musket and pike when we charge 'em? Or shrinking back like children in a lightning storm? Go, Watkins. Tell Meg to roar!'

Fire-worker Jonathan Blaze was perched on the edge of a supply wagon, a vehicle packed with bushels full of musket-balls, swords and spare tack.

He grinned. It was a strange sight for those standing around him, scuttling to adhere to his quick-fire orders, for his split lips and broken teeth made it more akin to a grimace. But a grin it certainly was. 'Thank you, Captain Stryker,' he said, as Stryker came to stand beside him. 'You have afforded me one last throw of the dice, and I cannot tell you what it means.'

'I have heard a great deal about you, Master Blaze,' answered Stryker truthfully. 'It will be an honour to witness you at work.'

'But you were at Cirencester, sir,' Blaze said.

'Aye,' Stryker nodded, 'but I have not seen you command a weapon such as this.'

Jonathan Blaze gazed down at the huge cannon's dark shaft, an almost loving glint in his swollen eyes. Roaring Meg had been hauled by the horses on to a temporary platform of wickerwork in order to minimize the effect of her monstrous recoil.

477

'She'll be half way into this mud, Stryker,' Blaze had said as the mattrosses laid out the wicker slats. 'Big guns like her have a kick like a thousand mules. Without the platform, she'd be embedded deep in the ground after the first shot, and I'd completely lose trajectory.'

Now that the wickerwork was laid out, and the demi-cannon in place, Blaze was busily adjusting the elevation of the vast black barrel, snapping sharp orders at the crew.

One of the gunners had placed a contraption, made of brass and the shape of a wedge of cheese, near the breech of the cannon. Its bottom side was curved in a gentle arc, and covered with markings that denoted a numerical scale. Stryker knew that the apparatus was a quadrant level, a device made of brass, attached to a dangling piece of metal called a plummet that looked similar to a builder's plumb line. The gunner adjusted the quadrant level so that it was aligned with the gun's axis, bending low to take the plummet reading from the numbers of the levelling arc, and shouted the information back up at Blaze, who considered each with a twitch of the nose, or gnaw of the lip.

Eventually the fire-worker nodded. 'We have our elevation, gentlemen, well done. Now, if you please, we will sight her. Will someone please help me down?'

Skellen and one of the mattrosses moved to take hold of Blaze's arms, together lifting him down, and soon he was at the cannon's breech.

'When used as a sight,' Blaze announced proudly, as though giving a lesson to schoolboys, 'the instrument is to be placed transversely across the barrel.'

One of the mattrosses turned the quadrant, and Blaze bent to look through the looped sight at its crest, wincing with the motion.

'Should he not see a chirurgeon?' Lisette Gaillard said as she came to stand beside Stryker. The captain had backed away from the cannon and its crew in order for them to ply their trade unhindered, and he was standing beside his horse, gazing up at the massed cavalry further up the grassy slope.

He looked down at her. 'He is gut-shot, Lisette.'

She nodded mutely. Stryker saw the sorrow in the Frenchwoman's face, and searched for some words of encouragement. None came. They had all failed the Blaze brothers.

'You look well,' Stryker said after a few awkward moments.

She smiled at him. 'I am recovering, sir, thanks to you.'

'Thanks to Doctor Chambers.'

'*Oui*, Chambers too. He is in the village, you know,' she said, pointing to the little hamlet of Hopton.

'He will tend the wounded there.'

Stryker sucked his teeth, thinking of the horrors Gregory Chambers would doubtless witness before this day was at an end. Lisette snaked an arm around the crook of his elbow and leant forwards to place her forehead against his shoulder. He wondered if she was thinking the same thing.

'I forgot,' Stryker said suddenly, bending to thrust thick fingers into his boot. Eventually he straightened, holding up a fist in which he gripped a long, pointed shard of silver that glinted like a slender icicle. 'Yours, I believe.'

The sapphire eyes enlarged in recognition. 'My hairpin!'

'More knife than pin.'

'But I keep it in my hair, so it is a hairpin.' She cocked her head to one side. 'I didn't know you had a penchant for such things, *mon amour*.'

He thought briefly of a sallow-faced man with malevolent green eyes and a wart-strewn face. 'More than you know.'

She gave a short laugh. 'Then keep it.'

He looked at the handleless dagger, turning it in his hand, remembering the moment when he had jammed it into Zacharie Girns's slim neck. 'I think I will.'

A rider approached from the direction of Northampton's cavalry. Resplendent in newly oiled buff leather, polished plate and visored helmet, he was clearly one of the earl's elite horsemen. Stryker handed the reins to Lisette and strode across the churned grass and mud to greet him.

'Who commands here?' the rider chirped as he brought his horse from gallop to trot.

Stryker lifted an arm. 'Captain Stryker, sir.'

The horseman stared at Stryker for a heartbeat, clearly pondering why the artillery commander did not wear a standard issue coat beneath his sleeveless buff jacket.

'Sir?' Stryker prompted.

'Compliments of his lordship,' the horseman said, blinking rapidly, 'and you're to pound the ridge forthwith.'

Sir John Gell sat atop his horse and stared, mouth gaping, at the red standards swaying at both ends of the ridge. His mind was racing, frantically churning facts and options, searching for a strategy that would bring him victory. Because his plans had gone stunningly awry.

Northampton had not flung his Cavaliers straight into Gell's brilliant trap. He had shown unexpected and infuriating restraint, and declined to fly headlong into the killing zone, instead sending his dragoons left and right to clear the Parliamentarian flanks. And those natural parapets of hedge and stone, breastworks harbouring Gell's drakes and muskets, had been utterly obliterated.

'We must recapture the flanks,' Sir William Brereton said at Gell's side, his voice strained with urgency.

Gell considered the statement. 'No,' he eventually replied, 'it is a blow, Sir William, I grant you, but the real fight will be here, at the centre. We cannot afford to lose men from our core force.'

'But, Sir John—' Brereton began.

Gell glared at him. 'Christ's bones, man, forget the damned flanks!' He turned to stare down the slope, eyes raking across the massed cavalry at the foot of the heath. 'Compton will come upon us soon enough. We must not weaken our main body. We shall stand firm and wait for him to break his mounts' legs in amongst the coney warren. Any that should make it through that treacherous field will be met first by your harquebusiers and then with pike and musket.' He looked at Brereton, fixing Parliament's Cheshire commander with a flinty stare. 'The day is not lost, so long as we do not break ranks.'

And then, from the very bottom of the slope, a cannon fired.

A collective intake of breath rippled across Hopton Heath's wide crest. Pikes swayed like monstrously over-grown reeds in a gale, gloved grips loosening as their owners peered skywards.

The cannon ball sailed above the cavalry at the bottom of the slope, always rising, cutting through the near dusk air at unimaginable speed.

Sir John Gell was in the centre of his great force. He stayed in the saddle. Deliberately conspicuous atop the big, sorrel-coloured stallion he had obtained at Lichfield, he watched the black dot carve through the heavens. He would not move. Would not be seen to move.

Voices shrill with panic sounded from somewhere behind Gell, and he twisted back angrily. 'Hold firm, damn your eyes!' he snarled, seeing that the commotion had originated with the inexperienced Moorlanders he had placed in reserve. 'Any man breaks rank, I'll kill him my goddamned self!'

When Gell turned back to face the heath, he could no longer see the oncoming missile. He squinted up at the clouds, trying to identify it, a black bird of prey moving faster than its own sound. 'Where are you?' he whispered.

The ball smashed into the front rank of the rebel army with a crescendo of noise and spraying blood and violence. It hit one of Gell's seasoned pike battailes, and the first men simply vanished, bodies reduced to nothing by the speeding lump of iron. But the lethal projectile continued its inexorable voyage, an angel of death with an appetite those first kills could not slake, and it drove onwards, taking the next ranks down in a maelstrom of screams and blood and of steel and bone and leather.

The blocks of musketeers either side of the damaged pike unit swayed away instinctively, sending a current of movement in both directions, causing men to step out of line.

Gell kicked his horse forwards and turned it back to face his army. 'Form up! Form up, damn you!' He thrust a hand towards the newly carved gap in the pike block.

From his high seat he could see that at least six men had been killed and almost the same number were injured. 'Close up there! Get those bodies to the rear and close up!'

To his relief, the men did as they were told, shuffling forwards to take the place of their fallen comrades and present a united and unflappable front to the enemy. He thanked God for the foresight to place the raw Staffordshire Moorlanders out of harm's way, for they would surely have cut and run had it been their friends and kin in that devastated pike battaile. His grizzled Derbyshire men had paid the price for their fearsome reputation, and he privately mourned their loss, but at least his army would survive the barrage.

Gell stared down at the Royalist army. 'What now?' he whispered.

Fire-worker Jonathan Blaze thumped a mutilated fist against the rear of the wagon. He had been returned to his perch in readiness for the gunners to touch their spark to Roaring Meg's charge. 'Damn it all!'

Stryker strode up to him as the gun crew began preparing the smoking demi-cannon for the next salvo. 'What vexes you, Master Blaze?' He stared up at the ridge. 'It was a direct hit!'

Blaze shook his head rapidly, evidently irked by Stryker's words. 'A direct hit for common bloody gunners, Captain, but not for me!' He thrust the congealed stump up at the Parliamentarian ranks. The pike block that had borne the brunt of Roaring Meg's first shot looked for all the world like an array of perfect statues; grey, undamaged and defiant. 'You are clearly used to this, Captain Stryker. Artillery employed to soften up the enemy before the *real* fighting begins.'

'That's exactly it, sir,' Sergeant Skellen interrupted. He was standing beside the cannon, watching its crew cluck about the red-hot barrel like so many hens. 'Blast the buggers for a while. Scare the green ones. Then charge.'

Blaze glared at Skellen. 'Scare the green ones,' he repeated the sergeant's phrase in a barely concealed sneer. 'And what if your enemy are not so green? What then? What, for instance, does your regiment do in the face of bombardment?'

Skellen shrugged. 'Ignore it in the main, sir. Field pieces don't do a great deal o' damage when all's said an' done.'

'Precisely!' Blaze bellowed hoarsely. 'And that is where I am different!' He stared up at the grey-coated ranks. 'This is not a field piece, Sergeant, but a siege piece. If I can find the exact elevation, I shall punch a hole so wide they won't be fit to reform, even if they wanted to.'

'Sir?' Gun Captain Porter shouted, louder than required, for his hearing had been dulled by the first blast.

Blaze looked down at him, and then shifted his pained gaze back and forth between the cannon and the ridge. 'A minor adjustment only,' he said absently, his voice soft, as though in a daydream. 'Help me down, Captain,' he snapped suddenly, looking at Stryker.

'Of course, sir,' Stryker replied, crooking an arm around Blaze's back and gently easing him to the very edge of the wagon. The movement smarted at the flesh wound beneath his armpit, but he bit down hard on his tongue, forcing the urge to cry out away.

'Gunnery is art and science intertwined, Stryker,' Blaze said as the captain and Sergeant Skellen helped him to the ground. 'The prediction of range in relation to elevation, which is the highest and most precise form of mathematics, enmeshed with something else. A sixth sense, if you will. Do you understand?'

Stryker nodded. He most certainly did understand. Perhaps not in relation to artillery, but he had experienced that intangible gut instinct, and had been saved by it more times than he cared count. In battle, the art of predicting where and when and how an enemy would strike was utterly vital.

'You require the quadrant again, sir?' Gun Captain Porter boomed.

Blaze waved him away and looked at Stryker, his face suddenly twisted. 'I am growing weak with every beat of my heart, Captain. I do not have long.'

Stryker helped him silently to the cannon, and the fireworker knelt as best he could behind the barrel. 'The quadrant can only calculate so much,' Blaze whispered, 'and then one must focus on the artistry. A great artilleryman must listen to his intuition, his impulse and his experience. Fortunately,' he added with a pain-racked cackle, 'I possess all three.'

Nearly a thousand horsemen gazed up at the massed ranks of Derbyshire greycoats. The Parliamentarians were crammed at the top of the slope, lining the ridge in deep blocks of musket and pike, awaiting the inevitable charge. The Royalists adjusted hats and helmets, checked buckles and sashes, slid swords in and out of scabbards to ensure they would not stick when the killing time came, and primed firearms. Some men prayed, others muttered jokes to stave off the nervous tension. One man vomited on to the ground, flecking his horse's dark fetlocks, another yelled a toast to the king that spawned a desultory chorus of huzzas along the deep line.

Spencer Compton, Earl of Northampton, was at their centre. He looked left and right, feeling swelling pride in these brave men. They were a fine force, expert horsemen who would destroy any that came before them. He watched them run through their final preparations, the stench of horse dung and sweat ripe in his nostrils, and drew his own blade.

'On my mark!' he bellowed at a pair of trumpeters, raising the sword high.

All eyes turned to him. Men tensed, horses shifted anxiously, trumpets were raised to lips. They had thought this day would see them charge headlong on to a heath covered on three flanks by enemy musketeers. It would have been a suicidal assault of impossible courage and certain death. But the dragoons had cleared both flanks, leaving only the men on the crest, and that, mercifully, was a far better prospect.

The wide line of cavalry was becoming ragged by the moment as they fought to curb the enthusiasm of horses eager to surge into the gallop they sensed was imminent. They would career up the slope and smash into the Roundhead infantry. They would carve a bloody swathe through the drab grey and turn the ridge into a killing ground.

They waited for the signal.

And, yards to the rear, Roaring Meg belched fire and smoke again. She jolted backwards, the recoil sending her big wheels rattling over the wicker platform, and then her voice, deep and terrible, like a dozen claps of simultaneous thunder, filled the air and shook the ground, and her fat iron projectile sailed high over their heads in a huge arc.

Sir John Gell swore viciously as the second Royalist salvo hit home. The first had been bloody but manageable. This time, though, he could sense the devastation would be greater, even before the whirring iron chunk reached the ridge.

When it finally came upon them, dipping sharply at the end of its arc, it hit the same pike battaile as before, but this time at a slightly raised trajectory. The ball clipped the heads of the first two pikemen, severing their skulls all the way down to their noses, and obliterated the faces of both men behind. Even as the wide, billowing spray of blood, brain and skull fragments showered across the battaile, the ball was angling downwards through the ranks, exploding through chests and stomachs, thighs and shins and ankles, shredding armour and pulverizing flesh all the way back to the very rear of the Derbyshire men, before finally burrowing a great tunnel into the soil in front of the terrified Moorlanders who stood further back along the ridge. And in the blink of an eye, it was over.

Gell kicked his horse into a gallop as he heard the screams. He raced along the front rank of his infantry-men, desperate to reform the shattered battaile and acutely aware that he would have to coordinate it himself. But when he reached the bloody gap, he knew it was a forlorn hope. The cannon had created such a wide fissure in the previously tight deployment that it would take far too long to clear the bodies and even longer to order, coax and threaten replacements to step forwards. Even as he gazed at the hideous carnage, the men around him were beginning to shift away from the scene, desperate to be out of the demi-cannon's vengeful path. Sergeants and officers stepped up, growling for silence and obedience, but heads were shaking and the terrified wails – from the mouths of greycoats and Moorlanders alike – were building to a horrified crescendo. And all the while the gap in the line was growing.

Stryker leapt up into the wagon as soon as he saw Jonathan Blaze slump back. He crouched next to the fire-worker, cradling his bloody head in his hands, and saw that Blaze's swollen eyelids were drooping.

'Master Blaze?' he said softly. 'Can you hear me?'

Blaze looked up at him, the simple act a hardship. 'Thank you for rescuing me, Captain.'

Stryker felt his cheeks burn with shame. 'I failed, sir. I am sorry.'

'But you killed Zacharie for me. For Lazarus. For that you will always have my gratitude.' He tried to laugh, but the gesture became a racking cough that sent a deluge of blood up from his chest. 'Not that such a thing is worth a great deal now.'

Stryker stared down at the dying Blaze. It was as though the effort of commanding Roaring Meg's crew had taken too heavy a toll on the fire-worker. As though the precision and skill required in delivering the perfect shot had sapped the last vestiges of energy from Blaze's broken body.

Blaze convulsed. He curled up like a foetus, ruined hands clutched tight to his pistol-ravaged guts, and unleashed a muffled scream into the wagon's timber base.

When the scream faded, he fell almost still, his body consumed by faint, frenetic spasms.

Stryker looked up suddenly, because another scream washed across the great heath like a sudden deluge. It was the sound of agony, but not the private kind suffered by Blaze. It was a scream set free by dozens – perhaps scores – of men, and it came from the high ground where the rebel army had gathered.

'You did it!' the Welsh gunner, Porter, was shouting from beside the still hissing demi-cannon. 'You did it, sir! Stone me, but you made them eat Meg's iron like you said you would!'

Stryker glanced from Porter to his own men, and was stunned to see both Burton and Skellen simply staring up, slack-jawed and silent, at the rebel horde.

'A direct hit.' The richly accented tones of Lisette Gaillard broke through Stryker's reverie, and he realized she was standing beside the wagon.

He looked at her. 'Like the last?'

Lisette shook her head, eyes full of their wicked brightness. 'Better. It looks to have taken out a whole block.' She glared up at the ridge, the old, incandescent hatred returning now that she was almost fully recovered. 'Bastards.'

Stryker followed her diamond-hard gaze. What he saw was the horizon. A wide space of open air, sliced into the very centre of the Roundhead battle line. Blaze, he realized, had shown his worth, and Roaring Meg had done her duty.

'*Jesu*,' was all he could think to say.

'Charge!' Spencer Compton, Second Earl of Northampton, swept his broadsword down sharply, revelling in its shrill zing, and his horsemen surged forwards. 'God and King

Charles!' he screamed, as his own mount's hooves skittered across the damp earth, but he knew none could hear the words, for the noise was deafening. Near a thousand beasts, huge warhorses bred for the hunt, thundered up the slope of Hopton Heath, and the sound and speed made it seem as though the heavenly host itself had joined them.

The earl dug his spurs as cruelly as he could into his horse's flanks, compelling it up the gentle gradient. He leaned forwards in the saddle, but craned his neck back so that he could see the ridge and the men waiting there. He was aiming for the hole. That great swathe of newly made cadavers opened up by the Royalist ordnance. He still could not quite believe it. He knew Stafford's gunners were good, but Roaring Meg had managed to send her searing iron ball straight into a pike battaile twice. And the second of those strikes had taken one of the heaviest tolls he had ever witnessed. One moment the rebel line had been a grand, unruffled, formidable wall of primed muskets and bristling pikes; the next, it had been split in two, a gruesome scar of corpses separating one half from the other. And into that scar would pour the Cavaliers.

'King Char—!' he began to scream again, but the word died on his lips as the ridge was suddenly obscured by the dark shapes of horsemen. They came from somewhere to the Parliamentarian left flank, like a shadowy, storm-swollen cloud rolling down a mountainside, enveloping the land to the right of the ridge, and then, at the last moment, sweeping in to engage the Royalists.

Northampton braced himself. There was no time to think or change tack or even retreat.

And then the two bodies of cavalry smashed home.

*

Stryker did not have spurs, so he ground his boot heels wickedly into the horse's flesh. He had left the rapidly declining Blaze in Lisette's capable care, and now he rode to war.

Stryker, Burton, Skellen and Barkworth were back on the mounts they had taken from Brocton, and, though not thoroughbred destriers, they were good, swift, oat-fed beasts that careered impressively up the slope in the wake of the Earl of Northampton's great charge.

Nearer the rebel-held ridge, perhaps two-thirds of the way up the slope, they watched the cavalry battle unfold. It was a surreal experience for Stryker, for he knew the sounds of rearing horses and clashing steel and the screams of dying men would be coursing across Hopton Heath, but he could hear nothing above the wind rushing about his head and the beat of his own horse's hooves.

They closed the gap quickly, for the Royalist charge had stalled in the face of the faster Parliamentarian horsemen – speeding downhill as they were – and very soon the engagement was a matter of moments away. Stryker could already see that the apparent silence belied a terrible carnage. The rebel harquebusiers were swift and brave, and had smashed headlong into the advancing king's men, but, though their numbers were similar, they were easily outfought and outmanoeuvred by the elite Cavaliers. Even from some distance away, Stryker could see that Northampton's men were already beginning to overwhelm the tenacious Roundhead force.

Stryker drew his blade. He caught sight of Skellen and Barkworth doing the same, and, though Burton rode on Stryker's blinkered left side, he knew the lieutenant would be hurriedly looping his reins over his withered arm, transferring control to his thighs, and unsheathing his own sword.

And then they were inside the churning mass of horsemen, pulses quickened by the sudden and irresistible battle-joy that made a man revel in the smell of blood and the demise of an enemy. But they could not wet their poised blades, or stare into the eyes of hated enemies, for there were none.

Stryker hauled his animal to a halt. It turned skittish circles in its excitement, but obeyed him all the same, and he scanned the scene, searching for the Parliamentarian troopers in the midst of Northampton's. But all he saw were their backs as they galloped, broken, terrified and chaotic, up the slope.

'On! On! On!' Northampton bellowed. He was exultant. He was jubilant. He had spilled Roundhead blood over the grass and the gorse, and had cut their cavalry to shreds in less than two minutes. Had Brereton expected anything else, he wondered? The king's army was filled by the nation's landed gentry, men who could ride and hunt as soon as they could walk. It was almost an insult to have to fight the common, ill-trained vagabonds Parliament thrust so readily into the saddle.

Northampton was at the head of his great, triumphal column, and, though it had temporarily stalled, he screamed encouragement back at the men, whipping them into fury and speed once more, urging them to chase the routed Roundheads all the way back to the ridge.

And there, on that ridge, he would set an example for those who would defy His Majesty, God's anointed representative on earth. And more rebel blood – infantry this time – would gush forth to stain the heath.

The Royalists returned to the gallop in moments, and soon they would be amongst that huge hole gouged so viciously by Roaring Meg. Northampton glared from behind the trio of iron bars that jutted across his face from the hinged peak of his pot, gauging the strength and resolve of the waiting units of foot, and prayed that he might cut through them like a needle through silk.

He jolted forwards suddenly.

He managed to right himself and then looked down at the browns and greens of the land as he raced across it. In amongst those colours were patches of black, and, with a sudden, heart-rending understanding, he knew why the Parliamentarian cavalrymen had launched their attack from the flank. Because the patches over which he and his men now charged were the cavernous mouths of holes. Too many to count. He had led his beloved cavalry into the very heart of a huge rabbit warren.

To his left he heard the horrendous crescendo of horse and man and steel crashing into the ground, and he knew that the warren had taken its first victim. Shouts of warning and terror rent the sky all around him, and a flash of reticence stabbed across his mind.

In a flash, another trooper went down, limbs of man and beast whirling in a cloud of tangled fetlocks and shattered bones.

Northampton cursed, consumed by sickening guilt and raging anger. It was a trap. Or, rather, a maze of a thousand traps, each one capable of wiping out a horse in the blink of an eye.

But the earl's son, Sir James, had taken the lead now, his sword drawn and held high above his head like a great standard, and men were following. Northampton bit back his trepidation then, all doubt giving way to a swelling pride in his gallant first-born, and he held tight to his thundering steed, praying that its hooves would stay firm and its balance would remain steadfast. They would make it. They *had* to make it.

And before he knew it, they were at the rebel front rank.

CHAPTER 22

Stryker somehow managed to thread his way through the treacherous warren and found himself just yards from the waiting grey-coated line. He did not know if Burton or Skellen or Barkworth had managed the same feat, or if they lay dying in his wake. At this moment he did not care. He could not.

On he raced, realizing now that this was to be an out and out confrontation between cavalry and infantry, for the rebel horsemen had been utterly routed and, he guessed, were already streaming away from Stafford like frightened mice from the jaws of a cat. For a moment he felt a pang of sympathy for the Roundhead Foot. As an infantryman himself, he knew how difficult it was to counter such a vast cavalry charge. But the brief professional empathy was gone as soon as it had come, and he set his mind to the business at hand.

Before him was the ridge's zenith, just yards away now, and across that great expanse waited unit upon unit of enemy soldiers. He recognized them as Derbyshire men, for he remembered their grey uniforms from Lichfield, and he knew that they would not fold as easily as their mounted counterparts.

He dipped his head and kicked on, desperate to get on with the killing. The line came up quickly, a deep array of glinting pike companies and musketeers, alternately deployed along the ridge, each block ready to go to work.

The infantry line exploded in a bright flash, orange tongues of flame lapping the ridge in one blinding instant, replaced by a cloud of smoke the next. The second rank fired immediately. Muskets crashed, more smoke belched around their heads.

Stryker felt the leaden balls whip past. One clipped his elbow, tearing the fabric of his sleeve, but only grazing the flesh beneath. He hunkered down, wishing he had taken the time to put on a helmet, wincing and gritting teeth and bracing for sudden death. Somewhere to the right, a rider was thrown clear of his horse, a musket shot having passed through his thigh to sting his mount's flank and set it rearing wildly. Another man's face exploded in a spray of red mist as a bullet took his jaw clean away.

'The breach! The breach!' the Royalist officers were bellowing, and Stryker saw that the majority of harquebusiers were funnelling towards the gap that still remained in Gell's formation, his men evidently too afraid of the cannon to step in and fill the hole.

Stryker steered his mount towards that target, and, like the parting of the Red Sea, he saw that the infantrymen nearest the ragged chasm were stumbling away, breaking ranks before the cavalry reached them.

A cry went up from the greycoats. 'Charge for horse!'

It was shrill and it was panicked, and it was much too late. Northampton's cavalry, his Cavaliers who had ridden and fenced and hunted all their lives, had rolled across the pitted warren like a shore-dashing wave, eating up the ground at a far greater pace than the rebels had anticipated, and they smashed against the grey line along the entire breadth of the ridge.

Those sections populated by Gell's musketeers had already loosed their shots, and they reversed their weapons, presenting the wooden stocks as clubs, and shrank back a pace so that the pikemen either side could thrust their ash poles – sixteen-feet long and tipped with a razor-sharp point – into the chests of the enemy horses and the faces of their riders.

But Stryker, along with most of the Royalist cavalry, surged into the gaping fissure in Gell's cannon-shredded formation, and he knew that it was here the battle would be won or lost. All around him the Cavaliers' faces were taut with grim determination, their eyes wide, almost glowing, in the late afternoon light. They brought only death at their heels.

The rebels instinctively backed away, their formation bowing and splintering with every second. They had had all the advantages this day. The high ground, the terrain, the element of surprise, and yet now, thanks to one monstrous iron gun and its frighteningly competent crew, a certain victory had been torn from their grasp in a welter of pain and blood.

The Royalist horsemen stood in their stirrups, hacking down at the heads and arms of the greycoats. They wheeled their animals round, pulling savagely on reins to bring their muscular mounts' bodies to bear as battering rams, forcing musketeers and pikemen back, allowing no choice but retreat.

Here and there, units of pike, appearing to Stryker like miniature battailes, offered more stout resistance. They jabbed up at the horses' chests and faces, forcing the animals to rear or twist away, but this demonstration of the effectiveness of well-ordered pikemen was too scant an offering to make any great impact. Still the Cavaliers hacked and whooped and cursed and crowed.

Sir John Gell was on the Parliamentarian left flank. He had galloped south and east along the crest of the ridge, from the centre of his dense human barrier of pike and shot, to the walls of the deer park, in order to organize that flank, making certain that the men deployed there would hold firm against the encroaching Royalist dragoons. He had lost both his flanks, and that was a devastating blow, but he would be damned if the Cavaliers would be allowed to circle behind his main body of infantry without first being made to fight.

In the event, he had successfully arranged the grey-coated defences, and had heard that the more competent officers sent to the hedges of the right flank had done an equally effective job. As a result, they were now engaged in bitter skirmishes on both of the ridge's peripheries, but at least, he reflected, the central infantry line had been able to face Northampton's cavalry charge without the added concern of dragoons at the rear. The rebels still had a chance at snatching victory.

But then Brereton's cavalry had been routed, and Sir William had led their ignominious flight from the field. And Gell's chance had dissolved.

'I'll kill him myself,' Gell hissed, as he stared across the ridge at the breach opened with so much carnage by just two shots from the Royalist artillery.

'Sir?'

Gell looked across at his aide. 'Sir William Brereton. I will kill that cowardly shaveling myself.'

Captain Mason winced at the coarse language, but nodded sombrely. 'If you can find him, sir. He'll be half way back to Nantwich by now.'

Gell nodded, hawked up a wad of phlegm and churned it with his tongue against the roof of his mouth. It was gritty with gunpowder and mud, and he spat it on to a patch of dark gorse, watching it break up on the sharp barbs and drip to the grass in sticky strands. 'We must step in, Captain,' he said eventually.

Mason's brow jumped. 'Sir?'

For an answer, Gell lashed at his horse with leather reins and metal spurs and the beast launched into a gallop that took him westwards along the ridge, across the back of his pikemen and musketeers. He lifted his backside off the saddle, straining to get a clear picture of the conflict. He could see Northampton's cavalry engaging his foremost ranks all the way along the great line. Too many had made it safely across the rabbit warren, and that fact, compounded by his severe miscalculation of their skill and bravery, was a painful truth to bear. For the most part, his Derbyshire men offered resolute resistance, but at the very centre of his line things were appallingly different. There, in the place where the demi-cannon had wrought its butchery and where the majority of enemy cavalry now concentrated their efforts, his beloved greycoats were dying and the line was beginning to buckle. That place, the eye of the storm, had become a hell on earth. A charnel house in the open air where the bodies of men and horses were grotesquely entangled; twisted and blood-drenched. Worse was to come. As Gell drew ever closer, he could see that his officers and sergeants were losing their collective nerve, allowing the infantry to back away from the slashing torrent, breaking ranks, making themselves easy targets for the exultant Royalist cavalrymen.

He looked right, to the northern slope of the ridge where the land plummeted down to a deep valley cut by the Trent. His reserves, the Staffordshire men, were supposed to be there, but now that land was empty. He drew his horse to a halt. 'Where are the bloody Moorlanders!' he bellowed towards the rearmost ranks of greycoats, those so far untouched by the cavalry.

A sergeant twisted back to see him. 'Gone, sir!'

Gell ground his teeth together until his gums stung. 'Gone? Gone where?'

The sergeant looked reticent. 'Just gone, sir,' he said gingerly. 'Turned tail and marched off.'

'God damn them! God damn the craven bastards!' Gell turned to Captain Mason, who had galloped up behind him. 'Our flanks are gone, the Horse have been routed and we have no reserve! We are on the very brink of annihilation!'

'Sound the retreat, sir?'

Gell glared. 'We will all die before that happens!' All at once he leapt down from the saddle and handed Mason the stallion's reins. 'Take him, Captain!'

'Sir?' Mason gaped. 'Where do you go, sir?'

Gell drew his sword and pointed at the breach. 'There.'

Stryker was in the midst of the fight. To his right, a red-sashed Cavalier, standing tall in flashing stirrups, battered down at a rebel officer. His heavy blow glanced off the Roundhead's blade and hammered against his shoulder, but the thick sleeve of the officer's buff-coat absorbed the impact and dulled the blade's edge. The Royalist urged his horse on, using the beast to force the infantryman backwards, and the rebel suddenly slipped in a patch of blood that still pumped from one of his fallen comrades. He took a knee, and the horseman sliced at his face, cleaving skin as though it were butter so that his cheek flapped open. The officer fell back, screaming pitifully, and the harquebusier kicked at his mount again, trampling him under pounding hooves.

Some yards away, a greycoat had discarded his musket and presented his tuck to parry a downward blow from one of the snarling cavalrymen. Steel met steel in a loud zing, and the rebel's blade snapped just above the hilt. The horseman's lips peeled back in a malicious sneer as he delivered a searing backhanded slash that sheered along the side of the Parliamentarian's pot, denting it and felling its wearer. The Royalist leaned across his saddle, taking aim with the point of his sword to stab hard at the fallen man's exposed neck, but the greycoat rolled away, snatching up an ancient shard of antler, bleached pearl-white by the elements, and jammed it into the horse's fetlock. The beast brayed in sudden agony, and reared, sending the Royalist tumbling across its rump and on to his back in the mud. He had lost his sword in the fall, and the greycoat was on him like a rabid mastiff, slashing at his face with the antler that now glistened red with the horse's blood. The cavalryman's face bars initially took the brunt of the attack, and he managed to scrabble with his buff-gloved fingers at the Roundhead's face, knocking the pot free from his head, but, with a grin of vicious triumph, the Derbyshire man finally found a way through with a hard jab, and the antler burst upwards through the Royalist's nostril, pulverizing his nose and eliciting a scream of utter terror.

Stryker kicked his mount so that he was above the pair, and he swiped down at the greycoat in his moment of victory, cleaving the top of his unprotected skull. The Roundhead immediately slumped forwards, dying on top of his own twitching victim.

Stryker looked up, staring all about, gauging the ebb and flow of the battle. The rebel line was disintegrating before him. Their reserves, held at the back of the ridge where the ground fell sharply down towards the river, had vanished, and he wondered if their officers had thought better than to dash them against the inexorable Royalist tide.

Another of the grey-coated Derbyshire men came at him then. The man was powerfully built, and he wielded a long halberd, scything the air in front of his chest as though he cut wheat at harvest-time. He lurched with more speed than Stryker had expected, leaping a twisted cadaver, swinging the halberd upwards to disembowel the Royalist's horse. Stryker hauled savagely on the reins, turning the beast away with barely a hair's breadth to spare, and the halberd's three-bladed point sung agonizingly close. But the huge blow had unbalanced the rebel, and Stryker turned the horse quickly back, beating down at the broad man's head with his sword. The edge clanged against the already dented pot, knocking the Roundhead further rearwards, and he surged on, battering again and again, not knowing which blows were successful, only aware of the rushing battle rage that quickened his senses and enlivened his muscles, and which found in him new depths of strength. And then the man was down, and Stryker was already looking beyond him, searching the scene for the next man to kill. He did not hate these men any more than he loved his king, but they were here, on this ridge, attempting to kill him. So he would kill them first.

He guided his horse towards a group of musketeers who were stumbling rapidly backwards, desperate to flee but too frightened to expose their backs. Stryker bolted into them, slashing down at bare and helmeted heads alike, cleaving indiscriminately, screaming unintelligibly.

Soon they would carve a swathe all the way through the enemy defences, splitting the Roundhead formation in two. After that, victory would come swiftly.

Sir John Gell's beautiful new sword was drawn as he reached the disintegrating centre of his line, and he pushed his way through from the rearmost rank to the very front, snarling and cursing at Parliamentarian and Royalist alike. He might have been abandoned by Brereton this day, and his yellow-bellied Moorlanders may have turned tail as well, but he'd be damned before he allowed his stout Derbyshire lads to lay down their arms so easily. Yet even as he waded into the very midst of the melee, he saw just how close his men were to capitulation. He was pleased to see that they were not throwing down their arms and sprinting down the escarpment towards the Trent, for that would see them cut to pieces in short order, but some of the more beleaguered units had shouldered pikes in preparation for an ordered retreat.

'To me! To me!' he bellowed, waving his sword as high as he could. 'God and Parliament!'

Men turned then. They recognized his voice, his armour and the face beneath the visor-obscured helmet, and they were torn between facing the demonic-faced king's men and the equally infamous ire of their commander.

Gell knew something had to be done. A grand gesture of strength and defiance. He stepped out of the line, parried the sword of the nearest Cavalier, dropped to a knee and chopped his own blade hard into the leg of the Royalist's horse. The beast screamed, shrill and blood-curdling, and it reared wildly, flinging its rider clear. Gell stepped over him, skewering the man's throat with the tip of his sword, and turned back to let his splintering line see the small victory.

The Derbyshire men cheered. They stepped forwards again, reinvigorated and anxious to show the same cour-age as their leader. Gell grinned, showing long white teeth, his blood-flecked face creasing with relish. 'That's it, my lads! Have at the malignant bastards!'

He stared around, seeing that some of the rearward pikemen still held pikes to the dark clouds, ready to affect a march, and shoved his way through the ranks to reach them. 'Hold, you buggers!' he bellowed. 'See your fedaries here? See 'em stand firm?' He paced across their front rank, knocking down their pike points with his sword. 'Fight with us, damn you! Fight!'

Suddenly, Gell heard a great, rippling cheer that surged up from the northernmost edge of the ridge, the place where the Moorlanders had been stationed. For a moment he wondered if those Staffordshire men had had a jolt of conscience and returned to the field, but then he saw the great taffeta standard hanging limp above their heads. It was Sir William Brereton's lost infantry.

And from the depths of the Royalist horde, trumpets sounded.

Spencer Compton, Earl of Northampton, was in the very epicentre of the roaring, screaming, flailing, blood-spattered morass.

They had been making ground, his brave Cavaliers, forcing the rebel forces back, driving a wedge right into the heart of their vast line. They were, perhaps, only moments away from achieving an all out rout, for an army carved in two would lose its chain of command and its sense of purpose and cohesion. And infantrymen without cohesion were the easiest of pickings for decent cavalry. But, just as Northampton had begun to imagine himself conveying news of a great victory to a grateful King Charles at Oxford, he had witnessed Sir John Gell step forward and bring order to chaos.

It had all happened so quickly. First the crumbling units of battle-facing soldiers had taken Gell's lead and pursued the fight with renewed vigour, then the deeper, hitherto unbloodied ranks behind had been physically compelled to stay on the field. And if that was not enough, a new force had suddenly, almost miraculously, arrived on the field to bolster Gell's beleaguered army. Northampton reckoned those newcomers probably only numbered three hundred or so, but they looked fresh, well equipped and determined.

It was enough for the earl to sound the retreat, and, as his trumpeters called the Royalist cavalry to disengage and regroup for the next charge, Northampton wheeled his own mount around.

He kicked hard, intending to be out of range before the enemy musketeers could target him, and the horse quickly picked up a thunderous speed.

And then the world turned.

Northampton's steed suddenly, inexplicably, pitched forwards, a thunderous gallop reduced to a rolling, crashing maelstrom of crunching bones and flailing hooves in the time it took to blink just once. The earl flew headlong through the air, hitting the debris-strewn earth with a sickening crunch that he was certain must have broken limbs.

He found himself on his back, staring up at the rapidly darkening sky. He pressed palms to the hoof-churned grass and gingerly pushed, lifting himself into a sitting position. There he sat for a moment, trying in vain to find his bearings, the fall having given his mind a terrible shake. He realized that he was staring down the slope, the village of Hopton at its very foot. Between him and those buildings was a broad, ever moving mass of mounted troopers, and, with an appalling rush of nerve-shredding understanding, he knew that they were his men. Which meant only one thing. He had been dismounted by the rabbit warren. And he was still near the ridge.

Captain Stryker, of Sir Edmund Mowbray's Regiment of Foot, much preferred to fight with his feet firmly on the ground, but today he thanked God that he was able to ride.

He was half way down the slope, just beyond the dangers of the warren, when he turned back to see the Royalist commander fall. It was not a matter of thinking, only reacting, and he wrenched hard on the reins with all his might, forcing his horse's head round, compelling it to slew about.

He galloped back up the heath, away from safety and into the jaws of a vengeful enemy. Once again his mount negotiated the deep and numerous burrow holes, and he cringed with every hoofbeat.

Up ahead he saw the earl struggle to his feet, stagger once, and draw his sword. He was no more than fifty paces from the Parliamentarian front rank, and a great many of those grey-coated men were already breaking away from the ridge and descending upon him.

Stryker kicked harder, screaming curse-laden encouragement in his mount's pricked ear, but the animal was exhausted, stumbling more than once on the difficult ground, and moving all too sluggishly.

Stryker watched helplessly as the rebel soldiers reached Northampton. He seemed to have regained composure now, and brandished his long sword out in front, gripping the hilt in both hands, crouching slightly like a cat about to pounce.

The first man, an officer, reached the earl, his own sword held high, and swung it down at the Royalist leader's helmeted head. Northampton parried the blow easily, letting the officer's blade slide along his own and twisting his forearm at the last moment. The motion tore the rebel officer's hilt from his grip, sending the weapon skittering away, and Northampton stepped forwards, viper-quick, felling his enemy with a backhanded blow from a gauntleted fist.

Another man came. He held a long pike and tried to spit the earl on its sharp point. Northampton, though, was far superior to the crude assault, and twirled away like an acrobat, allowing the pike to glide past until its owner was within range. The man died with Northampton's blade in his face.

More men reached the earl as Stryker finally drew close. He lashed at his horse's neck with his reins, urging it closer so that he could offer his commander the saddle, but some of the advancing rebels bypassed Northampton and went to engage Stryker, cutting him off and preventing any rescue.

Stryker caught a glimpse of the earl running the next man through, even as he faced his own would-be killer. A rebel musketeer, built like a bear, eyes rimmed with powder stains, charged headlong at his side, swinging his upturned musket like a great club. Stryker brought his sword down diagonally to meet it, and felt his wrist try to give way under the huge blow, but both arm and steel held firm. Before the big man could bring the heavy wooden butt back up for another swing, Stryker jabbed his blade forwards in a straight, rigged-armed riposte that sliced up the man's forehead, flicking his montero cap free and opening a huge, gushing swathe in his scalp. The man screamed, dropped the musket, lifted pawlike hands to his blood-blinded eyes, and Stryker stabbed him again, this time in the arm.

He moved on, urging his horse across a heath pocked with holes and littered with bodies, weaponry and armour. Up ahead he could still see the earl, fighting any who would face him. Like Stryker, Spencer Compton was a veteran of the Continental campaigns and was more than a match for the individual greycoats who stepped into his path. But before long, Stryker knew, those individuals would join to become a tide that would wash around the earl, surrounding him at first, and then enveloping him.

Another man ran at Stryker, stabbing up at him with his tuck. The attack was fast and well aimed, and the steel crept beneath Stryker's defence to jab at his guts, but the blade was poorly honed and not sharp enough to penetrate the thick hide of Stryker's buff-coat. He doubled over as the metal punched into him, sending a hot plume of vomit into his mouth, but just managed to stay in the saddle. The greycoat stabbed up again, this time missing, and Stryker kicked him in the face and squeezed his thighs together so that his mount lurched, barging the Roundhead out of the way as though he were a fly to be swatted.

Stryker was just yards from the earl now, but the enemy were already too numerous to push through. Swords lunged up at him, and he had to move quickly to parry each one, wheeling his horse in wide circles to keep the assailants back. Beyond them, the Earl of Northampton was completely surrounded.

'My lord!' Stryker shouted. 'My lord! To me!'

But Northampton did not hear. He was screaming his own curses at the Parliamentarians, who now encircled him like sharks.

'Quarter, my lord!' Stryker was relieved to hear one of the rebel officers call above the din. 'We offer you quarter! Lower your sword, sir!'

Northampton swung his blade in a wide, singing arc, forcing the poised enemy troops back a step, and grinned wolfishly.

'No, my lord!' Stryker bellowed over the heads of the men who kept him at bay. 'Accept quarter, I beg you!'

But either the earl did not hear Stryker's plea, or he chose to ignore it, for he leapt forwards, spitting a musketeer on his darting blade. 'I take no quarter from such base rogues and rebels as you!' he snarled.

'No!' Stryker screamed, unable to help the earl in the face of so many slashing blades.

The Roundheads surrounding Northampton surged on as one, like a pack of wild dogs, converging on the earl in an irresistible flood of violence. Stryker saw Northampton take another man down, but then a thrusting musket butt caught him on the side of the head, dislodging his helmet, and a halberd flashed in the melee, cleaving deeply into the earl's exposed skull.

Stryker watched helplessly as the earl dropped his sword and slumped to his knees. The halberd swept again, this time smashing into his face. And then the Earl of Northampton vanished, consumed within a torrent of stabbing steel and clubbing muskets.

Stryker found himself alone in the melee. A single Royalist horseman facing an entire army. The earl's killers now turned on him, and he realized that he would share Northampton's fate if he did not retreat immediately, but half a dozen greycoats had outflanked him and blocked his path with sword and pike. He kicked his horse, but the frightened animal would not charge into the pike points.

A howl, lingering, rising to a pitch that would have chilled the Four Horsemen, sounded from down the slope, beyond the enemy. Stryker knew that battle cry, had heard it across countless killing fields, and knew he had been given a chance to escape.

Sergeant William Skellen appeared to his right in a barely controlled gallop that sent him bowling straight through the backs of the pikemen. Two fell forwards, trampled beneath his hooves, the remainder scattered as though attacked by the Devil himself, and Stryker set upon them, hacking a path through the human barricade. Skellen wheeled his horse around, aimed it at one of the pikemen, and, as the rebel staggered backwards, snatched the long shaft from his grasp. In a flash he had reversed his grip so that he held it like a lance in his gnarled fist, and thrust it downwards, impaling its former owner through the soft flesh of his groin.

And then they were away, galloping south-west, straight down the slope, the encroaching rebel infantry at their backs and the regrouping Royalist column immediately to the front. They had survived, and Stryker knew he should feel happy, but a dull ache, put there by guilt and anger, twisted his innards. Because the Earl of Northampton was dead.

Sir John Gell had never felt so proud. His men, pounded by cannon, betrayed by their own side and harried by the enemy, had not been routed. They had stepped forwards at his back, found some deep reserve of courage, and had driven the Cavaliers away.

'Well done, boys!' he bellowed as the greycoats, their ranks augmented now by Brereton's late-arriving infantry, formed up into coherent ranks along the ridge. 'Well done, I say! Make ready your muskets! Present pikes for horse! We shall not break this day!'

Gell paced along the line, seeing the old breach finally close, his ranks tight and formidable once more. He sheathed his sword, forcing the blood-clotted blade back into the scabbard's throat, and gazed down at the Royalist army.

'We're ready for you. By God we are ready for you.'

And the king's cavalry charged again.

*

511

Stryker watched Sir James Lord Compton, now the Third Earl of Northampton, lead out the second charge, and saw the tears stream down the young man's cheeks.

'Shall we, sir?' Skellen said, drawing up next to his captain.

Stryker leant forwards, patting his mount's neck. 'Not this time, Will. She can barely trot.' He smiled ruefully. 'And I can hardly lift this damned sword.'

'We'll let the buggers show us 'ow it's done then, sir,' Skellen grunted.

Stryker nodded. 'And thank you, Will.'

Skellen casually loaded the carbine he had collected during the first melee. 'Welcome, sir.'

All around them the wounded were being ferried back to Hopton, where Gregory Chambers waited, and Stryker knew the doctor would be soaked to the skin in blood, cutting, sawing, tying, aided by a team of surgeon's mates who would be pinning down the badly wounded as their limbs were crudely and hurriedly butchered off.

'Sir!' Another voice reached them now. The speaker was trotting in their direction, a grin splitting his face. 'Lieutenant!'

'I bloody survived, thank Christ!' Andrew Burton exclaimed. 'Hot work though, eh?' He smacked his lips together. 'And not a drop to see me through it.'

Stryker chuckled. 'My compliments, Lieutenant. Have you seen Barkworth?'

Burton shook his head. 'He was in the melee. That's the last I saw of him.'

The three walked their mounts further down the slope to where the Royalists' only piece of artillery stood, silent and still, on its wicker platform.

Gun Captain Porter strode up to them. 'Sir, your lady took Master Blaze down to the village.'

Stryker nodded. 'How does he fair?'

Porter wrinkled his lips. 'He's poorly, sir.'

Stryker turned away, gazing up at the ridge from whence the next glut of Chambers's patients would soon come. The newest Earl of Northampton had already smashed into the waiting Parliamentarians and the battle raged all across the higher ground. But this time the rebels had kept their form and their discipline, and the pikemen, arranged in tight, bristling squares like vast iron-clad hedgehogs, were defending the units of musketeers, who spat leaden fury into the midst of the cavalry.

'Why don't 'e let us fire, sir?' Porter said, the frustration clear in his tone. 'Northampton, I mean.'

Stryker looked at the Welshman. 'Northampton's dead. His son commands now.'

'And his son did not see the damage Meg caused?'

'He is stricken with fury and grief, sir,' Stryker replied. 'He sees nothing but the need to kill.'

Porter shook his head angrily. 'But he charges against well-organized pike and shot, Captain. Without first making a few more holes, he will dash his men against them like waves at Rhossili's cliffs.'

Stryker did not answer but stared back up at the ridge, where, sure enough, the Royalist horsemen were already wheeling away, desultory musket fire and rising jeers chasing them across the bloodstained heath.

'Shit,' Skellen muttered.

Stryker dipped his head to Porter and kicked his horse into action. 'Enough rest, lads!' he called over his shoulder, and Burton and Skellen spurred their own mounts forwards.

They rode up to join the Royalist cavalry as the thousand horsemen reached the heath's lower third and circled round to launch another assault.

'You!' A voice cracked like a drake blast from the leading riders.

Stryker instinctively stared at the ground, urging his mount to move away.

'You there!' The snapping, aristocratic tones reached him again. 'The one with the scars!'

Stryker had wanted to avoid attention, but he could hardly ignore the more specific hail. He looked up, seeing the new Earl of Northampton cantering over to him.

Sir James Lord Compton raised the sliding nasal bar of his helmet and looked down at Stryker. His face was blackened by smoke, but the tears had scored vertical white lines down his clean-shaven cheeks so that now he appeared like an armour-plated jester.

Stryker lowered his gaze. 'My lord.'

'I saw you, sir,' the earl said levelly.

Stryker lifted his chin to look at the twenty-year-old. 'Saw me, my lord?'

The young man sheathed his sword and took a moment to wipe blood spatters from the gauntlet of his left forearm with the leather of his right. 'Try to save my father. Your name?'

'Stryker, my lord. Second Captain, Mowbray's.'

Northampton's brow wrinkled, this time spawning horizontal white lines. 'Foot?'

'Sir.'

The earl drew his blade again, making Stryker flinch. 'You showed great valour, Captain. Something I shall not forget.' He turned his horse. 'Form up! We charge again!'

It began to rain as the flying column hastened up the slope for a third time. The men were tiring, but anger at the loss of their leader drove them on. The great blade-flashing mass and the ground-shaking thunder of screams and whinnies thrashed across the rabbit warren once again. More horses fell, but as before the number to make it all the way through was a testament to the horsemanship of the riders. They hit the first Roundheads with bared teeth, snarled oaths and bloodied swords.

Stryker's horse went down. He did not know if the beast had been hit by flying lead or had simply snagged a hoof in one of the myriad holes, but before he could think, he was lying face down in the bloody grass. He patted himself down quickly, hearing the battle rage up ahead, and realized with relief that he was unscathed.

In a second he was up and running, pausing only to snatch up a discarded tuck, sprinting into the men of Gell's front line. The block he faced were musketeers in the main, but there were pikes there too, and he had to spin past a thrusting point to reach the Roundheads' waiting swords. He parried the first blow, gave three short stabs of his own, the second of which met with a wet smack against the bridge of his enemy's nose. The man reeled away, blood spurting freely, and his comrades either side hesitated in the face of Stryker's rage.

It was then that Stryker heard a voice he knew. One that brought with it a flood of memories: of booming mortar fire; of a dark, looming gallows; and of a sneering moustachioed face.

'Gell!' Stryker shouted, but all he could see were the nervous faces of grey-coated infantrymen, braced for attack behind their swords and upturned muskets. He spun on his heel, looking for some kind of leverage.

There, turning dazed circles at the edge of the fighting was a huge piebald horse, and he ran across to it. A man sat in his path, weeping inconsolably, his knee shattered by a musket-ball that would condemn him to a life of begging in some city gutter. Stryker kicked him out of the way, gathered the limp reins and heaved himself up into the black saddle.

He was at the battle line in moments and, from his new vantage point, could see a tall, slender man, with tight black curls cascading from beneath a pewter-grey helmet.

'Gell!' Stryker bellowed. 'Gell!'

The fight's din was deafening, but, eventually, the object of Stryker's focus looked up, a sudden flash of recognition igniting his features. And Sir John Gell grinned.

Stryker saw the blade in the Parliamentarian commander's hand, and recognized it immediately. It was madness, he knew, to throw away his life for a piece of metal, but something about Gell's mocking expression sent an incandescent rage coursing through his veins, and he kicked forwards.

Gell was three ranks away, a pair of sword-wielding greycoats standing in his way, but the first saw the fury on his face and began to step back, throwing the man behind off balance.

Stryker screamed and surged. The second man managed to raise his blade, its tip opening the flesh of the horse's rippling shoulder, but the animal was a destrier, a big, muscular, battle-bred beast, and, though it let loose a shrill whinny, it did not break stride.

And then Stryker was through, and Gell stared up at him, the grin gone, the moustache no longer upturned, but a black line adding definition to tightly pursed lips that showed only fear. Gell raised the blade he had taken from Stryker at Lichfield, and Stryker could immediately see that the Derbyshire man was trained in swordsmanship. But here, on a blood-reddened piece of Staffordshire heath land, such things counted for little. This would not be a gentleman's duel of dancing feet and flicking wrists. It was a brutal, dirty brawl. The kind Stryker had known all his life. The kind he liked.

Stryker wanted his sword back. It had been awarded to him by Queen Henrietta Maria, the best, most perfectly balanced weapon he had ever held, and it enraged him to know that another man wielded it. He slid from the saddle, walked up to Gell, and lifted the cheap tuck he had collected near the face of the melee. Gell darted forwards, but Stryker swept the blade up, knocking Gell's thrust aside with brute strength, and chopped downwards in a heavy blow that drove a great dent into the Parliamentarian's rounded helmet.

Gell staggered back, only just parrying a second chopping arc and barely managing to keep his feet.

'You're the one from Lichfield Close,' Gell hissed, stalling for time.

Aware that he was in the midst of the enemy, Stryker strode forwards. 'You have my sword.'

Stryker was thinking only of recovering his possession. Gell's exquisite blade was up in a flash, red edge gleaming, but Stryker batted it away contemptuously and lunged. The tuck might have been a cheap, standard-issue affair, but its original owner had still taken the time to hone it to a feathered sharpness, and that sharpness took its point through Gell's thick doublet and made short work of the collar underneath.

Gell screamed as Stryker's inferior weapon slashed across the base of his neck, opening a deep gash that immediately spurted a stream of blood down the Parliamentarian's chest plate.

Gell dropped the sword and stumbled backwards, gabbling incoherently as he clutched hands at the wound. Stryker went in for the killing blow, but already Royalist trumpets were loosing their querulous message, compelling his comrades to retreat, and a heartened swarm of rebels were coming to their stricken commander's aid. There were too many for Stryker to face alone, and he dived to scoop up the Queen's blade, its red garnet twinkling from the ornate pommel. A man wielding a savage-looking partizan challenged him as he straightened, but Stryker had no wish to linger, and threw the cheap tuck at the rebel's face. Partizan met blade, sending it skittering harmlessly away, but the move had given Stryker time to scramble back to his waiting destrier. As the vengeful rebels converged on him, he ground boot heels hard into the big piebald's sides, and the beast lurched violently away from the ridge.

Some two hundred yards from the battle's centre, at the very edge of Hopton Heath, on the Royalist right flank, a troop of dragoons cantered down the slope. They had been part of the force sent by the old Earl of Northampton to clear the walls of the deer park that had been manned by Gell's musketeers and his remaining four drakes.

Just like the dragoons of Northampton's left flank, their foray had been successful, and the walls had been taken after a short, bloody scrap. And now, as the Royalist cavalry disengaged all along the ridge, the troop, summoned by the new earl, were on their way to join the next charge. It was getting dark, so, the dragoon commander surmised, the Royalist commanders were becoming desperate and every available man would be required, even at the expense of the flanks.

'Down to the bottom of the slope,' called the leader, a muscular-set major with golden hair and moustache. 'They will wheel round and charge again. We must join them.'

The major looked across the ridge as he reloaded his weapons, a carbine and a brace of pistols, marvelling at the Parliamentarian change in fortune. He did not know how they had managed to hold the crest after being so near destruction, but now they were offering a stout, organized defence that would be extremely difficult for the Royalist cavalry to break down.

And then he halted. His horse, a capricious beast purchased only days ago in Stafford, stomped agitatedly at a patch of gorse, and he growled a low warning into its pricked ear. For he no longer wished to move to the foot of the slope.

'Sir?' a nearby officer prompted.

The major looked sharply at his subordinate. 'We are ordered to the bottom, so take the men down.'

'You're not joining us, sir?'

Major Henning Edberg shook his head slowly. 'I will follow presently.'

He had seen a ghost.

CHAPTER 23

Captain Stryker, the last man to break away from the melee, coaxed his piebald warhorse through the rabbit warren, flinching with each jolting hoof-fall. Behind him, shoulder to shoulder, stood the jeering ranks of Sir John Gell's Parliamentarian army. In front, some two hundred yards away, was the swirling mass of Royalist cavalry, regrouping for the next clash of flying mud and snorting horses, spraying blood and clanging steel. Far to his right horsemen streamed down the slope, the dragoons, he presumed, sent to clear the hedgerows. He wondered if Forrester had survived. To his left, riding parallel with Forrester's group, were the second detachment of dragoons, those men sent up to clear the walls criss-crossing the other Parliamentarian flank.

His eye lingered on the latter group. The dragoons, ambling down the edge of the heath, harassed – if not overly hindered by the musketeers on the crest, had something about them that snagged in his mind. It was not the small flag gripped at the head of the troop by a skinny cornet, for that declared allegiance to the Earl of Northampton. It was something else. Something Stryker could almost identify but that stayed tantalizingly obscured by rainfall and by the fog of war, nebulous and mocking.

Muskets still coughed from up on the ridge, but he was far enough away to be out of range for any but the best marksmen, and he began to relax, even as a lone rider broke away from the dragoons.

The rider cantered at an even pace across the heath towards him, and Stryker slowed his mount, lifting a hand in greeting. It was only when the dragoon was around fifty paces away that a flame of recognition scorched his mind. He had not thought to see this man again, but the yellow coat, the yellow hair and the yellow whiskers were all too real. And so was the carbine he now saw, jutting from the rider's outstretched arm, and so was its flame and its smoke plume and its sharp report.

And suddenly Stryker was galloping. Major Henning Edberg's shot had missed his thigh by an inch, finding a home in the piebald stallion's fleshy rump. This time the pain was too much for the stallion's training to absorb. It reared in agony, bolting down the slope in the direction of the gathering Royalists, and Edberg swerved his own mount to follow.

At the foot of the slope the king's cavalry were beginning to wonder if this was not to be their day. After a murderous, triumphal opening hour, they had failed to take the ridge. Moreover, the three charges had cost them scores of men and horses, several officers, and the Earl of Northampton himself.

'We must go again quickly, by Christ!' Sir James Compton, Third Earl of Northampton said as an aide fastened a tourniquet above his knee. 'It is getting too dark to continue, and the rain will make that damned coney warren even more precarious.'

Sir Henry Hastings, mounted at the young lord's right hand, nodded in agreement. 'But not you, sir.'

Sir James turned on him, the movement causing him to hiss through gritted teeth. 'It is not mortal, Sir Henry.'

'But it is bad,' Hastings warned. 'You are losing much blood. Any more and you will swoon, and even you cannot lead a charge like that.' Sir James sighed heavily, a gesture Hastings read as acquiescence. 'Thank you, my lord. I will take command.'

The younger man remained silent, and Sir Henry Hastings lifted his face to the brooding sky, feeling fat raindrops burst on his skin. 'Once more,' he said quietly, and then raised his reddened sword high for all to see. 'Once more!'

Sir James, Lord Northampton, left at the foot of Hopton Heath with a score of retainers, watched Hastings go and felt a burning shame, for the charge was his to lead. Yet the wound, for all his bluster, was severe, and it would be folly to ride with the fourth assault. He gazed at the backs of the galloping men, praying they would avenge his father before the day became too dark to continue the fight.

Another horseman caught his eye. It was strange to pick out one rider among so many. Yet this man was not charging up the slope, but down it, the horse taking a wide berth around the great, earth-shattering column. In the rider's wake came another man, one of the yellow-coated dragoons Sir James remembered joining the Stafford garrison after the fall of Lichfield, and his immediate instinct was to assume the first man must be a Roundhead.

But then he saw the rider's horrifically mutilated face, and recognized him as the only man to have gone to his father's aid, risking his own life in the process.

The earl turned to his nearest aide, as the pair sped past. 'Theophilus?'

'Sir?'

'What the devil d'you suppose they're about?'

Stryker ignored the charging throng of cavalry as he fought to regain control of the stallion. It careened as fast as its powerful legs could manage, ears taut, eyes like white plates, nostrils blasting, the pain in its rump having turned it from obedient steed to frenzied demon in the blink of an eye.

Up ahead was the very foot of the slope, and that area, parallel with the place he had left Roaring Meg, was studded with small, tangled copses. He gripped the reins tighter, if only to stay in the saddle, and looked beyond the stallion's big head. Sure enough, the crazed animal was headed directly for one such wooded grove, a place of trunks and branches and fallen logs. A place of untold peril for a bolting horse and anyone foolish enough to perch on its back.

So Stryker drew his sword, threw it on to the heath, and let go.

He was vaguely aware of a crashing sound as the stallion bolted through the copse, leaving a vast swathe of wreckage in its wake, but the fate of the wounded beast was the least of his concerns. The ground whirled around him as he hit the long, rain-drenched grass of the wood's edge, and he expected to hear the crack of shattering limbs. But he managed to curl into a fast, bruising roll that took the brunt of the impact, and though his whole body seemed to ache, he was able to scramble to his feet in short order.

He retrieved the blade, quivering tip-down in the mud as Edberg reined in above him. The dragoon pulled a pistol from his saddle holster and aimed it at Stryker's heart. 'I thought Gell stretched your neck.'

'He saw sense.'

Edberg's icy-blue gaze narrowed. 'So it would seem.' The hand holding the firearm twitched.

Stryker kept his face blank, though his heart gave his chest a rapid battering. 'Why does Crow want me dead?'

Edberg slid down from the saddle, his arm staying rigidly out in front, the pistol's dark barrel never wavering from its mark. At the top of the heath Northampton's cavalry smashed into the men holding the ridge, and Edberg paused until the initial crescendo had melted to a background roar before opening his wide mouth to speak. 'Because you killed two of his men.'

Stryker shook his head. 'They attacked me first, for God's sake! It was self-defence. No, this is more than that. Why did you lie at the hearing?'

Edberg casually inspected his front teeth with the tip of his tongue. 'The colonel bade me testify against you. I do his bidding.'

'The colonel—' Stryker began, but his protestation was abruptly curtailed by the snap of flint on metal. He flinched, expecting death to come quickly on the heels of a bright flash, but neither came.

Edberg looked down at the pistol as its pathetically fizzing cloud dissipated, his easy confidence evaporating as quickly as the spark.

'A flash in the pan, Edberg?' Stryker said. He held out his palms to catch the raindrops. 'Don't you know to keep your powder dry?'

Edberg tossed the rain-corrupted pistol away and drew his sword. 'If I must kill you up close, then so be it.'

The big mercenary charged straight at Stryker, forcing the latter to raise his weapon in a fraught parry that jarred all the way up to his shoulder. Stryker swept his blade round, lancing at Edberg's groin, but the major was equal to the riposte and countered it with a rapid block, letting his blade slide all the way up Stryker's so that he might cut at the captain's fingers. The razor edge ricocheted off the swirling bars of the hilt, and Stryker thanked God he no longer held the basic tuck, for his digits would surely have been shorn off.

They were close now, no more than five feet apart, and Edberg crouched low, ready to launch another attack.

When it came it was as fast as a viper's strike, and Stryker reeled backwards, needing all his speed to evade the Scandinavian's slashing advance. But he slipped on a slick patch of leaf mulch and sheep shit, taking a knee to regain his balance and dropping his sword. Edberg came on again, and Stryker had to abandon the blade, which the dragoon kicked away, and was forced to stumble rearward again, swaying out of the tip's slicing arc.

Stryker retreated – five, six, seven paces – and suddenly collided with the first of the copse's trees, the thick trunk slamming between his shoulder blades. He had nowhere left to go.

'What is the meaning of this?' a voice called then, sharp and commanding, and Stryker noticed for the first time that a small crowd had begun to gather nearby. Stryker looked beyond his attacker to see that the speaker had a bandaged upper arm, and realized that the men unable to fight, those wounded in the previous charges, had gravitated here to watch this private duel.

'This man is a wanted criminal!' Edberg shouted across his shoulder. 'He's mine!'

The man who had accosted them seemed to shrug. 'So be it.'

Edberg grinned, lunged at the Englishman in a powerful stab. The wickedly feathered edge cut through Stryker's scalp as he ducked, sending a pulsing gush of blood down his forehead and across his face, but it was a flesh wound, and Stryker twisted away. He now realized, when no second attack came, that Edberg's sword was stuck fast in the gnarled bark, a victim of its own huge force.

He wiped blood from his eye with a tattered sleeve and ran at Edberg before the bigger man could wrench the blade free. Clattering into the Swede's side, and eliciting a collective hiss from the crowd, he thrust the dragoon back with all the strength he could muster, sending them both on to the rain-soaked grass.

Immediately they were up. Standing. Knees bent. Fists balled. Poised for a brawl.

Captain Lancelot Forrester saw his old comrades as his dragoon company broke off from the melee. He had been ordered away from the hedgerows with the rest of the dragoons to bolster the Royalist numbers, had taken a new horse and stormed on as part of the cavalry now led by Colonel-General Sir Henry Hastings, and had harried a company of pikemen defending the ridge. But those pikemen were formed in square and charged for horse, and, like his comrades all along the bloody crest, he had been unable to break the enemy ranks.

And now, cantering out of range of the defiant rebels' crackling musketry, he spotted two horsemen among the rest. One tall and thin, competent in the saddle but not at home there, the other shorter, younger, with one arm cradled in a tight leather sling.

'By God's own fingernails!' Forrester declared as he steered his horse diagonally across the heath to greet them. He leaned over to shake the proffered hands. 'Where's Stryker?'

'Lost him in the charge,' Burton said grimly.

Sergeant William Skellen, afforded a higher vantage point than the others, pointed down the slope. 'Think I've found 'im again, sir.'

Beside the copse, Stryker was fighting for his life.

Edberg threw a broadly sweeping punch at the Englishman's narrow chin. It connected and, while only a glancing blow, sent Stryker sprawling. Stryker went for his boot, groped only at leather, and remembered with irritation the fact that his dagger was no longer there.

Edberg, however, had managed to produce his own dirk; a long, evil-looking piece of steel that was no wider than his forefinger. He waved it out in front, keeping it in line with Stryker's single grey eye, beckoning the shorter man on to the impossibly fine point.

For a second Stryker thought to reach for Lisette's silver hairpin. But what good could it do against such a formidable blade?

'Come, *javla svin*,' Edberg growled.

Stryker obliged. He jumped at Edberg, taking him by surprise, and twisted to the right as soon as his front foot was planted, letting the blade prick the air a reed's breadth from his arm. He gripped the Swede's wrist, pulling, keeping the arm stretched out, and jammed his spare fist into Edberg's locked elbow.

The major yelped as the joint cracked and his scarred fingers fell open. The dirk dropped, sticking hilt up in the soft earth, and Stryker kicked the dragoon in the balls. Edberg doubled over and vomited. Stryker hit him in the side of the face, hoping the punch hurt Edberg's big-boned face more than it did his stinging knuckles, and the major stumbled, tripped, and ended on his backside.

'Sir!' a man shouted from somewhere behind.

Stryker glanced around to see that the watching crowd had grown considerably, and absently noted that if so many men were congregating here, at the foot of the ridge, then the latest charge must have been aborted. At the front of the crowd he saw Simeon Barkworth. The little man, bloodied and bruised, was perched on his horse, and he held up a carbine. 'Allow me, sir!'

And then Stryker saw the others. Burton was there, sword drawn; Skellen too, his own carbine pointed at Edberg. With relief Stryker even noticed Lancelot Forrester, the captain's face a mask of grim determination. They would cut Edberg down in a heartbeat if he gave the word.

'No!' Stryker bellowed. He knew it was folly to deny their protection, but this duel was personal. He feared Edberg, knew he could never match the Scandinavian for raw power, but knew too that he needed to best the dragoon alone. 'He's mine.'

But when he turned back to Edberg the major was already on his feet. The Swedish warrior lowered his head, like a bull preparing to charge, and launched himself at Stryker. The Englishman reacted far too late and was taken at the midriff by the huge man's bolting assault, and they both crashed down on to the sodden earth.

Stryker thrashed wildly, desperate to extricate himself from the tangle of limbs before the stronger man could get a stable grip. A finger or thumb caught the Swede in the eye, making Edberg jerk back, and Stryker twisted away.

And then they were both on their feet again. Edberg lurched forwards, left fist lashing out. Stryker ducked, only just managing to avoid the heavy blow. The big mercenary threw his other meaty fist and caught the Englishman this time, clipping his temple and knocking him back a couple of paces.

Stryker's heel bumped against something hard, and he looked down to see Edberg's spent pistol skittering away. He crouched as he recoiled, snatching up the weapon and lobbing it hard. Edberg swayed out of the way, letting the short-arm cartwheel past, and he grinned maliciously behind his thick hedge of a moustache.

Stryker scanned the area quickly, this time spotting a fallen branch as long and broad as a man's arm. He ran to it, thrusting a boot end beneath it and flicked it up, plucking it quickly out of the air.

Edberg advanced, swung that big fist again. Stryker tried to block, but the branch was too heavy to lift in time, and the punch clattered his shoulder. It felt like a shot from Roaring Meg, and he had to jam the wood into the earth in front just to keep himself from toppling sideways. As Edberg came on again, Stryker heaved, propelling the branch sharply upwards, and the heavy club crunched into the dragoon's groin. Edberg howled. Stryker instinctively lifted the weapon, clutching the branch in both hands, and rammed it downwards, punching its jagged end into the yellowcoat's temple.

This time Edberg went down. He slumped to his knees, chest heaving, a hand pressed against the side of his battered skull.

Stryker hefted the branch, ready to swing, and loomed over the dragoon.

The crowd began to mutter, like the rustle of autumn leaves, a hundred voices all speaking at once, clamouring for ascendancy. And Stryker realized that some of those voices wanted to intervene on the side of the dragoon. Those, he supposed, who had heard Edberg declare him to be an outlaw. He thanked God that his own men were amongst that disquieted crowd, for it must have been their arguments that were keeping the mob at bay.

'You lied, Edberg!' he said quickly. 'To the Prince. You were never at the stable. Admit it!'

Edberg lifted his head a fraction, blue eyes fixing Stryker with a stare of sheer malevolence. 'No.'

Stryker lowered his voice. 'Admit it, Edberg, and I will spare your life.'

Edberg stared at him for a moment. 'I did as I was ordered,' he said eventually, evidently deciding that Stryker spoke the truth.

'Why?' Stryker said, loudly enough for the crowd to hear. 'Why did Colonel Crow give you such an order?'

Edberg's golden-haired head began to shiver then, and a low, coarse sound emanated from his mouth. Stryker realized that he was laughing. 'You do not know?'

'Know? Know what? Know what, damn you?'

Edberg's expression was withering. 'You have only to look at the colonel.'

Then a picture came into Stryker's mind. A picture of Colonel Artemas Crow. His short, squat body, and bushy hair and eyebrows. The fat, wet lips and huge, juglike ears. And next to that image came two more; of Saul and Caleb Potts. They were more youthful, more muscular, with darker hair and skin less ravaged by the passage of time. And yet . . .

'They were his kin,' Stryker said in sudden, mind-whirling understanding.

'Sons,' Edberg replied, dabbing fingers at the bloody wound on his temple. 'Did you not wonder how two such vile little turds as Saul and Caleb Potts were able to enlist with a troop such as Crow's?' He hawked up a globule of saliva and mucus, spitting it on to the mud a few feet away. 'Or how Saul was handed a goddamned commission?'

'His sons,' Stryker said absently.

'His bastards,' corrected Edberg, his voice full of scorn. 'But his sow of a goodwife is barren as a fucking desert. So Crow loves his bastards as though they were as legitimate as you or I. Well,' he added with a malicious grin, 'as I, certainly.'

'Jesu.'

'And you will die,' Edberg went on, 'because Crow will not rest until he can dance a jig on your grave! You will be hunted down like a dog. If not by me, then by Prince Rupert. Crow is powerful. Rupert will not cross him when there is proof you are a murderer.'

Stryker gritted his teeth in rage. 'But it is all lies, damn you!'

And Henning Edberg brayed. 'Who will believe you, Stryker?' He jerked his head towards the onlookers. 'This gaggle of clapperdudgeons?'

Edberg sprang up from the ground like a cat, pouncing at Stryker through the pulsating rain, and Stryker only realized the major had retrieved his dirk when its long, thin blade had already punctured his chest.

He crashed to the wet ground, impulse making him reach for the wound, and saw blood on his fingers. Thankfully the blow was not deep, for the buff leather of his coat had borne the brunt of the thrust, but now he was on his back, staring up at the darkening sky. And a huge man with triumphal grin and malevolent eyes came to stand over him.

'So tell me,' Edberg said. 'Who will believe you?' He did not look at the crowd, but gestured towards them with the blade, which was dripping with the captain's blood. 'Do they have the ear of Prince fucking Rupert?'

Edberg stepped forward.

The pistol crack startled everyone. Its high, ear-splitting report making men duck, some ready to run, others twisting to look back at the ridge, suddenly terrified of a Roundhead counter-attack.

Except one by one, people saw the small hole just below Edberg's right eye. It seemed like nothing more than a pimple. A red welt on the wide face. But then a trickle of blood seeped from it, welling like a teardrop, and tumbled down his cheek.

Stryker watched, dumbstruck, as his conqueror dropped the dirk and began to sway like a great oak in a storm.

A man limped out of the crowd; a tall man with clean-shaven face, dark eyes, long black hair and a bandaged leg. In his right hand was a pistol, its barrel still smoking.

'I believe him,' said Sir James Compton, Third Earl of Northampton. 'But, alas, I do not have the ear of Prince Rupert.'

Edberg stared at the young earl, his lips opening and closing, but no air or sound passed between them. His right eye widened, rolled so that it showed only white, and filled suddenly with blood.

'I do, however,' Northampton went on, 'have the ear of the King.'

Major Henning Edberg groaned, a deep, creaking sound that seemed to emanate from his very soul, and toppled forward, landing face down next to Stryker. It was over.

Darkness seeped across Hopton Heath like an unsanded ink stain blotting on parchment. Bodies were strewn across the reddened grass, tangled, contorted, stiffening. The stink of blood lingered, mingling with the sulphurous odour of black powder. The wounded men moaned, injured horses whinnied, looters rummaged and thieved.

Still Parliament held the ridge. Still the king held the town.

Captain Stryker left Edberg's body where it lay and made his way down to Hopton village. Now, as the armies faced each other in silent stand-off, he was bathed in the shards of a myriad refracted candle flames, the chandelier in the ceiling entirely at odds with the carnage of the floor.

Doctor Gregory Chambers, spectacles carefully balanced across the bridge of his nose, grimaced as he cast sad eyes across the rows of dead and dying. 'I commandeered this home to use as a hospital,' he said, voice oppressed by a desperate sorrow. 'It has become a charnel house.'

'Battle,' Stryker said simply.

Chambers looked at him. 'I pray I never become as accustomed to this horror as you, Captain.' Finally his gaze rested on one particular patient. 'He died just before you came in.'

Stryker looked at the still form of Jonathan Blaze. 'I don't believe I've ever met a braver man.'

Captain Lancelot Forrester came to stand beside Stryker. 'Without those two cannon shots, we might have lost the battle. Lord knows, we only really penetrated their line when they were too frightened to stand in the face of Meg's ire.'

'He should have let Porter pound them more,' said the exotically accented voice of a woman.

Stryker turned to look at Lisette, who stood with Burton, Skellen and Barkworth. They had all come to pay their respects to the fire-worker. 'Blaze had swooned,' he said.

'But he'd found the range,' Lisette replied indignantly. 'All Porter need do was fire the thing.'

'Sir James—the Earl,' Stryker corrected himself, 'was too consumed by grief. He wanted to break Gell's line himself.'

Lisette's nose wrinkled. 'Well, he got himself stabbed for his folly.'

'Least he didn't snuff it,' Forrester said to Stryker. 'He's your ticket to exoneration.'

Sir James Compton, Third Earl of Northampton, had vowed to repeat Edberg's confession to the prince. 'I saw you go to my father's aid,' he had said as the Swedish mercenary's corpse was stripped of its valuables. 'My family is in your debt. I will see this charge dropped, 'pon my honour, sir.'

Ordinarily Stryker might have thought such a promise far-fetched, for Colonel Artemas Crow was a powerful courtier, but Sir James's father had been one of King Charles's dearest friends. Stryker could not have wished for loftier patronage.

He knelt suddenly, grasping one of the coats that lay strewn between the battle's casualties. There were many such garments, all torn and blood-sodden, hurriedly removed by Chambers's assistants as he had tried to cauterize wounds and dig out lead. Stryker opened the coat out and cast it across Blaze's upper body and face. 'And now all three brothers are dead.'

'Where now for us, sir?' Barkworth asked.

Stryker twisted to look at him. 'We'll go to Oxford. Rejoin our regiment.' Barkworth nodded, and Stryker read the gloom on the little man's weathered features. 'But the regiment is under strength after Cirencester, is it not, Captain Forrester?'

Forrester winked. 'That it is, Captain Stryker, that it is.'

'Sergeant Skellen,' Stryker said, prompting the tall man to step forward a pace. 'Might there be room in our ranks for a former Scots Brigader, with a foul mouth and a quick temper?'

Skellen sniffed. 'Might be, sir. If we can find a coat to fit 'im.'

Stryker looked at Barkworth, single brow raised.

'Be an honour, sir,' Barkworth said with a gap-toothed grin.

EPILOGUE

The town was crowded.

The marketplace and all its tributaries were heaving, choked by the press of bodies come to leer at the morbid spectacle. Every door and window was crammed with the expectant faces of men, women and children, and rooftops were littered with more agile folk, perched there like so many rooks in a tree. Hawkers, pedlars, pickpockets and prostitutes moved about the throng, pie sellers dished out their still-warm wares, the tapsters did a roaring trade.

The roads themselves were only kept clear by ranks of grim-faced greycoats and the points of their glinting weapons. One man ventured beyond the invisible line defended by the soldiers. It was not clear whether he had meant the act or if he had been compelled by the sheer weight of bodies behind, but he was smashed to the ground by an iron sword-hilt. No one else crossed the line after that.

A huge cheer greeted the parade's arrival.

At the front, alone and resplendent in his garments of grey wool, amber buff and silver lace, rode the hero of the town. The man sat straight-backed and proud-faced, moustachioed lip turned upwards in a half-smile, round eyes gleaming beneath a high-crowned hat that sat at a suitably rakish angle atop his flowing black curls. A new rush of noise greeted each regal wave of his gauntleted hand, and he affected short bows to those he deigned to acknowledge.

At the rider's flanks walked servants clutching baskets of sugar plums. They handed the treats out to grateful children, the grime-faced urchins squealing with delight as cheeks bulged, their parents shouting words of loyalty to their benevolent leader.

A short phalanx of pikemen strode in the horseman's wake, and, as they came into the midst of the folk of Derby, a chorus of boos and hisses and catcalls reverberated around the town's walls and roofs. Fists shook, fingers wagged admonishingly. Preachers bellowed impromptu sermons.

The rising ire was not directed at the pikemen, but rather at the horse that followed them. It loped slowly, unbalanced by its unwieldy cargo, ears twitching in all directions as the angry, crushing sound grew with its every step.

'Down with the King!' a bystander bellowed.

'Down with the Pope and his devilish horde!' another responded.

A young man stepped out of the crowd, able for a moment to evade the cordon of soldiers, and hurled a clump of mud at the horse. It hit the man's corpse, stripped naked and slung across the animal's back, with a wet smack, eliciting another almighty cheer. The soldiers ushered the thrower back into the crowd. The parade's leading horseman twisted round to peer through the forest of pikes at the bloodied – and now muddied – cadaver, the corners of his thin lips twitching.

At the rear of the baying mob, two hooded men stood together in a low doorway. They had been given a wide berth by the rest of the townsfolk, for their diseased faces cast barbs of fear into even the stoutest of hearts.

'I told you,' one of the men said in hushed tones. 'Thick pottage, liberally daubed and left to dry, makes one look positively plague-addled.'

The second man kept his gaze on the parade. 'You never cease to amaze me, Forry.'

Captain Lancelot Forrester glanced up at the red kites circling overhead. 'They're desperate to dive down and pick at the flesh, but too frightened by the noise to dare.' He shuddered.

Captain Stryker followed his gaze. 'I'm just glad Sir James sent us. He would not have coped well with this.'

The pair stared back at the street and the macabre parade that had drawn such a crowd. 'Gell lords it up as though he won the day,' Forrester said after a time.

'He held the ridge,' Stryker replied quietly. 'How we didn't break them, I'll never know.'

'As the rebel diurnals have such delight in reminding us,' said Forrester ruefully. 'But we held the town. And we captured all those guns of theirs.'

'A stalemate, then.'

Forrester looked at his friend sharply. 'The prize was not a ridge on a barren piece of scrubland, Stryker. It was Stafford. And Stafford belongs to the King. Ergo, we carried the field.'

'It is a hollow victory when the rebels are able to show off our commander's rotting corpse through the streets.'

Forrester hissed a vicious oath as more mud came from the crowd to splatter the stiff cadaver. '*Sir* John Gell,' he said through gritted teeth. 'The man's a knight of the realm, for God's sake. We are witnessing the very death of chivalry, Stryker.'

'Has there ever been any in war?'

'I suppose not. But this is beyond anything I expected to ever see in England.'

Stryker shrugged. 'He wanted his guns back.'

Forrester turned to look at him, the layer of pottage unable to conceal his outrage. 'And it's reasonable for him to parade Northampton's carcass though the streets because Sir James refuses the ultimatum?'

'No,' Stryker said. 'But understandable.'

'*Piffle.* And the new lord was in no position to oblige anyway. Captured cannon belong to the King. He'd have had no right trading them for his father's body, even if he'd had a mind to.' Forrester's head moved to the left, his eyes drilling into the silver-laced man riding at the column's front. 'I'm glad you chopped the bugger's neck open.'

Stryker looked at Gell, whose neck, he presumed, must still be well bandaged under all his finery. 'I thought I'd hurt him worse than that.'

'Perhaps next time.' A small patrol of musketeers stalked past suddenly, and the Royalist spies dipped their heads, staring at boots while hearts thundered. 'What do we tell the earl?' Forrester mumbled when the immediate danger had gone.

Stryker blew air through pursed lips. 'The truth.'

Forrester's stare was sharp. 'I'll leave that delicacy to you, old friend. I'm sorry, your lordship, but the bastardly moldwarp Gell paraded your late father's corpse, naked and stinking, through the streets of Derby.'

Stryker winced. 'He'll find out soon enough, Forry. Better that it comes from trusted men than from Gell's bloody pamphleteers.'

Forrester nodded glumly. 'You're right, of course.'

The pair watched the spectacle until it had progressed well beyond their position and the crowds were beginning to dissipate. 'I've seen enough,' Stryker said. 'Let us find the earl.'

'Where will he be?' Forrester said as they stepped carefully through the squelching mud.

'At the King's new capital.'

OXFORD, 30 MARCH 1643

It was with a heavy heart that Stryker made his way up the wide staircase of the lavish Lion Tavern, for his report had engendered a flood of tears from the dashing Earl of Northampton. Sir James had doted on his father, and the brutal truth of Gell's provocative action had cut the young man to the quick. Stryker had vowed to kill Gell. He hoped one day to make good on the promise.

Now, as night fell across the labyrinthine university city, Stryker returned to his billet. He reached the top of the staircase, turned to his left, and paced along the candlelit landing.

The first thing he saw when he opened the iron-studded door was a pair of long, dark riding boots lying side by side. He kicked off his own boots and padded across the bear-skin rug to the bed.

She was there, pale face peering at him from the gloom, pristine sheets pulled right up to her chin. He thought of what was beneath those covers and it set his heart frantic. 'Madam.'

Lisette smiled sweetly. 'I am pleased you could join me, sir. I thought the Prince might have thrown you back in gaol.'

'I wondered,' Stryker said truthfully, for the audience with the king's nephew had been a nerve-fraying affair, 'but Northampton was true to his word.'

A hand appeared from beneath the sheets to twist at a tress of golden hair. 'You are a free man?'

Stryker nodded. 'For the moment. Crow is in Cornwall. He will have something to say upon his return.'

'Do you blame him?'

'No.'

She patted the bed. 'Come.'

Stryker hesitated. 'You will leave again?'

She rolled her eyes. 'Why do you even ask, Stryker? Now that I am fully recovered I must go to my queen. You know that.'

'York?'

'York. Until she marches south, of course.' Her blue eyes glinted suddenly. 'We will sweep the rebellion into the sea.'

'God's blood, Lisette,' he said angrily, 'will you not stay in Oxford just a little while—'

She stared at the ceiling beams. '*Merde*, Stryker, but you are an infuriating man!'

'And you are the most maddening wench I ever bloody laid eyes upon!'

'Eye,' she corrected caustically.

Stryker approached, teeth gritted, fists balled.

They fell silent for a while, angry stares the only thing to pass between them. Eventually the corners of Lisette's mouth twitched, and she pushed the sheets down to her bare waist. 'Did you really come here to argue, *mon amour*?'

Stryker swallowed thickly, unbuckled his belts, letting sword, dagger and bandolier clatter to the floor, and knelt on the edge of the bed. She sat up, leaning forward, grasping his wrist with a slender hand and pulling him towards her.

For a moment Stryker stared at Lisette. The woman as delicate as porcelain and as hard as diamond. The woman he loved but could never keep. The woman whose very presence invigorated and infuriated him in equal measure. The old anger burned at his insides.

But when he felt her tongue on his, he forgot everything. Because she was alive. He had evaded a prince's justice and a colonel's wrath, survived a brutal siege and lived through a bloody battle. All, at the end, for her. For Lisette. It was enough.

ACKNOWLEDGEMENTS

Once again, I find myself indebted to a great many people. Firstly, I am tremendously grateful to my editor Kate Parkin, for steering me through this process. Her incisive criticism, encouragement and patience have made this second instalment a thoroughly enjoyable and rewarding experience. My sincere gratitude to everyone at John Murray and Hodder for making *Devil's Charge* a reality. Particular thanks to my copy-editor Hilary Hammond, and to Caro Westmore, Susan Spratt, James Spackman, Ben Gutcher and Lyndsey Ng for all their hard work. Thanks too to my agent Rupert Heath, who has remained committed to the Stryker Chronicles since long before *Traitor's Blood* saw the light of day.

A huge thank you to Malcolm Watkins of Heritage Matters, for revisiting Stryker's world to cast an expert eye over the manuscript, and to John Paddock of Cotswold District Council, for helping me iron out the detail of Cirencester's dramatic fall. Also to Richard Foreman, whose important introductions are very much appreciated, and not forgetting Jeff Wheeler for his continuing support.

Special thanks, as ever, to my parents. From general words of encouragement, to proofreading, web design and even bookmark production (!), their efforts during this continuing adventure have been as vital and priceless as ever. And of course, much love and gratitude to Becca and Josh, for everything.

HISTORICAL NOTE

By the winter of 1642/3, the English Civil War had fractured into a series of regional conflicts. Though this pivotal year would eventually see major battles fought all across the country, one of the first engagements was fought at the Parliamentarian town of Cirencester.

The storming of Cirencester unfolded much as I have described in the book. Though relatively small, this town was strategically important – especially so for King Charles. The Royalist faction was strong in Wales and the south-west, so it was necessary to unite those two regions by securing the fortified towns in between – one of which was Cirencester. The town had already declared for Parliament by early 1643, and Prince Rupert's first attempts at taking the settlement (with the offer of free pardons for all) had been stoutly rebuffed. No doubt irritated by the response, Rupert returned in February at the head of a 7,000 strong force, only to find the majority of the defenders had marched to nearby Sudeley Castle. Cirencester was ripe for the taking, and the young general wasted no time. On 2 February he launched a major offensive from the west, risking a frontal assault against the town's better fortified positions in the hope that it would provide the shortest route to the town centre and avoid a difficult river crossing in the process.

The most solid defences to be overcome were the walls around Barton Farm, but, as noted in *Devil's Charge*, these were blown up in advance of the main assault. It is generally accepted that a well-aimed grenade might have done enough damage, but I have taken the liberty of giving the honour to my fictitious fire-worker, Jonathan Blaze, and his petard of black powder. Rupert's cavalry did indeed face fierce resistance from the locals, and had to cut their way through chained harrows blocking the streets, but in the end his superior numbers overwhelmed the Parliamentarians. The fight lasted two hours, costing the lives of more than three hundred defenders, and the town was subjected to a brutal three-day sacking. Rupert's forces took as many as 1,100 prisoners who, as the book suggests, were promptly roped together and marched barefoot to Oxford, where they were pardoned in return for their submission to the king.

At around the time Prince Rupert was taking Cirencester his aunt, Queen Henrietta Maria, was preparing to return to England. On 2 February the northern Royalists were strengthened by the arrival of weapons, munitions and troops sent ahead of the queen from the Continent. Having initially been thwarted by storms in the North Sea, the queen's personal convoy finally landed at Bridlington on the 22nd, escorted by the Dutch Admiral Tromp. The following day a squadron of Parliamentarian warships commanded by Vice-Admiral William Batten bombarded Bridlington, endangering the queen's life (as mentioned in the book, a cannon ball hit the house in which she was staying, and the queen famously took shelter in a ditch) and menacing her supply convoy, until a threat by Admiral Tromp forced Batten to withdraw. The queen, styling herself 'Her She-Majesty Generalissima', rested for a few days and was then conducted to York, where she arrived on 5 March. Colonel Abel Black is a fictitious character, but I imagine there were plenty of men (and women) like him in the formidable queen's service.

Another settlement upon which the Great Rebellion would leave an indelible mark was the small cathedral city of Lichfield. The city had neither walls nor castle, so the Royalist commander, Philip Stanhope, Earl of Chesterfield, chose to garrison the walled Cathedral Close.

Though Stryker himself is a figment of my imagination, many of the characters involved in Lichfield's dramatic first siege were real. Lord Brooke and his purplecoats did indeed bombard the main gate with a demi-culverin, and, unlikely as it seems, Brooke really did die in the manner described in *Devil's Charge*. John Dyott, deaf and dumb from birth, is said to have shot the Parliamentarian general through the left eye when Brooke ventured too close to his siege works. That event, of course, precipitated the arrival of Sir John Gell, who took command of the besieging forces and eventually captured Cathedral Close. Like Brooke, Gell found the defenders a tough nut to crack (the ambush and rout of his men at Gaia Lane is a real event), and eventually he employed a huge mortar to dissolve the Royalists' morale. The incendiaries, as described in the book, did not wreak the havoc the Parliamentarians had hoped for, but with dwindling supplies and no obvious sign of any relief force, the Earl of Chesterfield was forced to surrender. The earl, his son

Ferdinando, and some of the highest-ranking officers were conveyed to London and imprisoned in the Tower, but, to Gell's credit, he did allow the majority of Lichfield's defeated garrison to walk away with their lives. His reputation, however, would be forever tarnished by the events following the Battle of Hopton Heath.

Lichfield would be subjected to two more sieges before the war's end, one of which would feature the first-ever explosive mine detonation in an English siege. It was a torrid and dramatic time for Lichfield and its poor citizens, but I must refrain from detailing its fortunes here, for it is likely Stryker will return there before too long. In the meantime, those who would like to know more about the fascinating history of the city during the Civil War period need look no further than Howard Clayton's fantastic book, *Loyal and Ancient City: Lichfield in the Civil Wars* (1987).

During the action at Lichfield, the king had sent orders to the Earl of Northampton, Spencer Compton, to lead a relief force out of Banbury Castle to support the besieged Royalist garrison. Unfortunately for Stanhope and his beleaguered supporters, Northampton arrived too late to intercept Gell. He had, however, received intelligence as to the next target on the Parliamentarian agenda. Sir William Brereton, Commander of the Parliamentary forces in Cheshire, had sent correspondence from Nantwich to Gell at Lichfield, requesting him to combine forces at Hopton Heath for an assault on Stafford. By taking Stafford, Parliament could create a vital territorial chain across the Midlands. The Earl of Northampton, having caught wind of Brereton and Gell's plans, reached Stafford with a force of 1,200 men (1,100 of whom were cavalry and dragoons) on or around 16 March 1643. He set about clearing the area of rebel garrisons, and fell back on Stafford to await the arrival of the Parliamentarian force. He did not know exactly where Brereton and Gell would rendezvous, but he was certain battle was imminent.

Hopton Heath is around three miles north of Stafford on the south bank of the River Trent, on terrain of open rough pasture between the villages of Salt to the north and Hopton to the south. To the east of the heath was a walled deer park and on the western side lay arable farmland with ditches and hedgerows separating the heath from the cultivated hay fields. At the narrowest point of the heath a ridge ran between the enclosures to the east and west. Gell arrived on the morning of 19 March, and immediately took up position on the high ground, realizing it would be an excellent position from which to face the experienced Royalist cavalry.

Word had by now been sent to Northampton, who was at a church service in St Mary's, Stafford. The earl set about mustering his force from scattered billets around Stafford and arrived on the heath at around 3 p.m., though not before Brereton had linked up with Gell on the ridge. In Brereton's haste, however, he had left his infantry miles behind, so he was given command of the horse, numbering around 1,000, while Gell took the foot, consisting of some 1,200.

Formed up along the ridge, the Parliamentarian force must have seemed formidable to the first Royalist cavalrymen to ride out from Stafford. The Parliamentarians had tactical and numerical advantage, were protected on either side by flanking breastworks in the hedgerows of the hay fields and behind the walls of the deer park, and had eight fieldpieces angled down the slope to create a lethal cross-fire covering the Royalist approach. Furthermore, the main body of infantry, still awaiting Brereton's foot, was protected by a vast rabbit warren that spanned the entire breadth of the ridge, rendering a cavalry charge exceedingly perilous. With all the apparent advantages, Gell must have felt extremely confident as his enemies massed on the lower part of Hopton Heath. A frontal assault by Northampton would surely have seen his horse delayed by the rabbit warren and eviscerated by cannonades and musket fire from three sides.

But Northampton did not fall into the trap. Instead, he deployed his seasoned dragoons to clear the flanks of the breastworks, a task they managed to execute with few casualties while inflicting severe losses on the rebels and capturing eight cannon, thereby nullifying Gell's planned crossfire. While his dragoons skirmished so successfully, Northampton's artillery piece, a huge 29-pound demi-cannon, began to create mayhem on the ridge. I have given the honour of commanding the cannon to Jonathan Blaze, but the event itself is real. Contemporary accounts record that the first blast from Roaring Meg killed six rebels and injured four. The second cut such a swathe through the rebel ranks that the gap was never filled.

Spying such a 'swathe' must have given Northampton great encouragement, and he immediately released his cavalry, who swept Brereton's horsemen from the field and fell upon the infantry holding the ridge. With the rebel flanks destroyed, Brereton's cavalry scattered and their front ranks disordered by cannon fire, the Staffordshire Moorlanders, held in reserve by Gell, promptly fled the field.

But, as described in the book, at the very point of annihilation it was Sir John Gell who steadied the Parliamentarian ship. Seeing several of his greycoated units shoulder their pikes in readiness of retreat, he dismounted and ran into their midst. Contemporary accounts talk of him knocking their points down with his sword and ordering them to stand firm. Having reformed his men into coherent defensive formations, Gell was able to repel the Royalist charges time and again. Each time the king's men galloped up the slope, his troops held their ground and fired devastating volleys into the charging Royalists, who reached the line each time only to wheel away as they fell upon the rebel pikes.

In one of the early charges the Earl of Northampton was killed. His son, Lord James Compton (now the third earl) was wounded, as was Sir Thomas Byron. Sir Henry Hastings led the fourth charge and then decided that further attempts at breaking the rebel formation would be foolhardy, despite his own reputation for reckless bravery.

As the day drew to a close, the Royalists retreated to the low ground on the heath. Gell and his forces remained on the ridge, but withdrew towards Uttoxeter during the night. Although the battle concluded in a stalemate, Parliament could at least take pride in the avoidance of a rout; for the Royalists, it was a bitter-sweet day. They had saved Stafford and inflicted heavy casualties on the rebels, despite being heavily outnumbered, but they had lost many of their senior officers, including their overall commander.

Accounts differ on the exact nature of Spencer Compton's death. How he got to be isolated by Gell's infantrymen is a mystery, but it seemed logical to me that the rabbit warren might well have unhorsed him. We do know, as I have described in *Devil's Charge*, that he died fighting on foot, surrounded by rebel infantry. While on foot, Northampton killed a rebel officer and a number of ordinary soldiers prior to being overwhelmed. He was given the option of quarter, but refused with the famous dying words, 'I take no quarter from such base rogues and rebels as you are.' Having refused quarter, he was struck on the head from the rear by a halberd.

As alluded to at the end of the book, Gell took Northampton's body from Hopton Heath to be used as a bargaining tool. James Compton, third Earl of Northampton, sent a trumpeter to Gell at Uttoxeter requesting his father's body, but Gell refused, issuing the reply that he would exchange the dead body for the eight captured cannon. Compton refused, as the cannon belonged to King Charles and not him personally. In what became the defining act of Gell's career, he had the dead earl stripped naked and the body slung over the back of a horse. He transported it to Derby and paraded it through the streets. When King Charles got to hear of the events at Derby (he was a lifelong friend of Northampton), he immediately put a price on Gell's head. I feel certain Stryker and Gell will cross paths again . . .

The Blaze brothers are entirely my own creation, though many men like them had enlisted in the armies of King and Parliament at the outset of war. They were often (though not exclusively) Frenchmen, experienced in the use of black powder, who had plied their trade for the vast European armies in the wars of the 1620s and 1630s. Consequently, these fire-workers – men like La

Riviere, La Roche, St Martin and Montgarnier – were highly prized assets in the various field armies.

Stryker and his men have made it through a difficult winter, but the campaign season is only just beginning. The spring of 1643 will see some of the bloodiest engagements in British history, and I'm certain the men of Mowbray's Regiment of Foot will be right in the thick of it.

Captain Stryker will return.

Book 3 of The Civil War Chronicles
available now in hardback

HUNTER'S RAGE

MICHAEL ARNOLD

After a daring raid on a Roundhead arms cache, Captain Innocent Stryker and his men find themselves hounded across Dartmoor by the formidable Colonel Gabriel Wild and his elite cavalry unit. Surrounded by Wild's troops and battling almost impossible odds, Stryker will need all his military skill and ingenuity to avoid complete annihilation.

There is more at stake, however, than mere survival, and Stryker is not the only Royalist at large on the moor. What he cannot know when he comes to the aid of the beautiful and mysterious Cecily Cade, is that she carries a secret that may prove the key to Royalist victory – and may also prove Stryker's undoing.

Now read on . . .

www.michael-arnold.net

PROLOGUE

The soldier had hidden himself well, the thick under-growth at the road's edge providing ample camouflage for a patchy coat of russet and dark green. It was a dry day, the first since the battle, and he was thankful that his backside would not get wet as he sat on his haunches, waiting impatiently for the cart to arrive.

He checked his twin pistols one last time, ensuring flint, powder and ball were all in place. He was not fond of the weapon, preferring the robust reliability of a musket rather than that of the small-arm, but this brace, stolen from a Swedish cavalryman's saddle holsters, would suffice for today's task. He hefted the pistols in gloved hands, hoping the weapons would lend a fearsome edge to his appearance. The soldier had wanted to burst from the tangled bushes with the ferocity of a demon, all howls and savagery, but he suspected, at just twenty years of age and with a slim frame and long, straight, sable hair, he would appear more feral vagabond than terrifying monstrosity. He had been told that his pale eyes, lupine in their grey depths, gave him a certain roguish quality, but he was beginning to wonder whether that would be enough to cow the men on the cart.

Feeling a tickling sensation cross his knee, he looked down to see a fat bumble-bee crawling across one of the stains that speckled the wool of his breeches. His clothes had collected as many dark, crusty splatter marks as they had lice since he'd enlisted with the company, but this one was different. It still carried that telltale rusty tinge that spoke of its macabre origin. It was a fresh stain and was all that was left of that flashing, screaming, panic-fuelled moment when a man's life had ended. The soldier shuddered involuntarily. His latest kills had been only days before, on a blood-soaked field at the crossroads between three villages whose names he could not even pronounce. The Swedish army, of which the soldier's company of English mercenaries had been a part, had finally triumphed over their enemies in the Catholic League, but at a cost that made him shiver.

Feeling sick at reliving that day of death, he flicked the bumble-bee on to the overgrown grass and forced his mind back to the one thing that made life in this war-torn, hate-filled, plague-rotten part of Europe more bearable.

Beth Lipscombe. He smiled at the thought of her. That fiery hair, the lily skin, the heart-searing gaze, the honey voice.

He tilted his head suddenly. There was a sound of something different and not entirely natural above the gentle thrum of the countryside. He waited, breath held, eyes clamped shut.

There it was again: the creaking of wheels.

The soldier took up the pistols in each hand and thrust himself upwards into a squatting position, careful to remain concealed behind the wild chaos of mouldering bracken and tall grass. The sound of wheels was growing ever louder now, joined in discord by the low murmur of voices and the groaning of wood. Using the muzzle of one of the pistols, the soldier eased the undergrowth apart so that he could catch sight of the road. At first he saw only mud, hoof-churned and undulating like a freshly ploughed field. He let his gaze snake to the right, tracing the road until it reached a gentle bend. And there, drawn by a couple of bored-looking ponies, was the cart. His quarry.

The undergrowth grasped and clawed at the soldier's tall boots as he burst forth from his place of concealment. His knees protested sharply, for he had been concealed there the entire half-hour since sunrise, but the exhilaration of the moment quickly chased the pains away. He turned right as his first boot touched the road, pacing purposefully towards the cart. The driver, he saw, had already spotted him and was desperately hauling back the thin ropes that served as reins. He raised both arms, levelling the twin pistols at the frightened-looking man, and was rewarded to see the lumbering vehicle judder to a slanted stop in one of the road's deep ruts, one of the rear wheels left to spin in mid-air.

The soldier did not stop. He picked up his pace, eager to be up at the cart before its startled occupants had time to respond. He saw four fellows leap awkwardly from the rear, making the cart rock like a skiff in a gale, and immediately trained one of his firearms on them, keeping the other firmly fixed on the driver. The men were all of similar age, though very different in appearance. Two of them, burly of shoulder, rough of face and dressed in everyday shirt and breeches, were clearly locals. Farmers or millers, the soldier presumed. Labourers of some kind.

The other two faces the soldier recognized instantly. Clothed in more expensive attire than their companions – pristine shirts, black cloaks and high-crowned hats – they had softer features and slimmer frames. Both clutched Bibles. The soldier had never met either of them, but had studied them from afar, and knew them to be clergymen of some kind. He hawked up a dense gobbet of phlegm and spat on the road.

'*Was soll das bedeuten?*' one of the priests called out.

The soldier was within ten paces of his captives now, and he brandished what he hoped would be a suitably wolfish grin. 'Don't *sprechen* the tongue, Herr Canker-Blossom.'

The priest, a man perhaps ten years the soldier's senior, pulled a sour expression, wrinkling his hooked, beaklike nose. 'I asked, what is the meaning of this?'

The soldier frowned, as annoyed at the man's evident lack of fear as he was surprised to hear the accent. 'English?'

'Aye, sir,' the priest called back, 'and a saddened one to learn that he may be robbed by his own countryman.'

The soldier shook his head vigorously, sending the dark locks cascading about his shoulders. 'No robbery here, sir. Merely rescue.'

'Rescue?' the black-cloaked man repeated incredulously, but then his small eyes, brown and intelligent, narrowed, and he looked up at the cart. 'And the Lord sheds light.'

The soldier stepped a pace closer, stabbing the air at his front with the pistols. 'Release her, sir, or so help me I'll stick lead in your face.'

The locals, judging by their plate-eyed expressions, probably did not comprehend a word of the exchange, and began stumbling backwards at the renewed threat. The driver stayed in his seat, careful not to move an inch lest he draw the young brigand's attention.

To the soldier's surprise, the English priest stared directly down the mouth of the pistol barrel and shook his head slowly. 'We take this witch to the hanging tree, where she will know God's judgement.'

The soldier gritted his teeth. 'Have a care for your words, fellow.'

'The witch must hang!' the priest bellowed suddenly, his expression darkening with explosive anger. 'Hang, I say!'

A new face appeared then, popping up from within the cart. Narrow and white, with high, delicate cheekbones and glittering hazel eyes, all framed by a shock of flame-red hair that flowed like a sun-dappled waterfall. 'Hang me, you dry old bastard, but then you'll never get your privy member polished.' She grinned; an expression of wickedness and defiance, of pearly teeth and crimson lips.

To the soldier at least, it was a smile of flesh-scorching beauty. He winked at her.

'This wench is a harridan of Satan,' the second priest spluttered. He was fresher-faced than his compatriot, tall and willowy.

The soldier tore his gaze from the girl to meet that of the new speaker, who, to his surprise, was also English. 'She truly looks a frightening creature, sir.'

'She is a witch!' the first priest interjected with outraged indignation. 'I have proof she worships Lucifer.'

A chorus of low mutterings came from the driver and the locals. They may not have been able to comprehend the discussion, but they all knew the name of the Devil well enough. The second priest sketched the sign of the cross over his chest.

'*Proof*!' the girl screeched from up on the cart. 'And I got proof of no wrongdoing!' Her hands were bound in front, but somehow she managed to angle them so that her long, thin fingers could fish for something from within the neckline of her bodice. When she withdrew them, they grasped a glinting disc of metal. 'The king's shilling! Payment for a night's work,' she jerked her chin at the taller priest, 'with this young gentleman!'

'She bewitched me!' the second priest wailed, his tone shrill and desperate. 'Befuddled my senses!'

The soldier's lip upturned in an amused sneer. 'Turn your head did she? She's a rare beauty, I grant you.'

'I—I—' the willowy priest stammered, unable to find a suitable retort.

'What are you, son?' the soldier went on. 'Sixteen years? Seventeen? I bet she befuddled you well.'

'She is the Devil's whore!' the older priest bellowed.

The soldier shook his head. 'She's a whore, certainly, sir. But more angel than demon.'

'*Blasphemy*!' The priest almost spat the word. 'You should have your neck stretched beside her!'

'Perhaps,' the soldier replied casually, 'but at least I can sleep at night. You goddamned priests want her just as any other man, and hate yourselves when you've shot your bolt. You would see her hang to salve your vile consciences.' The younger priest's pale face immediately reddened, and he knew he had spoken true. He glanced up at the cart. 'Beth! Get down here!'

Beth did as she was told. Wrists still bound, she swung her legs over the side of the vehicle and dropped down to the road with a squelch, pushing her way past the indignant men to stand beside her rescuer. She held up wrists that had been rubbed raw by the coarse bindings. He handed her one of the pistols, and she trained it on the group as, with his free hand, the soldier drew a small blade from his belt and cut her bonds.

He grinned as she pecked him on the cheek.

The locals began to mutter their dissent at her release, but they remained frozen to the mud, frightened by the pistols into bovine acquiescence.

The soldier pursed his lips and gave a short, high-pitched whistle. The undergrowth at the road's edge immediately began to rustle and crack as branches, vines, bracken and grass were thrust aside and a bay mare trudged on to the rutted road.

'Get on, Beth,' the soldier ordered, taking back the pistol and backing slowly away from the group.

The younger of the priests simply stared mutely at the ground as the object of his lust clambered up into the waiting saddle, his thin lips working frantically in what looked like silent prayer.

The senior priest took a step forwards, dropping his voice to a low growl. 'She seduced this God-fearing, Christian man, sir. Poisoned his mind with wicked desire. And she *will* swing for it.'

The soldier's angular jaw quivered as he gritted his teeth. 'Not today.'

The shot echoed about the trees as a fat halo of acrid smoke obscured the air around the soldier. He heard the priest scream and knew the ball had found its mark, but did not wait to see the result until he was safely in the saddle, Beth Lipscombe's lithe arms snaked tightly about his waist.

Only when he had holstered the spent weapon and handed the remaining pistol to Beth did he look down at the men gathered around the cart. The priest was rolling in the sticky mud, a hand clutched at the tattered flesh of his backside.

'Let that be a lesson to you, sir!' he called down at the wounded, writhing man. 'And be thankful I showed you the mercy you would not have shown this woman.'

The priest looked up at him, blood seeping through fingers held tight to his breeches, face creased with fury and pain. 'I will find you, witch's helper! I will hunt you down, so help me God! I may not have your name, but—'

'No, sir, you will not!' the soldier called. 'For we will be long away from this cursed country by the time your arse heals! So you may have my name.' He grasped the reins, slashing them against the bay's broad neck, propelling them on in a surge of power and a spray of mud. He crowed his victory to the thick canopy above, glancing back only to shout his name. And they were gone.

CHAPTER 1

Captain Innocent Stryker was in a foul mood. It might have been late afternoon, but it was still warm, too warm for a man in a woollen coat and breeches, and the Devon sky was smothered in a pelt of pregnant clouds that made the skin prickle with humidity. The steepness of the hill seemed to make his pumping chest burn and tightening calves ache. All these things made a march difficult, and, in turn, his mood darken. But worse still, Captain Innocent Stryker was running away. And that, more than any other trial, turned his temper as black and as explosive as gunpowder.

'Maybe we could go back?' a voice came from behind him.

Stryker rounded on the speaker, causing the long line of scarlet-coated soldiers to halt their march. 'God's blood, Ensign Chase! I'll send you back down there alone if you say something so dull-witted again.'

Chase, the man charged with bearing the company standard – a large square of blood-red taffeta, with the cross of St George at the top corner and two white diamonds in the field – stared into his captain's face. That face was narrow, weather-hardened and spoiled by a mass of swirling scar tissue in the place where his left eye should have been. He swallowed hard. 'Sir.'

The tremble of shoulders caught Stryker's lone grey eye. He turned to glare at a man who stood taller than any other in the company, a man whose amber-toothed smirk immediately vanished. 'And you'll join him, Sergeant Skellen, do not think I jest.'

Skellen's face, layered with dark stubble and criss-crossed with its own creases and scars, became a well-practised mask, blank and unreadable. 'Wouldn't dream of it, sir.'

Stryker turned away to stare back down the road. 'Got out just in time,' he muttered to no one in particular.

They had marched out of Bovey Tracey some three hours earlier, with word of an advancing Parliamentarian unit hastening every step. Stryker eyed the town's thatches, tiny smudges of gold and russet from this distance, huddled at the foot of the tree-choked hill his men now climbed. With the uneasy truce in the south-west close to ending, Hopton, the Royalist general, had become increasingly nervous, and Stryker had been stationed here, at Dartmoor's south-eastern fringe, to guard one of the few routes into the bleak wilderness. But now he had been driven to the hills like a deer in the face of hounds. He swore viciously.

'Least they didn't catch us sleeping,' a new voice reached Stryker from further down the road.

Stryker peered along the line of soaring pike staves and shouldered muskets until he saw the speaker, a man whose hard face and battle-ravaged body belied the fact that he was only in his late teens. Stryker nodded acknowledge-ment to his second-in-command. 'That is something I suppose, Lieutenant Burton. Still, I hate to turn tail.'

Burton smiled. 'Strategic retreat is not cowardice, sir.'

Stryker glanced at him, single brow raised. 'When did our roles reverse, Andrew?'

'Sir?'

'It was not so long ago that you were as green as cabbage,' Stryker said, though without malice. 'Now you offer me advice.'

Burton absently adjusted the leather sling that cradled his right arm. That arm had been shattered at the shoulder by a pistol ball the previous year and was now withered and next to useless. 'Seen a deal of soldiering now, sir.'

That was true, Stryker reflected. Youthful innocence had been marched, slashed and shot from young Burton, so that the lieutenant was now an extremely proficient officer, and one of the few men Stryker trusted with his life. He was proud of Burton, strange though it was for him to admit.

'We'll rest here,' he ordered suddenly. He looked at Skellen. 'See to it, Sergeant.'

Burton moved to stand at his captain's side as Skellen sent word down the line. The lieutenant kept his voice low. 'What if they send men after us?'

Stryker pulled the buff-gloves from his fingers and scratched at the puckered skin that served as a macabre lid to his mutilated eye socket. 'A force that size? They were to garrison Bovey Tracey. We're of no concern.' He took off his wide-brimmed hat, rapping it with his knuckles to send a cloud of dust into the breezeless air before tossing it on to the grass at the road's verge. 'Besides, if they send cavalry we will be caught. Would you march another hour and be tired when finally they're at our backs?'

Burton shook his head. 'I would rest now and fight them afresh.'

'So we rest.' Stryker unbuckled his sword, dropping it next to the hat, and sank to his haunches. 'And hope the bastards don't come.'

Burton removed his own hat and sat beside Stryker, running a hand across his forehead to shift thick tendrils of sweat-matted hair. 'A good match, wouldn't you say?'

Stryker followed Burton's gaze to where Ensign Chase was attempting to prop the company colour against a broad tree trunk. 'Match?'

'The new coats, sir. Captain Fullwood has some experience in the dyeing trade, apparently. According to him, getting the right shade of red – or any colour for that matter – is the devil of a job.'

Stryker stared at Chase as the company's most junior officer continued to struggle with the large standard. The regiment had been supplied with new coats after Cirencester had fallen to Prince Rupert earlier in the year. The Stroud Valley was a prolific centre of wool production, and many of the king's regiments had taken the opportunity to replace their threadbare coats and breeches with the sudden availability of material.

'They might have ended up in blue,' Stryker replied eventually. 'There was more blue than anything else.'

Burton sniffed his derision. 'Well I for one am pleased Sir Edmund insisted upon red. Goes with the regimental colours, after all. Slightly darker hue than our flag, I grant you, but it's not too far off.' He glanced down at his own coat, a nondescript shade of brown, and fingered the sleeve of his limp right arm. 'Perhaps I should have taken the opportunity to replace this old thing when I had the chance.'

Stryker shook his head. 'The prince would not have been pleased.' He might have been an infantry officer, but Stryker and a select group of comrades were often enlisted by the king's nephew, Prince Rupert of the Rhine, for special – often covert – tasks.

Burton chuckled. 'Aye, I suppose he would not wish us parading around in nice, bright red. Still, the fact remains,' he went on, his attention back on the rank and file, 'they look a far more imposing body now.'

Stryker did not much care for coats or colours, and he allowed his thoughts to drift elsewhere. To old battles and fallen friends, to the most recent horrors he had witnessed on the killing field of Hopton Heath, and to the bitter siege he had barely survived before it. And then, inevitably, to the person whose presence had drawn him to the ill-fated little city of Lichfield. A woman with long, golden hair and sapphire eyes. Who could be dainty as a flower one moment and hard as steel the next. A woman who beguiled and infuriated Stryker in equal measure.

'Is she still in Rome?' Burton's voice stabbed through his reverie.

Stryker looked up sharply, and the lieutenant's face paled, his eyes immediately studying the ground. 'Christ, Andrew, but you're becoming as impertinent as Skellen.'

'Beg pardon, sir, I overstepped,' Burton muttered sheepishly.

'Yes, you bloody did,' Stryker replied, though he could feel the anger already begin to seep away. He sighed heavily. 'Aye, she is still in Rome.' The image of Lisette Gaillard leapt back into his mind's eye, and for a second he allowed himself to luxuriate in the memory of her voice, her touch, her scent. But even as those fine thoughts swirled, they were intertwined with sadness. She had left England back in March, shortly after the bloody fight outside Stafford, a fight that saw the last great act of a master fire-worker, the death of an earl, and the restoration of Stryker's reputation. For Lisette was Queen Henrietta Maria's agent. Messenger, spy, assassin. Ever at the monarch's beck and call. And that meant she could never be truly Stryker's. He didn't know if he loved her or loathed her. 'So far as I goddamn know,' he added bitterly.

Burton opened his mouth to speak, but another glance from Stryker's forbidding grey eye made him think twice. Instead he watched Stryker unlace his sleeveless buff-coat and fish out a folded piece of paper. The captain opened the greasy square carefully, staring down at the hand-drawn features adorning its surface.

'Where now, sir?' Burton said after a few moments.

Stryker squinted to discern the black lines of bridle-ways from the paper's myriad creases. He indicated a particular point with a grubby finger. 'We're here. Outside Bovey Tracey.'

'Never to return.'

Stryker thought of the large Parliamentarian force they had seen approach the town and felt a wave of relief that his company had been organized enough to take their leave in good time. 'Aye. And here,' he continued, tracing one of the meandering ink strokes westwards with his nail, 'is the road we'll follow.'

'The Tavistock road.' Burton glanced up. 'Back to Launceston?'

'Naturally. General Hopton will wish to know why we abandoned our post.'

'Will it go bad for us, sir?'

Stryker could sense Burton's concern and he looked up. 'He sends a single company to guard a road, and the enemy appear with a whole bloody regiment.'

'Not a great deal we could do, was there?'

'I fear not.' He leaned back on his elbows. 'Justice will out, Andrew. Hopton's no fool.'

Burton nodded. 'So we must trudge back across the moor.'

Stryker read the bleakness in Burton's expression. 'You do not relish the task?'

'Dartmoor is such a desolate place.'

'You listen to Sergeant Heel too readily, Lieutenant.' Stryker sat up and slapped Burton on the shoulder. 'Tall tales of men vanishing in the mists and swallowed by bogs. The fact remains that we are here,' he said, tapping the map, 'in the south-east, and, as of this morning, so are the enemy. Further east we have Exeter—'

'Rebel town.'

'Indeed.' The captain's finger moved upwards across the page. 'And to the north they hold Okehampton. In short, Launceston is the only safe town for us hereabouts. So we must head due west, back into Cornwall.'

'Across Dartmoor,' Burton said glumly.

'Damn these boots!' Sergeant Skellen's coarse tone – honed in the taverns of Gosport – rang out nearby.

Stryker and Burton looked to where he sat a short distance along the road, long arms wrestling to pluck a ragged-looking bucket-top boot from his huge foot.

'Thought you said they was the best ever crafted,' one of the soldiers said.

'Stitched by the fair hands of a dozen maids, you said, Sergeant,' Lieutenant Burton chimed in.

Skellen let out a heavy breath through his nostrils. 'Indeed an' I did, sir.' He struggled a while longer, amused smirks breaking out all around, and looked up when finally he had relieved his feet of the offending items. 'Took 'em off a dead harq'busier after Kineton Fight. Comfy as a night in the Two Bears down in Southwick.' He closed his small, dark eyes at the memory. 'A buttock banquet before bed, and tits for pillows.'

The men laughed raucously, and Skellen offered an amber-toothed grin.

'What's the matter with 'em now then, Sergeant?' a man asked.

'The wenches at the Two Bears? Absolutely nothin' I hope, lad. For I shall visit them again soon, God willin'!'

'The boots, Sergeant,' the man clarified.

'Kineton were months ago, Harry lad, and I've marched many a night and fought many a day since. Now the buggers are torn up like a pair o' shot-through snapsacks, and my feet are sufferin'.'

'And ripe as old milk!' Stryker added, sniffing the air, and was rewarded with more laughter.

'*Sir!*' The call reached Stryker from perhaps fifteen paces further up the road. 'Horses, sir!'

Stryker scrambled quickly to his feet, spinning on his heel and fixing the nearest men with a look they had come to know well. Wordlessly he gestured that they should stand. Rapidly, and in deathly silence, the red-coated ranks took to their feet, buckled belts, emptied pipes, crammed on helmets, took up weapons and formed into their squads.

The man who had raised the alarm was now at his captain's side, and Stryker looked down at him. He was an incongruous sight, equipped in full military regalia and dressed in the grey coat and breeches of the feared Scots Brigade, for the man's head did not reach a great deal above Stryker's waist. He was tiny, a dwarf whose clothing and weaponry made him appear for all the world like a child playing at soldiers. But it was a sight to which Stryker had grown accustomed in the weeks since Simeon Barkworth had joined his company. He had also grown used to trusting the little man's judgement. 'Certain?' Stryker asked.

''Course I'm certain,' the Scot responded tartly.

Stryker glowered. 'You may not carry rank here, Simeon, but I'll bloody break your nose if you address me like that again.'

Barkworth's eyes were a luminous yellow colour, putting Stryker in mind of a cat, and they narrowed at the taller man's threat. But he evidently thought better than to argue, and instead reined in his temper. 'I apologize, Captain. Aye, I'm certain of what I heard, sir.'

'Good enough.'

And then Stryker heard it too. The soft whicker of a horse, hidden somewhere within the phalanxes of ancient oak. Stryker saw Burton and Skellen staring at him intently, their faces questioning. 'Hear that?' he said, voice quiet now, senses alert.

Skellen frowned after a while, but even as he began to shake his head, a horse whinnied. 'Christ!' he hissed, hooded eyes widening in alarm. 'It can't be!'

Stryker thought for a moment, but shook his head. 'They're not from the town. They'd never have reached us this soon.'

The horse's call carried to them again. Burton pointed to the right of the road, where nothing could be seen for forty or fifty paces through the dense woodland. 'Over there.'

Stryker turned to Simeon Barkworth. 'Take a look.'

Barkworth nodded once and immediately plunged into undergrowth. The company watched as the little man leapt branches and dodged trees, his movements agile but soundless, until his silhouette was swallowed by the gloom.

They waited in near silence for two or three minutes with only the birdsong for company. Stryker studied the sky. It was still warm, the prickling at his sweating armpits all the more irritating now that they were not on the move, but he noted how grey the thick clouds had become, and quietly ordered the men to protect their powder in case it rained.

When Barkworth eventually returned, his expression was one of excitement. 'Land—falls—away—' His voice, throttled to near destruction by a hangman's noose more than a decade earlier, was never more than a rasp, but the sprint had rendered him breathless, and virtually impossible to understand.

Stryker held up his palms. 'Hold, Simeon. Catch your breath.'

Barkworth nodded, took several deeper lungfuls of the muggy air, and looked into his commander's keen eye. 'The land falls away to a shallow bowl. A clearing in the forest. They're there.'

'They?'

'A dozen, cavalry all.'

Stryker's eye narrowed. 'Ours or theirs?'

Barkworth's face creased in an apologetic frown. 'Can't be certain, sir.'

576

'Field sign?' Lieutenant Burton asked.

Barkworth glanced at him. 'Black feather, sir.'

'A black feather?' Skellen interjected. 'Never heard o' that one.'

Barkworth stared up at him. 'And you're the authority on the subject, you lanky bastard?'

'I'd wager I'm an authority greater than you, you bloody puck-eyed dwarf.'

'Enough!' Stryker ordered. The mostly good-natured sniping between Barkworth and Skellen had become part of the company's fabric since they had first encountered the Scot – working as the Earl of Chesterfield's bodyguard at the time – at Lichfield the previous March, but now he required their undivided attention. 'Simeon, you're sure that was the only field sign? Skellen's right, I've never seen one like that.'

Barkworth nodded. 'That's the sign, right enough, sir. Big thing, too. Pinned between the helmet tail-plates.' He moved a hand across his skull from neck to forehead. 'The plume curves right over, like this.'

Stryker looked at Burton. 'Lieutenant?'

'We assume they're Cropheads until we're certain.'

Stryker nodded. 'Indeed we do.'

Barkworth stepped forward, his yellow eyes suddenly bright. 'Set about them, sir?'

Stryker rubbed a hand across his stubble. 'I'm inclined to let them be, Simeon. I do not wish to draw any undue attention to our small force.'

'Aye, sir,' Barkworth replied casually, 'as you order.'

Stryker stared down at the little man, suspicious at the ease with which Barkworth's notoriously flammable battle-lust had dissipated. 'Simeon?'

Barkworth's gnarled features cracked in a sharp-toothed grin. 'You might like to take a peek at what they have with them, sir.'

Stryker, Burton, Skellen and Barkworth crouched low behind a close-cropped group of trunks and studied the strangers at the foot of the slope. The clearing was indeed the shape of a bowl, a circular patch of sunken, bare land in the forest's depths with wide oaks lining its rim. At its far side was an opening in the trees where a narrow track ran away to the north, quickly swallowed by the darkness.

There were, as Barkworth had said, twelve cavalrymen. All but one was mounted, though there seemed no urgency about their movements. One leaned back to take a long draught from a leather-bound flask, another picked at his teeth with a thin dagger, and at least three were sucking lazily on clay pipes. None of the riders wore their helmets, but those Stryker could see, slung at the sides of saddles or propped under their owners' arms, were adorned with the large black feather Barkworth had described.

Stryker's attention turned to the object that had so excited Barkworth. It was a wagon. An inauspicious affair of half-rotten planks and rickety wheels, drawn by a pair of gaunt nags, and with a nervous-looking man in a brown farmer's shirt who kept his gaze fixed on his reins.

'See there?' Barkworth rasped, indicating the vehicle. 'Worth a scrap, wouldn't you say?'

Stryker eyed the wagon's contents, and his heartbeat immediately began to accelerate. The bed of the vehicle was crammed full of objects. Stout little barrels, bulging cloth sacks, coils of thin rope, and bushels full to the brim with fist-sized orbs. Ammunition. Powder, shot, grenadoes, match.

As he studied the vehicle with growing excitement, Stryker noticed a man emerge from a pit at the wagon's rear. It was narrow, its mouth perhaps a yard across, but evidently deep, for the man had required a ladder to climb out. 'It's an arms cache,' he whispered.

Barkworth evidently read the expression on Stryker's face, for his dirk was suddenly in his little fist and his grin full of murderous relish. 'Fucking rebels.'

'*If* they're rebels,' Burton said soberly. 'And there may be more of the buggers about.'

'Aye, that there may,' Barkworth replied, 'but aren't we to engage the enemy where possible, sir?'

Stryker glanced at them both, weighing up his options. To fight here would be fraught with risk, for the gunfire would likely carry all the way down to the Parliamentarians in the town, but he could not help but think of the rich prize that awaited them. A huge enemy ammunition dump was difficult to ignore. If they were the enemy.

'How do we get close enough, sir?' Skellen asked dubiously. 'Bastards'll ride off soon as they see us comin'.'

Barkworth's grin soured, and he grunted reluctant agreement. 'Ninety-five men ain't on the quiet side, sir.'

Stryker looked at the Scot. 'Aye. If we could get this done with fewer. Twenty perhaps.'

Barkworth's grin returned, his eyes narrowing to gleaming slits. 'Enough to batter this lot.'

'Split the force?' Burton asked.

The question seemed to pour icy water on the fire that was steadily growing in Stryker's belly, and he sighed deeply, impressed with the younger man's cool head. He rubbed a hand across the bristles of his chin. 'You're right, Andrew, of course. I have been in a black mood of late, and my judgement is not what it ought to be.' He turned to Barkworth. 'We should not risk this. There may be a larger troop nearby, and that dozen would send a rider out to fetch them as soon as they heard our approach.'

Barkworth grimaced. 'But sir—'

'And hear us they most certainly would,' Stryker added, cutting Barkworth's protest dead.

The trees began to whisper then. A crackling in the canopy above their heads, as though the branches were passing ancient secrets to one another. Stryker instinctively looked up, wondering at the noise that was already growing louder, more insistent, a chatter rather than a whisper. In seconds it was louder still, a rushing sound that seemed to engulf the forest.

When the first cold drops finally hit his face, Stryker allowed himself a small smile.

'Will, Simeon,' he said as the rain thrashed through the leaves and branches to soak the earth at their feet, 'bring up the men.'

'If they're rebels,' Burton said again as they watched the company's tallest and shortest men vanish with equal stealth into the trees.

Stryker patted the lieutenant's good shoulder. 'Let's find out.'

The two officers met the red-coated ranks some forty paces further back from the clearing. As expected, Stryker saw that his musketeers had wrapped lengths of oiled cloth around their weapons so that the rain would not dampen their firing mechanisms or permeate the black powder within. The pikemen had no such worry, though their lethal staves had to be carried horizontally at waist height to prevent the ash poles, each more than sixteen feet long, from snagging on the boughs above.

'Sergeant Heel,' Stryker said, his voice low, urgent.

Moses Heel, the bullock-shaped native of Tiverton, paced quickly up to his commander. 'Sir.'

'See we're covered.'

'Sir,' Heel said, and abruptly turned to the company. 'Jack and Harry Trowbridge.' He paused as two musketeers, both long-nosed and blue-eyed, with tendrils of blond hair poking out from beneath their pot helmets, stepped briskly out of the line. 'You've got the sharpest eyes, so get your bliddy arses on that road. One north, t'other south.' He looked back at the company. 'Lipscombe and Boyleson, where are you?'

'Here,' was the response as a pair of men came to stand by the Trowbridge brothers. They wore the red coats of the ranks, but instead of pike or musket they carried large drums, slung at their midriffs by thick cross-belts.

'Go with the twins,' Sergeant Heel ordered. 'If they see somethin' worthy o' tellin', hammer it out. Understand?'

'Sergeant,' one of the drummers responded, and the four paced back in the direction of the road.

Stryker nodded acknowledgement to Heel, and turned to Burton. 'Lieutenant, you command the men. Hold them here but spread them wide, and be ready with point, steel and shot on my mark.' His eye winked mischievously. 'I am to go fishing.'

Burton's mouth twitched in half-smile. 'We'll ready your net.'

*

Stryker led Barkworth and Skellen, chosen for their lack of conspicuous company coats, at a rapid pace towards the clearing. They snaked through the trees, edging ever closer to the black-plumed horsemen, the rustle of their footsteps masked by the rain as it crashed through the canopy. Fat droplets pounded the branches above and the leaves at their feet, exploded against hat rims and raced across the surface of impervious buff-coats.

Stryker halted half a dozen paces before the trees started to thin, knowing the land would soon begin to slope away. He glanced over his shoulder and scanned the trees further back towards the road. He was pleased to see no sign of Burton or the rest of the company.

Skellen appeared at his side. 'What now, sir?'

Without reply, Stryker crept forwards, dropping to the lowest crouch possible as he reached the edge of the clearing. His knees burned keenly as he held the position, but he wanted a moment to study the strangers, to check the group had not been joined by more horsemen in the minutes Stryker had been organizing his approach. There they were: twelve only.

He stood, drawing his sword, easing it slowly from the scabbard's throat so that the rasp was inaudible above the dashing rain. Still the horsemen did not notice his presence. Stryker swallowed hard, took a steadying breath, and stepped out into the open.

A shout went up almost immediately, a high-pitched cry of warning from the base of the shallow bowl, and Stryker wondered whether the cavalrymen would charge him down without pausing to discover his allegiance. But, just as the lobster-tailed helmets were shoved unceremoniously on to their heads and the huge horses were coaxed out of their lethargy, one of the strangers walked his mount out from the group.

Stryker took a couple of tentative paces down the slope, not taking his gaze from the man he presumed to be the small troop's leader. It was difficult to discern age from a face obscured by the three vertical face bars of the helmet's visor, but from the lines at the corners of his eyes, the confident bearing and the thick, pointed beard at his chin, Stryker guessed he was in his early thirties. He, like his comrades, was equipped in the manner of a typical harquebusier, with buff-coat swathing his torso beneath gleaming back- and breast-plates, a long sword at his waist and a carbine slung at his side. Stryker suspected there would be a smaller blade and a brace of pistols about the man's person as well, and he approached with caution.

'Greetings, sir,' he said, keeping his voice loud and steady, for the rain still roared around them.

The leader of the horsemen kicked his mount on a touch, and glared down at the man on foot, pale-blue eyes appearing like orbs of glass beneath the coke-black plume of his helmet. 'Who the devil are you, sir?'

'Captain Stryker, Mowbray's Foot.'

The horseman's nose wrinkled. 'I am Colonel Gabriel Wild. Have you no Christian name?'

'None worth mentioning, Colonel,' Stryker said, and stole a furtive glance at the ammunition wagon that was now firmly screened by the dozen harquebusiers. 'King or Parliament, sir?'

Wild's expression remained stony. 'The latter, sir,' he said with deliberate slowness. 'And you?'

Stryker could now hear his own heart above the rainfall. 'The former.'

In a flash Colonel Wild's sword was free, its tip levelled at the Royalist's throat. Stryker saw that it was not the delicate, probing rapier he had expected to see, but a brutal, wide-bladed, broadsword. The weapon of a trained killer.

'Hold, sir, I urge you!' Stryker called, forcing the tension from his voice. 'For you are at a disadvantage.'

Those final words gave the cavalryman pause, for he seemed to take a moment to consider the situation, glancing into the trees at Stryker's back. 'How so, Captain?'

'I have men in these trees, Colonel.' With that, William Skellen and Simeon Barkworth emerged from the tree line, muskets trained on the enemy officer. 'You are sore outnumbered.'

'Lies!' Wild spat the word. 'Why are they not here if you have them? You are three only. Nothing more than brigands, wagering at my timidity! You insult my intelligence, sir.'

Stryker ignored him. 'I merely want your wagon, Colonel Wild. Surrender it now, and take your leave.'

Wild tilted his head back so that raindrops soaked his face, and brayed with laughter. 'Such nerve, sir! Such goddamned nerve!' The gesture he made was barely discernible, a mere flick of the wrist that made his heavy sword waver slightly in the air, but Stryker read it and recoiled instinctively, even as one of Wild's men burst forth from the group. The horseman's arm came up, straightened, levelled in line with Stryker's chest, and he saw the glint of metal in the gloved hand. He scrambled back up the slope to the protection of the oaks beyond. The pistol flashed, but the sound was more muffled cough than sharp crack, and he knew the horseman's powder had become damp. The rider looked down in horror at his impotent weapon, and Stryker threw himself on to the higher ground of the forest, screaming at his comrades to follow.

Immediately hooves pounded at their backs, more thunderous than the rain lashing about them, and the three Royalists sprinted for their lives, weaving in and out of the thick trunks of oak, hurdling fallen branches and rotten stumps and powering through grasping thickets of bracken. Stryker's feet and legs and chest blazed with the effort, but still he could sense the cavalrymen gaining, could hear their murder-tinted snarls and imagine the gleaming blades lofted high above their heads, poised for the killing blow.

'Charge for horse and give 'em some fucking steel, boys!' a voice bellowed from somewhere to Stryker's left. He could not see the speaker, for a significant portion of his left side had been left black to him by the bag of gunpowder that had taken his eye, but he knew the voice well enough. He ran towards that voice, immediately rewarded by the black-bearded grimace of the Cornishman, Jimmy Tresick, musket nestled at his shoulder, a seemingly endless length of match-cord wound loosely about his wrist. But the corporal did not pull his trigger for suddenly other men were at his shoulders. Strong men in steel morion helmets hefting long shafts of ash upwards at an angle, the razor-sharp blades embedded in their tips hovering menacingly at eye-level. Or, more importantly, chest-level with a horse.

Stryker threw himself on to the wet earth, rolling under the first of the pike points, and knew that his experienced redcoats would be stepping up to close the trap. He turned just in time to see the first of his

Parliamentarian pursuers hit home amid a crow of triumph. But instead of glory, the cavalryman would find only death in this hunt. He was galloping too fast to slow his mount, and though he managed to tear the beast's head back with a savage pull on the reins, the hooves continued unabated and slid in the deepening mud, scrabbling violently for purchase until its heaving chest thudded on to the tip of a waiting pike. The pikeman was driven backwards by the sheer force of the beast, but he did not let the tapered stave go, and the blade drove deeper and deeper. The animal toppled sideways, crashed into the rain-soaked blanket of leaves, and two musketeers, in position behind the pikemen, stepped forward with naked swords. They drove them into the horse's chest, stabbing manically for the heart in order to stop the beast's dangerous thrashing. Its rider was trapped beneath the huge bulk, and he received a blade too, so that both man and horse fell silent together.

Stryker stared left and right, and felt a rushing pride for the men of his company. Burton had hidden them well, and had released them at precisely the right moment, so that the redcoats emerged from behind the trees in two concentric circles, pikes in the front rank, muskets behind. He looked up at the milling cavalrymen, black-plumed heads darting all around, searching for a way through. But he knew there was none. They would see a line of wicked-tipped pikes, offering death to their horses, and, should they break through, they would be cut down in short order by the primed muskets.

Stryker studied each anger-etched face within the circle until he found the one he wanted. 'Do you yield, Colonel Wild?'

Wild turned his mount to face him, and Stryker thought for a moment that the proud officer, incandescent with rage, would launch a suicidal charge, but instead he merely spat a yellow gobbet of phlegm on to the soggy mulch.

'I said, do you yield?' Stryker shouted again.

'Your powder will fail!' Wild shrieked. He lifted his blade, whipping it in a tight circle above the now limp plume of his helmet. 'God and Parliament! God and Parliament!'

But none of Wild's horsemen moved, for their mounts would not charge the hedge of pikes, let alone the muskets beyond.

Stryker shook his head. 'Their charges are dry, sir, unlike your own. For one shot at least. And I think one shot for each of my men will comfortably win this fight, don't you?'

Wild's desperate gaze flicked from one musket to the next and gradually the belligerence began to drain from his face as he noted the oiled cloth wound around each weapon. 'My regiment are nearby, Captain. Four hundred elite horsemen. Four hundred swords that will enfilade your meagre force in a heartbeat. They will be here in minutes.'

Stryker shook his head slowly. 'I think not. You were wrong to give chase, Colonel. Do not make another such mistake, for I would not wish further bloodshed.' He glanced down at the dead rider and his still-twitching horse. 'But be certain I will have the rest of you slaughtered here and now if needs be. I merely want your wagon. Or rather its contents.' He turned to Tresick. 'Fetch it, Corporal.'

With a snarl of pure rage, Colonel Wild flung his sword to the earth, the tip driving into the mud so that the ornate hilt was left to tremble in the rain.

'God and *King*, sir,' Stryker said as he pulled the weapon free.

The languorous frame of Sergeant Skellen came up beside him, a grin splitting the tall man's face from ear to ear. 'And a pox on Parliament.'

A short while later Captain Stryker's Company of Foot were arranged in the formal line of march and ready to take their leave. Stryker was thankful that the rain had finally stopped, for the storm would have made their march into Dartmoor much less bearable.

'You did well,' Stryker said when he found Lieutenant Burton inspecting the heavily laden ammunition wagon. The company had ensured the subterranean cache was truly empty, and now they would take their loot back to the army in Cornwall.

Burton gave a short snort in a futile attempt to hide his pride. 'Men did well, sir.'

'Either way, it was the perfect trap. Exactly as I had imagined.'

Burton went to ensure the bolts at the wagon's rear were locked tight. 'And without a shot fired,' he said when he stepped back.

'That was crucial, Andrew. The wagon is a rare prize, but not one worth losing the company for. Our musketry would have alerted the Roundheads down in the town.'

Burton nodded, perhaps considering the thought of what horrors might have come from Bovey Tracey had their guns burst into life. 'I still cannot fathom how you knew Wild's powder would be damp.'

Stryker looked at him, acutely aware of the guilt that must etch his face. 'A guess, Andrew.'

Burton's mouth lolled open, but Stryker turned away, unwilling to discuss his folly further. And folly it was, he knew, for he had taken a great risk in gambling on the pistol's misfire. But he had wanted that wagon. He chuckled silently, mirthlessly, chiding himself for a fool. She had made him angry, and he had wanted a fight.

'You are nothing but common thieves, sir!' a bellowed voice carried to him, and in a strange way Stryker was almost relieved to have his dark thoughts brought back to the here and now.

He paced across the clearing and to the edge of the tree line. 'You are alive, sir.'

Colonel Gabriel Wild, stripped of weapons and armour, wrists bound tight at his back and kneeling at the base of a tree, was older than Stryker had thought. Perhaps, he guessed, near 40. His hair was light brown, left long so that it just reached his shoulders, and bisected by a bright streak of silver that ran through the very middle of his head, putting Stryker in mind of a badger. His brown beard had lost its waxed precision amid the chase and the rainfall, but Stryker remembered how well kempt it had been when first he had seen the cavalryman. His grooming, his expensive weaponry, and the well-equipped nature of his troop told Stryker that Wild was a man of status, and of wealth.

'Christ's robes, you damnable peasant,' Wild continued as though Stryker had not spoken. 'I will have every man here hanged by his own entrails!'

Stryker stared down at the line of kneeling, pitiful cavalrymen. 'We are at war, Colonel.'

'War? What do you know of war, eh?'

Stryker heard Skellen grunt in amusement nearby. 'I know enough, sir.'

Wild glared up at his captor, pale eyes glittering with white-hot rage. 'Then you will know that this is not war. It is simple brigandry. You know what I do with footpads on my estates, Stryker? I exterminate them.'

'So I will look forward to when next we meet,' Stryker said, turning to his sergeants. 'Skellen, Heel. The wagon is ready. See Colonel Wild's horses are tethered behind, and his plate and weapons loaded in the rear. We leave now.'

'By Christ, Stryker,' Wild almost spat his words now, 'you will never make it back to your lines! I will hunt you down and use your stones as paperweights, 'pon my honour I will.'

Stryker rounded on the colonel, patience finally at an end, and kicked him square in the chest, so that Wild was flung on to his back, filth spattering in all directions. 'Enough of your threats, you pribbling bastard! Be thankful you lived today, for I am in a cave-dark mood, so help me God!'

Wild kept his mouth shut this time, though his eyes were a veritable blaze of hatred.

'Another mortal enemy, sir,' Simeon Barkworth croaked as Stryker turned away. 'You seem to attract them like flies on . . . well, I'm sure you grasp m' meaning.'

Stryker sighed deeply. 'Aye.'

'Think I'd cut 'em all down here and now, sir.'

'I dare say you would, Simeon,' Stryker replied. 'Which is why I thank God you are on my side.' He glanced back at Wild and his trussed cavalrymen. 'He is no threat now. We have his wagon, his horses, his weapons and his clothes. They have a long walk ahead of them.'

'At least you left them their boots.'

'I might not have, but we do not need them.' A thought struck him then, and he scanned the area for the man whose head he knew would rise above the rest. 'Skellen!'

'Captain, sir,' Skellen said when he had jogged across the clearing to where Stryker waited.

'They lost a man today.'

The sergeant sketched the sign of the cross. 'May God see him rest in peace. A good lad, I reckon, sir. Brave to charge our pikes. And tall.'

'Quite.'

The corners of Skellen's mouth twitched. 'Similar sized feet to mine, I'd imagine, sir.'

'They're yours.'

Skellen affected a deep bow. 'You're a grand man, sir.'

'Spare me, Will,' Stryker said, turning away.

'As you wish, sir.'

Stryker looked to the company. 'Prepare to march!'